She stepped ... de Base, Level F... he feeling of familiarity with the layout of the Main Dome, which she had gained from months spent "rehearsing" FS-6's mission in the training center mock-up, vanished at her first sight of the massive destruction of supplies and equipment eerily illuminated by the faint phosphorescent red-orange glow of the level's emergency lights and exit markers. Equipment lay strewn around the room with vandalistic capriciousness. Paper refuse littered the floor, and, worse still, the neutral pale-yellow walls were heavily defaced with sinister-looking nonsense words, phrases, numbers, and symbols scrawled in soot-colored chalk and black spray paint, which overlapped and obscured each other.

Tseng scanned the walls, reading to herself: "dead . . . dead . . . dead . . . eat death."

"Food for the Moon," a phrase she'd seen scrawled on a wall in one of the last FS-5 video transmissions, was prominent. Tseng could feel her expectations sinking. No one was waiting for the rescue team's arrival, and there was evidence of violence here—insane violence. . . .

BLOOD MOON

Sharman DiVono

DAW BOOKS, INC.
DONALD A. WOLLHEIM, FOUNDER
375 Hudson Street, New York, NY 10014

ELIZABETH R. WOLLHEIM
SHEILA E. GILBERT
PUBLISHERS

ACKNOWLEDGMENTS

Many people helped in many ways. Special thanks to Lt. Nils R. Linder of the Los Angeles County Coroner's Office, Dr. Bruce C. Murray and the California Institute of Technology's Planetary Sciences Department, and Richard Landers MD, for their technical assistance. Any inaccuracies are mine.

PART ONE

Po Tseng felt the thud of impact, then a momentary stomach-churning, falling sensation as the cushioned-landing system settled the *Collins* onto the lunar surface. "We're down, Houston," she said.

"We copy you down at eighty-four hours: thirty-two minutes: zero-five seconds Ground Elapsed Time, *Collins*," Dave Christiansen's voice came over the COMM.

No one at Mission Control would say it, and none of the *Collins'* crew would say it either, but Tseng knew it was on everyone's mind—the possibility that they'd made this trip to the Moon only to find their friends and colleagues, the astronauts of the fifth construction mission to Far Side Base, dead. "Roger, Houston. Hope you're comfortable in that CAPCOM chair, Dave. This is going to be a long night," Tseng said instead.

"I copy you, China," Christiansen responded. "For you, Jerry, and Joe: in the interest of maintaining the schedule for EVA-1, you should proceed with your landing checklist."

"Roger, Dave," Pilot Jerry Cochagne acknowledged from the next seat.

Tseng pulled the landing checklist clipboard out of its bracket and passed it to Copilot Joe DeSosa, seated behind her. After the weightlessness of deep space, in the Moon's one-sixth gravity it seemed heavy. She glanced down at the new silver eagles of full Air Force Colonel which stood out on the collar points of her one-piece blue Air Force-NASA flight coveralls. Perhaps it was just the psychological weight of the task ahead of her that she felt.

Shutdown of the *Collins'* flight systems had to proceed "by the book." They performed, then crossed off, the various tasks on the list. Professionalism demanded following routine and being calm under pressure. Deep down, she was impatient, and she sensed a similar underlying tension in Cochagne, DeSosa, and the other four members of her crew. They were all anxious to find survivors.

☾

Far Side Moon Base Project Director Dolores "Dee" Bianco felt compelled to move; to busy herself with a technical task. However, there was nothing for her to do right now except to stand at the back of the cramped control room, maternal, available, but out of the way, while the Houston Mission Control team members sat hunched and sweating over their computer terminals monitoring the mission.

She hated the damned waiting.

The last few weeks had been measured not so much by days and hours as by the stages of the crisis. Again, her thoughts escaped to the chilling events she'd been forced to hear about over the COMM and to see on the video monitors and telemetry screens. . . .

Yet again, she heard the dialogue that neither she, nor anyone in Mission Control, could forget. . . .

"Houston . . . ar Side Base. We have . . . ad situation . . . ere . . . problem . . ."

"Far Side Base, this is Mission Control. We're losing your signal again. Can you compensate?"

". . . assive systems malfunction . . . we have it . . . soon."

"Far Side Base, we are unable to duplicate your problem with our computer. . . . Far Side Base, do you copy?"

". . . ar . . . d . . . life support . . . diagnostic . . . intermittent . . ."

"This is Control. Say again, Far Side."

". . . component . . . ailure . . . work . . . to . . . repairs. . . . up recovery sched . . . ?"

"Far Side Base, this is Mission Control. Do you copy? Repeat. Do you copy?"

Bianco glanced at the Mission Clock and saw that it had stopped at seven thirty-two PM, Eastern Time. It would be nine o'clock before Tseng and her crew could leave the *Collins* and begin to probe the extent of the disaster at Far Side Moon Base. What she wanted most, at the moment, was a drink of water, some aspirin, and a few precious minutes to herself.

In her private office in the Houston Spaceflight Center, two floors up from Mission Control, Bianco luxuriated in the feeling of being "home." In the midst of chaos and crisis, she felt renewed as she relaxed into the womblike security of the room which was crammed with several decades of souvenirs from the U.S. Space Program. Star maps, autographed pictures of astronauts, and photos and artists' renderings of space vehicles covered the walls. There was a photo of the International Space Station next to a movie "one sheet" from *2001,* the venerable icon of science fiction movies. The movie poster made the International Space Station look primitive. To any science fiction fan it was. To those science fiction fans like herself, who, motivated by tales of far-flung space exploration, had pursued careers in the real space program, it was a heartbreaking sight. Almost two decades since the time frame of the movie, neither American, European, Japanese, nor Russian space technology had progressed far enough to make a ship like the *Discovery* possible.

A chunk of *Apollo 15* Moon rock in a vacuum case weighted down a large pile of papers in a stack on top of the desk next to the computer and an old portable TV. They were both surrounded by a litter of empty thermal foam coffee cups. There were a few pieces of old "hardware" lying around, too. Some mementos were grim reminders of the primitive past, such as the photo of the charred insides of the *Apollo 7* command module, crematorium for three of the early astronauts.

Apollo 7 had happened before she was born, so she'd learned about it in school, but she'd been an eyewitness, along with millions of people throughout the country and the world, to the *Challenger* explosion. As an engineering student, she'd studied every detail of those accidents.

Her gaze returned to the picture of the Space Station. Tonight, it brought back memories of the disaster that had changed her life. She'd just been promoted to management in the Space Habitat Division of Rockwell when a berthing interface on one of the Station's modular sections malfunctioned during an orbital attitude correction maneuver, killing the four technicians aboard.

She remembered the dark days that had followed at the plant as everyone from the front office to the assembly line tried to deal with the feeling of having the blood of those four people on their hands. She was chosen to head the company's investigation into why the part had failed, depressurizing the module and setting it adrift, and had soon thereafter found herself in the "short course" at the astronaut training center, in preparation for a job on-site, as a supervising mission specialist at the Space Station.

Work in space could mean prestige jobs and promotions in the private sector, Earthside. It was the "fast track" to the top. Fortunately—or unfortunately, depending on how she was feeling about herself at any given moment—she had chosen to stay with NASA . . . only to inherit her very own disaster, it appeared.

A steady stream of data flowed into the Mission Control computer network from the *Collins.* Bianco kept an eye on her computer screen, but switched on the television. She was anxious for the distraction and curious to see what was happening outside Mission Control— outside the microcosmic maelstrom that the Moon base disaster had now become.

The TV picture came up on the tail end of a replay of the FS-5 crew's departure, a month ago, from the Cape. As it ended, the words UBC NEWS SPECIAL BROADCAST, and CRISIS AT FAR SIDE were superimposed on the screen. There was a cut to a live shot from a telephoto lens that showed the activity around the Houston Spaceflight Center at close range, and Bianco heard the voice of Ted Guest, the network's star news anchorman, over it.

"There hasn't been an accident in space in this decade," Guest began. "Now, there's still no word from NASA officials as to the condition of the fifth Far Side Base construction crew." Ted Guest—ageless, intense, serious—appeared on the screen, and Bianco saw that he was standing outside, near the hangar designated to accommodate the Far Side Base mock-up. His right hand was cupped over his right ear where a tiny receiver was nestled and, as he talked, Bianco could tell that he was also listening to instructions from his director stationed in the news truck outside the security perimeter. The newsman looked cold and uncomfortable in spite of the heavy overcoat he wore over his network sport coat.

"It'll be another twenty minutes before the crew of the *Collins* will emerge onto the lunar surface. We have a

special report now from UBC Science Editor, Gene
Reynolds, at the Jet Propulsion Laboratory in Pasadena.
Gene. . . .”

There was a cut to the inside of the auditorium and
the camera pushed in on Reynolds, distinguished, professional. Bianco couldn't remember when the man
hadn't been a part of any background news story concerned with space. She'd been interviewed several times
by Reynolds, and she admired the veteran newsman's
knowledge and integrity. There was a rumor that he was
being forced to retire. In a visually oriented, multilingual
society where news and information were communicated
in short-duration, digital video clips selected for maximum shock value—sight-bites that were a direct assault
on the visual cortex—the network powers-that-be
evidently felt the public was too impatient with the
thoughtful, in-depth news coverage that was Reynolds'
style.

The auditorium was set up for the NASA press confer-
ences concerning the experiments at Far Side Base that
were being monitored at JPL and, for dramatic effect,
there was a static display containing models of the equipment being used in the experiments.

“FS-1, the first mission to the Far Side Base, commanded by Brigadier General Jack Bucar, was more than
a token mission,” Reynolds said, walking slowly through
the display as he talked. “It was a two-week, ground-
breaking, flag planting ceremony and, at the same time,
heavy equipment and building materials were transported to the site. Lunar Sciences Engineer Po Tseng,
known to her friends and colleagues by her Air Force call
sign, 'China,' took her first steps on the Moon. FS-2, also
a two-week mission . . .”

A knock at the door caused Bianco to look up as one of
the project engineers leaned in. “When are you going
back to Mission Control, Dee?”

"In a few minutes," she answered. "I'll let you know what's happening as soon as I can." The engineer nodded and left.

". . . and the FS-5 crew was the first to live inside the base," she heard Gene Reynolds continuing. "They were scheduled to stay just short of two months to continue the major construction of the base, and to complete the testing of the base computer, but two weeks into the mission, a series of equipment malfunctions began which led to a blackout of all communication with the Moon base just nine days ago.

"There has been much criticism of former astronaut, and now Far Side Project Director, Dr. Dolores Bianco, for her refusal to disclose any details of this potential tragedy . . ." Reynolds looked down, listening to the voice in his earphone, then he looked straight into the camera. "Okay, back to you, Ted."

Ted Guest came back on the screen. "Thank you, Gene. We're at the mercy of NASA's schedule here . . . so, while we're waiting for a news update, we're going to replay video shot by the astronauts at Far Side Base approximately two weeks ago, according to NASA officials."

Bianco focused her attention on the TV, intent on watching the network's presentation of the last good picture transmission from Far Side that she had allowed the press to have. The TV picture changed from network quality to a grainy, jumpy, amateur exterior shot of Far Side Moon Base, with the monochromatic, barren lunar landscape in the background.

"The far side of the Moon is the dark side, the unexplored side, the side that looks out into the depths of space," Guest narrated, somewhat melodramatically, Bianco thought.

"For eight days, there has been no contact with the astronauts at Far Side Base, located in the South

Pole-Aitken Crater, on a site carefully chosen by NASA, and Boeing and Shimizu Corporation engineers because of its peculiar positive gravity field which gives the base personnel slightly more than the normal one-sixth gravity of the Moon. The layout of Far Side is reminiscent of 'Little America,' Admiral Richard E. Byrd's famous Antarctic base camp, where, less than a century ago, scientists and explorers lived and worked below ground to escape harsh surface conditions. . . ."

The jumpy, handheld camera footage had been shot by Shinobu Takizawa, one of the civilian mission specialists on the FS-5 team. It featured the rectangular, sliding outer air-lock hatch and the surface of the habitat—the dome, which was the roof over the structure's aboveground Fourth Level. Formed of layers of polyurethane micrometeoroid net sandwiched between layers of spun Kevlar and aluminum multishock shielding, the dome's weight was supported by an aluminum and graphite strut reinforcement. The outer surface was covered with the lunar surface material extracted from the foundation's hole for the dome's three subterranean levels. Each of the four levels of Far Side Base provided ample living and working space.

A fast, nausea-inducing pan to the right took in the base of the communications tower, the tripod-mounted dish antenna for high-gain transmission and reception, and the support structure for the first telescope in what would be the Lunar Telescope Array, a system of eight electronically linked telescopes aimed outward into deep space.

In the background, Bianco saw the bare, weblike "rafters" of the second dome, slated to be the Science Dome. All science experiments were currently being conducted out of the "basement," or Level One, of the Main Dome, but the Science Dome would house a lab, an infirmary, and the controls for the telescope. When completed, the Science Dome would be connected to the Main Dome by an enclosed, pressurized walkway. In the years to come, the base facilities could be expanded by adding more domes, with the Main Dome acting as the central information hub of the colony complex.

The camera stopped on the air-lock hatch and lingered for a few seconds on a metal plaque bearing the project symbol composed of the NASA emblem and the Boeing and Shimizu company logos, which stood out smartly against the metal surface. That was sheer corporate promotion. Takizawa worked for Shimizu, a Japanese construction company, one of three thousand civilian subcontractors in the Far Side project and Boeing's major subcontractor for the domes.

When she'd first viewed the film, Bianco had been glad to see that the construction work had progressed as far as it had, what with all of the other problems, both technical and personal, that had begun to plague the six-person FS-5 team.

There was a crude jump cut to the interior of the Main Dome. The picture quality was poor because no attempt had been made to adjust the lighting, but it showed four of the crewmen gathered in the wardroom on Level Two.

Bianco told the voice-activated remote control to enhance the picture on the TV screen to maximum as Ann Bisio, a mission specialist with Cray Computers, Bob Faden, the computer systems specialist, Frank Drzymkowski, the structural engineer, and Shinobu Takizawa all acknowledged the camera. They were displaying a surprising lack of showmanship for astronauts, and that was partly due to heat exhaustion. The climate control system had been one of the first systems to malfunction.

There was no excuse for the crew's apparent disregard of strict hygiene and proper decorum, however. Bisio and Faden were scantily clothed, Drzymkowski had tousled hair and a two-day growth of beard stubble, and looked as though he'd gotten out of bed just for the occasion, and, instead of regulation NASA uniform clothing, Shinobu Takizawa was wearing a Japanese kimono. None of the crewmen looked as though they had used the hygiene station's shower in several work cycles, a situation that could promote the spread of disease.

This video had been shot by Louise Washington, the pilot and communications specialist, because, at that moment, the remaining crew member, the mission commander, Colonel Mike Mobley, walked into camera range, looked straight into the lens and then walked out of the shot.

Mobley was only on camera for a few seconds, but the image was haunting. He was the only one heavily dressed—as if for the Antarctic, by comparison to the others. His sandy-brown hair was uncombed and he'd grown a beard and a mustache, but neither were trimmed. He looked tired. He moved like a sleepwalker, unaware of what was going on around him. ". . . and there you see Mike Mobley, the FS-5 Mission Commander," Guest finished his narration. His face reappeared on the screen. "It's clear that there has indeed been a massive equipment failure at Far Side Base . . ."

The phone rang. Bianco felt a rush of adrenaline as she picked up the receiver.

"They're almost ready to go outside. About twenty minutes," the flight director told her.

"Okay, thanks," she answered automatically. The news was a welcome relief from the waiting. For the first time in more than nine days, she relaxed.

In the history of the U.S. Space Program, there had never been a rescue mission. Things happened too fast in that inhospitable environment, so there was no hope of rescue anyway. The accident at the International Space Station which had propelled her into the astronaut program was a case in point. Death by implosive decompression had come in a split second for the four techs. There was nothing anyone could have done at that time.

This situation was different. Tseng's FS-6 mission had already been in the final stage of preparations for its scheduled launch. Any effort to delay it, with the fate of Mike Mobley and his crew unknown, would have been inexcusable. In the face of an outcry for the shutdown of the space program pending an investigation, she'd rallied the necessary support to reconfigure FS-6 as a rescue mission.

It had meant that, on the verge of countdown, the FS-6 crew assignments had had to be reviewed for who was expendable and who wasn't.

The flight crew was not expendable. Po Tseng, mission commander, Jerry Cochagne, pilot and base systems specialist. Joe DeSosa, copilot and communications specialist. All were going up.

That had left the four mission specialists. Dick Lebby, computer system specialist. Chris Sweet, construction engineer. Arminta Horo, geologist. Chuck MacCallum, astronomer. Each of these four had been important to the original FS-6 mission. Each had spent years in training for the possibility of getting a mission and months more training to be part of Tseng's team.

But FS-6 had had a new set of mission priorities thrust upon it. The first had to be the rescue, or, in the worst case, the recovery of remains. There was also the mandatory detailed analysis of what had happened and a critical damage assessment. The last priority would be to push forward with any original FS-6 and Far Side program objectives, if at all possible.

For the oldest member of FS-6, Dick Lebby, a veteran of FS-3, getting bumped would have meant the end of his chances for another mission before retirement. Fortunately, Lebby's ride was as secure as the flight crew's. He'd overseen the development of the major computer hardware as well as the software—right down to the highly sophisticated and exotic grid-generation program and the hyperspectral, digital, topographical, and geologic imaging mappers. There was no one better to probe the system's failure. Bianco knew she wasn't the only one who believed that. Besides, her own days in the astronaut corps had taught her that the strength of the mission would be rooted in the core personnel, the operations specialists, and then in the integrity of the entire team. Experience had put her on solid ground in the fight to preserve the vital core of FS-6 as much as possible.

Of the remaining three mission specialists, only Horo had kept her seat. The thirty-six-year-old African-American woman and Tseng had a special friendship, developed during their shared experience of FS-1. However, the reason Horo had remained on the FS-6 crew was that she was inseparable from one of the most important pieces of equipment transporting up with FS-6, a mining and geology robot, already stowed aboard *Collins* when disaster struck.

Sweet and MacCallum had been bumped for a medical team.

There was a deadened, tomblike hush in the building. The concentrated activity surrounding the FS-5 recovery was now dispersed into specialized areas of expertise. Technicians in Mission Control were still trying to reestablish the computer-communication links with Far Side, still monitoring the equipment around the clock, alert for any changes, any signs of life. Soon they would have their first clues to the mysterious disaster at Far Side.

She picked up the vacuum case containing the small chunk of Moon rock. It was a sample of the dull grayish breccia, that, when put under a microscope, exploded with color, revealing quantities of silicon, aluminum, iron, titanium, and magnesium. For the last fifteen years

she had made her living helping the United States
Government and private enterprise achieve the goal of
establishing a fully operational base on the Moon with
international cooperation. Was it the spirit of exploration, the ceaseless quest to chart unknown waters? Was
it because of the seemingly limitless profit potential in
this small piece of rock? At times the whole effort—and
her job—seemed silly, considering that, with Japanese
backing and Russian technology, Mars was now quite literally on the verge of becoming the "Red Planet" joked
about for three decades in the space program, before the
collapse of Communism and the dissolution of the old
Soviet Union.

Two decades ago, there were those in Congress and in
the scientific community who had favored a space program scenario which bypassed the Moon altogether,
channeling proposed Far Side project money directly
into a Mars mission with international participation.
They were in the minority. The Moon base project was
voted in and scheduled to follow the International Space
Station with Mars as a distant third priority.

In spite of their outward technological crudeness, in
the final analysis, the Russians had looked farther ahead
than the Americans during at least three critical periods
in the twentieth century. Mars had been their goal as far
back as the first U.S. landing on the Moon, and, whereas
the U.S. Space Program with all of its superior technology had floundered, a victim to protracted accident
investigations and the fickle tide of domestic and political policy changes, the Russians had viewed space as a
national priority, and they had moved doggedly ahead
with their research. Now they were in lead positions in
the program to colonize Mars. There might be nothing
anyone, not even the United Nations, could do about getting them to relinquish control.

Future plans for Far Side included expansion of the

launch-landing facility as a jumping-off point for deep space missions—another step in the "serial" approach to space that the U.S. had always favored. But there was heavy debate in Congress about a Mars mission now, and there was a real danger that a disaster at Far Side Base could fatally sidetrack the future of the Moon base project.

Bianco stood. It was time to go. Her eye was drawn to her copy of Tseng's crew patch laying on her desk. Shortly after their selection, the original members of the sixth mission to Far Side had chosen an enthralling picture of the Moon base with a telescope array pointing out into space to represent their mission. The legend read, "FS-6: Looking Outward." She was reminded of her own mission patches stuck in a drawer somewhere, either at home or in her office. She couldn't remember. It wasn't that their importance had dimmed with time. They were just a painful reminder that she was an astronaut. Now it seemed she was destined to be "dirtbound" for the rest of her life.

She checked her reflection in the window glass, and a little of her self-confidence returned. Even after making the decision to stop campaigning and hoping for one more mission, to focus her energy and talents on becoming a program director, she'd remained conscientious about her physical condition. At five feet eight inches, she was still muscular and solidly built with no sign of the professorial softness common to middle-aged scientist-administrators. Instead, she had the fit, athletic handsomeness of an outdoorswoman. She was an avid tennis player, a cyclist, a horsewoman, and a golfer, and she'd kept her auburn hair long. She pulled it back into a ponytail or neatly coiled it when working, but she refused to defeminize herself by chopping it off as most mature women did.

Why did she keep driving herself? The answer was

simple. She couldn't bring herself to give up. She'd wanted to go up with Tseng and her crew. She'd put her best arguments forward, but the powers that be had denied her the opportunity. She turned away from the window. She had to stop beating herself up. It was too late in life.

On the TV, a commercial had just begun when the network cut away to a live shot outside the space center, which happened to catch Shinobu Takizawa's wife and Louise Washington's parents in a tearful embrace. It was an intense, raw, emotional moment, callously exposed to public view by the camera, then lost, when the network cut back to the hangar area. Bianco left the office as Guest appeared on camera again to make a smooth transition from the background story to the story that was now unfolding at Far Side Base.

☾

The sound of her own breathing was loud in Tseng's ears. While still inside the *Collins'* payload bay, she'd made several fine adjustments to the controls of her "Snoopy hat"—slang for the communications carrier, a close-fitting World War I-style head covering worn inside the helmet of her space suit—but sound still resonated inside the closed atmosphere contained by the helmet. The Snoopy hat contained the headset and mike allowing her a choice of frequencies to hear and talk with Joe DeSosa, standing by in the *Collins,* Mission Control, Arminta Horo, Dick Lebby, Jerry Cochagne, and Paul Manch and Iona Greer, the medical team. She could talk to them on separate channels or all at once over an open mike called the "hot mode." Mission Control had decided that the first extravehicular activity would definitely have to be on the hot mode.

Tseng felt the pressure of every moment of elapsed

time. At least they were within sight of their objective. She hurried to join the crew members lumbering slowly ahead of her toward the *Aldrin*. They would have to pass by FS-5's LLM, sitting dead and lifeless at the opposite end of the landing pad, on their way to the base; it had been decided that they would take pictures of it so that Ground Control could visually inspect the hull for damage.

In the Moon's gravity, she did not feel weighted down by her space suit, which, on Earth, weighed one hundred and eighty pounds, nor was she thrown significantly off balance by the massive Portable Life-Support Subsystem—the PLSS—on her back, as long as she remembered to lean slightly forward as she walked. The weight of the PLSS backpack tended to pull an astronaut backward, so to compensate it was necessary to lean into the direction of travel, as in cross-country skiing. The skiing analogy could be particularly apropos if one lost one's balance or footing because lunar soil, composed of microscopic beads of glass, could be as slippery as ice, and that made recovery difficult.

The simple act of ambulating on the Moon resulted in exertion. Unlike deep space, on the Moon Tseng had the feeling of being somewhere, and, though walking in one-sixth G felt like taking a stroll on a trampoline, there was a sense of direction and a feeling of the physical force needed to get around.

A solid-state camera and lights were also incorporated into the PLSS backpacks. They were controlled from a panel mounted across the chest of the suit's "hard shell" upper torso section called the Display and Control Module. The module contained all the suit controls plus a microcomputer which monitored everything including the wearer's vital signs. The camera lens in a box assembly crowned the PLSS backpack and extended out over the space suit helmet. Unfortunately, its fixed angle made the camera useful only for long-distance panoramic shots, so Tseng carried a compact handheld digital electronic video camera for close angle shots plus its rechargeable power supply.

The more detailed close-ups were Jerry Cochagne's responsibility. For that purpose, the astronaut had a specially adapted Nikon digital electronic still camera and light gun, encased in a dust-proof housing. The still camera was designed around a basic F4 35mm camera body, lenses, and accessories. A charge-coupled device, or CCD, and electronics replaced the film cartridge. Both the video camera and the still camera stored the captured images in digital form on a computer hard drive attachment. This enabled image playback, manipulation, and, in the case of the still camera, printing via a downlink with a computer, or by direct transmission to the most favorable remote receiving locations. The Space Station, California's Jet Propulsion Lab, Connecticut's Goddard Spaceflight Center, and Mission Control in Houston could all get images through the digital downlink system on the *Collins* and later, from Far Side's own digital downlink system. Even now Cochagne's pictures were being received by Goddard and then transmitted to JPL for detailed imaging, manipulation, and analysis. The video was being received by Goddard and transmitted to Houston. In the event of a communications breakdown, both cameras were capable of storing recorded data for later playback and downlinking.

Manch and Greer carried satchels of emergency medical supplies and instruments which looked like oversized "black bags." Horo had the rescue bubbles, inflatable, completely enclosed pouches which could be fully pressurized and were each capable of carrying one astronaut tucked into a fetal position. They would be needed to transfer the critically injured personnel back to the LLM. In addition to the small tools of his trade as base systems specialist, Cochagne was also prepared for a forced entry into the Main Dome, if necessary.

Tseng slowed her pace and positioned the portable camera with her arms tightly against her chest to give it a tripodlike stability.

"Houston, this is Far Side. Before I give you a test shot, how are you reading me? Over."

"Far Side, Houston. We're reading you loud and clear, over," Christiansen answered.

"*Collins,* how are you reading me?"

"Loud and clear, China," DeSosa answered from the LLM. The speech of the quick-tempered, thirty-nine-year-old copilot and communications specialist, a Mexican Air Force pilot with the rank of captain, was characterized by the particular care he took to enunciate in English.

The *Collins* was their communications relay center until they could get the base system back on line. DeSosa was staying behind to make sure that nothing went wrong with communications . . . and to survive, if something went terribly, terribly wrong during the EVA. If that happened, Tseng and the others knew that DeSosa would do everything he could to help them, but that there were certain types of disasters where he would have to simply fire up the *Collins* and head for home without them.

The chances of a disaster of that order of magnitude seemed remote to all of them, and Tseng sympathized with DeSosa's frustration at having to be left behind with so much of the mystery about to be uncovered.

"Far Side, Houston. I'll give you a time hack on the Ground Elapsed Time . . . on my signal it will be eighty-six hours: ten minutes . . . MARK eighty-six hours: ten minutes Ground Elapsed Time," Christiansen said.

"Roger, Houston," Tseng acknowledged.

"It's show time," Christiansen said.

For a moment, Tseng was all too cognizant that, four hundred thousand kilometers away, the world was watching and waiting. The attack of "stage fright" passed quickly. She was careful to properly frame the *Aldrin* before transmitting.

Tseng put the specially molded eyepiece of the hand-held video camera against her helmet glass and did a slow pan of the *Aldrin*.

The LLM's outer hull, covered with multiple layers of very thin aluminum and ceramic-metallic tiles, was undamaged as far as Tseng could tell. The MMSTRP, the Multishock Meteoroid Shield and Thermal Radiation Protection Assembly, was based on the theory that incoming meteoroid projectiles could be broken up on impact with the first layer, and the fragments could then, in turn, be broken up further by each subsequent layer. Impact pressures heated the fragments, melting or vaporizing them before they reached the spacecraft. The same shielding concept was being used to protect the Far Side Domes from micrometeoroid bombardment.

The air-lock hatch, located beneath the flight deck, also appeared undamaged, but there was something wrong with the flight deck and cabin windows. They looked as though they'd been painted from the inside. It reminded her of the windows of New York subway cars defaced by spray-painted graffiti. There was no black spray paint at Far Side, so the substance had to be the dull black liquid polymer used to join and seal the seams of the base's prefabricated deck panels.

Economic considerations had forced the space industry to resort to the concept of rocket staging for all classes of the orbital transfer vehicles now in operation by NASA. Far Side Base's three lunar landing modules were the "workhorses" of the space program and ungainly looking spacecraft not designed for atmospheric flight. The lunar landing modules were referred to as "lems" because of the acronym, LLM. The naming scheme honored the crew of the first lunar landing, Neil *Armstrong,* Edwin "Buzz" *Aldrin,* and Michael *Collins.*

The *Collins* and the *Aldrin,* two of three LLMs were now on the lunar surface, a situation that had been foreseen, but not under these circumstances.

The LLMs used retrievable, reusable stages for the trip out from Earth, and an escape-assent propulsion system, for their return. Why hadn't the FS-5 crew tried to escape, Tseng wondered. *Aldrin, Collins,* and *Armstrong* were designed to be foolproof. They could be launched during lunar night, or full darkness on the far side, the coldest period in the Moon's extreme temperature cycle. The LLMs' escape-assent propulsion engines were based on proven technology, designed to be as simple as possible for extremes of temperature in space and on the lunar surface. Engine ignition for this stage was dependent only on the chemical reaction of a hypergolic fuel to trigger the liquid hydrogen and liquid oxygen.

Few of the LLMs' precision computer and life-support system components could be expected to function reliably at a temperature of one hundred and eighty degrees below zero, Celsius, but once in orbit the astronauts could initiate a passive thermal control maneuver, which would cause the LLM to revolve slowly around its longitudinal axis. The LLM controls and instrumentation would "thaw" and begin functioning again for the ride home.

At one hundred and eighty degrees below zero, conditions were at their worst and there was always the risk that the fuel metering system's sensors, valves, and orifices would be cold-soaked—frozen solid—and that ignition would be impossible. Tseng glanced at the flight deck windows again. The way they'd been painted over disturbed her.

"Houston, Far Side. We're continuing to the base."

"Copy that," Christiansen responded.

Exasperation at the hostile environment that prevented her from crossing the distance between the pad and the Main Dome at a run and throwing open the door to shout, "We're here!" fueled Tseng's impatience. She and the others would each have to be especially careful that, in the excitement of this first EVA, their physical efforts did not exceed the rated capacity of their suit cooling systems.

At the moment, Tseng could not see the faces of her companions because the astronauts all had their gold-covered EVA sun visors down over their faceplates for the trip to the base. But, after the months of training together, in and out of the lunar surface simulator, she could distinguish Cochagne's movements from Lebby's and Horo's, even at a distance. As for the two new crew members, Manch was five inches taller than Greer. Fortunately, fitting a space suit was a simple matter of adding arm, glove, and trouser segments with molded boots in small, medium, large, and extra large to the one-size-fits-all shell of the upper torso.

Of all the decisions about the FS-6 crew, to the rank and file on the inside, the choice of Manch as medical officer was the most obvious indicator of the prevailing theory for a disaster scenario among the NASA hierarchy. He was not the only MD in the astronaut pool, but of all the candidates, Manch clearly had the strongest background in the areas of emergency space medicine and forensic pathology. He and Greer had worked together in the past.

Greer was on indefinite loan to NASA from the British Astronaut Corps. She was an MD-PhD with a background in psychiatry, and had recently served a three-month tour of duty at the Space Station before returning to Houston to begin work on a report about environmental stress. She'd been the logical choice to do the stress analysis on Mobley's crew as the situation at Far Side deteriorated.

It was hard to think of Manch and Greer as part of the team. Intuitively, Tseng knew they felt like strangers, too. Flat spots on a wheel. That they might "meld" with the others during the mission was too much to hope for, but she wondered if Greer, at least, would be able to bridge the psychological gap, overcome the awkwardness, and solve the interpersonal conflicts.

The lunar rover was directly ahead of them. It had been overturned. Beyond it, Far Side Base broke the monotony of the lunar horizon where, just nine months ago, only the jagged ridge of Mare Basin could be seen against the star field. Tseng triggered the PLSS camera and turned toward Far Side Base. The domes, the radio antennae, and the cluster of inflatable shelters, put up originally to house the first construction crews, and then to store construction and scientific equipment and supplies until the base's completion, would be an impressive sight from this angle.

"We're sixty meters from the Lunar Roving Vehicle," Tseng said. "Everyone's moving at his own pace. The other crewmen are walking ahead of me. There is no discernible activity outside the Main Dome. . . ."

"This is one for our scrapbook, Doc," Tseng said to Horo in a subdued, but more familiar tone. As colleagues during FS-1, she and Horo had spent hours helping to survey the surface and plan the layout of Far Side. They were looking at the result of those efforts.

"If you ask me, it's an illusion created with lights and mirrors," Horo replied.

Tseng heard DeSosa chuckle and she smiled at her friend's use of a favorite "comeback." During the most serious situations facing astronauts in space, there had always been lively exchanges of joking banter that relieved the stress and pressure of the moment. Later, De-

Sosa would have the opportunity to marvel at the transformation of the once barren site at his leisure.

"Far Side, Houston. We're getting a picture. You are looking very good, over."

"Far Side, *Collins,*" DeSosa said, "you are looking good from where I sit, too."

Lebby and Cochagne lumbered into her frame, followed closely by Manch and Greer. The crewmen were excited by something. Cochagne's concentration and his camera lens were focused on the ground near the rover. Lebby was tapping him on the shoulder and pointing—directing Cochagne where to shoot.

"Astronauts Paul Manch, Iona Greer, Jerry Cochagne, and Dick Lebby are stepping in closer to get detailed photos of the rover accident site," Tseng said.

"What have you got there, Pops?" Horo asked Lebby.

The question startled Lebby into looking up, and he made a hand gesture of caution. "Be careful as you move in here," he warned.

"Houston, we're examining a grouping of boot prints near the LRV," Cochagne elaborated.

"We'd appreciate confirmation from JPL on the transmission," Tseng told Christiansen.

"Far Side, Houston. You'll have it the moment we do."

"Unfortunately, the tracks overlap," Manch said.

"Far Side, *Collins*. Can we get a real-time transmission?" DeSosa asked.

"I'll be up there shortly," Tseng answered. Cochagne's still pictures would reveal more detail because his camera could provide higher resolution and a vastly broader gray scale capable of revealing more fine detail than the pictures from the solid-state video camera. The live video was serving to keep those in Mission Control abreast of the EVA's real-time progress.

"Far Side, Houston. We have confirmation from JPL

on your transmission. They like the quality they're see-ing," Christiansen said.

"I'm in a good position to shoot from the passenger compartment side with the handheld camera right now," Tseng said. She turned her body slowly, panning away from the crewmen, then she used the camera's zoom lens to get a closer look at the overturned vehicle. Horo triggered her PLSS camera, though the closer she approached, the more her body would block her own camera lens. However, the transmission would provide another angle on what might prove to be a clue in the Far Side disaster.

To Tseng, the visual evidence had a sinister overtone; a subtext of violence. The rover was the most expen-sive all-terrain vehicle NASA money could buy. An off-roader's dream, it sported a wide wheelbase, a four-wheel-drive independent suspension and damper sys-tem, and deep-tread balloon tires. It was specifically designed not to flip over in the roughest terrain. More-over, the area in which it had overturned was part of the broad upper basin of South Pole-Aitken, and the flattest spot in the vicinity of the base. The launch landing zone was the only spot on the Moon where the dust had actu-ally been sifted for rocks during the construction and layout of the base.

Construction tools and the contents of six galley stor-age containers, packets of dehydrated foods and bever-age boxes, littered the ground where they had spilled out of the rover. They were unsecured, probably hastily piled on the back of the vehicle, and had thus been thrown off in the accident. It appeared to Tseng as though in des-peration a person—or persons—unknown had looted the base, and had scavenged all they could carry from the galley.

"The LRV was carrying dehydrated foodstuffs, and I

see tools," Tseng continued. "It appears that these items were being transported to the *Aldrin.*'

Tseng motioned Manch, Greer, Lebby, and Cochagne to back out of the camera frame. Cochagne was in a semi-crouched position, shooting pictures at a furious rate. Lebby acted quickly, moving in to gently pull the others back.

She gratefully gave the senior astronaut the "okay" sign and approached the rover along the path he was pointing out for her. Through the camera lens, she saw the tracks that had caught the crew's attention.

"Houston, we have boot prints leading away from the rover, but they disappear into a well-worn footpath that leads to the *Aldrin,* " Tseng said. "They're dug in at the toe, and based on the length of the strides, I'd say the individuals were running."

Tseng followed the trail backward with the camera lens and lost the tracks at the rover. Here, the ground was heavily trampled. From the way the tracks overlapped, and from other scuffle marks and imprints in the lunar dust, it appeared to Tseng that a fistfight had ensued among the crewmen there, with the tools being used as weapons.

"Far Side, Houston. You are to proceed with your objective of gaining access to the base," Christiansen said.

"Copy that, Dave," Tseng answered. "We'll come back here later for more pictures. We're proceeding directly to the Main Dome now. Over."

☾

In Mission Control, Bianco remained silent as techs replayed Tseng's video on an auxiliary monitor. Theoretically, boot prints on the Moon stayed forever until obscured by other signs of movement. The jumble of footprints and unidentifiable depressions at varying depths and angles all around the LRV added credence to a worst-case scenario. The rover accident was a sign of physical violence among Far Side crewmen, and evidence of a complete breakdown of discipline on a level that neither she nor anyone else connected with the project could have anticipated. Until now. The possibility chilled her.

Individuals seeking careers as astronauts worked their way up the ladder of eligibility by means of either the corporate system or the military system. Her own rise through corporate ranks had resulted in the opportunity for her to become a mission specialist for the post-accident reconstruction of the country's first orbiting space station. For the flight crewmen, in particular, military flight training was the means to a career in space.

At no time had she, personally, ever expected to find herself in a combat situation in the space program. She doubted that Po Tseng, who had taken the military route to the stars, had ever entertained such a possibility either.

In her mind, she tried to picture a scuffle with space-suited crewmen brawling in slow motion. Who were the combatants? What conditions or series of events had driven them to such an extreme?

There had never been a reason to send armed astronauts into space. Even the idea of using weapons—projectile weapons in particular—was ludicrous in an environment where humans depended on an enclosed, pressurized life-support system.

Again, Bianco tried to imagine the FS-5 crewmen in a killing frenzy, tearing at each other's throats. Her scientific mind balked at the idea.

☾

"It's like a ghost town," Tseng said quietly. Cochagne and Lebby, working on the control panel to the Main Dome's air lock with tools and test equipment, nodded agreement. "All we need is a dry, desert wind to kick up the moondust, a few creaking and banging window shutters, and tumbleweeds blowing down the main street."

There were no signs of life, and there was no way to tell how recently anyone had been active on the surface, but the exterior condition of the base and its equipment bespoke deliberate destruction. The flat-panel blackbody radiators, vital for temperature control inside the dome, lay overturned; the small dish antenna for high gain communication and image transmission also lay facedown in the dirt. Abandoned equipment, discarded parts, tools, and construction debris littered the ground. The base wasn't a living thing, but the notion of its "murder" occurred to her as she surveyed the destruction. Far Side had been rendered deaf, dumb, and blind with clear intent.

Tseng directed the portable camera toward Horo and shot the astronaut setting the dish antenna upright on its base. Then she focused the lens on Cochagne and Lebby. The astronauts looked small against the backdrop of the shrouds for the vanes of the oxygenation system and the fuel cell modules of the energy storage system for the concentrator solar array, which were all grouped together outside the dome on a poured concrete slab for ease of maintenance. Sighting through the lens, she saw Cochagne put away his tools and step back from the air-lock control panel, a sign that he was finished.

"The entire base is operating on manual control," Cochagne cautioned as the astronauts converged on the air-lock hatch. "There's generated and stored power available. The precipitator will function, but I suggest we exercise considerable discretion before throwing any light switches inside."

"Far Side, this is Houston. We concur. You are GO for ingress into the Main Dome at eighty-six hours: fifty-eight minutes: seventeen seconds GET."

"Roger, we are GO, Houston," Tseng acknowledged, then stood aside as Manch and Greer carried their supplies into the enclosed portico in front of the air-lock hatch and passed through the center of two rectangular doorframes constructed of metal plates. Like many of the base's applications systems, the electronic precipitator, designed to keep the powdery and invasive moondust out of the Main Dome, was based on long-proved, simple, reliable technology which employed few moving parts. The precipitator was a set of oppositely charged electronic doorframes. The first put a negative charge on any dust particles clinging to a surface. The second frame, which was positively charged, attracted the dust particles, instantaneously cleaning space suits, boots, and anything carried in.

Tseng followed Manch and Greer and helped them load their supplies and equipment into the air lock. It took all of Tseng's agility, strength, and suppleness to keep from pinching or snagging her suit, or bumping the camera, while she carefully squeezed herself into what little space remained inside. There was a sensation of increased weight and balance as the magnetic soles of her boots made contact with the air lock's black, steel-reinforced polycarbonate flooring, and it made tight maneuvering more difficult in the cramped space. The flooring was a big advantage inside the base, however.

It was annoying that muscles atrophied so rapidly after only a few days of weightlessness. She felt muscle cramps in her legs as she braced herself next to Greer.

With an exaggerated "good-bye" wave of his thickly gloved hand, Lebby closed and sealed the hatch.

"See you inside, guys," Tseng said to Horo, Lebby, and Cochagne on the radio. She rolled back her helmet sun shield and nodded approvingly as Manch and Greer followed suit, then she stretched, and finally reached for the valve for the positive pressurization cycle, which allowed air from the air-lock tank to pressurize the air-lock chamber. She tried to ignore the pain in the muscles of her calves and thighs and shifted her weight experimentally to get the most comfort and relief possible.

Constructed much like a deep-sea compression chamber, the air lock was compact, of necessity, to reduce the power requirements, not of filling it with air, but of purging it. Air entered the chamber from a pressurized main tank through a valve, but a vacuum pump/compressor was needed to pump the atmosphere back up to pressure and into the main tank to create a vacuum in the air lock whenever anyone went outside. The design was a compromise between functionality and cost-effectiveness.

Cost-effectiveness. The bottom line. How cost-effective would Far Side Base be now, Tseng wondered. There was no question in her mind that a catastrophe at the lunar base could only enhance the outlook for redirecting Far Side money to the funding of the Mars mission.

That was Dee Bianco's worry.

The sensor and gauge readings from inside the dome were her worry and they were disturbing to her. "Houston, *Collins,* this is Far Side. Do you copy?"

"Far Side, *Collins.* Go ahead," DeSosa answered.

"Go ahead, China," Dave Christiansen echoed.

"The atmospheric pressure inside is in the normal range, at seven pounds per square inch, but we have a high carbon dioxide level, high level of trace contaminants, high internal temperature reading at thirty-two degrees Celsius, humidity high at eighty percent," Tseng finished.

"Bad air," Manch said.

"Stagnant, hot, and muggy air," Tseng added.

"Far Side, Houston. Keep your helmets on when you get inside. Over."

"Roger, Houston," Tseng said. "Everybody copy?"

"Affirmative, China," Cochagne acknowledged.

The next few seconds passed in silence. Greer appeared absorbed in her own thoughts. Tseng continued to watch the air pressure gauge. A forty/sixty percent oxygen and nitrogen mixture at seven point five psi was the standard for Far Side, where frequent EVAs were necessary. In their space suits, they were now breathing pure oxygen at a pressure of four point three psi. Lower pressures had been used since the twentieth century, when it was discovered that, although the atmospheric pressure on Earth averaged out at just under fifteen pounds per square inch, since eighty percent of that was nitrogen and only twenty percent was oxygen, the partial pressure of oxygen in the lungs was normally only twenty percent of fifteen psi—three psi. This pressure was sufficient to cause the right amount of oxygen to pass through the membranes of the alveoli of the lungs and into the bloodstream.

Breathing pure oxygen at four point three psi allowed flexibility and freer movement while working in a space suit. It had proved to be life sustaining and more than enough pressure to maintain all body fluids and gases in their normal state—except for nitrogen, always present in the tissues under normal atmospheric conditions.

Nitrogen was known to come out of solution at an atmospheric pressure of three point seven psi causing the "bends" or decompression sickness, a painful, potentially fatal condition well-known to divers. Space crews coming from Earth and Earth-normal conditions, such as the Space Station, routinely prebreathed pure oxygen for at least an hour before the start of an extravehicular activity in order to denitrogenate.

Tseng had had her crew begin the gradual process of acclimation to lunar working conditions soon after touchdown in order to maximize valuable time. Nevertheless, it had taken them over an hour to get outside.

Manch was also studying the instrument displays. "The high carbon dioxide level could mean that the air purification system is malfunctioning, but it could also be an indication that there are corpses putrefying somewhere inside."

"Gas composition will not affect the air recirculation purification and ionization subsystems. They may be getting only partial oxygenation, but a more likely cause is a fouled polarized CO_2 concentrator," Tseng said.

"Far Side, Houston. The high ratio of trace contaminants detected by the filtering systems inside the dome would support either theory, so we'd like you to proceed on the assumption that there are injured survivors, over."

It had taken one minute for the pressure inside the air lock to reach equilibrium with the dome. Tseng maneuvered past Manch and Greer, slid the inner air-lock hatch open, and stepped out into the semidarkness of Level Four.

The feeling of familiarity with the layout of the Main Dome, which she had gained from the months spent "rehearsing" the mission in the training center mock-up, vanished at the first sight of the massive destruction of supplies and equipment eerily illuminated by the faint phosphorescent red-orange glow of the level's emergency lights and exit markers.

Her eyes grew accustomed to the available light, but there was so much chaos that she dared not navigate through it in the dimness, risking a fall and a punctured suit. She switched on her suit lights and drew her utility flashlight.

This was the only part of the subterranean Moon base visible above ground. It was the EVA Operations Center, and it was equipped for servicing and storage of EVA equipment such as air tanks, suits, helmets, gloves, and boots. That equipment now lay strewn around the room with a vandalistic capriciousness that was inconceivable considering the intellectual caliber of the personnel responsible for it. It reminded her of a messy attic. Paper refuse littered the floor; worse still, the neutral pale-yellow walls were heavily defaced with sinister-looking nonsense words, phrases, numbers, and symbols, all scrawled in a soot-colored chalk and black spray paint, which overlapped and obscured each other. The only way to describe the effect was as ghetto graffiti.

Tseng scanned the walls, reading to herself: *dead . . . dead . . . dead . . . eat death. Food for the Moon,* a phrase she'd seen scrawled on a wall in one of the FS-5 video transmissions, was prominent. There was more graffiti, but it was incomprehensible to her. She could feel her expectations sinking. No one was waiting for the rescue team's arrival, and there was evidence of violence here; insane violence with overtones that Tseng could only describe as satanic. She remembered Manch's speculative remark about putrefying corpses. With her suit and helmet on, there was no way of knowing how the air smelled. That was a blessing, she concluded grimly.

She helped Manch and Greer pull their equipment from the air lock, then she secured the hatch behind them and touched the controls for depressurization. She was reassured to feel vibration of the vacuum pump/compressor through her gloves as the purge cycle began. The evacuated air would be pumped back into the main tank for reuse by Horo, Lebby, and Cochagne.

"The oxygen resupply tanks are at a hundred percent, so the air system is working," Manch confirmed.

"Houston, Far Side. I'm barely able to transmit a pic-

ture at this time because of poor lighting, so stand by for
what could be lousy video," Tseng said.

"Go ahead, China."

Greer unclipped the flashlight from her utility belt.
She let the beam travel up graffiti-covered walls and
bulkheads. Tseng triggered the camera and followed the
light beam with the lens.

"Houston, the interior wall surfaces have been defaced
with random words and a great number of scribbles, doo-
dles, and numbers that are recognized occult symbols,
most notably the star configuration known as a pentagram," Greer said. "A transcript of the following should
be given to my colleague, Dr. Birnbaum at Bethesda
Hospital, as soon as possible: 'moongrems . . . Moon kils
grem vix . . . bitch . . . whore . . .' " The psychiatrist's
British accent made each word clipped and precise. Her
tone of voice was dispassionate, as though she were
dictating into a recorder for transcription by a secretary,
" ' . . . dead . . . dead . . . eat death . . .' and here's our favorite, 'Food for the Moon . . .' The number, six-six-six,
has been written repeatedly. Supposedly, that's the
devil's number according to occult science—and that's
an oxymoron if I ever heard one," Greer interjected, with
quick sarcasm, then continued, "any reference you
can obtain for me on the obscurer terms will be much
appreciated."

"We copy, Far Side."

Just hearing the childish gutter talk made Tseng feel
foolish, but having it referred to as "occult" was more
disturbing, and the concept of "occult science" was a
downright contradiction in terms, as Greer had been
quick to point out.

The air lock was cycling again as Tseng directed her
camera and lights in a wide arc that took in an auxiliary
computer terminal, one of several portable plug-in units
which provided access to the Far Side main computer

from anywhere inside the base. The keyboard was torn apart. The screen was shattered.

The air-lock hatch opened and Lebby emerged, followed by Cochagne and Horo. They immediately switched on suit lights and drew flashlights, adding more illumination to the grisly scene.

"We're getting a better picture now," DeSosa told her. "It's better than nothing, anyway."

Tseng followed Lebby with the camera while he crossed to the auxiliary computer terminal. The astronaut fingered the hanging wires and cables.

"Someone went to a lot of extra trouble to disconnect this terminal from the system," he mocked. Tseng caught the sarcasm.

"Mike Mobley's space suit is gone," Horo said. "Faden's, Washington's, and Bisio's suits are here. Takizawa's is missing . . . so is Drzymkowski's," Horo added.

"I hope we don't have to go looking for them outside," Manch said.

"Just what we need," Tseng answered. A sudden, blinding explosion of light from Cochagne's flash gun made her wince and turn away as the astronaut captured details of the damage with the still camera.

"As there may be casualties below, let's move down to the lower levels and do the detail work later," Tseng said.

They were working efficiently with six sets of lights. Everyone was careful not to turn the wrong way and blind the others with their backpack lights. They cleared the Level Four fire-safety hatch of debris, lifted it, and latched it in the open position. Tseng wedged the portable camera under her arm and climbed down the companionway in the orange glow of the exit markers.

Tseng's lights revealed more destruction on Level Three. The nature of it gave her an eerie feeling: the entire area was emptied of furnishings. The Base and Mission Operations Center on Level Three was the heart of the Far Side Base. The Far Side computer's main terminal, the communications equipment, and primary work areas were here. Where there should have been chairs, tables, and other workstation furniture, the room was bare, except for the built-in electronic equipment. Everything else had been wrenched from the low-gravity safety hold-downs and removed.

Where?

Tseng moved out into the room with her eyes down, being careful to wade smoothly through the debris of paper and package wrappers on the floor so as not to kick anything airborne. Suddenly, a dark spot appeared on her helmet faceplate. It disappeared just as suddenly, but reappeared a second later, lower down on the faceplate. It scurried across her line of vision, and she blinked and stared in disbelief, then brushed at it with her gloved hand. Again, it disappeared, only to return a moment later to continue its journey across her faceplate.

It was a fly.

She gasped and jumped back, startled, as something brushed the top of her helmet with the sound of tree branches in the wind.

"Far Side, do you copy? This is Houston! What happened?" The alarm in Christiansen's voice was like a shout in her earphones. The concerned voices of the other crewmen were an incomprehensible jumble.

"Situation nominal. Repeat, the situation is nominal. Everything's under control. I'm okay," Tseng said quickly, catching her breath. She backed up and aimed the flashlight upward. Its beam revealed broken electrical wires, delicate and potentially dangerous tendrils, dangling from an overhead panel that was ripped open.

"What happened?" she heard Cochagne's anxious voice in her earphones.

"I jumped out of my skin, that's all." Tseng suppressed

the urge to laugh, even with relief. "I encountered exposed wiring. Everybody, check ahead of you as well as at the floor and eye levels . . . and there's something else you all won't believe. I just saw a fly."

"Say again?" Joe DeSosa exclaimed.

"Did I hear you say that you have sighted a fly?" Christiansen's voice betrayed his skepticism.

"Roger, Dave," Tseng said. "I realize how incredible that sounds, but I know what I saw. I'll keep you posted and confirm as soon as there is another sighting."

Cochagne, Horo, Manch, Greer, and Lebby reached the deck. Lebby crossed directly to the main computer terminal. Tseng saw that the housing was off and the circuit boards were ripped out and left to dangle. Someone had disemboweled the machine. FS-5's video camera, which had been left dangling from the bracket which was used to transmit a hands-off view of the room, was battered and the lens was smashed.

"We're descending to the next level," Tseng told the listeners in Mission Control and DeSosa in the *Collins.*

Level Two, the Crew Support level, contained the sleep stations, the bathroom, the galley, the wardroom, and the recreation area.

Manch's flashlight beam illuminated the galley, and he moved toward that area to examine the litter of empty food trays and packages scattered around the preparation area. "I found something," he called out excitedly.

As Cochagne, Horo, Lebby, and Greer hurried to join him, Tseng immediately saw what had caught the physician's attention. One of the covered TV dinner-style meal trays was out on the countertop. Two selections had been poured out into the divided sections of the square plastic tray. The food was now dried and crusted. Spots of blue-and-white mold, which had dotted the surface, were now black spots and there were other signs of spoilage. According to the empty package labels, the dried brown lumpy substance in one section of the tray was curried chicken. The other empty package had contained apple cobbler.

A standard meal in space consisted of an entree, a vegetable, a starch, and a dessert. The food was arranged on a tray, then the entire meal heated in the galley's microwave oven. Meal selection was left up to the individual, and there was enough variety in all categories to stimulate the appetite. There were also chocolate bars and packets of nuts and raisins available in unadulterated form. There were strict nutritional guidelines and the minimum and maximum calorie intake range was determined for each crewman to maintain his or her weight, though astronauts always lost weight on a long mission, regardless.

Tseng studied the evidence thoughtfully. She was sure the meal in the tray contained a double ration of apple cobbler.

Manch picked up a fork and broke the surface of the chicken mixture. Three flies alighted and crawled over it. He brushed at them and they flew a short distance away, then circled stubbornly before alighting again on the food. "Houston, the fly sighting is confirmed. I'm afraid there may be a major infestation of the little buggers in here."

"We copy. We'll have to get back to you about the problem." Christiansen sounded exasperated.

"Whoever was preparing this tray was interrupted, and never came back to it," Greer said.

"Then there could be at least one survivor," Cochagne said.

Tseng felt a twinge from the renewed anxiety that they were too late.

The area on the other side of the companionway was partitioned for privacy. There was a passageway through the two rows of six sleep stations. Eleven of the twelve cubicles were designated by a number. There were brackets for removable nameplates which identified each crewman's choice of quarters. One sleep station was designated as the "CDR" quarters. Mobley had not bothered to put up his nameplate, Tseng noted. The other FS-5 crewmen had followed his example.

"We'll have to do a room-by-room search through here," Tseng told the others. "We'll split up, and I'll start with Mike Mobley's quarters."

There were nods and grunts of assent from the others as they shuffled away.

Tseng parted the black soundproof privacy curtain at the entrance to the compartment labeled "CDR" and stepped inside.

And saw a crewman in a space suit, laying faceup on the bed pallet. A swarm of flies floated lazily above the figure like a black cloud.

She drew a single breath, and in that time, her mind separated the total picture in front of her into its component parts. In a quick series of memory snapshots, she saw that the suit was large enough to be Drzymkowski's, and that there was no portable life-support system connected to it. Instead, the suit's umbilicals and electrical connections dangled from it with the ends resting limply on the floor like severed puppet strings.

Drzymkowski was in Mobley's quarters, and there was something wrong with his suit. It looked overpressurized, like a balloon ready to burst or a giant inflatable rubber astronaut doll.

She felt as though her bowels were falling in an express elevator. A flush rose up from her chest, back, and shoulders as pinpricks of heat. Like electric current, the pinpricks raced up her spine and continued past the nape of her neck. Intense heat and pressure suddenly enveloped her face and head in a "flash vaporization" or "frisson" of nerves and synapses. The need for relief from the shock forced Tseng to look away—especially from the fogged helmet faceplate.

Breathing required a great effort. Tseng suddenly needed more air than it seemed possible to get from her suit tank.

She forced herself to approach the body. She could feel her heart pounding. She hyperventilated. The muscles around her eyes felt tight. The hand that held the flashlight shook.

The inside of the helmet faceplate was wet and dripping with condensation. Through the wetness she saw purplish muscle and ligament tissue clinging to a hairless skull with a smashed-in forehead. The grinning death mask was surrounded by lumpy green gelatin mottled with black patches.

Prior to launch, a hastily arranged private briefing at the county morgue and a macabre slide show of the faces and attitudes of death had served as the team's preparation for a "worst-case scenario" at Far Side. They had all looked at death for hours until saturation boredom set in.

Nothing could have prepared her to see this death face. None of the morgue pictures had been of a friend.

There was no sound in her ears except her own heartbeat and breathing. She continued to stare, transfixed. How much time had passed? Sudden awareness broke the horrific spell. There was an explosion of sound and voices, snatches of cross talk from the other crewmen and from *Collins* and Houston. She forced herself to speak over them. "Houston, I've found a body. It's Drzymkowski." In her earphones, Tseng heard groans from the other crewmen, and from DeSosa in the *Collins*.

"We'll be right there," Manch said.

"Hang on till we get to you," Lebby said anxiously.

In her mind, Tseng saw Drzymkowski alive. She remembered conversations, training exercises, meetings with the affable Army civil engineer, a construction worker with a Masters degree from MIT. On FS-2, he had bossed a crew whose education and experience was in the building trades rather than in the sciences. A widower, he had remarried four years ago. There were no children. Among the astronauts hardest hit by the news of his death would be Chris Sweet, foreman of the FS-3 building crew and the engineer bumped from FS-6, and Ralph Stromeyer, scheduled to ride up with FS-7. Stromeyer's construction crew would complete the Science Dome. The three civil engineers were . . . had been close colleagues. Stromeyer and Sweet fostered a running gag about proposing that Drzymkowski be sent up to build Far Side by himself in an afternoon as a project cost-cutting measure.

All five crewmen crowded into the doorway at once, then Manch pushed through, followed by Greer. Lebby, Horo, and Cochagne lingered near the entrance.

Tseng stepped back from the body. Manch peered in through Drzymkowski's faceplate, then turned to look at her. "Are you okay?"

Tseng felt weak, but nodded assent. "The worst is over."

Manch turned back to the body. He studied the skull through the faceplate, his expression thoughtful. "Houston, the subject is enclosed in a space suit. It's inflated with the gases of decomposition, and the pressure has already stabilized at approximately ten psi above normal suit atmosphere. This is a very advanced state of decomposition—approximately seventy to eighty percent skeletonization." Manch glanced at Greer for confirmation. Greer nodded agreement. "The subject has certainly been dead for more than a week . . . I'd guess almost two weeks," Manch finished.

"The space suit is the only indication we have that this is Drzymkowski's body," Greer interjected.

"The body will be tentatively identified as that of Frank Drzymkowski," Christiansen responded.

Tseng aimed the handheld camera and shot a few minutes of video of the body, all the while remembering Mobley's video and her last sight of Drzymkowski alive. They would have to move the corpse out of the dome and, eventually, to the *Collins* for transport back to Earth. How did one carry a space suit filled with two hundred-plus pounds of gas, jellied remains, and bones? The grisly thought sent another stab of what felt like electric current up her spine.

"Houston, from marks on, and damage to, the front of victim's skull, I'm confident that the cause of death can be listed as blunt force trauma," Manch said.

"Far Side, Houston. Roger. We copy." There was a brief pause, then in a more spontaneous, emotional tone, Christiansen added, "Our hearts go out to you guys. Sorting this thing out has turned into a nightmare job."

"Thanks, Dave. We all appreciate your concern and your empathy," Tseng said. "Are there any special instructions as to how we should prepare the body for return transport?"

"You'll have to stand by on that."

"Roger, Houston," Tseng acknowledged.

"Someone had enough presence of mind to enclose the corpse to prevent contamination of the dome's air supply," Horo said.

"There was no alternative, if the others were to survive," Lebby said.

"There's almost nothing of him left to examine, is there?" Tseng asked.

"X-ray and toxicology analysis can still be done on these remains, but that's all," Greer said.

She turned to Cochagne. "You'd better get pictures of this, Jer."

Nodding, Cochagne moved forward with the reluctance of a man steeling himself for a grisly sight.

"Far Side, the consensus here is that as long as there's no damage to it, the suit will continue to contain the remains with no problem, for the time being. Just don't open it under any circumstances, and don't let it get punctured."

"We copy that." Tseng answered.

"That stuff must stink. What if that smell were to spread through the entire base?" Horo asked.

"Not only that, the organisms in the putrid gas can carry contagious diseases," Manch said to the group.

Tseng saw his expression become apologetic when he turned toward her. "In addition to a rescue and recovery operation, it appears that we also need to conduct a crime scene investigation."

"I'm relying on your judgment, Paul," Tseng replied.

"Since this will be the first such investigation in the history of the space program, we'll need expert help," Manch said. "That being the case, Dave, we should leave everything in the area untouched for now, until we've been through the rest of the base."

"That's a good plan," Christiansen said. "For your information, as I look at the hard copy of your biomedical telemetry readings, I see they were all off the scale there for a few minutes," the CAPCOM added. "There were terrific increases in heart rate and respiration across the board. It's understandable."

"Roger on that," Cochagne said. "Houston, there are no bodies in any of the other sleep stations. It's a real mess in here, and we'll have to sort it all out and take pictures . . . but I think you might want to take a look at Bob Faden's quarters now."

"We can only take a moment for that," the CAPCOM replied.

"I know. I just think it's important," Cochagne said.

While the others were filing slowly out of the CDR sleep station, Tseng took a last look around. The compartment looked like a hotel room with all the signs of a month's occupancy by a person who was less than tidy. The ordinary complement of work and off duty clothing and personal hygiene articles was scattered haphazardly through the room, rather than stowed neatly on the storage shelves provided by the habitat designers. Judging merely from the sizes, they belonged to Drzymkowski. Where were Mobley's things, she wondered. Pictures of Drzymkowski's wife and other small personal possessions and mementos were scattered about in keeping with personal habit and astronaut tradition, such small reminders of home serving to add warmth to a hostile environment and a much-needed feeling of privacy in what was otherwise a cramped communal living situation. There was even a miniature chess set left out on a table and captured pieces from both sides were arranged at each end, making it appear as though the big engineer had played a game with someone and had stepped out of the room for a moment. She emerged from the CDR sleep station to find the other astronauts gathering around the entrance to a room farther down the passageway.

The moment Tseng looked inside the cubicle there was no doubt in her mind that it had belonged to a madman. Obscene and satanic words and phrases were written or painted over and over again in layers of black paint until every hard surface was painted nearly a solid black. Splash stains from spilled liquids radiated out from the center of the room. The bed linens were in a pile on top of the sleeping pallet. They were stained with blood. The room was cluttered with paper refuse from the computer's printer, small scraps of building materials, pieces of lunar rock, family photos carried up from Earth, and snapshots taken with the personal camera that lay in broken pieces on the table.

The others crowded in close behind her to look inside and then stood staring, their whispers of shocked amazement and disgust flooding the COMM link for a few moments, until she interrupted impatiently with, "Houston, I'm in Faden's quarters now." Instead of elaborating on the radio, she raised the camera to her eye and shot video. "I don't know how well this room will photograph under these conditions," she said. "Through the camera lens, it looks like we're in a mine shaft."

"It looks that way to us, too," Christiansen said.

"Not all of this stuff belongs to Faden," Lebby said. "Some of Takizawa's pictures and personal effects are here, too."

"Do you have any thoughts you'd care to share about all of this?" Tseng asked Greer.

"It's a certainty that rituals of a satanic nature have been performed in here, in this room," Greer said. "It has the characteristics of a shrine. I'd like to reserve any further speculation until such time as I can do a more thorough analysis, however."

"Let's move on, then," Tseng said. She followed the others out into the passageway, and they moved as a group toward the recreation area and the wardroom. As she passed the Personal Hygiene Station, the base's combination washroom, shower, and toilet, a glance inside caused her to stop and to aim her camera lens into the room for the benefit of the watchers in Mission Control.

The cover of the base's first aid kit, a molded plastic box stowed in a wall bracket, hung open. The entire contents—patches and rolls of sterile gauze, adhesive tape and Band-Aids; oral and injectable medicines, a hypogun and disposable thermometer strips; ointments, disinfectants and astringents—most in sanitary wrappers for individual application, were strewn about the floor of the compartment.

Along with the words "Drink blood" and "Food for the

Moon," more obscenities were scrawled across the mirror with the reddish-brown substance, but now it also coated the walls and it was streaked across the surfaces of the plumbing fixtures. It had proved impossible to tell what it was in Mobley's stills and video, but now Tseng had to master a strong feeling of revulsion and mortification. The compartment looked as though it was painted with the menstrual blood from the blood-soaked tampons which littered the floor. She glanced at Horo. Her friend's expression confirmed her conclusion.

"It's in worse condition than it looked in the FS-5 video," was all Cochagne said.

Tseng avoided eye contact with the male astronauts as she left the compartment, though she was annoyed with herself for doing so.

In the recreation area, the wardroom furniture and the furniture from Level Three was piled against the wall across the room, together with various hand tools, articles of clothing, a mattress from a sleep station, wads of paper refuse, and the exercise equipment, benches, and fitness accessories. It formed a densely packed "junk mountain." Here, too, the surrounding walls were defaced with obscenities written in paint, marking pen, and dried blood. This room was the site of a strange incident known as "the phenomenon," in one of FS-5's last video transmissions. No one had yet come up with an explanation for it.

"Unrestricted playtime at the insane asylum," Cochagne mumbled.

When Tseng turned to regard him, he gave her a reassuring wink. His face had a comical, boyish twist that made her smile. He had the reputation, in the media and in the astronaut corps, of being a ladies' man. He was one of the few single men in the astronaut program. Was the reputation the result of unavoidable publicity, or was it an indictment of his character? Having trained with him prior to the Far Side project, Tseng knew that the darkly handsome astronaut, a Marine-trained pilot, was the consummate professional. She had deliberately and aggressively campaigned to recruit him for the FS-6 team, and during the long training phase for the mission, he'd exhibited just the right amount of natural charm and professional detachment in his attitude toward Arminta Horo and toward her. That he appeared to take pleasure in being the "class clown" for the team and for her did not diminish his ability on the job in her eyes.

Dismayed, Tseng studied the pile. Swarms of flies darted in and out at certain places. She noticed that Greer, too, was staring at it fixedly.

Greer reached into the dense tangle and yanked at a chair embedded in the wall of the junk mountain. It came loose, and she tossed it aside carelessly.

The chair bounced toward a bank of controls, but Lebby caught it just before the impact. "Be careful of the equipment," he said sharply.

Greer ignored him and pulled at another chair in the pile with all her strength. "Help me," she said, gasping for air from the physical effort.

His body language showing his reluctance, Lebby lumbered forward.

Tseng crossed to her in floating strides. "What is it?"

"A feeling. A hunch. I . . . I don't know . . . !" Greer panted.

Tseng unshouldered the portable camera and put it aside. She grasped the center post of the card table and pulled. The refuse was tightly packed. Many of the pieces were interlocked, and she found it difficult to brace herself against the effort in the lighter gravity. "Give us a hand," she called to the others. The rest of the team converged on the pile and their added strength succeeded in disentangling the pieces of the wardroom's gym equipment.

Someone was imprisoned inside the stack. At the same moment Tseng recognized Louise Washington, other exclamations of "Washington!" sounded like a hurricane in her earphones. She redoubled her efforts to clear away the debris.

"Houston, we have just located a second crew member, Louise Washington. We're working now to ascertain her condition," Tseng announced, her voice breathy with excitement.

"Far Side, Houston. We're standing by."

Washington was clad only in a uniform tank top and gym shorts, and her shoulder-length red hair hung over her face in stringy clumps. She was cut, bruised, and filthy. Where there were no purplish bruises, the skin tone was pale blue. The blood on the numerous scratches covering the body was dried. There was a scab over the deep cut on the left side of her scalp where she'd been struck by a flying object during "the phenomenon." The larger, oozing wounds were alive with flies.

As they removed more of the debris imprisoning Washington, Tseng strained to see every detail of the astronaut's physical condition, searching for a sign of life. Had the dry, cracked lips moved? When Washington's eyelids fluttered, Tseng called out, "Washington is alive, Houston!" She was overcome with relief and thrilled with elation. She did not care about being pushed rudely and hastily aside by Manch when he crowded in to get at Washington with an oxygen mask.

"Give us more light," Greer ordered, moving to assist Manch.

Horo, Cochagne, and Lebby directed flashlights into the tangle.

Tseng retrieved the camera. The scene through the lens was grainy, but the figure of Washington was recognizable. She did not try to control the excited tremble in her voice when she announced, "Houston, we have just located one survivor, pilot and communications engineer, Captain Louise Washington. The medical team is effecting rescue." Through her headset, cheers from Mission Control and the *Collins* were deafening.

Only Manch and Greer were oblivious. They moved Washington out of the pile of debris with care and laid her out flat on the floor.

"There are definite signs of dehydration," Manch said in a tone that cut through the cross chatter. "Dry mucus membranes, collapsed external jugulars, skin texture thick and parchmentlike."

Greer was already wrapping an electronic device with a wide cloth cuff attached around Washington's upper arm. "The automatic blood pressure monitor is on," she said.

"Set it to read at Q2," Manch said.

"Q2 means at intervals of two minutes," Greer told the others. She set the blood pressure control function and the cuff inflated itself. "In a normal situation, Paul and I would communicate strictly in medical terms. We'll try to remember to translate."

"Houston, we're establishing peripheral I.V. access through the antecubital veins to administer electrolyte solution," Manch said, inserting intravenous needles into the crooks of Washington's arms. He secured them with tape while Greer pulled two clear plastic I.V. bags filled with solution from the black bag she had carried over from the *Collins*. Tseng marveled that Manch and Greer could be so deft in their movements, even in space suits, and with heavy gloves.

Greer plugged the tubes into the I.V. needles, then began to squeeze the contents of one bag into Washington's arm. From her own point of view, Tseng reasoned, it was important to stay focused on the relevant action, to frame and shoot only the details that were important, not the whole hodgepodge of activity going on around Washington. She kept the camera on the unconscious astronaut while the others moved in the background or entered the picture from off frame.

"This is real 'frontier medicine.' One of you needs to help," Manch said, glancing up.

Cochagne moved to Washington's side and Manch handed him the second I.V. bag.

"The solution won't flow fast enough in lunar gravity, and we don't have a pump, so you'll have to squeeze the bag," Manch told the astronaut. "Harder," he said, as Cochagne gingerly closed his hands around the bag.

Tseng experienced a squeamish feeling as Cochagne squeezed the bag hard, pumping the solution into Washington.

Manch yanked Washington's tank top up to her neck to bare her chest, then he took a small electronic box from his own black bag. He affixed its three electrodes across Washington's chest and over her heart. "Houston, I've just placed the monitor leads across the precordium," he said.

"BP is eighty-five over fifty, Paul," Greer said worriedly.

Manch switched on the monitor, and Tseng saw the heartbeat function displayed as an oscilloscope pattern with high rounded peaks and deep valleys. Something about it looked wrong to her, but she did not want to interrupt Manch and Greer with questions.

"Pulse is one-twenty."

"Sinus tach . . . Houston, sinus tachycardia . . . rapid heartbeat. It's not unusual in cases of dehydration," Manch said, "but it's cause for concern."

Washington's eyes fluttered, then slowly opened.

"She's conscious," Tseng said excitedly. She got down on her knees and moved in for a closer shot, expecting to see recognition and relief in the astronaut's eyes.

The anticipation changed to alarm and confusion as a

look of pure terror twisted Washington's features into a grotesque mask. The astronaut screamed as though, instead of her rescuers, she beheld demons from the depths of hell reaching for her.

"Louise, you're going to be all right! I'm a doctor," Manch yelled, but it was useless trying to overcome the sound and tactile barriers the space suits were creating between them and Washington.

She could hear the woman's screams of hysteria through her helmet faceplate, but the sounds were muffled. The FS-6 astronauts were all linked to each other, to Earth and to the *Collins* by radio, but not to the reality outside their suits, Tseng realized. It was something about that reality that was terrifying Washington. Her face was red from the strain of her hysteria. Tseng could see but not hear her gasping for breath, and the violent heaving of the woman's chest told her that the fright she was experiencing, known only to her, was a threat to her survival.

"What's wrong with her? We're here to save her," Lebby shouted, his voice strained with emotion.

Washington continued to scream. Her body writhed and convulsed with the effort of her dry throat. Unexpectedly, she flailed her arms and both I.V. needles were torn out, spattering Greer, Manch, and Cochagne with blood.

Lebby and Horo lumbered forward and grabbed Washington's arms and legs. They pinned her down, but her struggles did not cease.

The importance of getting pictures kept Tseng behind the camera lens. She and it were moving and seeing as one.

"Far Side, what's happening?" Christiansen asked anxiously.

"Washington is delirious. She's fighting us, and we don't know why," Tseng answered. She had worked to keep alive the hope of a joyous reunion with the FS-5 survivors; now, she felt her expectations and her emotions plunging. "Can't you do something?" She glanced helplessly at Manch and Greer.

Neither one acknowledged her. Instead, Greer kept her eyes on the monitor. The rhythm of the heartbeat was clearly changing and it looked perilously abnormal even to Tseng's untrained eyes.

"V tach," Greer said.

"We have a ventricular tachycardia, Houston," Manch said. "Let's reestablish the I.V. through central access," he told Greer.

"Subclavian vein?"

"Too risky under these conditions. Internal jugular."

Tseng winced when Greer inserted a large I.V. needle at the base of Washington's throat and slowly pushed it in.

"I'm giving her an amp of lidocaine," Manch said, grabbing a disposable drug ampoule from the bag. He snapped it open, inserted it into the I.V. needle, and pushed the contents in.

"BP is eighty systolic. I can't get a diastolic," Greer said.

To Tseng, it appeared that the drug was taking effect as Washington's body relaxed and she stopped struggling, but on the monitor, the heart line was now beginning to resemble a seismometer readout during an earthquake— it was extremely irregular and jumping all over the scale.

"V tach is now V fib," Greer said. Her voice was calm yet quietly urgent.

"I'll check another channel," Manch said, stabbing clumsily at the pressure pad controls with his gloved fingers. There was no change in the heart line. "I've got V fib on both channels—ventricular fibrillation." Manch reached into the black bag and pulled out a box with two paddles attached. "She's in clinical death. I'm going ahead with defibrillation."

"No blood pressure reading," Greer said. She reached into Manch's bag, drew out two large pads, and placed them onto Washington's chest.

"The paddles are revved. Everyone has to be clear of body contact when I give her the juice," Manch said.

Greer withdrew her hands and moved back; Cochagne, Lebby, and Horo did the same. Tseng continued to shoot the scene with the portable camera while she leaned back on her haunches, making sure that she was not touching Washington.

"All clear," Manch called out. He put the paddles of the defibrillator over the chest pads and pushed the buttons. Washington's muscles contracted with the electrical charge, causing her body to jump. Manch watched the monitor for precious seconds, but it showed no change in the uncoordinated heart rhythm.

"Recharging the paddles to three hundred joules," Greer said. Tensely, they watched the machine's charge indicator.

"All clear," Manch called, then pressed the paddle buttons again.

Again, Washington's body jumped with the shock.

Again, the rhythm on the monitor did not change.

"Full cardiac arrest, Paul," Greer said.

"Bag her," Manch responded.

Greer pulled an oxygen mask with a bag attached and a small tank of oxygen from the black bag.

"I have to pump for her heart," Manch said, placing his hands on Washington's chest on the lower portion of the breastbone. He pushed hard, then repeated the action, rocking his body back and forth rhythmically, as Greer put the mask over Washington's face and connected the air tank. She turned the valve on the tank, then squeezed the bag in sync with Manch's pumping. Manch was panting from his effort and his voice came in explosive grunts over the COMM as he said, "I'm going to intubate now—to insert an endotracheal tube."

Manch stopped pumping as Greer handed him a straight-bladed instrument and a piece of plastic tubing. Tseng nearly gagged as he lifted the mask from Washington's face and inserted the instrument into her throat. He followed with the tube, then replaced the mask and bag over the astronaut's mouth and nose. "I only hope that I've threaded it right," he said tensely. "Normally, I would be able to use a stethoscope or put my head on her chest to listen. With the helmet on, I can't tell. We may be putting the air into her stomach." Manch began the chest compressions, again, as Greer squeezed the bag, but, after a few seconds he said, "I need Iona to take over for me with the chest compressions, so someone else has to keep pumping the oxygen bag."

Lebby moved quickly to take Greer's place as Greer took Manch's. He tried to time his squeezes to Greer's pumping, but his movements were clumsy, and the rhythm was not as smooth as Greer's and Manch's. The two doctors were an efficient team and it was apparent to Tseng that they had worked in tandem in an emergency room environment many times before.

"How am I doing?" Lebby asked worriedly.

Manch was rummaging in the drug bag, and he withdrew an ampoule. After a quick glance at Lebby he said, "That's good. Squeeze hard, but not too fast. "I'm going to give an amp of epinephrine q5, Houston," he said as he snapped the ampoule open and inserted it into the I.V. access. "While we're waiting for it to take effect, I'm going to draw blood from the femoral artery and check blood gases and chemistry."

He took the sample and placed it into a small electronic device, which Tseng recognized as a blood analyzer.

"Bad numbers. She's acidic as hell," he said, a moment later. "Sodium level: one-fifty; potassium at three point two; BUN: thirty-three; creatinine one point four; PCO_2 is thirty, the PO_2 is four hundred-twelve. The pH is seven point zero six."

The numbers were meaningless to Tseng, though she knew a little about metabolic readings from monitoring her own fitness level. What affected her was that they were, in Manch's words, "bad numbers." It meant Washington was slipping away from them.

"The pH indicates lactic acid accumulation from anaerobic activity," Manch said.

"The PCO_2 shows hyperventilation from being bagged," Greer elaborated.

Manch took a drug ampoule from the black bag. I'm giving her an amp of bicarb," Manch said, pushing the contents in through the I.V. He turned and watched the monitor for what seemed like an eternity. "No joy on the epi," he said. "I'll shock her again."

Tseng felt herself giving up hope. It was a physical feeling of "letting go"; a sensation of release. She was distancing herself emotionally from Washington. The worst part of it was that the FS-5 astronaut was dying from fright, and it made no sense.

"The paddles are revved," Manch said. "All clear!" Again the astronauts withdrew from the patient. Tseng heard the dull thud through her helmet as Manch fired the charge. "Recharging the paddles ... all clear," Manch said again, and again he pushed the buttons. The seconds ticked by. On the monitor, the heart line was flattening out, but Manch and Greer were not ready to give up. Tseng felt a twinge of guilt. The camera was the omnipotent watcher.

"I'm giving an amp of bretyllium," Manch said, pushing the drug in through the I.V. needle.

The line on the monitor was now flat.

"I'm going to shock her again," Manch said stubbornly. "All clear!"

Washington's body jumped with the electric current once, then again. The line stayed flat.

Manch withdrew slowly this time. Tseng could tell he was drained physically and emotionally.

"It's eighty-nine hours: fifteen minutes Ground Elapsed Time," Christiansen said.

"Paul, it's been over forty minutes," Greer said quietly.

"You're right. I'm sorry, Houston," Manch said.

"Thanks for your efforts," Christiansen said.

"I'm stating the cause of death as cardiac arrest promoted by underlying electrolyte and acid based imbalances," Manch said.

Tseng lowered the video camera. "What made her go berserk the way she did? She was terrified?"

"The air is bad in here. It could have been as simple as an hypoxic hallucination from the reduced oxygen," Manch said.

"The electrolyte imbalance alone was enough to make her become unstable under stress," Greer said. "Fright then triggered the arrhythmia—the malignant heart rhythm."

"Dr. Ramirez requests that you bring blood and spinal fluid samples back with you," Christiansen said.

"We copy," Manch answered.

"The flies are still attracted to something deeper inside there," Cochagne said in a low voice, angling his flashlight beam to illuminate the swarms of iridescent black insects darting in and out of the gaps between the piled objects. "Can we move Washington?"

Manch removed the I.V. needle from Washington's neck and the portable oxygen mask over her mouth and nose. "We can move her now," he said.

Tseng put down the camera to help with Washington. Anxious moments passed while they lifted the astronaut's body clear of the debris. Then, spurred on by the need to finish the job, as well as the hope of finding another crewman alive, Cochagne, Horo, and Lebby removed more pieces of the piled up furniture and refuse.

The first glimpse of Ann Bisio's corpse turned Tseng's stomach and left her shocked and stunned. The rotted, bloated body was suspended upright in the tangled debris, impaled through the abdomen by a piece of the lightweight aluminum pipe stock, the basic structural member which formed the sturdy tetrahedral trusses, the support pillars and beams for the Space Station "power tower" and the framework of the Far Side structures. Bisio's eyes were frozen open in terror and surprise, and the protruding tongue was black and swollen. Gases of decomposition had raised oozing blisters on the blackish-blue skin which was crawling with flies. Where the blisters were eaten away, the open cavities were alive with flies and maggots and pupae of flies.

Flies swarmed in Bisio's open mouth, and flies crawled across her swollen, distended eyeballs. The blood from the open puncture wound had turned black along with the flesh around it. There was discoloration around her mouth, neck, wrists, and ankles.

"Houston, Far Side. We've just discovered the remains of crewman Ann Bisio," Tseng said mechanically. There were groans and sighs from Mission Control. She heard Horo choke back tears.

"Mother of God," DeSosa said softly on the COMM.

Tseng closed her eyes, overcome by the horrendous sight. To control the urge to retch, an action that could be dangerous and even fatal to her inside her space suit, she took several deep breaths and steadied her nerves before opening her eyes again.

When she did open them, she found herself looking into Jerry Cochagne's face. He had leaned forward until the faceplate of his helmet was almost touching hers. The astronaut's deep blue eyes regarded her face intently. Though he remained silent, there was something compelling about his intensity. It stirred up emotions within her that were disturbing.

Was she merely disconcerted to discover an aspect of the carefree and jovial astronaut's personality that she had never seen before? His attention was focused on her exclusively. For a brief moment, she could only stare back at him, dumbfounded and tongue-tied in amazement. Then her mind quickly rationalized Cochagne's behavior. They had all been profoundly affected by the evidence of the horrible deaths of their friends and colleagues. It was a normal reaction for them to pull closer together as a team, now, while seeking solace and comfort from each other in the face of such a shared ordeal.

But the expression in Cochagne's eyes went beyond anything she could conjure up to safely depersonalize the moment. He was looking at her . . . into her, and she knew that she was seeing Jerry Cochagne, the man, for the first time.

Manch's voice broke the euphoric spell. ". . . and there are signs of trauma on the body. Bisio has been dead approximately two weeks also, so her death may be connected to Drzymkowski's . . ."

Tseng did not know how long the physician had been speaking to Mission Control, but the feeling that time had stopped, for herself and Cochagne, was unsettling. She positioned the camera and shot video of Bisio.

"Far Side, we copy, and we want to emphasize the advisability of extreme caution in your reconnaissance of Far Side Level One," Christiansen said.

"Roger, Houston," Tseng replied. "I'm taking Horo, Cochagne, and Lebby with me. The medical team will remain with Washington and Bisio. Over."

"Roger, Far Side."

Lebby was moving restlessly through the room, as if

searching for anything that might be a clue, but without knowing what to look for. He was the first to reach the hatchway to Level One.

"What could have happened here that caused this . . . this insanity?" he asked anxiously.

Though directed at everyone, Tseng knew the question was not rhetorical. Lebby's technical mind desperately wanted a technical answer.

Cochagne's shrug looked exaggerated because of his bulky space suit. "It's hard to conceive of a handpicked team of trained scientists and engineers behaving like homicidal maniacs, isn't it?"

Tseng had to turn her body to look at the pilot when he spoke, and it put Greer in her line of sight as well. The nervous urgency in the woman's actions, while she worked with Manch to examine Bisio, was a sign of strain. Tseng was aware of how much her own nerves were on edge from exhaustion.

The flash of Cochagne's photographic strobe interrupted her thoughts. He was shooting pictures of Bisio. Every detail of the nauseating sight would have to be shown to Mission Control. Tseng raised the video camera to her eye and began to transmit more live video. Through the lens, she saw the corpse illuminated by the strobe again, but now the image was surrealistic, the body like a ghoulish figure in a wax museum Chamber of Horrors suddenly revealed by a dramatic flash of lightning. She found herself continuing to stare in macabre fascination long after she'd captured enough video of the scene.

Feverish excitement over finding Washington, then deep depression over losing her had given way to revulsion and disappointment over the discovery of Bisio. Now, with every step downward to the "basement" level, the feeling of apprehension became more and more oppressive to Tseng. She felt even more sickened, physically exhausted, and emotionally burned out than she had on the upper levels. Despite her feeling, she continued her descent, followed by Horo, Cochagne, and Lebby.

Pausing halfway down the stairs, she directed her suit lights into the cavernous space. There were no injured crewmen, nor were there any dead bodies, but the signs of violence were unmistakable. Pieces of the lab equipment and a quantity of supplies and fragile electronic components destined for the Science Dome had been set up in one area to serve as a makeshift lab. The area was ransacked, and broken laboratory glassware covered the floor.

Up to now, this level was to have been used mainly for the storage of the construction and scientific equipment. After completion of the Science Dome, Far Side would have a fully functional lab. This space would then be partitioned into an official sick bay and more sleeping quarters, so that the number of mission specialists in residence at the Moon base could be doubled by overlapping the crews and extending the length of stay for certain astronauts.

"Another auxiliary computer terminal has bitten the dust," Lebby said, directing his flashlight at a pile of debris. Tseng saw a ball-peen hammer lying near it. She thought of Drzymkowski's crushed skull and shuddered. In her earphones, Manch was describing the condition of Bisio's body to Houston in medical terms that were no less horrifying and graphic than a layman's description in every detail.

"This place reminds me of a mad scientist's lair," Cochagne said.

They reached the bottom of the companionway. Horo threaded her way slowly and carefully through broken glass to a long worktable made from a prefab wall panel supported in the middle and on each end by containers of lab equipment. It was covered with notebooks, NASA charts, and scraps of paper.

Horo played the beam of her flashlight over the table. "There are lunar geological charts and plans of the base and its systems here," she told them. "The notes are in Mike's handwriting. He was working on something down here."

"Mobley wanted to work alone," Tseng said. "He wanted to be away from the others. Why?"

"And why was his 'sanctum sanctorum' invaded and destroyed?" Lebby added.

Cochagne's flashlight beam found a picture of Mobley's wife and two sons propped against a wall next to a bed assembled from chair cushions and the light synthetic blanket the mission commander had worn wrapped around himself the night of the phenomenon. Someone had taken care to align the cushions, and the blanket was folded and tucked around them according to a strict military standard. "He was sleeping here, too . . ." Cochagne let the sentence trail off suggestively.

"He came back here after the destruction," Lebby cut in. "Look how his things are arranged." She joined Horo and sifted through the papers on the worktable, careful not to disturb the order with her bulky gloves.

Mobley had tucked pieces of scratch paper with handwritten notes and mathematical calculations between the charts and blueprints. Glare from the lights on her helmet visor made the handwriting impossible to decipher, but the thought—messages from the grave—flashed into her mind along with "mental highlights" from the hours she had spent, as CAPCOM, talking the commander through a series of mystifying technical problems while the patently unexplainable transpired all around him.

At the time, she had sensed there was much Mobley was not telling her. On occasion, he had sounded exceptionally vague. Wild speculation over the COMM would not have been professional or acceptable. Looking at the destruction, she now understood. How could Mobley have talked about the insanity that had gripped him and his crew? No one would have believed him or listened to him. To technicians, scientists, administrators, it would all have sounded like the babbling of an insane man. It would have meant the end of a brilliant military career.

Had Mobley preferred death to dishonor?

To Tseng that was totally out of character for him. And yet . . .

Early studies about possible problems in group psychodynamics on long duration space missions were based on Admiral Richard E. Byrd's journals of his Antarctic expeditions. Studies conducted at the Space Station proved that the initial conclusions were still valid, because the two environments had much in common: they were sensory-deprived and spatially restricted. The hazards of "wintering over"—that is, remaining alone and isolated at base camp through the Antarctic winter—could include insomnia, carelessness, depression, and irritability. Astronauts were prescreened for high resistance to these problems, yet each member of FS-5 had manifested them to such a degree that it had impaired their efficiency. It didn't take a military genius to see that a total collapse of discipline had occurred here.

Tseng was conscious of a void, both personal and professional, caused by Mobley's absence.

It was a terrible emotional letdown. More than she wanted to admit to herself. It was hard to sort out her feelings. It was not that they had started a long-distance love affair, or a romantic obsession, a syndrome that often developed with electronic communications especially between strangers of the opposite sex—the mysterious became alluring, then erotic.

While Mike Mobley was no stranger, and their relationship was not personal, still, the daily interchange was a challenge requiring her total focus. After a while, she had looked forward to her link with the FS-5 commander, even coming to prefer extra time on the COMM to personal time.

Telepathy was not something she believed in. Had there been an empathic link between herself and Mobley? Maybe. Toward the end, it had taxed her willpower to remain objective and aloof from the commander's problems at Far Side.

Emotions aside, the base commander's death created a serious information void. Astronauts drew heavily on each others' experiences. In Mobley's case, there could be no mission debriefing; no orderly transfer of command.

Would any of the slips of paper randomly tucked between the charts and diagrams refer to things that happened during the days of radio silence with Earth? She needed help to piece together the chronology of events leading to the whole Far Side disaster. "Houston, it appears that there are no more survivors inside the Main Dome," Tseng said. "That leaves Mobley, Faden, and Takizawa still unaccounted for. I'd like Greer and Manch to go back to the *Aldrin* with me."

"We have no problem with that," Christiansen said. "Because of the exposed corpse, you will have to take a few special precautions inside the dome. We'll discuss some procedures down here and then run our ideas by you. We'll outline a procedure for the fly infestation as well, though, for the life of us, we can't explain it down here."

"We copy that, Houston," Tseng replied mechanically.

☾

From the GO for lunar orbital insertion, through descent, EVA PREP, Far Side, ingress to Far Side Base, and reconnaissance, the rescue saga had lasted more than twenty-six hours, all in the hope of finding survivors inside the Main Dome. Bianco felt weighted down with her own exhaustion, and depressed over the grim discoveries and events at Far Side.

It was one-thirty in the morning, Houston time. The only routine changes of shift in Mission Control had occurred among the flight controllers and the CAPCOMs. The red team had monitored the *Collins'* landing. However, EVA-1 had not begun until after nine PM Houston time, so the night shift—the black team—had monitored it. They had lived every moment of the rescue attempt on the edge of their seats, and they were emotionally wrung out. Since the last live video of Bisio's corpse, a ponderous silence had settled over them. Unfortunately, the green team was not scheduled to relieve them for another four hours.

It was the middle of the night and Bianco longed to tell Tseng . . . What? That she was directing things at her end, which, as everyone knew, was too far away to be of any real help at all? Everyone at Mission Control was a bystander. It was more important, at this stage, to tell Tseng only what she needed to know.

She felt inadequate on that score. The events of the last few hours were completely out of her realm of expertise. Here on Earth, one called the cops in situations like this.

Bianco stretched her body until her tired muscles were on the verge of cramping. The area near the CAPCOM console looked like, and was, a nomad encampment. A circle of chairs with an outer perimeter of the discarded package refuse from meals from the snack bar marked the boundary. They were all eating, working, and napping in the chairs, getting up only to stretch, pace, or make a hurried trip to the public restroom down the hall.

Everyone was keeping in touch with the outside world via television news reports and the phones in Mission Control.

There was a sense of close family support among the group of technical advisers keeping the vigil with her. No one wanted to go home until the latest set of problems was solved. The trouble was, for every solution, a new problem arose to take its place. Bahija Fayyad, Al Weinstock, and Ralph Stromeyer, part of Dave Christiansen's FS-7 crew, were using their training and expertise to guide their fellow astronauts at Far Side. For them, the time spent in Mission Control was also the final phase of training. If something happened to Tseng and her crew, it would be their only preparation for what they might encounter. Their opinions and comments were being given a certain deference in recognition of that fact. Jack Bucar was on hand as a veteran military man and astronaut. The commander of FS-1 was regarded as the father figure among them.

Also present were Ignacio Ramirez, the astronaut-MD who had assisted in Mission Control during the attempted rescue of Washington, and Engineer Chris Sweet, and Astronomer Chuck MacCallum, the mission specialists from FS-6 who had lost their seats to Manch and Greer. There were still more astronauts and scientists working with the group on a drop-in basis when they could take time out from their own work.

Tseng, Manch, and Greer were en route to the *Aldrin*. Expectations of what they would find there were low. Tseng had the camera, but they would be lucky to have video from the inside of the powered-down LLM.

The flight director for the shift had made notes on a sheet of paper, which he handed to Christiansen. The astronaut glanced at it before opening the COMM link.

"We all consider EVA-1 a complete success. We really appreciate what you're going through." Christiansen paused for emotional emphasis, before continuing with the necessary technical exchange of information which was, by comparison, dispassionate. "We've got a couple of schedule updates and your fuel and consumable updates, but we'd like to talk candidly about your assessment of the immediate situation at Far Side."

"From the standpoint of the medical team, the next few days will be critical," Paul Manch's voice came over the COMM. Fatigue had put a hoarse edge in it. For Bianco, it was a sharp reminder of the reason that working in space could never become routine. There were too many ways to die. Man was too dependent on artificial life support. Another tragedy at Far Side, this time due to the fatigue of the FS-6 crewmen, must be avoided at any cost.

"Dr. Greer and I would like to learn anything we can from postmortem data on Washington and Bisio," Manch continued. "We're in agreement that an examination of Drzymkowski is beyond our capabilities at the present time."

"One question," Christiansen said. "What's the outlook on the technical side?"

"Jerry Cochagne and I feel we can be operational inside of eighteen hours," Lebby responded.

"We're still analyzing your live transmissions, but the damage looks superficial," Christiansen said. "We're looking forward to the still photos, which should reveal more detail."

"We'd appreciate a GO for a full week to recover all casualties and to do our on-site investigation," Tseng said.

"We'll have to get back to you on those decisions," Christiansen told her.

Bianco studied the faces of the assembled astronauts. They were a formidable talent pool, representing a cross-section of disciplines, experience, and backgrounds. "As it shapes up, we have two missing, one accident-related death, and we have at least two . . . suspicious deaths," she said. The word "murder" had stuck in her throat. "Also, from the recorded video it looks like . . ." she searched for an appropriately neutral word, ". . . acts of vandalism have taken place inside the base. Are any of you familiar with the words and the numbers . . . the "occult science" thing Dr. Greer mentioned?"

The question was met with a tense and awkward silence. It verified her gut feeling of the mood among the astronauts. Based on her own experience, she doubted that any of them had gone through their entire childhoods and young adulthoods without exposure to horror movies, stories of the supernatural, or other elements of superstition, such as devil worship and witchcraft. They were tightly woven into the fabric of human history. It would be extraordinary if these highly educated people had not studied the Middle Ages, the Spanish Inquisition, or the Salem witch trials. But to avow such knowledge now might arouse suspicion, and mere suspicion could destroy careers and lives. With the very real possibility of a witch hunt facing them, the subject was taboo; verboten. No one was going to reveal any knowledge by coming forward even to speculate.

Even Christiansen remained mute, yet the expression on his face told Bianco that there was much the devoutly religious astronaut wanted to say. If Christiansen did not want to speculate openly, perhaps it would be possible to draw him out privately, though Bianco wondered if there was anything valuable to be gained from it. The astronaut's point of view in the critical areas would hinge on a specific faith and dogma instead of general mythology.

"This is bad business," Jack Bucar said with a sad head shake. His voice, made gravelly by decades of command, cut easily through the ambient noise.

Dee Bianco genuinely liked Bucar, and valued his experience and knowledge of space craft systems. He had the deep squint lines that were burned into a veteran pilot's face by years in plexiglass cockpits, and he'd earned a star for leading a squadron of fighter jockeys during the bloody five-year Philippines Conflict of a decade ago. He was the first one-star on active duty to go into space. Though he was only in his mid-fifties, he was still their "old man"—the oldest astronaut in the program.

"Remind them to get as much photographic coverage of Bisio as possible before they move the body," Bianco told Christiansen, and the astronaut leaned toward the mike. "Far Side, this is Houston. Do you copy?"

"Go ahead, Houston," Tseng answered.

"We have a request . . ."

". . . we heard, Houston. We'll get full photographic coverage of Bisio before attempting removal of the body," Tseng said.

"Will the regular disinfectant that they have up there mask the odor of the decomposing body inside the Main Dome?" Sweet asked.

"Nothing's been invented that will take away that stench," Ramirez said.

Sweet grimaced. "They'll just have to live with it, then."

Sweet, Stromeyer, and a Japanese mission specialist named Yoshio Adachi had each accepted the news about Drzymkowski and Takizawa with stoic silence. Whatever mourning they might do would be in the elite company of their construction crews. For now, they were all grim-faced with determination to see the situation through.

"They're going to be dealing with three decomposing corpses," Stromeyer said.

"The rate of decomposition varies with temperature," Ramirez answered, "but there's no way to preserve

the bodies inside the Main Dome. They just don't
have sufficient space, nor is there enough capacity for
refrigeration."

"Except outside, on the lunar surface as they enter the
night phase," Al Weinstock, FS-7's physicist, added.
"Unfortunately Far Side will be in the sun for three more
days and the outside temperatures are still high."

Bianco said, "That's an approach worth considering."

"Prior to the FS-6 crewmen's departure, Paul Manch
oversaw a retrofitting of the *Collins* designed to convert
the LM into a hospital ship, or a flying morgue, whichever
the case might be," Bucar said.

"If, however, we load the remains of Washington,
Drzymkowski, and Bisio aboard now, and there's damage that causes leakage, the entire spacecraft will be con-
taminated," Fayyad said.

"When the issue becomes the safety of the FS-6 crew,
versus bringing back the remains, the remains will be
left behind," Bianco said. "That's always been NASA
policy. Incidentally, I have the crew chief's report on the
Aldrin. Other than superficial interior damage, all primary systems checks were well within the specs. When
they get it, they're going to pull the computers, gut the
interior, and update the control systems so they're esti-
mating the turnaround time at right around seven
months. This has no impact on FS-7's schedule as you're
still going up in the *Armstrong*."

"Go easy on that bird, you guys. We absolutely can't
afford to have the *Collins* wind up in dry dock along with
the *Aldrin*. That would shut the program down for sure,
and ground FS-10, Jer," Christiansen said.

"Don't even say that in jest, Dave," Cochagne
responded.

"Houston," Tseng's voice came over the COMM. "In
times of war, the policy in dealing with remains of battle

casualties is to return as much of the body as possible to the family for burial, is it not?"

Bucar nodded thoughtfully. "That's true."

"What would happen if the bodies were taken out on the surface and exposed to several days of sunlight?" they heard Tseng ask.

"Provided the bodies are not enclosed, at lunar surface temperatures, about the same thing that will happen to your Thanksgiving turkey if you leave it in the oven for fourteen or fifteen hours. They will dry up. Mummify," Manch answered.

"And how does that affect any laboratory testing they might want to do on them?"

"I don't think it would pose any problems at all," Manch replied, "but in the case of Drzymkowski, it means opening the space suit and releasing what's inside—which is under pressure, don't forget—into the lunar environment. We're talking about massive organic contamination of the Moon."

"What's the consensus there, Houston?" Tseng asked.

Bianco looked to Ramirez for a reaction. The astronaut shrugged thoughtfully. "Some strains of bacteria might be sterilized, but others are known to go into stasis or hibernation under those conditions. They revive when conditions are right again . . . and viruses don't even need air to survive. I have to think about this more . . . maybe talk to someone more knowledgeable in this area . . . but, getting back to the other question, I agree with Paul. Chemical analysis of tissues will not be affected and, actually, the resulting weight and size reduction from evaporation of the liquids would be a minor advantage in handling and transporting the remains."

"I'd like to blow the atmosphere inside here and purge the oxygen recirculation ducts. That should kill off the flies, too," Tseng said. "That's contamination of the lunar atmosphere."

"Do we have any experts here on the life cycle of flies?" Bianco asked.

"Both the *Skylab* and the *Discovery* Space Shuttle experiments proved that they can live and reproduce in weightlessness, but I don't think they exposed the flies or their eggs to vacuum," Ramirez said. "There is something that we have to consider, though. They've had an exposed corpse, so the place is crawling with microbes and bacteria. The flies have spread that all over the interior, and they've laid eggs."

"We're already resigned to a major scrub down of the base," Tseng said.

"There is radiation in the lunar environment and, due to that, we could have considerable mutation in the bacterial strains carried by the flies," Ramirez said. "We already know that radiation causes mutation in the flies themselves. Any contact with living tissue and/or oxygen and moisture will revive dormant bacteria. People have been known to get very, very sick after examining Egyptian mummies, for example."

"Is that the mystery of King Tut's curse?" Sweet asked.

"Exactly. We might have to contend with diseases we've never seen before, and against which we have no immunity. That being the case, we have to prepare for a quarantine of the entire crew when they return," Ramirez finished.

"Will Earth be safe from the return of the mutant astronauts?" Cochagne quipped.

There was quiet, sympathetic laughter among the astronauts.

"Why can't they just stay at Far Side for as long as it takes, then?" Chuck MacCallum spoke up. "I'm in favor of letting them do as much science as they can fit into their schedule. There's bound to be a slowdown in the program after this mission. Who knows how many months it will be until we can get back there?"

MacCallum's comment was met with a glum silence from the FS-7 astronauts, but for everyone, it was a reminder of something else that could have a major effect on careers. Some mission specialists now in training in the Far Side program might never get the chance to fly if the slowdown lasted long enough.

"We're getting ahead of ourselves," Bianco said in an attempt to get their attention and put the discussion back on track.

"We have to solve one problem at a time," Christiansen said. "We're up against a time factor here—you guys have had one heck of a long day and it's not over yet. We have to get the bodies out of the dome."

"The only one that could present a problem is Drzymkowski," Tseng said on the COMM. "It will be tricky taking him through the air lock. The change in pressure could cause that suit to leak."

"Can they put him into a body bag?" Ramirez asked. "The pressure inside the bag should make the suit hold its shape."

"Paul, can we get him inside one?" they heard Tseng ask.

"It would be a tight fit even if he didn't have the suit on," Manch responded. "All we can do is try it."

Bianco stole a look at her watch, then glanced at Bucar. Bucar was waiting to catch her eye. With a tired smile, the astronaut rose from his chair. "I bid you all a good night. I'll be taking off for a while to sleep."

"The question we'll all be asking ourselves tomorrow is, 'Will show biz spoil Jack Bucar?'" Ralph Stromeyer said.

"The secret's out about the UBC TV deal, eh?"

" 'Fraid so," Bianco said. She stood up, taking her suit

jacket from the back of her chair. "I need some air. I'll walk you out of the building."

"There's going to be a squabble in Washington over investigative jurisdiction," Bianco said, when they were in the hallway, and out of earshot of anyone in the Mission Control room. "If I'm not careful, I could get caught in the cross fire between the Department of Defense, our own security boys, the CIA, FAA, and the FBI."

Bucar's reaction was a guffaw. "I can imagine, but not for the reason you think," he said. "From what I know, the DOD has no power here. We're not a branch of the military. NASA is a civilian operation that employs military personnel, but my 'orders' don't come from the Air Force. Now, in the services, when a crime is committed off base involving military personnel, if the Military Police, Shore Patrol, or Air Force Police can get there first, they get their people out fast and keep everything 'inside.' Otherwise, it's in the hands of local civilian law enforcement.

"As for SID, the NASA Security Investigation Department is geared for things like industrial espionage and petty theft on NASA property, but it's not a law enforcement body, and certainly not an extraterrestrial law enforcement body. I'm sure the CIA would get all excited, if there was a proven international espionage connection, but, again, what happened at Far Side isn't what they're set up to deal with.

"In the case of the accident at the Space Station, there was no serious challenge to the FAA's claim to jurisdiction, since crash investigation, with or without political sabotage, is what they're set up to investigate. In this instance, though, you're investigating the possibility that a "capital" crime was committed on the lunar surface, so any FAA claim would be weak.

"Far Side Base is United States territory. In my opinion, that puts the whole thing solidly in the lap of the

FBI. The trouble is, the FBI has a miserable record when it comes to solving crimes. They have one hell of a crime lab and database, but they don't have experienced manpower out in the field. The Bureau recruits kids out of college with no law enforcement experience, issues them a badge, a gun, and a "Most Wanted" list, and then sends them out into the world to fight crime. But if I was in administration at the Bureau, I wouldn't want this case. If I was with the CIA, the SID, or the FAA, I wouldn't want it, either. For the sake of my career, I wouldn't want to come within miles of an investigation like this."

"There's no other alternative than to appoint an Accident Investigative Committee, then," Bianco moaned. "They could drag the process out for a couple of years."

"Initially, the FBI will get stuck with it," Bucar said, "but, yes, a commission is inevitable because of the circumstances."

Bianco was surprised when Bucar slowed his pace and stepped closer, lowering his voice for emphasis.

"Dee, once the Feds come in, you'll have to cooperate with them, but don't get into a situation where they make you feel like you have to defer critical mission decisions to them. They know nothing about monitoring a mission. You've got people up there, and you owe it to them to keep those bastards from running amok in here."

"I intend to stay on top of it. . . ." Bianco pulled the packet of six sheets of paper, folded in thirds, from her inside jacket pocket. "That's why I've prepared this."

"It had better not be work I'm supposed to take with me," Bucar said in a mock warning tone.

"I'm counting on you to help keep us out of trouble tomorrow," she said, handing the thick fold of papers to him.

Bucar grinned. "God knows, I've been through the mill before." Bianco waited in silence as Bucar scanned the pages. "These are the official answers to the questions you think they may ask?"

"Based on the information we've released—and are going to release—to the media, yes."

"If this should get into the wrong hands . . ." Bucar said warningly, waving the papers.

"I forgot to tell you. It's also your in-flight meal," Bianco quipped. She got the laugh she'd hoped for from Bucar.

They reached the outside door and Bianco saw an Air Force car waiting at the curb.

"I'll have plenty of time to go over it on the plane . . . and I'm flying military, not commercial," Bucar said, refolding the sheaf of papers and tucking them inside his jacket. "I'll be back."

"Take it easy, Jack."

"One thing, though," Bucar added, lingering at the door, "you know that, ultimately, there's nothing you can do to stop the information you're trying to suppress from leaking out. It's a question of when it will get out, not if."

"I'm aware of that. Too many people know too much. I'm just trying to buy as much time as I can."

Bucar appeared satisfied. "I figure you've got a day— a day and a half, at the most—to play with."

Bianco watched Bucar's Air Force car drive away until it was out of sight. She sincerely hoped the "old man" would be able to sell the official story in New York. As for the real story, the practical strategy was to go with her first impulse. The idea brought back a flood of personal memories of the chaotic days following the accident at the Space Station. With the memories, came a rudimentary plan of action that could be set in motion with one phone call—to the Houston Police.

"I'm cracking the inside hatch," Tseng announced on the COMM. She caught herself holding her breath as the

Aldrin's inner air-lock door swung open. She switched on her backpack lights to dispel the darkness inside the payload bay. Manch and Greer followed her out of the air lock with their equipment and did likewise.

Tseng raised the camera and looked through the lens, but the picture was murky and grainy.

The inside of the Lunar Landing Module was a disaster. She'd expected that. It looked just like the inside of the Main Dome, with the bulkheads defaced with painted obscenities and the phrase, "Food for the Moon," and the deck littered with the debris of carelessly discarded tools and equipment. Tseng unclipped her flashlight, letting the beam play across the scene of destruction to make sure, but she saw no space suits or other EVA equipment. It didn't mean there wasn't anyone aboard. She shuddered, remembering her first sight of Drzymkowski. She doubted she would ever forget it. On the hot mode, she said, "Houston, this is *Aldrin*. How are you reading me? Over."

"*Aldrin,* your audio is good," Christiansen responded. "We'll just have to live with what we can see."

"There isn't much to see," Tseng said. "*Collins*? How do you read me?"

" 'Same as Houston," DeSosa responded.

"We're heading for the mid-deck now," Tseng told them.

As they moved toward the companionway leading up to the mid-deck, Tseng steeled herself for the moment when she would see the first dead crewman.

There were no bodies on the mid-deck, but, through her helmet faceplate, she heard a faint sound. Like an animal whimpering.

"Do you hear something?" she asked Greer and Manch.

"I hear it," Greer said.

"*Aldrin,* what's happening?" they heard Christiansen's anxious voice.

Tseng directed her flashlight beam around the

mid-deck, illuminating torn furnishings, broken controls, and . . .

On the hot mode, everyone heard Manch's audible intake of breath.

"*Aldrin,* do you copy?" Christiansen barked.

For a moment, Tseng couldn't speak. Instead, she aimed the camera lens. Crouched in the farthest corner, of the auxiliary crew station, she saw a solitary naked figure, clutching a space suit helmet. It was Bob Faden. His body was covered with sores, fresh bleeding wounds, scratches, and his own excrement. Saliva dripped from his chin, and oily, dirty strands of his hair were stuck to his skin. The hands clutching the helmet were stained with dried blood. "Houston, we've just found Bob Faden . . . alive," she said, at last.

"Faden appears to be in a state of dementia praecox, or 'no awareness,' " Greer said.

"I can't imagine how he could have survived a takeoff, let alone a return to Earth in his condition," Manch said.

"We can barely see him," Christiansen said. "What's he holding?"

"He's got Shinobu Takizawa's helmet. I don't see any sign of Takizawa or Mobley yet." She climbed the companionway to the flight deck and swept the area and the smashed control consoles with her flashlight beam. "Houston, there's no one on the flight deck," she reported, before returning to the mid-deck.

Through the camera lens, she watched Greer take a step toward Faden. He cringed and whimpered incoherently.

"Will someone say what's going on?" Christiansen insisted.

"S–sorry, Houston," Greer mumbled. "Faden's physical condition isn't good. He's in shock, and he's suffering from a variety of minor injuries—cuts, bruises, lacerations. There's also dehydration and symptoms of jaundice."

"Where are the others? Where are Mobley and Takizawa?"

"I don't think we'll get any information about the others out of him right now," Manch said.

Greer motioned to Manch, and they moved toward Faden in unison. The deranged man edged away from them.

"Let's give him an amp of Seconal," Greer said.

"Sounds like a plan," Manch responded.

Tseng followed the two doctors with the camera lens as they moved to corner Faden.

Suddenly, the astronaut let go of the helmet and sprang forward with a high-pitched animal cry of anger. Greer made a grab for him, but instead of evading her, he leaped at her, clawing savagely at her helmet ring. Manch pulled him away and pinned his arms. Tseng hoped the video was good enough to let the Ground see what was happening.

There had been nothing sexual about the attack on Greer, but Faden's penis was obscenely erect. In his struggles it flopped grotesquely. Faden fought them with the strength of ten men. Tseng doubted the two doctors could hold him.

Tseng laid aside the camera and was about to move in to help them when Faden broke loose and rushed toward her. Tseng set herself to grab him, but Faden stopped short of her—to stare at his own dirty hands. He looked at the dried blood on his fingernails as if unable to believe it was there. He licked at it, then his body was racked by the spasms of an orgasm. Tseng stumbled back to avoid being soiled, but the semen splattered her suit and the deck.

Faden started to cry.

Mortified, Tseng felt the heat of the blood rushing to

her face as a thousand pinpricks, and she suppressed the ridiculous urge to laugh from embarrassment, revulsion, and helplessness. Her mind shrank away from the raw vulgarity of what she'd just seen.

Faden collapsed to the floor, then he drew his knees up to his chin and hugged them. He rocked back and forth, whimpering softly.

Greer reached into the medical bag and pulled out a pneumatic injection gun and an ampoule of what Tseng guessed to be the Seconal. She mumbled something to Manch about needing a straitjacket. Tseng could see she was badly shaken. Faden did not resist when she put the hypogun's barrel against his arm.

"This will quiet him down," Manch said.

Tseng couldn't hear the gun's pneumatic hiss, but Faden's body went limp. "Houston, *Aldrin.* Faden is sedated," she said.

"Let's find a blanket to cover him," Manch said to Greer.

"Houston, how do you want us to proceed on this?" Tseng asked.

"The consensus here is that you should move him to the *Collins.* Can you get him into his suit ASAP. . . ?"

"His suit isn't aboard," Tseng replied. "There is no EVA equipment aboard."

"But . . . how could that be?" Christiansen asked in disbelief. "How did he get there?"

"I'd say he was marooned here by design, by the others," Tseng responded.

"They took his suit, but you didn't find it in the Main Dome, did you?" Christiansen asked.

"It's missing, along with Mobley's and Takizawa's suits. Only Takizawa's helmet is here," Tseng said.

"We'll move him in a rescue bubble when we're sure he's stabilized," Manch said.

After a few seconds of silence on the COMM, Christiansen said, "We've got a lot to do. We need Po and either Paul or Iona back at the Main Dome as soon as you can manage it."

"I'll stay here with him," Greer said.

"I'll keep her company on the COMM," DeSosa said from the *Collins*.

☾

Tseng and Manch found Horo, Lebby, and Cochagne on Level Two.

"We heard what happened," was all Cochagne said.

Manch busied himself with unpacking a microgravity surgical bag, and three of the body bags with which they had also come equipped. Developed for use at the Space Station, the disposable clear silicon surgical plastic bag was designed to contain surgical waste, specifically blood and tissue, and prevent it from contaminating the fragile artificial environment inside the medical lab module. A subject was sealed inside the bag; the bag was then inflated with a mixture of oxygen and inert gases to become a sealed, anti-inflammable, portable, sterile operating theater. Surgeons operated using glove-shaped access points with the set of instruments that were prepackaged inside each bag. Manch would use the bag to perform the autopsy on Washington.

The body bags were also a product of Space Station technology, but they owed their origin to the accident. They drew on space suit technology and were, basically, inflatable coffins. The opaque front panel could be folded back to view remains through a clear plastic window.

"Houston, what's the status on that technical help I requested? We still have quite a dilemma here because we will have to move these bodies and we don't know what to touch or where to walk, or what to do with ourselves," Tseng said.

"Far Side, Houston. At this time, we have to ask you to please just stand by," Christiansen answered. "Dee Bianco's been working on the problem, and she found somebody. From what I understand, there's going to be a short delay until he gets here."

"Roger, Houston," Tseng sighed. The priority task of the FS-6 mission, the search for survivors at Far Side, was finished for the moment, and she was becoming more and more aware of her fatigue. Strangely, unlike the experience of finding Drzymkowski, looking at Bisio's corpse did not make her remember Bisio. It did not even make her sad. Less than a month ago, Bisio had been a living person; a fellow astronaut; a professional colleague; a friend; someone's wife; mother; daughter . . . a link in a chain woven into the infinite mesh of humanity. Yet Tseng was conscious of feeling nothing. Something inside of her—a safety mechanism?—was refusing to make the emotional connection between the rotted thing impaled inside the junk pile on the Moon and the woman she had known on Earth.

Or maybe, she was finally numb from all the horror. She recognized the irony of that and felt tears welling up at the realization.

☾

Bianco judged the man jogging easily across the parking lot toward her to be in his late thirties, tall, trim, and wiry like a marathon runner. His facial features resembled those on the faces seen on the ancient stone carvings of Mayan ruins. "Lieutenant Gutierrez? I'm Dee Bianco. Welcome to the Johnson Space Center," she said when he was close enough to hear her.

Gutierrez caught up to her. Without ceremony, Bianco started back into the Mission Operations building.

"We're going directly up to Mission Control," she told the detective.

Bianco set a fast walking pace. Gutierrez matched her stride effortlessly. They crossed the parking lot, entered the Spaceflight Center and got into the elevator. " 'Sorry to get you up in the middle of the night, but we have a serious time constraint," Bianco apologized.

"I'm used to it. Homicides rarely happen in broad daylight. I got here as fast as I could, although I'm not sure why I'm here or what you think I can do. I'm no rocket scientist."

"I have all the rocket scientists I need," Bianco said. "What I don't have is someone trained in homicide investigation. You're here as a technical consultant."

"Has something happened here?"

"No. Have you been keeping up with the situation on the Moon?"

"When I've been able to, yes. I've had to glean whatever I could from the TV and radio reports."

Bianco could not suppress the urge to wince at the misinformation the detective might already have. "I'll bring you up to date. There are three confirmed deaths at Far Side Base at this time."

"Three," Gutierrez echoed.

"We also have two crewmen missing, the commander and one mission specialist. We have one survivor. They found Bob Faden, the computer system specialist, marooned in the *Aldrin,* but he's not in any condition to tell us what happened."

"You said 'marooned'?"

"That's right. He was shut up in there without a space suit. It was deliberate. We've had fatalities in the space program before but not a situation like the one I'm about to show you. One death occurred at the scene, but we're certain that, in the case of the other two bodies, the deaths were not accidental. We don't know what part Faden played in this."

The homicide detective's surprise was perceptible, though subtle—a spark from his black eyes. "What you're telling me is that you think you have a crime scene," he said.

"That's correct."

Gutierrez "hmmmed" comprehension. "When I think about astronauts and scientists and the space program, it's incongruous—something as base as murder, I mean. I'll give you whatever help I can."

As they left the elevator and headed down the long hallway toward Mission Control, Bianco said, "There isn't much time left in this EVA." At a questioning look from Gutierrez, she said, "Sorry, 'Extravehicular Activity.' Everyone talks in acronyms around here. The astronauts entered the Main Dome about five hours ago and found one survivor, who died, and the two bodies. We had live coverage. Everything we're getting from the Moon is being recorded. The actual close-ups will come from the still shots. Those will be transmitted from the *Collins* to JPL for imaging. We'll have them shortly thereafter. All of it is available to you."

At the door to the Mission Control room, Bianco paused. "Two things I want to emphasize to you. First of all, after a lot of bureaucratic fuss, a federal agency will probably be brought in on this, and they'll want to be in total control of the information flow. By bringing you in, I'm sidestepping the bureaucracy. Just don't be surprised at anything that happens."

Gutierrez responded with a knowing smile.

"The other thing I want to mention comes under the heading of my being able to rely on your sense of professionalism. I discussed this with your department chief, and his recommendation of you was based on that as well as on your ability and qualifications. There's no rule of secrecy being enforced, but there's a need for discretion."

"Understood."

"Good." Bianco said. She hoped that, upon finding himself in the company of those in Mission Control, the homicide detective would not become so overawed that he proved ineffective. She liked Gutierrez's intelligent, soft-spoken manner. It was hard not to be attracted to him.

She needed to squelch those thoughts.

Heads briefly turned in their direction when they walked into Mission Control, then turned just as quickly back to the mesmerizing scene on the huge main monitor. Tseng's portable camera was focused on Manch performing the postmortem on Washington's body by flashlight illumination. Every few seconds, Manch would brush nervously at the flies crawling across his helmet faceplate.

"Washington, the pilot and communications officer, died shortly after they got to her," Bianco told Gutierrez quietly. "We have the recorded video of what happened, as well as the discovery of the other two bodies."

Bianco left Gutierrez alone for a few moments, to absorb the scene while she retrieved a printout of Manch's report on the deaths from the computer, then she guided the detective toward Christiansen's console. The astronaut's face had assumed a steady, neutral expression which Bianco recognized as a mask of fatigue.

"This is our principal CAPCOM, Dave Christiansen," Bianco said. "Lieutenant Gutierrez . . . I'm sorry . . . your first name is . . . ?"

"Lol. It's a nickname, short for Lorenzo."

Christiansen grunted an acknowledgment.

"I'd like to make notes as we go along," Gutierrez said. "They'll go into my murder book. No one outside Homicide will see them. Is that okay?"

Bianco nodded.

"Okay, show me what you've got."

"Far Side, this is Houston," Christiansen said into the mike. "We have your expert here with us. Can we get shots of Bisio?"

"Houston, Far Side. Roger on that," Tseng replied offscreen.

"Colonel Tseng has the video camera," Christiansen told Gutierrez.

Tseng did a slow pan from Washington to Bisio. Bianco noticed Gutierrez's doubletake when the frame caught the phrase "Food for the Moon" scrawled on the wall and surrounded by graffiti. The detective made a quick note. The camera pan stopped on the corpse.

"This is Mission Specialist Ann Bisio," Tseng said.

"Will I be able to speak directly to the crew up there?" Gutierrez asked.

"Normally, that's against procedure and protocol . . ." Bianco said, letting the sentence trail off thoughtfully. She saw concern, then anger rise to Christiansen's face and ignored them. "In this case, I believe we are forced to make an exception."

Bianco gave Gutierrez the medical transcript, and the detective spent a few moments alternately studying it and the picture of Bisio on the screen.

"After a few weeks it's so hard to tell anything about a body," Gutierrez said. "Colonel Tseng, what is she wearing?"

"She's in a tank top and shorts—her fatigue underclothing. Washington was dressed the same way," Tseng answered.

"Any special reason for that?"

"Yes," Tseng answered. "They were having a problem with the environmental controls. Up here, the problem is not heating the base, it's getting rid of the heat produced by the base. There are three underground levels, and the deeper you dig into the Moon, the hotter it gets because you're getting closer to the planetary core. Added to that, we have heat produced by all of the equipment inside the dome. Lunar soil has very poor heat transfer properties, so getting rid of the heat can be a problem. It's about thirty-two degrees Celsius—that's ninety degrees Fahrenheit—in here right now. We have radiators and thermoelectric heat pumps, but quite a bit of that system hardware is down at this time."

"I don't understand exactly what that means—I'll just take your word for it. That kind of technical stuff is over my head, Colonel. Have you examined the area around the body very closely?"

"No, and unfortunately, we've already tramped through this entire place like a herd of elephants," Tseng said.

Gutierrez grimaced worriedly. "What's done is done, but before anybody else walks into the area, I'd like one person to go through it again with me."

"I'm in charge of all this, so it should be me," Tseng said. "Doc, take this camera. I want my hands free."

They waited while Tseng passed the portable camera to Horo, then moved in front of the lens. The light reflected off her helmet faceplate, and Bianco could not see her face distinctly.

"Organization and documentation will be very important here. I'm going to have you search the area in a tight spiral pattern, moving from a corner of the room toward the body. If you see anything, avoid picking it up or touching it with your gloves."

"We've already found a hammer on Level One that could have been used to kill Drzymkowski. I'm glad we didn't touch it," Tseng said.

"That's good," Gutierrez said. "We'll get to it later. Right now, let's concentrate on this area."

"I have a pair of forceps, if you need to pick anything up," Manch said.

"How about good old-fashioned pliers," Lebby volunteered. "I'll have an easier time manipulating the pliers, Paul," Tseng said to Manch.

As Lebby handed the pliers to Tseng, the gesture appeared to be in slow motion. It brought Bianco sharply back in touch with the reality of what they were seeing and the problem of distance for Gutierrez, who was examining a crime scene three hundred thousand plus miles away.

"Now, can you give me a close view of the deceased from all angles?" Gutierrez asked.

The full body shot of Bisio steadily became a closeup as Horo moved forward and then went beyond the optimum focal length of the camera lens. The distortion twisted what was left of Bisio's face and body into bulges and wavy ribbons of rotting flesh. The flies were still swarming around the body. The sight made Bianco shudder. She looked to Gutierrez for a reaction, but the detective's concentration had not wavered. Had he seen worse? Bianco tried to imagine what "worse" was.

Horo adjusted the picture by stepping back. The camera made a slow circle of the body.

"Stop," Gutierrez said as the strut impaling Bisio was revealed. "What is that shaft?"

"It's a piece of aluminum pipe from the construction site," Tseng answered.

"It's very likely the murder weapon. We can't know for certain yet, but let me see the point of entry."

The camera angle changed to show more of Bisio's wound and Gutierrez squinted, trying to see details in the dim light.

Bianco felt a pang of anxiety. Had she caused the delay for EVA-1 only to run up against the limitations of the poor photographic conditions? "After computer enhancement of the stills, you might have a better chance of seeing the details," she said hopefully.

"Okay. Under normal circumstances, it's sometimes possible to tell if a wound was made before or after death," Gutierrez said.

"Jer, do you have any close-ups of this?" Tseng asked.

"I'll make sure it's covered," Cochagne replied.

"For the present, don't touch the strut. I'll tell you how to deal with it in a few minutes. I want her clothes, too. Try not to shake them. Make sure any blood on them is dry and then wrap them in paper," said the detective.

"Dr. Greer and I will take care of it," Manch said.

"Was there any friction between Bisio and the other members of this crew?" Gutierrez asked.

"None that I know of," Bianco replied. "You can ask those questions of the crew at your leisure, though."

"I understand," Gutierrez said, then, with a pained look on his face he added, "I apologize for being a little confused at the moment. Which astronaut has the camera?"

"Dr. Arminta Horo," Bianco answered.

"Oh . . . that's 'Doc.' Are you by any chance the gold medalist of Olympic track and field fame?" Gutierrez asked.

"Yes, Lieutenant," Horo answered off camera. "I'm flattered that you would remember."

"I'm a runner myself," Gutierrez said shyly and with awe and admiration in his voice. "Okay, Dr. Horo," he continued, "if you could show me more of the body . . ."

The camera resumed panning the corpse. The detective studied the picture.

". . . and stop here. See those wounds on the palm of the right hand? Those look like defense wounds. The other hand, too. My guess is, she tried to fend off her attacker."

Bianco was caught off guard when Gutierrez suddenly turned to regard her intently, and then said, "I'm assuming that you want me to try to reconstruct what happened.

That may not be possible, even if I have all the time I need. What exactly are your expectations as far as my input is concerned?"

"I guess I just wanted a chance to see this mess through your eyes; to try to make sense of it," Bianco replied slowly. "We have to get on with this mission, and we don't have the luxury of leaving things as they are here. We've slipped the schedule as much as we can, and we're coming up on a twenty-six-hour day—almost seven of those hours in space suits—for this crew. They're exhausted and they've pushed themselves—and we've pushed them—way beyond their physical limits, and they're still not finished. They have to get inside the *Aldrin* and move Faden. They have to move the bodies, and some critical decisions have to be made on procedures that cover problems we didn't foresee. By the way, are you considering Bob Faden a witness . . . or a suspect?"

"Since he can be placed at the crime scene legitimately— he had every reason to be there—there has to be something unique about a piece of evidence tying him to the actual crime of murder," Gutierrez said. "Fingerprint evidence on a murder weapon is unique. DNA evidence is unique, but, in this case, hair, skin cells, and other 'microevidence' might not help reconstruct the crime unless these substances can be found on the murder victim and identified as having come from the murderer during the commission of the crime. That's 'convicting evidence.' Thinking of Faden as a suspect creates certain problems for me at this point, because my judgment will be prejudiced, and there's a danger I might misinterpret something. I don't want to have any preconceived notions or theories." Gutierrez turned his attention back to the monitor. "How are you doing, Colonel Tseng?"

The camera moved to get a shot of Tseng, bent over and studying the floor with the aid of her flashlight. "I don't see anything here. I wish I knew what to look for," Tseng said.

"Don't forget to look up," Gutierrez told Tseng. "Never forget to look up and down, and at eye level."

Bianco heard gasps of concern and guffaws from the other astronauts in Mission Control. To Gutierrez's look of puzzlement at the reaction, she said, "That's very tough to do in a space suit." They watched while Tseng bent precariously backward in order to look at the ceiling. She stabbed a gloved finger upward excitedly.

"I see something up here! It's black like smoke or greasy soot—Doc, get a shot of this for them." The camera lens tilted upward and Bianco and the others saw an irregular black blotch that covered several of the modular ceiling panels.

"So. Now we at least know that they may have had a fire. Tell me about that writing all over the walls."

"We don't know what to make of it," Tseng said.

"From what I can see on the monitor, they are occult symbols and words," Gutierrez said, then he made a wry face. "I've seen a few occult crime scenes. Satanic cults. Ritual killings. Colonel, go back to the body. Look for marks on the wrists and ankles that look like the victim was tied up."

On the monitor, Tseng lumbered slowly toward Bisio. "The flesh around the wrists and ankles is discolored and puffy, Lieutenant," she said after a few moments.

"Let me see the other body."

Tseng and Horo walked the short distance to the CDR sleep station with the camera on.

"Drzymkowski was the engineer, but he was quartered in the commander's sleep station. The commander, Mike Mobley, was sleeping down on Level One. We don't know why," Tseng said.

Gutierrez "ummed" an acknowledgment, then said, "It's like the inside of a submarine in there."

"A corpse in a space suit," Gutierrez exclaimed, as Horo shot Drzymkowski from the doorway and then walked the camera in for a close shot of the body.

"It's little more than a skeleton, according to Dr. Manch," Bianco said.

"Deterioration would be very rapid in this case. You would have a greenhouse effect," Gutierrez said. "What's the cause of death?"

"Blunt force trauma," Manch answered on the COMM. "There is damage to the skull which appears to have been made by a heavy tool such as a hammer."

"We found a hammer on Level One," Cochagne volunteered.

"That's encouraging. Tell me, though, how hard would it be to put a dead body inside a space suit?" Gutierrez asked.

"At times, it's tough to get a live body in one," Tseng responded, "but it looks like he actually came in from outside because he's wearing a liquid cooling and ventilation garment—space suit underwear to you, Lieutenant."

"A keen observation. You're doing great, Colonel," Gutierrez encouraged.

"It's easier to look at him this time than it was when I discovered him. The first shock was terrible . . . another thing I just realized . . . he's not wearing his communications carrier for the radio."

"Without touching or moving the corpse, look closely at the suit fabric. I want you to look for evidence that the body was moved, so look for scuff marks on the hard surfaces and wrinkles on the suit that are dirty on the outside and clean in the folds. If the edges of the wrinkles are down, he was dragged headfirst. If they face up, then he was pulled feetfirst. Also, are there any stains on the outside of the suit?"

On the monitor, Tseng bent over the body. "I do see

wrinkles defined by Moon dust. By your logic the body was dragged both ways," she said. "There are no scuff marks on the back of the helmet and no stains on the outside . . ."

"Might he have been interrupted during the process of taking off the suit when he was killed?" Gutierrez asked. "They could always stick the helmet back on afterward to seal the suit, couldn't they?"

"That sounds viable to me," Tseng said.

"Why didn't they take him outside, then? Why drag him down two levels, rather than dumping him in the air lock?

"I can't answer that, Lieutenant."

"Neither can I," Gutierrez said. "Certain actions reflect the killer's state of mind or the conditions prevalent at the time of the murder. I'm going to treat this entire base as one big crime scene, so I'd appreciate it if you'd give these questions some thought."

"I copy . . . I mean, I'll do that," Tseng replied.

"What about blood and toxicology on him? Dr. Manch, are you going to post this body?" Gutierrez asked.

"We can't open that suit," Manch answered. "We're not equipped to deal with the consequences. So, no postmortem on Drzymkowski until we get back to Earth. Sorry."

"As you look at the body, does anything else come to your attention, Colonel?" Gutierrez asked. "Something might appear unimportant at first. Don't overlook anything no matter how insignificant it appears. Mistakes made now can't be rectified later."

"I can't see anything unusual," Tseng answered, frustration evident in her voice, "except that I believe whoever moved him had a very hard time."

"A big man?"

Bianco gave an affirmative nod when Gutierrez looked to her for confirmation.

"Let's assume it took more than one person to move him, then; two women, for example," the detective continued. "We may have a conspiracy. That's frequently the case in satanic cult crimes."

Bianco stiffened, her indignation rising at the implication.

"Have you gone through his pockets?" Gutierrez asked Tseng.

"I didn't even think of it."

"Better do that now."

They waited while Tseng opened the suit utility pockets and reached inside.

"He's not carrying anything; not even his tools," she said.

"Let's have a look at that hammer," Gutierrez requested.

They heard the muffled heavy shuffle of boots when Tseng and Horo moved out of the CDR sleep station and into the passageway. Horo continued to shoot video which documented the interior damage to the Moon base during their passage down to Level One. The picture on the monitor had all the annoying, unsteady qualities of a handheld "traveling shot," but Bianco appreciated the close look it was providing at the graffiti scrawled on the walls.

"Can I see what you've written, Lieutenant?" Bianco asked.

Gutierrez handed her the notebook, and Bianco scanned the pages, reading to herself. "Food for the Moon??? Victim: Female. Found at the crime scene. Apparent cause of death: piercing stab wound in the upper abdominal cavity. Victim: Male. Enclosed in a space suit. Victim was moved. No visible damage to the suit. Victim died in the suit. Blunt force trauma. Victim: Female. Died of injuries at the scene. Two crewmen, male, still missing. Fire damage on ceiling of Level 2. Why was

Bisio killed? Why was Drzymkowski killed? Why is he in a space suit? In CDR's room. Why are Mobley and Takizawa missing? What is tie-in with the occult?"

Bianco handed the notebook back. "I guess we're really at a dead end, eh?"

"On the contrary. It's shaping up nicely. I'm sure this will help," Gutierrez said, holding up the transcript. He folded the papers and put them in his inside jacket pocket. Bianco caught sight of a gun in a shoulder holster and a set of handcuffs in a case clipped to the waistband of the detective's pants.

Gutierrez checked his watch. "When will it be possible for me to see all the video and still photos you have?"

"I'll set it up for you for tomorrow," Bianco said.

"We're down on Level One," Tseng said, on the COMM. The image of the hammer grew larger on the screen as Horo "walked" the camera in on it. "Has anyone touched or moved it?" Gutierrez asked.

"No. We didn't know what to do with it," Tseng said.

"Believe me, you did right to leave it alone."

"I can't see any blood on it," Tseng said.

"It can still be examined for microevidence," Gutierrez replied.

"What about fingerprints?" Bianco asked.

"Latent prints are a good possibility. The biggest obstacle we face in gathering biological evidence is that the specimens are a few weeks old, but there are ways of surmounting that. Dr. Manch, what's your opinion?"

"I've been busy up here on Level Two, so I haven't seen the hammer yet," Manch said.

"Can you take time out and have a look, Paul?" Tseng asked.

"I'm coming down," the physician answered.

"In the meantime, tell me about the hammer," Gutierrez said.

The camera tilted down and then homed in on the

hammer. Bianco could see neither bloodstains nor any other signs that identified the tool as a murder weapon.

"It's a nine-kilogram ball-peen hammer; stainless steel head; a thirty-six-centimeter composite plastic shaft. Made for Shimizu by the Dogyu Tool Company," Tseng said.

"What size?" Gutierrez asked incredulously.

"Nine kilograms. Up here, in one-sixth gravity, that's the equivalent of a standard three-pound hammer."

They heard the sound of Manch descending the companionway, and then the physician's feet entered the picture frame. He squatted on his haunches for a close look at the hammer.

"Look at it, but don't touch it," Gutierrez cautioned.

"Just looking at it, I can tell you that there's at least a possibility that the indentations on Drzymkowski's skull might very well have been made with it. However, if so, the hammer head was wiped clean," Manch said. "I can bag it for you, if that's what you think should be done."

"I don't want it put in a bag until it's been dusted for fingerprints and photographed," Gutierrez replied. "The head should be pitted from use. If the hammer was only wiped, there will still be microscopic traces of blood, tissue, and hair, and, possibly, skull fragments in those crevices."

"I can run tests on it," Manch said.

"I know zip about fingerprinting, but if you tell me what to do, I'll shoot stills of the handle and transmit them along with the rest of my film," Cochagne said.

"There's an advantage in having those test results sooner rather than later," Gutierrez told Bianco. "They might help us all to look at the crime scene from a more accurate perspective, while it's still relatively unspoiled."

"It's your call, Lieutenant," Tseng said.

"I'm aware of that. We need to devise a way for

you to make any prints visible, so that they can be photographed."

"Whatever you decide, make it fast. We have to get on with this EVA," Christiansen said.

Bianco glanced at the Mission Clock. "Let's not do anything about the hammer this instant. It's not going anywhere. I want to get these people back to the *Collins* with a good margin of safety. I'll definitely need you back here tomorrow, Lieutenant."

"No problem."

"Then that's all the amateur sleuthing we have time for tonight, boys and girls," Dave Christiansen said, taking over the mike.

On the monitor, Bianco watched the astronauts head for the companionway as the camera was turned off. Despite the hour, she saw that Gutierrez was reluctant to leave Mission Control. "I have a question for you, Lieutenant," she said. "It's about jurisdiction. Say you and several other law enforcement agencies all arrive on the scene of a murder at the same time. How do you determine who gets the case?"

"In most states, the cities and the counties are broken up into districts, so it can depend solely on geography. Sometimes it's more complicated, though. If there's an out-of-state stolen car involved, or a kidnapping in connection with the killing, then the FBI comes in on it and we all have to cooperate. So, what I'm saying is, where there may be a conflict, the motive can determine the jurisdiction. Does that tell you what you want to know?"

"That's moderately helpful," Bianco said. "Now tell me how much cooperation is really involved between agencies?"

"People think that law enforcement personnel all work together to fight crime. That's a myth. We're not all on the same team. There are times when we have to 'pocket' certain information in order to keep another agency from screwing up an ongoing investigation. We may secretly withhold the name of an informant, for example, or not come forward with the knowledge of the existence of a piece of evidence in order to protect ourselves. Otherwise the other agency might want to go in and make a high-profile arrest on a lesser charge that will forever end our chances of solving a murder case. Same thing happens to us. And there are all kinds of deals struck on cases, too. A few years ago, we had a big investigation going where we wanted to arrest a guy. We were all ready to move on it, and the FBI got wind of our plan and said 'back off.' The suspect was working for them as an informant in a big drug case, unrelated to what we had on him, and they couldn't afford to have him taken out. We had to wait until they were done with him.''

((

"Houston, we'd really like an estimate of when you may be ready to discuss what the next procedure should be," Tseng said.

"Far Side, this is Houston. When do you think you'll be ready to start back?" Christiansen asked.

"Paul has indicated to me that he's just about finished with Washington, so, provided we grind out the solutions to our current problems, say, in about an hour?"

"Stand by a minute, and I'll give you a time hack on the GET. Stand by . . . MARK ninety-four hours: thirty-seven minutes: ten seconds Ground Elapsed Time."

"We're right on, Dave. Thanks."

"Far Side, at this time, you are GO for two days. We'll review your status at the end of that time. It's the best we're willing to do until further notice," Christiansen said.

"We copy, Houston," Tseng replied, glancing at her crew. It was a letdown for her; a punch in the gut.

She saw it in the postures of the others, too, and she wondered if those in Mission Control sensed their disappointment.

"We have a schedule update. You were originally scheduled for live TV coverage at the base. In view of what has happened at Far Side, that's been changed. Your sleep period will be followed by a press conference from the *Collins* at about one-zero-six hours: twenty-eight minutes Ground Elapsed Time, which will be carried live on TV."

Tseng heard the collected—though subdued—sigh of relief from the other crewmen. "Thanks, Houston. We appreciate it."

"We're still coming up with creative ways to get rid of the flies, but we want to try your suggestion about depressurizing the Main Dome and exposing them to vacuum," Christiansen told them.

"We copy," Tseng acknowledged. "At this time we'd like to get on with it, then."

"You're GO for egress," Christiansen answered after a short pause, bracketed by a muffled mike.

Remembering the hushed, abbreviated comments given in response to questions and requests from Mike Mobley and the others during her own shifts in Mission Control, as FS-5 CAPCOM, Tseng wondered what was being said during the pauses. "The next order of business is taking care of Bisio, then," she said. "Is that homicide detective still around? We could use his expertise."

"I hate to sound crude, but it's going to be a little like trying to get a toasted marshmallow off of a stick as intact as possible," Tseng heard Gutierrez say, in the background.

At the same moment that she winced at the raw "gallows humor," she heard a cacophony of startled vocal reactions from the people in Mission Control who were nearest the CAPCOM mike.

"In the future, you should refrain from remarks like that around here," Christiansen blustered angrily, on mike.

Christiansen could be touchy about banter that he considered irreverent, callous, and disrespectful. His strong religious feelings were common knowledge in the astronaut corps, but Gutierrez couldn't know that. She heard his muffled apology and felt embarrassed for him—not so much for the remark, itself, because, from their prelaunch briefing at the morgue, Tseng knew that gallows humor was common among the assistant coroners and law enforcement people who were constantly exposed to death, and, in particular, to violent death. She sympathized with the position Gutierrez found himself in at Mission Control, that of a fish out of water; an outsider thrust by circumstances into a tightly knit community into which he had not yet been accepted.

How would Christiansen have reacted if another astronaut had made the comment? Mild annoyance probably, though Christiansen's attitude could be rigid even toward colleagues at times. Looking around at the graffiti covering the walls of the Main Dome, Tseng wondered how he would be handling the present situation if their missions had fallen in reverse order.

For that matter, how had Mike Mobley dealt with it? The commander set the tone for a mission. Often, his or her crew reacted to problems based on the commander's behavior. One clue might be that Mobley had separated himself from the others.

"Lieutenant Gutierrez says the body will have to be wrapped in something, or it might not hold together," Christiansen said, his voice still bristling with anger.

"I'll see if there's an extra blanket in one of the sleep stations," Cochagne said.

"There's one on Mobley's level. It's on the bed. Use that one," Tseng said.

"How are we going to deal with that?" Lebby said, pointing to the aluminum strut protruding from Bisio.

"Houston, can you give us a procedure for pulling out this strut?" Tseng asked.

"The lieutenant wants it put aside for fingerprinting, and he wants you to avoid handling the shaft with your gloves," Christiansen said.

Manch turned to Lebby. "I've examined the problem from all angles and, if you have that pair of pliers handy, I think that's the way to go."

"I was going to suggest that if you didn't, Paul. I'll get them."

Cochagne reentered the recreation area carrying the thin, acrylic blanket. A space suit increased the difficulty of the most basic task, and Tseng had to help Cochagne and Manch unfold the material.

Her reflexes caused her to pull back as the act of draping the blanket over and around the body like a shroud sent a black swarm of flies into the air. With the body at least covered, Tseng felt relieved. She no longer had to look at—or avoid looking at—Bisio's death face. It also spared anyone from having to contaminate their suits by touching the body itself.

Even though, through the bulky space suit there was no tactile sensation at all, Tseng's nerves and muscles recoiled in revulsion when she grasped Bisio. She held the corpse while Lebby gripped the edge of the strut with the pliers and pulled. The pipe came free, and she had to support the body to keep it from falling. She was surprised that it felt so fragile and light. It was not just from the Moon's gravity. She was handling a desiccated shell of flesh.

A bloodstain and hardened jellylike tissue marked the section of pipe that had penetrated and remained inside the corpse. Horo and Cochagne wrapped the blanket around it to further support the body as they gently lowered it into the body bag. Lebby deftly manipulated the pliers to place the bloody end of the pipe on a sheet of compressed fiber cloth which Manch laid out for him.

Tseng had the urge to comment on the uncanny accuracy of Gutierrez's "marshmallow on a stick" remark, but decided to say nothing that would further agitate Christiansen. "Houston, Far Side. If Lieutenant Gutierrez has no further questions, Bisio's remains will be sealed inside a body bag," she said, making a mental note to tell Gutierrez of the pun, privately, face-to-face.

"You can wrap it up, Far Side."

"Okay, we're going to go ahead and transport all the casualties up to Level Four. In Drzymkowski's case, though, there's that minor problem with the air lock which we think can be overcome in the way we discussed. We'll keep you posted on that," Tseng said.

"We copy," Christiansen said. "No one down here has a better idea, China."

An hour later, Tseng took a last look around, then tucked herself into the air lock. "*Collins,* Far Side. We're just leaving the Main Dome. We'll be on our way home shortly, Joe."

"I copy," DeSosa answered.

"Far Side, this is Houston," Christiansen cut in, "you're coming up on eight hours, and you still have Faden's evacuation from the *Aldrin* to handle. We'd like to have you back to the *Collins* with a reasonable safety margin on your oxy and consumables."

"Rog, Dave. It took us a bit longer than we expected to finish up here. All three bodies are on the lunar surface and the Main Dome is secured for depressurization and egress."

"Are you the last one off the ship?"

"That's right, Houston. I'm keying the manual depress to vent the atmosphere to the outside. . . . pressure is dropping . . . there are going to be a lot of dead flies in here, shortly . . . I hope . . . down to six point two pounds . . . I'm out of here." Tseng secured the interior hatch behind her, evacuated the atmosphere from the air lock, then opened the outer hatch and climbed out into the glaring lunar "afternoon" where Lebby, Manch, Horo, and Cochagne stood waiting with the three lozenge-shaped body bags.

Drzymkowski had, indeed, presented problems for them. The first attempt to move his body from the bed pallet had caused the liquid inside the suit to slosh up into the helmet. By mutual agreement, they had lowered the gold sun shield down over the faceplate before inserting him gingerly into the body bag. There was little room to spare inside of it.

"I've been thinking about where to lay them," Lebby said. "In my opinion, the best place is that knoll about fifty meters out from the dome. That way, we avoid the path of the communications cable, and the concrete slab, and they'll be away from vehicular and foot traffic routes."

"I agree with that suggestion," Tseng said.

"This is just a reminder about the elapsed time," Christiansen said.

"We copy, Houston. We can go to our reserve oxygen bottles, if necessary, but we've got three quarters of an hour before we have to do that. I just can't leave them out here and walk away . . . even if it's only a token gesture. It's better than nothing."

"Po . . ." Christiansen began, then hesitated in apparent exasperation.

"I'm with China on this one, Dave," Cochagne said.

"Same here," Horo spoke up.

"Count me in," DeSosa said from the *Collins.*

"It would mean closure for everyone," Greer said, from the *Aldrin.*

Christiansen's silence on the COMM was enough to express the helpless frustration that everyone in Mission Control must be feeling at her stubbornness, Tseng reflected.

She thought about what to say at the site as they walked slowly away from the Main Dome. They were bearing the first humans to die on another planet. The moment demanded that something be said. Ashes to ashes, Earth dust . . . to lunar dust?—if not for the non-biodegradable shrouds, maybe, but it sounded too melo-dramatic and awkward. Anyway, she agreed with the final decision to keep the body bags sealed for transport back to Earth.

Though it would not happen this time, she could not suppress a thought about bodies decomposing in lunar soil. Was there a question here of the right that human be-ings had to contaminate another world with Death? No one had come here intending to die or knowing they would die. Death happened when it happened, and death was necessary to replenish life on the Earth. But nothing would grow out here on the surface. Back on Earth, the successful results of early agricultural experiments in-volving crops grown in lunar soil had proved that moon-dust was not infertile, just inactive in its natural state.

To die in a place where death was truly the end was of concern only to the living. But to die and be buried on an-other planet, even if only for a short time . . . it was something she had not considered in depth before. She felt the pressure of their circumstances. They were reaching the limit of the portable life-support systems, yet . . . the thoughts and images of Mike Mobley, and an obligation to him, especially, persisted.

There was no religious feeling involved. No question of interpreting God's will. It was a sign of human audac-ity and egocentric thinking that mankind could conceive of a supreme being capable of creating the universe, then believe that they could miraculously read his mind, and speak and act for him. A bloody world history vouched for the error in that way of thinking.

Her scant knowledge of Buddhism's teachings came from the Vietnamese side of the family. The other relatives were Protestants—mainly Baptists. Somehow she had managed to emerge with no allegiance to an organized faith, merely a jumble of vague beliefs in a "higher power," an afterlife of the soul, and a value system based on situation ethics.

They had all lowered their gold sun visors before emerging from the air lock. Now, her reverie was cut short by the sudden awareness that the faces behind five golden mirrors were turned toward her in anticipation.

"I didn't prepare anything to say," Tseng told them. "I wasn't prepared for this moment, but there are a few things I do want to say. Unknown to the crewmen of FS-5, they brought death up with them to the Moon. Perhaps it was always here; always waiting for us. On Earth, death brings forth new life. Here, on the Moon I am struck with how much of an end it is. To die on a dead world such as this one is really to die in vain. That's why we are committed to bringing our friends home to a final rest.

"In human civilization the ceremonies of burying the dead go back so many thousands of years that we know it is the nature of our species to search for the meaning to existence. We, in the role of colonizers, bring our rituals and customs to this barren place, this dead planet, if only temporarily, as in the case of Louise Washington, Ann Bisio, and Frank Drzymkowski. Still, we must accept that, if it is the destiny of man to colonize space, then he will experience death on other worlds. We can only hope that he will be able to reconcile this in his mind and allow his soul to rest in peace far from the fertile ground and grass-covered hills of Earth.

"At this juncture, let us also remember our missing colleagues, Mike Mobley and Shinobu Takizawa. All those who can might want to take a few moments to pay their respects in their own way," Tseng finished.

"We copy, Far Side," Christiansen acknowledged.

For the first time in many hours, there was silence on the COMM. It felt oddly unnatural to Tseng. Though she tried to focus her mind on the dead astronauts, it was not they whom she pictured, but Mike Mobley. She could not rid herself of disturbing thoughts which were loud in the silence.

Lebby's sudden movement distracted her. She watched the astronaut reach into a hip pocket of his suit and pull out a small camera. She hadn't thought to bring a personal camera on such a grim assignment, but she understood Lebby's desire to save this moment for his own collection of personal mementos.

☾

"Moments of silence" were always awkward intervals, as far as Bianco was concerned. At the moment, all she could think about were the problems facing her. Gutierrez, and Adachi, Weinstock, Ramirez, Fayyad, Stromeyer, Sweet, MacCallum, and the flight controllers stood with heads dutifully bowed. She saw Christiansen sitting with his eyes closed, his elbow resting on the console, his head bowed, forehead supported by thumb and forefinger. To the casual observer, the act might go unnoticed, but Bianco knew he was praying for his dead and missing colleagues.

Christiansen had never made his religion an issue that affected his performance as an astronaut, yet Bianco was both deeply moved and uneasy about the astronaut's actions now. The uneasiness she thought she recognized as stemming from her own mistrust and lack of faith in anything incorporeal or insubstantial.

"We're proceeding to the *Aldrin,* now, to move Faden to the *Collins,*" Tseng said.

On the monitor, Bianco watched Horo's video of Tseng, Lebby, Cochagne, and Manch moving toward the *Aldrin,* which could be seen in the background of the shot. Then the transmission ended. "So what are your impressions of Mission Control, Lieutenant?" she asked Gutierrez.

"In some ways, you're not as organized as I thought. To the average person, it looks like you guys—the scientists and astronauts and all the other technical experts— have it together. We think that you know what you're doing every second. But you're really 'winging it.' Take this debate about the body in the space suit. It looked simple, but I can see it was a major problem."

Bianco nodded sagely. "Techniques for dealing with fatalities in space were developed before the big accident at the station, but it was all theory. When the accident occurred, some procedures had to be revised on the spot, based on practical experience. Things that everybody thought would work, didn't. We had to improvise. It's been my experience that no matter how much preparation you do, each situation is unique. At Far Side, we've run into an entirely new set of problems, and there are no procedures to cover them. We've had to put our heads together and work them out. You were a part of that and I appreciate your expertise. I hope you're not too disillusioned."

"If I am, it's a good thing," Gutierrez said. "A minute ago, you spoke about the Space Station accident like you were there. You were an astronaut at that time?"

"Yes, I became one because of the accident. I had the qualifications and the technical background, though not the astronaut training, but they gave me the 'short course,' and then sent me up to diagnose and solve the problem. It was an unforgettable experience," Bianco said, watching for Gutierrez's reaction. She was not disappointed. The detective's eyes sparked with interest.

PART TWO

Tseng found Cochagne and DeSosa in the *Collins'* wardroom. "When you guys get inside the base and unsuit to do your repairs, we and the Ground will lose touch with you," she said. "The way around that problem is for you to use the portable camera."

Cochagne looked up from the photos and diagrams he was studying with DeSosa and Lebby. Earlier, he'd removed the hard drive from the digital still camera and had downloaded the pictures it held into the computer for storage, playback, and printing by the crew. Lebby had drawn diagrams, and he and Cochagne had spread them out on the wardroom table to reconstruct the sequence of events during the EVA for DeSosa.

"I figured one of us would just stay suited up," Cochagne said, "but having the video camera is a good backup."

"They'll be happier if they can see what's happening," Tseng said.

"I don't know why they scheduled the live interview *before* today's EVA," DeSosa said without looking up from the pictures and diagrams. No one was more impatient than the moody, often mercurial, Communications Engineer to suit up for the second extravehicular activity, during which he would finally lay hands on Far Side's malfunctioning communications equipment.

Tseng merely glanced at the clutter on the table. She

wasn't eager to look at the photos of horrors she had seen firsthand. "Why don't you begin clearing this up now?" she said. The aft crew section, which functioned as a dining hall, lounge, and conference room, would function as a television studio today, and they had all agreed that it should not appear cluttered to the "viewers at home." It was important to convey the subliminal message that the FS-6 crewmen were alert, on top of the situation, and following a proper military regimen. For the occasion, all the astronauts had donned fresh and crisp-looking three-piece uniform fatigues with the FS-6 and Far Side program patches. "Jerry, are you hooked up for the video?"

Cochagne hefted the camera experimentally. When he aimed it at her, Tseng saw herself on the compartment's monitor. The picture from the video camera was not a good substitute for a mirror, she reminded herself. At least the puffiness that came from fluid retention in the upper extremities, always experienced in zero gravity, had diminished in the moon's one-sixth gravity. She believed her appearance was an acceptable compromise between her vanity and military neatness.

"You're gorgeous, China," Cochagne said, grinning wolfishly.

Tseng felt another hot flush of embarrassment at having her thoughts read so easily. Annoyed, she looked away from Cochagne deliberately, and heard him chuckle. She glanced at Horo for a reaction and saw her friend's raised eyebrows. It didn't seem possible that Cochagne had been making a pass at her.

Tseng chafed inwardly. To hide her reaction from Cochagne and Horo, she crossed to the galley. She made two cups of microwave coffee, then headed for the sleep stations that Manch and Greer had converted into an intensive care unit for any survivors during the last minute emergency refurbishing of the *Collins*.

She recalled her thoughts and actions during the memorial service. At the time, being unprepared to speak had not deterred her from eulogizing her colleagues. She'd felt instinctively driven to memorialize them. It had helped her deal with her guilt at having to leave their remains on the surface. She couldn't call it a funeral, considering the interim status of the casualties. Greer had called it "closure." She could accept that.

Later, back in the *Collins,* the experience had bothered her. Such bouts of rumination were rare for her, but she had just spent a restless, sleepless sleep period worrying about the ramifications of what she'd said at the memorial. It was inevitable that her extemporaneous words would be dissected, analyzed, and clutched to the sorrowing bosom of an entire planet. Horo had assumed custody of the portable camera and had transmitted the scene for posterity. Tseng wondered how well she had weathered the first crisis of this high-visibility command. She was afraid to see that video. How had the gesture looked to the world?

A morguelike silence had prevailed throughout the *Collins* after their return from the EVA. Everyone had been exhausted and in shock over the events of the day. Washington's death had had the most profound effect on them. Not that she was any more a colleague than Bisio, Drzymkowski, or Faden. They'd tried to save her and they'd failed.

Faden was alive, though both his condition and his circumstances were mysterious. The *Aldrin*'s life-support systems had been functioning on stored power alone. Therefore, he'd been imprisoned in the ship for no more than two days. Had FS-6 arrived one day later, Tseng believed they would have found Faden dead, too.

As things stood now, the Faden they all knew was among the missing.

In the course of astronaut training, she'd come to know the young computer expert on a personal basis through close daily association and after-hours socializing. Saturday backyard barbecues and an occasional round of golf as well as casual meal breaks in the Space Center commissary were routine.

She hadn't considered him a close friend, merely a professional colleague, somewhat boyish and socially unsophisticated for his thirty-two years. She had never gone so far as to think of him as an egocentric "computer geek." Others had. Faden's behavior as an astronaut might even have been called juvenile at times and yet, she had to admit that occasional displays of childish immaturity did sometimes occur between astronaut colleagues. A career in the sciences required a lot of years in school, and that meant a very cloistered existence.

During her years at Caltech, while working for her doctorate, the four or five subjects Tseng had taken per semester required at least three labs per week, during which she'd done assigned research and worked out the answers to complex problems as classroom exercises. Each of the labs had been three hours, but it had taken an average of twenty-three hours to write up the results of a lab. Classwork and preparation had thus added up to nearly eighty hours a week in school, and it had meant several years of never going to bed on Thursday nights because of the lab reports due on Fridays.

In the pursuit of a career in the sciences, "life" was looked upon as a pass-fail course that was not an academic requirement for a degree. Thus, one never had time to include it in the course of study. It was no mystery to Tseng why a thirty-two-year-old man might have the emotional maturity of a fourteen-year-old boy.

Prior to the mission, Dick Lebby, Faden's senior, mentor, and "guru" on the all-systems-encompassing Far Side computer, had known him better than anyone. Lebby's particular genius at the keyboard led him to seek unorthodox solutions for difficult problems. Faden had been his most attentive devotee.

But what about the problems with the Far Side computer that had baffled even Lebby? In her capacity as principal CAPCOM for FS-5, she had relayed the consensus of the experts on the ground to Faden. The simulations run on the "twin" of the Far Side computer indicated the possibility of a sophisticated "virus" in the software. Lebby and Faden had brainstormed novel ways to cleanse the system, but without success.

She realized that she was now thinking about Faden in the past tense most of the time. It was tantamount to writing him off as dead. They had tried to save Washington. She was real to them. The tragedy of her death was real. Faden was a phantom by comparison.

Tseng drew aside the privacy curtain across Faden's quarters and peered inside.

Faden was still in a drugged sleep, it appeared. Before the start of their sleep period, she and the other crew members had helped Manch and Greer shave the astronaut and give him a hospital bath. They'd also cut his hair. Military style. They'd covered his body with a hospital gown, then they'd wrapped him up in a bedsheet like a mummy, with his arms pinned to his sides. They'd wound a cargo strap tightly around him to further secure him.

Greer stared back at her through exhausted, bloodshot eyes. "What time is it?" she whispered.

"Half-past two, Houston time. Here . . ." Tseng handed a coffee to her.

"Thanks." Greer accepted the cup and took a cautious swallow. She winced as though she'd scalded her tongue. "This is very strong," she said. "The last thing I remember is sitting down and closing my eyes for just a moment . . ." Greer glanced at her watch. ". . . for twelve minutes, so it appears."

"How's it going?" Tseng whispered.

"As well as you'd expect," Greer answered.

Greer's ice-blue-gray eyes seemed to be looking through her, breaking her down into component parts and then examining each one individually. Tseng made an effort to shrug off the feeling. She respected Greer, but the psychiatrist had an intensity that was disturbing. It was as though there was something boiling inside of her, a tremendous pressure just behind the stone mask of her face or below the surface of her humanity, that needed to be contained.

Greer took another swallow of the coffee. From her grimace, it was still too hot, but she seemed impatient to be fully awake.

Tseng recognized the signs of the awkward standoffishness that Greer habitually exhibited to anyone whom she felt might want to get too familiar. Indicating the second cup of coffee she held, she asked, "Where's Paul?"

"Next door."

Tseng leaned over to look into the sleep station. Manch had fallen asleep with his back to the bulkhead, his knees pulled up to his chin. He had spent an hour at the Herculean task of "posting" Washington. He'd taken samples of blood, tissue, and hair. Tseng suspected he and Greer had spent most of their sleep period going over their data on all the casualties and packing the samples.

"It's a little too soon to know anything." Greer glanced at her watch, and added, "I should take his vital signs again."

When Greer touched Faden's wrist, the astronaut's eyes opened wide.

Shock reverberated through Tseng when Faden turned his head and smiled at her. He looked hollow-eyed and feverish under the harsh lights in the sleep station. His wasted state suggested that his present recovery bordered on the miraculous. A glance at Greer told her that the doctor was equally as surprised and disconcerted by the astronaut's sudden return to consciousness.

"Get Paul," Greer murmured.

Tseng reached next door to pull aside the sleep station curtain. Manch was awake. "We need you," she said.

"I'm coming," Manch muttered, stumbling forward.

Tseng handed him the cup of coffee in her hand. He took a tentative sip, then drained the cup in two gulps, while walking. Tseng stepped aside to let him enter Faden's sleep station.

"So . . . how do you feel, Bob?" Greer asked Faden.

To Tseng it was a lame question, but it might get Faden talking.

"Fine, I guess," the young astronaut replied in a "chatty" tone of voice. "I'm very, very, very alert. I can't relax at all, you know. Everything that's going on . . . I pick it up. I'm talking to you right now, but I can hear everything that's going on up here."

"Up here?" Manch asked. He plunged the empty coffee cup into the room's trash receptacle.

"On the Moon, you silly cocksucker. You're a putrid lump of dirt. Who are you?"

Manch paled. "I'm Paul Manch. I'm a doctor. You already know Dr. Greer."

"Oh, yes, Greer. How well do you suck cock?" Faden asked her.

Tseng cast a shocked, questioning glance at Greer, but the woman's expression remained neutral. "Jerry! Get in here with the camera, ASAP," she called out.

Faden struggled experimentally against the sheet and the cargo strap holding his arms. He said, "This is a straitjacket, isn't it?"

"Yes, Bob," Greer said, her tone that of a stern adult reprimanding a child. "You were delirious for a while, and we were afraid you would hurt yourself."

Faden's features distorted with an emotion that Tseng could only define as animal rage. The expression was fleeting. A moment later, the astronaut's entire body went slack. He surveyed the room with a dreamy, half-lidded expression.

Tseng was relieved to hear running footsteps. Cochagne arrived with the camera. Horo was with him. She stifled their questions with a negative headshake and pointed to the camera, then to Faden. Cochagne began to shoot.

Manch moved closer to the bed to distract his attention. Faden acted unaware of the camera. "We want to bring Mike and the others home if we can, Bob," Manch said. "Perhaps you can tell us where they are or what happened to them?"

"Everything is in pieces," Faden said, as if he hadn't heard Manch. "You get a picture in your head piece by piece. It's in your head, but it's like a photograph that's torn up into little pieces. It's into your head. It's like a photograph that's torn in pieces and put together again. The picture I have in my head is all broken up. I don't like moving. I'll break apart into pieces if I move too quick . . . my arms, my legs, my hands, my feet, my head, my eyes, my ears . . . they'll just break apart. I feel myself going into a kind of a trance. It scares me to death. I can be just walking around and I feel it coming on. I start to think so deep that I leave this world. I get scared that I'm going to go so deep that I'll lose myself, and then I can't move. There's too much noise. People are talking and laughing. I have to stop and listen. I could be walking across a room, and when I hear the voices, I freeze like that for a day or two. I can't help stopping to listen. It happens when I'm in bed, and I can't sleep. There's too much noise going on, and I can't move. I listen to sounds and voices all the time. I can't tell if they're separate from me." A look of stark terror came over Faden's face.

"He's going to kill me. He's watching me. I know he is. Waiting to kill me. They're burning me up! I'm coming apart, and I can't do anything about it."

"Who is going to kill you?" Greer asked trying to break into Faden's stream of consciousness monologue.

The astronaut's muscles tensed spasmodically. He stopped talking and stared fixedly at Greer. Then his demeanor changed. He became sly and smiled wolfishly at her. "How well do you suck cock?" he asked again.

Tseng turned at the approach of DeSosa and Lebby. She silenced them with a finger to her lips.

"I'm always dead," a voice that was lower pitched and harsher-sounding than Faden's said.

Tseng turned back to see Faden smiling impishly.

Greer appeared genuinely curious when she asked, "Why are you always dead, Bob?"

Tseng wanted to laugh at the ridiculous question Greer had asked in such a serious clinical way, but she controlled the urge.

In answer, the astronaut launched into a series of grunts and squeals in imitation of a pig, then the voice that was not Faden's voice giggled and twittered.

Faden's mouth articulated the sounds, but Tseng wondered how his vocal cords could make them.

"What the hell . . . ?" Lebby mumbled.

"I hate you," a new Faden voice hissed at them, and bewilderment was suddenly clearly visible in the astronaut's eyes. In his own voice, Faden shrieked, "Get out," and strained at his bonds.

"Let's give him another amp of Seconal," Greer said to Manch. Manch nodded. Faden hissed at her when she rushed by him to get to the medical supplies. She took a small ampoule of the drug out of a medical bag and quickly and expertly loaded it into a hypo-gun as easily as an experienced hunter might load a rifle cartridge.

Faden pulled against his restraints. His face turned dark red and his eyes bulged with the effort. Suddenly, blood gushed from his mouth and nose.

"God! Has he ruptured himself?" Tseng swore.

Manch shook his head. "Broken blood vessels."

Greer approached Faden with the hypo-gun at the ready. The astronaut bared his teeth and growled at her like a mad dog.

"Help me," Greer said.

Tseng was already in motion toward Faden, and she heard Lebby, DeSosa, and Horo behind her. She was glad Cochagne was capturing the scene. She grabbed Faden's shoulders, pinning him to the bed. His breath smelled like decomposed flesh.

Greer jammed the hypo-gun barrel against his neck and pulled the trigger. The drug was pneumatically forced through the skin and into Faden's bloodstream with a staccato hiss.

Tseng relaxed her grip on Faden, expecting the astronaut to succumb immediately to the powerful sedative as he'd done the night before. Instead, Faden lunged at her and tried to bite her arm.

She jerked away, then got a new hold on Faden. Greer, Manch, Horo, Lebby, and DeSosa combined their strength with hers to push Faden down on the bed. All the while, the astronaut struggled to free his trapped arms. His features contorted with effort and with a violent rage that was definitely inhuman to Tseng's perception. Blood and thick saliva cascaded over his chin and onto his chest.

"He should be out," Greer panted. "I don't understand . . ."

Faden squirmed against the hands holding him. His body bucked and twisted. The snakelike movements loosened the cargo strap wrapped around him. He pulled one arm out of the sheet. The sheet came loose and he freed his other arm. "We'll take you to hell with us," Faden shrieked in a new voice that was higher pitched than the others, and he waved his arms wildly.

"Give him another shot!" Tseng ordered.

"I can't! It would kill him," Greer fired back.

Faden hissed at them.

"Pin his arms!" Greer shouted. "We have to subdue him until the drug gets to him!"

Manch grabbed Faden's arms and tried to cross them over his chest while the others bore down on him. Tseng could see his arm muscles bulging with the effort. Faden was winning the battle. Summoning his strength, Manch backhanded Faden, slamming him down against the bed pallet.

Faden strained forward, then all the fight left him. He fell back, drained, limp, and unconscious.

Trembling with relief, Tseng released her hold. Relief changed to alarm. Faden wasn't breathing.

Manch pulled her aside and felt Faden's neck for a pulse.

"Is he dead?" Tseng asked, remembering Washington.

"No. His heart's still beating," Manch said.

Faden's eyes opened. His lips stretched tight over yellow, bloodstained teeth in a ghoulish smile. He made a guttural sound deep in his throat. "Watch out, he's back," Manch warned. Greer, Horo, Lebby, and DeSosa converged on him and used their body weight to help him force Faden to stay down. Blood oozed out of Faden's mouth, staining his gown and the bedsheet around him. Horo looked away from the revolting sight.

The astronaut's mouth twitched hideously. He spit up foul-smelling blood onto his chin. "I'm always dead," he choked out in a harsh voice. Then, he collapsed into unconsciousness again.

Whatever the thing in the bed was, it wasn't Bob

Faden, the astronaut and the man she knew, Tseng told herself. The spark of energy, the essence, the personality, the psyche, the very soul that was Faden was gone.

Cochagne switched the camera off.

With firm but gentle pressure, Manch pried Faden's mouth open and peered inside. "It's just as I thought. He bit his tongue." He looked up. His eyes sought Greer. "Let's get him cleaned up. Then we need to figure out a better way to restrain him."

"Maybe we should approach this as an engineering problem," Cochagne suggested.

Tseng nodded agreement.

"You know, we're really not equipped to handle something like this here," Greer said.

"Collins, Houston, do you copy?" Shah Zia's voice came over the COMM.

Tseng had been sitting alone at her console on the flight deck. She leaned forward and snatched up her communications headset as Cochagne emerged from the companionway, followed by Horo.

"Houston, *Collins.* Good afternoon," Tseng said.

"Collins, Good morning to you. It's one-zero-four hours: fifteen minutes Mission Elapsed Time. According to our crew status report for sleep, you all only had five hours' sleep out of ten, Commander. Tsk, tsk, tsk . . . Shame on all of you!"

Tseng laughed off the gentle but firm reprimand from Mission Control. "We've been busy up here," she said.

Cochagne and Horo rolled their eyes, but said nothing.

"Where's Pops Lebby? I want to send my greetings and felicitations," Zia said. Shah Zia, a computer specialist in the astronaut program, had trained with Lebby and Faden.

"Greetings and felicitations to you," they heard Lebby call out, his voice cutting through the hushed atmosphere in the *Collins* like a piercing yell. The senior astronaut was again at the computer. He was playing back Cochagne's video of Faden and making hard copies of selected frames for reference.

"Pop's busy, so he can't come to the phone right now," Cochagne said.

Zia laughed in response. He and his wife, Bahija Fayyad, had met and married while in the astronaut program. Tseng knew them well and liked them. Shah and Bahija would have the best shot at making the transition from the Far Side Program to a Mars mission, because the space agency was looking at sending married couples on the two-year round trips.

Outwardly, they appeared to have achieved the perfect balance in their relationship; they were partners in life with no conflicting professional interests and a mutual tolerance for difficult work schedules. It was a type of contentment that had eluded her for so much of her life that Tseng had become resigned to living without it.

In retrospect, there could be little doubt that her emotional growth and maturity were "stunted" by the choices she'd made to pursue her career. That conclusion was undeniable, and a result of the merciless self-examination she'd done lately—that was one of the "perks" of going into space; it took one out of the normal routine of daily life on Earth. The long duration of a spaceflight meant time spent gazing out at the stars. The time was conducive to introspection.

"We have news for you, people," Tseng said. "Bob Faden came out of his coma for a while, a short time ago. Unfortunately, he didn't say anything that made sense to us before we had to sedate him again."

"Can you give us the details?" Zia asked.

"I was just about to downlink some video. He's still critical. That's all I want to say right now, until you've seen for yourselves," Tseng replied.

There was silence on the COMM.

Horo looked at her with mock scorn and raised her eyebrows for emphasis.

The reaction made Tseng smile. She was about to give the Ground information about something they could do nothing about. They'd been given the GO for the mission, so until such time as the Ground felt Faden's condition threatened to have a direct and immediate impact on crew safety or on the success of the mission, they would press on with their agenda. Any change in plans would be the ground's call. It was better to let them come to their own conclusions.

"Houston, are you still there?" Horo asked "What about this live interview you've volunteered us for?"

"Sorry for the delay," Zia said. "We'll take that downlink when you're ready. We promised them a live interview, it's in the schedule, and we feel obligated to keep our word. We've prepared a script for you, which you'll get on the teleprinter shortly. It's based on the questions that are going to be asked."

"You're giving us a script?" Tseng said loudly, her indignation rising. Interviews with astronauts in space had been "scripted" only a few times in the history of the program. Each time, such attempts at control from the Ground had resulted in protests by the crews. In the end, such a directive had to be obeyed. There were cases of passive resistance which took the form of childish demonstrations or pranks—one Space Station crew having gone so far as to sever all communications with Mission Control for an entire day as retribution for "spur of the moment" additions to their workload which they considered excessive—but usually, no one dared to "cross the line" in such earnest.

Still, this felt like a usurpation of her authority.

"Dee Bianco hopes it will cut down on wild speculation," Zia said. In a more rebellious tone, he added, "I know how you feel. I'd resent it, too. In addition, we're about to beam you the 'pre-interview interview'—a news broadcast from one of the major networks. We've released some of your footage to the news media and you'll be seeing it. That will give you an idea of how much they know—which is not much. They've been driving us crazy! No pictures of Bisio or Drzymkowski. We didn't want them to focus on the gory details. That should be your cue: spare them the details and don't make any speculative remarks. We'll alert you when it's time for your TV debut."

"Stand by for the downlink," Lebby's voice broke into the COMM.

"Just questions and answers from a panel of representatives from the networks and wire services, no surprises?" Cochagne asked, the question heavily laden with sarcasm.

"Roger. That's it for now. Look on the bright side. You guys should feel important. After all, you're preempting the soap operas in this time zone."

"Damn right we feel important! Not everybody has the clout to do that," Horo fired back.

"We've got your downlink, *Collins,* stand by for the TV feed. I'll give you a short count . . . five . . . four . . . three . . . two . . . one . . ."

A network quality telephoto shot of the Moon appeared on the flight deck monitor. The words, "UBC NEWS: THE FAR SIDE CRISIS" were superimposed along the bottom of the screen and an announcer's voice proclaimed, "This is a UBC News special report: Crisis at Far Side. Here's Ted Guest in New York."

"They must have taken that picture a couple of nights ago," Cochagne said.

The picture dissolved into the handsome, serious face

of the well-known newscaster seated behind a desk in the network newsroom.

"We're coming to you live from the studio, where we have an update."

Guest's face was replaced with network-shot live footage of the FS-5 crew leaving the ready room, shortly before launch. His voice-over continued. "Before the FS-5 launch went off, I guess it wasn't paid any closer attention to than by the folks in Lincoln, Nebraska. That's where the ever popular Louise Washington hailed from. There, she had so many fans and so many friends who were praying for her survival and rescue."

The picture changed. Tseng recognized her video of their attempt to revive Washington. "It's been computer enhanced and filtered," she told Cochagne and Horo, "The frame lines have been changed to cut out as much of the background as possible."

"You're watching a recording of what happened shortly after midnight, Eastern Standard Time, yesterday," Guest continued narrating. "Today, we're sorry to report that FS-5 Pilot Louise Washington must be added to the list of fatalities at Far Side."

Guest appeared on camera again. "In a few minutes, we'll be going live to the Moon to talk with the mission commander of FS-6, Colonel Po Ming Tseng and her crew. Astronaut Bob Faden, apparently the only survivor of the Far Side disaster, has not regained consciousness. Doctors are hopeful of his recovery. However, his condition is still regarded as extremely critical."

The camera moved in dramatically on Guest's face. "Tragedy, today, with the confirmed deaths of three of the six crew members of the fifth mission to Far Side Moon Base. Two more crew members, Commander Mike Mobley and Mission Specialist Shinobu Takizawa, are listed as missing and presumed dead. This brings to a total of ten the number of deaths in space since the turn of the century. Parallel to the sadness that has been felt all over the country at this latest loss of Americans who have challenged the reaches of space, comes the support of people from all over the world of America's pursuit of space ventures. The Russian Commonwealth issued a statement on behalf of the Russian people expressing condolences on the loss of American lives.

"Reporter Charles Nader is standing by at the White House. Charlie . . . ?"

The picture cut to a man wearing a trench coat to shield him from the chill wind, standing at the front gate of the White House.

"Charlie, what happened when the news was announced there, and what has happened subsequently?" Guest's voice asked.

The reporter looked into the camera, a serious expression on his face, as befitted the occasion, Tseng observed.

"Ted, just a few minutes ago, the President came into the room, where a few of us were being briefed. He explained how they had come and told him about the reports from Far Side. He told us about the incredible sense of shock he felt, and he said, 'Our hearts go out to all the families,' but he also said that 'when something like this happens, Americans just don't throw in the towel and quit.' He said, 'This program has to go on.' "

The picture cut back to Guest. "Thank you, Charlie. We'll be checking back with you a little later." The camera angle on Guest widened again. Tseng, Cochagne, and Horo saw Jack Bucar seated at the desk next to Guest. There were exclamations of amusement from Lebby and DeSosa, watching from the mid-deck.

Tseng had heard rumors, before launch, that Bucar was being courted by a network news agency, but she'd kept quiet. She was glad the secret was out, and happy for Bucar.

"Here with me is General Jack Bucar, UBC's special correspondent and technical expert, veteran of the space program and the Commander of FS-1, the first mission to Far Side Base."

"The old war horse looks tired," Horo said with affection.

"I'm sorry I never had the chance to serve under him," Cochagne said.

"You missed a good experience. You just can't buy that kind of education," Tseng said.

"Amen," Horo added.

To the world, FS-1 was a perfect mission. Only the astronauts who'd flown it and the Mission Control team that had supported them were aware that everything had not gone as smoothly as reported. The tendency of sophisticated machines and computers to fail at critical moments was legendary in the space program, but FS-1 had experienced more than its share of potentially life-threatening glitches. Bucar's command skill, his resourcefulness, and his stubbornness had brought them through, and they had come home as heroes. More importantly, they'd come home.

It was doubtful that Bucar would get another ride into space. He was a combat veteran and astronaut on the verge of being put out to pasture. It was a difficult phase to get through and some did not make it easily or gracefully. Many fell prey to alcoholism. This was an audition for Bucar, and Tseng hoped that the UBC TV consultant contract would be lucrative for him. He deserved to make some real money after years of drawing a military salary followed by the prestigious but low paying job as an astronaut.

Considering the low pay, the wealth of education, experience, and talent in the astronaut pool was astounding. With the advantages of perfect eyesight, hearing, and general health, she had planned her own career down to the last detail. As a graduate of Caltech's prestigious Aeronautics program, she had substituted experience as a test pilot for combat experience. Most mission specialists had PhDs. Some, like Paul Manch and Iona Greer, had medical degrees and a doctorate. That represented many, many years of schooling. Once accepted into the astronaut program, two to five more years were required preparing to get a mission because it was NASA's philosophy to "despecialize specialists" with cross-training in other aspects of spaceflight.

What the job offered was the chance to go into space. In Tseng's opinion, no other job could compare with it. It was that attitude that she and Arminta Horo had in common, and it had made them close friends.

Compared to the money Horo could be making in the private sector, her astronaut's salary was a joke. Ukita Corporation had tried to recruit her for the last two years and, recently, she'd fielded offers from Shimizu and Matsushita. Technically, she was working for Matsushita on the robot project. Tseng knew Horo was beginning to think seriously about the money they were offering.

"Before we look at the pictures from FS-6, I have a question," Guest said on-screen. "The fire which killed *Apollo* astronauts Grissom, Chaffee, and White: you people—that is, NASA—knew right away the cause of that fire. You always knew that using pure oxygen to pressurize a space capsule was risky, yet it took the deaths of three astronauts to change things.

"The *Challenger* explosion: within minutes of the accident, you knew what had gone wrong. Again, NASA had been aware of potential problems with the seals, yet no one did anything about it until lives were lost.

"The accident at the Space Station . . . yet again, you knew the cause immediately, because the problem with the capture latches on the berthing interface had been identified, and had been called to your attention repeatedly.

"The disaster at Far Side: you knew immediately that the communications problems at Far Side were being caused by electromagnetic interference. You knew there was a problem. Why wasn't it corrected before the loss of life occurred?"

"Oh, geez, what an all-around oversimplification! We could be in for a very hard time!" Horo warned.

There were groans and nonverbal sounds of agreement from Cochagne, Lebby, and DeSosa. On the monitor, the camera angle changed from a two-shot of Guest and Bucar at the news desk, to a close-up of Bucar, in anticipation of the astronaut's answer to Guest's question. Bucar's on-camera presence reassured Tseng.

"I don't know that you can compare the situation at Far Side with the other accidents you mentioned," Bucar answered slowly and deliberately.

"Five more astronauts are dead, General," Guest said.

"And we're working very hard to find out why," Bucar answered. "I don't want to sound callous about the loss of life we've had in the U.S. Space Program. That's a terrible, terrible thing which is felt very deeply in the spaceflight community, just as it is across the nation, except that with us, there are close friendships and working relationships of long standing involved. I can say very truthfully that we have never knowingly put lives in jeopardy.

"To say that, because of budgetary problems, we've had to do things the cheapest way we can, which has not always been the best way, is a weak defense, but, like it or not, that has been, and still is, a factor in the way we do things . . . and in view of that, our safety record is still outstanding when you think of what's been accomplished and when you compare our record, with, say that of the old Soviet Union and its successor, the Russian Republic. . . ."

Bucar paused to gather his thoughts. In the studio, the moment of silence and contemplation was evidently a signal for a change in the camera angle. The shot widened to include Ted Guest, but just as the anchorman opened his mouth to speak, Bucar spoke. Guest forced a smile and did not interrupt as the astronaut continued with, "You know, Ted, it's come to light, in recent years, that loss of life in the Soviet space program was far greater during the time period you mentioned than in the U.S. space program. Their systems lacked the sophistication of ours, so they went ahead and tried a lot of things in space without the benefit of being able to run elaborate simulations on the ground first to get the bugs out of procedures and equipment to diminish the risks to their astronauts. They sent a lot of people up there to try out complex systems and to perform difficult tasks for the first time, hoping everything would work. Sometimes they were lucky, and they scored a big public relations coup for their country, but a great deal of the time, they weren't lucky. They've only been using simulators for the last two decades or so, and that's only because we shared that technology with them.

"They haven't talked openly about their fatalities during the early days and they didn't suffer the delays in their program after every accident that we did, because of their political system and because their scientific community was firmly committed to the value of being in space and of having a space program. They accepted the risks inherent in their method, corrected their mistakes, and kept moving along. However, let me tell you that their safety record stinks to high heaven, and, frankly, that's what I call a callous attitude about human life. That has never been our policy at NASA. We are professionals who work in a very dangerous environment where, despite all the elaborate safety precautions we take, anything can happen."

"Thank you for sharing your point of view on that with us, General," Guest said, then he looked into the camera and said. "These pictures have just been released by NASA. As a former mission commander we'd appreciate your interpretation."

To Tseng, the anchorman's attitude was a dismissal of Bucar's statements.

She was caught by surprise as the picture cut from the live studio shot to her video of the overturned rover. The network had chosen to use her slow pan from the passenger compartment side. Her critical eye noticed every flaw in the camera technique. Would she ever be more than a talented amateur with the camera? she wondered, and felt mildly embarrassed that her "flawed work" was being seen around the world. An annoying start-up chatter from the *Collins'* teleprinter, which threatened to drown out any dialogue from the news program, caused her to lean forward in her seat and scowl at the screen.

"This is the LRV, the Lunar Roving Vehicle," Bucar's voice narrated the footage. "From the evidence, we think that the FS-5 crewmen may have been transporting consumables to the *Aldrin* with the intention of making an early departure. We think that, during this operation, the rover hit a soft spot or sinkhole in the lunar surface and overturned. We can see the footprints of the crewmen as they might have attempted to right it. They were unable to do this, so they abandoned the effort. They may not have had time for a second attempt."

"That being the case, they just left the things in it," they heard Guest say. "Isn't that odd?"

"They were out of communication. That put them under a lot of pressure," Bucar countered. "Beyond that, we just don't know."

On-screen, there was a cut to a scene showing the approach to the base. Tseng recognized it as a PLSS back-pack camera shot.

"We're seeing the exterior of the Main Dome," Bucar said. "Beyond it, you can see the framework for the Science Dome. There doesn't appear to be any damage to the outside of the structures."

Guest replied with a thoughtful, "Ummmhumm," which, to Tseng, expressed his deep-down personal mistrust and disbelief of the facts he'd been given, then he said, "We have some pictures of the inside of the Main Dome. Perhaps you can explain what we're seeing, General."

"The lighting was very poor in there. It gave us limited photo ability. There's been damage to the interior since the last transmission from FS-5."

"Where are we?" Guest asked.

"This is Level Three. The computer mainframe is located here, along with the communications equipment. It's the work center of the base."

The next cut was to the attempted rescue of Washington. "We're showing you the recorded footage of the FS-6 medical team's attempts to revive Louise Washington. We can't see much of the background, General."

"Colonel Tseng just did not have the light. I can tell you that Washington was found in the recreation area on Level Two, which is the crew support level."

"Drzymkowski's and Bisio's bodies were also found on Level Two."

"Yes, that is correct."

Bucar and Guest appeared on camera again. Guest gave Bucar his most penetrating glance. "Why didn't NASA disclose the information about the fly problem prior to this?"

"We didn't know about it," Bucar answered, with a touch of righteous indignation in his voice, Tseng thought.

"Somehow, they took a fly—or, likelier still, one or

more fly eggs—up with them," Bucar continued. "There are any number of ways that could have happened. We try to prevent it, but it has happened before. We're investigating this thoroughly, so it won't happen again."

"Will any further attempt be made to locate the bodies of Mobley and Takizawa if FS-6 cannot recover them, General Bucar?"

"We intend to make every effort to account for the entire crew of FS-5. I have every confidence in Commander Tseng to do a thorough investigation at Far Side, within the time constraints that may fall on this mission."

"And, from what I'm given to understand there are very serious time constraints," Guest emphasized.

"Yes. As you know, we have two FS-5 astronauts still missing. Any investigation we do out on the lunar surface must be done before the base and the surrounding area are in total darkness. At that point, the temperature will drop below the safety margins. Extravehicular activity will be severely limited."

Guest reached off camera, then placed a globe of the Moon on the desk in front of Bucar. "We have a model here. Perhaps you could show us what you mean."

"I'd be glad to," Bucar said, picking up a pencil from the desk. "When we see phases of the Moon, here on Earth, what we're seeing is something called the lunar terminator line—the edge of the shadow caused by the angle of the Sun. It moves from east to west at about nine and a half miles an hour at the Moon's equator. Faster in the upper and lower latitudes. The base is in the lower latitudes, here . . ." Bucar pointed at the site, ". . . near the upper edge of South Pole-Aitken Crater. South Pole-Aitken just happens to be the largest mascon on the far side."

"What is a mascon, General?" Guest interrupted.

"A mass concentration. Mascons are found in the lunar impact basins, the craters, and marea of the Moon, the sites of meteor strikes. Mascons are very large concentrations of basalt, a highly reflective, igneous rock formed of titanium-rich magnetic iron and other minerals." Bucar rotated the Moon globe to the near side. "We're used to seeing these dark areas on the near side, the side that faces Earth. They form the face of the 'man in the Moon.' Lunar mascons represent quite a potential for commercial exploitation."

This was the frustrating part of a live interview like this one, Tseng reflected. The media were asking questions. They demanded to know the answers. The problem was, the answers were not easy to understand.

"What does this mean in relation to the communication problems at Far Side?

"One of the Moon's scientific mysteries is that, while it has no magnetic field of its own, there is residual surface impact magnetism," Bucar said. "We can theorize that this phenomenon is due, in part, to the influence of the Earth's magnetic field on the native iron; however, we have been conducting spaciography experiments since before the *Apollo* program days. The high point, of course, was the data gathered by *Lunar Prospector* in the late nineteen nineties. Spaciography is the science which studies stellar and planetary magnetic fields. The studies reveal that the magnetic activity is higher at some points in the lunar rotation cycle than at others. The likelihood is that this is a function of proximity of the Earth and the Moon because at certain stages in the cycle, the gravitational fields also interact. The Moon passes through the Earth's magnetotail. This behavior is characteristic of a binary system and, here on Earth, this has bearing on the strength of ocean tides."

"Another of the FS-5 scientific objectives was a follow-up on peripheral data from the *Apollo 17* Lunar Ejecta and Meteorites experiment conducted on the near

side. In that experiment, an increase in surface micropar-
ticles carrying a high electrostatic charge was recorded
during the passage of the terminator over the instrument.
FS-5 was the first mission since that time to have
the opportunity of observing this phenomenon. Unfortunately, PERM, the Particle Event Rate Measurement
instrument package, has also stopped transmitting.

"In constructing Far Side, surface electromagnetic effects were anticipated and the equipment was shielded
accordingly. Two weeks ago, electromagnetic field activity in the vicinity of the base intensified to such a
degree that it seriously effected the Far Side team's experiments across the board. We're fairly certain that electromagnetic interference had a marked effect on the
base's communications equipment.

"Joe DeSosa and Dick Lebby were working with Bob
Faden, the FS-5 Computer Systems Specialist, and with
Takizawa, Bisio, and Drzymkowski also, to determine if
the shielding on the base's power supply was inadequate,
and therefore adding to the malfunction problems. I need
to reiterate that we checked many possibilities in order
to isolate the problems at Far Side. At one point, we also
suspected a malfunction in the signal handoff between
the two Lunar Tracking and Data Relay Satellites. The
L-TDRS make it possible for us to maintain constant
communications with Far Side. Normally, we'd expect
to get data from the base's computer, but the system kept
crashing, and then, as you know, it finally went down
and has stayed down. We were forced to rely on our
Earth-based equipment, which told us that the L-TDRS
were okay. That possibility was then eliminated," Bucar
finished.

"We began to focus on the shielding question. The
principal habitat of the base is underground for radiation
and thermal shielding, but there's also electromagnetic
shielding. Far Side power requirements are met in two

ways. There are six fuel cells that are energized by the photovoltaic solar array during lunar day, and then they provide stored power during the lunar night. Electrical currents passing through cables and wires create electromagnetic fields and, whenever there's communications equipment and/or a computer system involved, there has to be shielding that prevents it from being affected by these fields. At the base, it's necessary for us to generate a substantial amount of power. The source is shielded from the equipment, and the equipment is shielded from the power source. One of the things we are given to suspect is that the shielding on the base's generating system is inadequate and that there is magnetic leakage. Combined with the Moon's own electromagnetic activity, and the fact that the base is sitting on top of an iron-rich source, the total disturbance is most likely destabilizing the computer and communications equipment."

The news anchorman looked mildly skeptical, but as media coverage went, Tseng felt Bucar had conveyed more genuine information that was closer to the working theory of the actual problems than the anchorman had any right to expect without a security clearance.

"What are FS-6's chances of finding Mobley and Takizawa?" Guest asked.

"We're approaching the full Moon as seen from Earth," Bucar said. On the far side, just the opposite is happening. Once this terminator passes over Far Side Base, the surface temperatures will drop dramatically—eight degrees an hour. Work on the surface will become increasingly difficult."

"But the FS-6 crew might be given the go to stay at Far Side through the lunar night phase?"

"That's correct, Ted."

"A lot depends on how efficiently Colonel Tseng conducts her investigation, then."

"I wouldn't go so far as to say that. There are a lot of factors involved," Bucar said, his tone mildly reprimanding.

Tseng was silently grateful for the show of loyalty.

"It's purely a matter of how much we are able to learn over the next day or so," Bucar concluded.

"This next piece of video we're about to see, General . . . this was taken by one of the other astronauts. Perhaps you can tell us about it."

On the monitor, Tseng saw herself, Manch, Greer, Lebby, and Cochagne standing in a semicircle near the body bags. All had their heads bowed. The shot emphasized the barrenness of the setting and added a powerful pictorial impact to the moment that Tseng had been oblivious to at the time.

She suddenly felt queasy as she stared at the scene captured by Horo for all time. The memorial service had been attended by millions of TV viewers. She was now looking at what they had seen. It was like seeing through the eyes of someone else. She heard her voice, but it sounded like a different person.

"I wasn't prepared to say anything. I wasn't prepared for this moment, but there are a few things I want to say. Unknown to the crewmen of FS-5, they brought death up with them to the Moon . . ."

"All the FS-5 astronauts will be brought home for burial with full honors," Bucar said. The sequence ended, and the network cut back to the studio.

"There's a degree of detachment among all of you, in the space program, in view of the magnitude of this tragedy," Guest said to Bucar. "Some of us, in the media, have found that disturbing."

"Our attitudes may very well seem 'detached' to you. They may seem frivolous, irresponsible, and insensitive," Bucar answered. "You have to understand that we'll never forget our colleagues, nor do we want to trivialize what happened there. But we can't dwell on the deaths, nor do we have the luxury of a prolonged period of mourning. In the case of the FS-6 astronauts, the memorial was their way of dealing with that, and of putting it behind them.

"Now, it's imperative for them and for NASA to move on. That's more of a tribute to Bisio, Drzymkowski, and Washington, and to Mobley and Takizawa, than if we mope around in a morbid state of mind and miss something that may turn out to be extremely important in getting to the bottom of this. That would be very unprofessional."

Guest smiled at Bucar and said, "Thank you, General." Then he looked into the camera. "Evidence of man's fascination with the Moon's mysteries is found in the earliest examples of recorded history. He has deified it, worshiped it, attributed awesome powers to it, and he's been terrified by it and its 'supernatural' effects. In the Far Side disaster, we add yet another mystery to its mythos, but one which we're looking to modern science to solve, and, given the right tools and clues, the people at NASA will solve it.

"We at UBC find the words of Commander Tseng apropos to this moment, for 'Unknown to the crewmen of FS-5, they carried death up with them to the Moon. But, as we reflect on it, perhaps, it was there all along . . . waiting for them.' We're going to take a short break to let the local stations identify themselves. For now, this is Ted Guest on behalf of my colleagues, and for UBC News, in New York."

The network cut away from Guest to the film of the memorial service on the Moon, and technical credits for the news segment rolled over the bleak scene.

Tseng realized she'd been holding her breath and she let it out with a long sigh. Her moment, captured on

video, was history. As for Bucar, he had put the limited
information NASA had released into an order that made
sense. It was a truthful scenario, but not the truth; a rough
sketch, but not the complete picture.

"The old man was great," Horo said.

"He had a presence that they were able to exploit to
dramatize the moment," Tseng said. "I'm going to miss
him."

"He's not quitting yet, is he?" Lebby asked.

"I haven't heard anything to that effect," Tseng said.
"However, from now on, it will be different for him—
like going home again, once you've left. There's a certain feeling of distance. Knowing Jack Bucar, it will
make him want to get on with his life rather than to ret-
rogress and hold on to the past."

On the monitor, the TV camera was again moving in
on Guest. The newscaster adjusted his earphone. He continued to talk while listening, but his voice was hesitant
with the divided concentration. "We do learn, at the moment, that, while NASA was ready to hold its news conference five minutes ago, there appears to be a hang-up.
If anyone there is listening, perhaps they can give us an
indication of what the hang-up is . . ." Guest let the sentence trail off and waited through a long pause. "Our information is sketchy," he resumed, "but we've just been
informed that Mission Control received a video transmission from the *Collins* a short time ago."

Tseng heard the teleprinter stop. She retrieved the
six-page printout and returned aft. Lebby, Horo, and
Cochagne crowded close to read over her shoulder while
she scanned the printed pages. DeSosa got up from
the stack of hard copy photos he was studying and
joined them.

"It's more of a detailed guideline than an actual
script," she told them.

"What are we going to do about it?" DeSosa asked. "It's a P.R. maneuver, there's no question about it.

"Unfortunately, we have to think in terms of the consequences if we ignore it," Tseng said. "What do we have to gain by open rebellion? Do we want to look like a bunch of jerks, or do we want to be perceived as part of a team?"

"I still don't like being told what to say," Horo fumed.

"That was my initial reaction, too," Tseng said. "However, after watching this newscast, at the present time, it's better not to interpret it that way. Instead, try looking at it as an official position on what had better be left unsaid at this point . . . for the good of the Far Side program and everyone in it. Especially us."

Horo continued to glare angrily, but she remained silent. "Regardless of how you all feel personally, I'm passing this around for everyone to read," Tseng added.

"If you've just tuned in, again, we mourn the loss of five Americans, crew members on the fifth mission to Far Side Base," Guest said. "That brings the number of Americans who have died in the space program to a total of twenty-two."

Guest put a hand to his earphone again. "I apologize . . . again, if you've just tuned in for the news conference, there's been a slight delay in the schedule . . . at the moment, we have a report from Gene Reynolds, who has been out at the Jet Propulsion Laboratory in Pasadena, California. Gene . . . ?"

There was a cut on-screen and Gene Reynolds was looking into the camera from JPL. To Tseng, it was a face from her childhood. Reynolds had covered the Space Station construction missions.

"I've been talking to a number of people today," Reynolds said, "and, first of all, nobody really knows anything yet, but I've been talking to a former astronaut on the Space Station program, who, like General Bucar, thinks there may have been a last, desperate attempt by the astronauts to escape from Far Side Base, and that the deaths occurred subsequent to that accident, maybe even as a result of it. If we could just roll that footage of the rover again . . ."

The camera cut back to Guest. "We have it for you, Gene. We're putting it up now . . ."

The footage of the rover appeared on the screen. "There you see the rover—the Lunar Roving Vehicle, or LRV, in space parlance—and there are a lot of boot prints around it," Reynolds said, off camera. "Obviously, the rover contained supplies for an escape attempt. That attempt may have failed when the rover hit a soft spot or a hole and turned over."

Cochagne groaned. "A soft spot? A hole? Don't they realize that the whole damn place is a soft spot riddled with holes?"

Manch emerged from the flight deck hatchway. He looked pale and drawn with fatigue. "As nonscientific guesses go, that's a reasonable one," the physician said. "It's clear they've run out of real news. When that happens, they fill in the time with wild speculation."

Tseng noticed that he worked to keep a straight face. "How magnanimous you are when it comes to the technical domains of others," she said.

"Magnanimity is my middle name."

"Okay, but wait till the tables are turned and they come out with an outrageous medical theory," Horo said.

"What's your best guess, then?" Manch asked. "It's time we heard an expert speculate."

"The LRV isn't very heavy," Tseng responded. "Any time it gets stuck, we just pick it up and carry it out of trouble. That's a two-man task—except someone like Drzymkowski could pick the thing up by himself. My best guess? There was a fight over it. The winner, or winners, overturned it," Tseng said.

"You didn't come up here to discuss the rover," Cochagne said.

"You're right. I wanted to let you know that Greer thinks we should start Faden on Thorazine as soon as possible. I agree. Thorazine is an antipsychotic drug. It's not the best one, but it's all we have available. However, I have to warn you that our medical supplies are limited. That's going to impact the mission."

"Thanks for that information," Tseng said.

On the monitor, the video footage ended, and Reynolds appeared on camera again. "I don't want to take this too far, Ted, because it's dangerous until we really know what happened."

The network cut back to Guest in the studio for a reaction shot. "I agree, it's very dangerous," Guest said thoughtfully. "Gene, if you had to make a guess at this point, and I realize that it is only a guess, would you think, based on your association with both politics and space, that the Far Side program would have a serious slowdown?"

At JPL, the camera moved in on Reynolds for a close-up. "A serious slowdown? Absolutely. I don't think there's any question. I think it is also true that they will do their investigation, find out what happened, and surmount it . . . and I can't imagine that this will be the end of the Far Side program. They've got a lot of work to do, but having done it, they will be a lot better off for it."

Guest appeared on the screen again. "Thank you, Gene. As we mentioned earlier, NASA has scheduled a live interview. We'll shortly be talking to Po Tseng, the commander of the mission on which the hopes of the nation hung for a considerable length of time . . . how this will be accomplished . . . NASA has selected a panel of broadcast journalists . . .

On the monitor, Guest bent his head as though listening to a message on his earphone, then he looked into the camera, making eye contact with the viewing audience of millions he could not see. He possessed an instinctive feel for the theatrics of the medium, Tseng had to admit.

Dee Bianco was fond of portraying the broadcaster as an "evil nemesis" for her own amusement, and when it suited her purpose. Perhaps there was something to be gained from adopting that attitude for the upcoming interview. Wasn't it a newsman's job to put news makers—people already under pressure—on the spot, in the hope they might make more news? She would have to thwart any such attempt.

She doubted that Guest really had much control over the content of a story, and over which stories made the news and which didn't. Maybe star anchorman status gave him clout in those areas, but he was only the "on-camera talent." The network news department was the entity pulling his strings.

In the days of the "big three" competing networks, Guest's face on-camera might have made a difference in the ratings for whichever one he represented. With control in the hands of one big entertainment conglomerate, United Broadcasting Company could create another Ted Guest any time they needed one. She wondered if that knowledge kept Ted Guest awake at night. It was certainly keeping him on his toes for the coverage of the "disaster" at Far Side.

"I've just been informed of the reason for the delay of the start of the live interview," Guest said. "Word from NASA is that while we will have a live interview with Colonel Tseng and her fellow crew members, it will be from inside the lunar module, *Collins*. It appears that there are still too many technical problems to surmount inside the Main Dome.

"A reminder, we will be staying on the air for a follow-up after the live interview, which is due to start any time now. While we're waiting for NASA, we have a special report from Beverly Ochoa, our correspondent at the Johnson Space Center in Houston."

Tseng was amused when the scene on the screen changed from a live picture to a scene of giant mutated ants spewing acid as they attacked a helpless human settlement in a remote southwest desert setting.

A young-sounding female voice narrated over the old film clip. "Such movies as *Them,* seen here, were produced around a theme popular in the nineteen fifties and sixties, a period sometimes referred to as the "Atomic Age" or the "Cold War Era" in our nation's history. They depict the bizarre effects of radiation on Earth people, insects, and animals."

There were gasps of surprise and guffaws of amusement from the other astronauts as more film clips, all from the days before computer generated special effects, featured other radiation-enlarged monsters.

"Go, Godzilla," Horo shouted, when the giant lizard exhaled "atomic breath" on a monstrous flying insect called Mothra.

Another clip featured a thirty-foot queen wasp and thousands of her offspring menacing humanity.

"I've seen this one," Cochagne grimaced, racking his brain for the title.

Ochoa's voice-over narration identified it as *Monster From Green Hell.*

In quick succession, a giant octopus destroyed a seaside town in *It Came From Beneath The Sea.* A film montage showed a giant black scorpion, a giant tarantula, a praying mantis, a caterpillar, and hundreds of killer shrews proceed to inflict horrible deaths on their human victims.

The films were far-fetched and ridiculous. Tseng hadn't seen them in at least a decade. She was a NASA astronaut in command of a Moon mission, using the *Collins'* sophisticated communications equipment to watch Hollywood's interpretation of the challenges, mysteries, and dangers of science and outer space. However, they made her feel nostalgic, too. She remembered how many of the films she had seen as a child, when she was hungry for any information that would feed the fantasy of being a scientist and going into space. Such childhood sources of inspiration were something many of her friends and colleagues in the astronaut corps had in common.

For her, the appeal of those childhood fantasies of the distant future, and of galaxies far, far away, had matured to a more intense yearning, a more all-consuming curiosity, a more heady excitement about space, and a desire to be out there. She had become a scientist and an astronaut to acquire the tools to help make a future that she would live to see. It was current technology that had put her on the threshold of a vast unexplored frontier. *These* were the most exciting times in space exploration.

The film montage ended. The cut to a live shot of Ochoa revealed a plumpish brunette with a polished sorority girl smile. She stood on what looked like a stretch of airfield tarmac, but Tseng didn't recognize the site. Familiar places looked different on camera.

"Here at the Johnson Space Center, there is real concern about the ramifications of the fly infestation at Far Side Moon Base," Ochoa said. A timely cut from Ochoa to a recorded close shot of houseflies swarming over and on a large piece of discolored, slimy, rotten meat in a laboratory beaker conveyed the appropriate effects of shock and revulsion. "These are common houseflies of the order: Diptera; species: Musca domestica," Ochoa continued, again in voice-over narration. "They transmit such dreaded human diseases as typhoid fever, cholera, dysentery, and are carriers of such internal parasites as tapeworms and hookworms. There is concern at NASA about the infestation at Far Side Base, but should there also be concern over the effect on the insects of long-term exposure to the unfiltered radiation in space which bombards the lunar surface? At Far Side, flies have already mated under these conditions, with as many as three generations continuing to live and breed unchecked." The camera pushed in on Ochoa for a dramatic close-up. "Could this be the reason for the deaths of the FS-5 crew? Will the FS-6 astronauts unwittingly bring home a breed of 'super fly' against which the Earth has no defense? The possibility gives a chilling new meaning to Colonel Tseng's words, "Unknown to the crewmen of FS-5, they brought death up with them to the Moon . . ."

Tseng groaned.

There was a cut to a film clip which showed Martian ships crashing in the streets of a major city. "In the movie version of H.G. Wells' *War Of The Worlds,* the Earth is saved by the effects of the common cold virus on invaders from outer space. But even more frightening is the possibility of mass death on the Earth from a 'space plague.' "

Would they be ambushed with this question during the live interview? Tseng wondered. It seemed inevitable.

There was a cut from the taped footage back to a live shot of Ochoa. It was a long shot which revealed that the reporter was standing on the tarmac outside of an old building on the Space Center grounds, a place that Tseng knew well.

"This building housed the Lunar Receiving Lab during the *Apollo* days," Ochoa said. The camera moved dramatically in on her. "The first lunar explorers spent twenty-one days in quarantine here because medical scientists did not know what effect extended time on the Moon's surface would have on the astronauts, or if they would unwittingly bring a terrible epidemic back to Earth.

"Now there is talk among some experts about the threat of this new menace from outer space and what to do about it. Upon their return from Far Side, Colonel Tseng and her crew may be forced to endure at least a month in isolation, under the strictest quarantine as test subjects of experiments which harken back to the last century. This is Beverly Ochoa at the Johnson Space Center in Houston."

". . . and stay tuned for *The Invasion of the Diseased Mutant Satan-Worshiping Astronauts!*" Cochagne said, imitating the style and delivery of the announcer.

Tseng laughed with him, though there was an underlying element of truth in the joke which she could not dismiss lightly.

The picture on the monitor jumped, and a computer-animated model of the Moon and Far Side Base appeared on the screen. "From New York, this is live UBC News coverage of the live interview from Far Side Base," the network announcer's voice boomed.

"*Collins,* Houston," Shah Zia's voice came over the COMM. "Are you ready for TV?"

"Houston, *Collins.* Roger, we're all set," Tseng answered.

☾

Bianco expected Gutierrez to follow her into her office. When he didn't, she turned to see him still standing in the doorway. His eyes roamed the room, taking in every detail, it seemed to her. It made her self-conscious about the clutter. She could see how it might be overwhelming at first sight, and how he might be intimidated by an astronaut's lair. She tried not to notice how good he looked in his blue-gray sport coat, gray slacks, and sapphire-blue shirt, and how well his broad shoulders, wide chest, and hard, flat stomach made the clothing fit. She was drawn to the masculine strength in the planes and angles of his face.

What was she thinking? She'd calculated an age difference between them of at least five years.

Not much more than that.

She hoped.

She didn't want to feel old around him.

How long had it been since a man had caught her attention this way? Too long, obviously. So this was what they called a "midlife crisis."

Maybe not. She felt tired and wrung out, and emotionally vulnerable as a result. She'd rushed home a few hours ago to grab a nap, a shower, and clean clothes. She'd rushed back to the space center wearing a black knit suit, with her hair pulled back in a ponytail while it was still damp from washing. Black was easy and fast. So was a ponytail. It wasn't sophisticated, but she'd given up sophistication years ago, a few minutes into her first mission. One couldn't be sophisticated while floating weightless in a cramped Space Station habitat module, surrounded by male crew members.

She would coil her ponytail into a chignon later.

She wrenched her mind back to the business at hand. "The office is a mess, but the privacy is necessary," she said, as she snatched an empty Styrofoam coffee cup from her desktop and threw it into the trash. She moved her Moon rock from in front of the TV monitor and motioned for him to sit in her chair.

Gutierrez crossed to the chair, but didn't take it. "Where will you sit?"

Bianco pulled her visitor chair around the desk and arranged it beside the desk chair. "I'll sit here," she said. "I want you to have the best view. I've seen this video."

Gutierrez sat.

"We'll be looking at the last live video transmission

from FS-5," Bianco said. "The FS-6 astronauts, including Dr. Greer and Dr. Manch, have seen it. You'll understand why it hasn't been released, and why, at this time, it's classified as 'sensitive.' There was massive signal interference, so we had a lot of trouble acquiring it, and we had to spend considerable time cleaning it up. I won't say anything more until after you've seen it."

Bianco withdrew two laser disks from her suit jacket pocket. "Shinobu Takizawa shot most of the live picture transmissions from Far Side with the same model of digital video camera that the FS-6 astronauts are using. Mike Mobley's hobby was photography, so he preferred the still camera."

"Did you know him well?"

"The mission training schedules are pretty intense. You spend a lot of time with your people. You're a family. Yes. I knew him well."

"I'm sorry."

Bianco nodded her thanks and turned her face away, so he wouldn't see that the sincerity that had come through in his simple remark had brought tears to her eyes. She turned on the TV and the disk player and inserted a disk.

The scene that came up on the monitor was of the personnel quarters on Level Two. Takizawa could be heard arguing with Frank Drzymkowski, who'd been a big man with the well-defined, well-developed muscles of a serious bodybuilder. The sound quality was bad. The brief, heated exchange was still partially unintelligible, after all the efforts made by the techs in Houston to enhance it electronically. The FS-5 Japanese mission specialist had tried to document something—what they had come to refer to in their final voice transmissions as "the phenomenon."

"The big guy is the one they found in the space suit," Gutierrez said.

"Yes," Bianco verified.

In the video, Bob Faden and Ann Bisio, awakened from their sleep cycle, staggered out of their compartments like inmates in an asylum and into the confusion of the motley camera procession heading for the recreation area and the wardroom. Mobley was ascending from Level One, and he was wearing a blanket wrapped around his body over his fatigues. Faden and Bisio were in T-shirts and underwear. The picture went dark for a second, as Drzymkowski moved in front of the camera lens. Like Faden and Bisio, the structural engineer was in his underwear.

The principal light source in the picture came from flashlights. Everything in the immediate foreground had an overexposed, high contrast harshness. Everything in the background was murky black. The camera was equipped with a short focal-length lens, for close quarters, but Takizawa was too close to Mobley, Drzymkowski, Faden, and Bisio, and the distorted, fish-eye effect made everyone look foreshortened, abnormally bloated, and bizarre.

Even the pixieish Bisio, with her delicate Latin features, looked gnomelike. "Wha . . . ?" they heard her mumble sleepily. Voices faded in and out. ". . . wardroom?" she asked anxiously.

Then the view changed and widened. The camera was carried into the recreation area. It was darker there, and inhabited only by Louise Washington. The lanky redhead's eyes were wide with fear. She glanced around the room furtively as if expecting something to happen.

Takizawa panned slowly through the room. The exercise treadmill, the recumbent rowing machine, the bicycle ergometer, and the card table and chairs were discernible in the available light, and the taller framework of the electromagnetic weight machine loomed over them in the background.

Suddenly, a frightened squeal of pain was heard from

off camera. There was a blur of motion as the camera panned back to Washington. She was crouched on the floor, crying and holding the left side of her head which was oozing blood. There was confusion, and panicked voices drowned each other out as Bisio moved rapidly to Washington's side, stripped off her own T-shirt and pressed it against the wound. Bisio exhibited no self-consciousness about being nude from the waist up, and no one else took any notice, caught up in the moment as they all were.

A spearlike object flew diagonally at the camera. The meteoric speed with which it appeared, shot across the frame from left to right and continued off, was shocking. Bianco heard a sharp intake of breath from Gutierrez.

Takizawa evidently ducked and then lost his balance, for there was a crazy kaleidoscope of color and motion as he and the camera tumbled. The object struck something off camera with a metallic sound. They heard Drzymkowski swearing. His vocal stress level was high.

The camera was still on, but focused on a wall panel for a few seconds. They heard Washington pulling herself together. The camera was picked up.

"Mike . . . over here," someone—Bianco agreed with the experts who'd guessed it to be Faden—said, off frame.

"So it's Mobley who has the camera now?" Gutierrez asked, turning to her.

She nodded in confirmation.

The careful slowness with which Mobley panned across the room made Bianco impatient, but it was evidence of the man's determination to maintain his professionalism despite the stress that he'd been under at this point in the FS-5 mission. The pan stopped on Faden, Takizawa, and Drzymkowski, who were crouched over a metal bar lying on the floor.

Drzymkowski picked it up and held it toward the camera.

"Get a shot of this," he said defiantly.

"What the hell . . ." Mobley was heard to say as he "walked" the camera in on the solid length of metal bar stock with a ring welded to the midpoint which, as an unguided missile, had had the mass to do Washington serious damage. "This is the 'lat' bar belonging to the electromagnetic weight machine," he added, narrating the footage he was shooting.

The camera panned over to, and stopped on, the weight machine, a simple framework which supported a pulley over which the cable to the variable-strength electromagnet was threaded. The "lat" bar was for building up the latissimus dorsi muscles of the upper back. The last user of the machine—and Bianco's guess was that it was probably Drzymkowski—had put it aside in favor of the short contoured push-down bar for working the muscles of the forearms, and had left that bar connected to the working end of the cable.

Bisio giggled nervously, off camera, ". . . a weird . . . magnetic effect?"

Mobley turned around in time to catch Washington and the others leaving the wardroom.

The picture ended as though the camera had been shut off. Gutierrez remained silent.

"There's more," Bianco said.

A shot of Louise Washington sitting on the lid of the low-gravity commode with Bisio, Faden, and Takizawa crowded around dressing her head wound appeared on the screen. Washington squirmed and yelped in pain as Takizawa dabbed—a bit roughly, Bianco thought—at a deep cut just above her temple. A vain and flamboyant redhead with a fashion model's cheekbones, it was rare to see her without makeup, and rarer still to see her sloppily dressed and careless about her hygiene.

The sound quality was much better here, though the voices echoed as though coming from inside a cave.

Washington looked into the camera angrily and screamed, "Will you get out of here?"

"Well, I didn't do it," Drzymkowski said, off camera. It was an angry salvo in an argument that had apparently begun before the start of the transmission.

"Who's got the camera?" Gutierrez asked.

"Mobley," Bianco said.

"Get out," Washington yelled at the camera again, and reached out as though to strike the lens. Takizawa and Faden held her back.

"Somebody did it," they heard Mobley say.

"Why are you sending 'em this, Mike?" Drzymkowski yelled off camera.

The camera panned, found Drzymkowski, and pushed in on him. He was angrily trying to wipe something that looked like smears of dried paint off of the bathroom mirror.

"Move away," Mobley ordered.

"You can't transmit this," Drzymkowski bellowed.

"I said move!"

The big engineer stepped aside reluctantly. *Food for the Moon* had been scrawled across the mirror in blood. Below the mirror, the washbasin looked as though someone had slit their wrists and bled to death in it, but all the crewmen were accounted for. Drzymkowski lunged forward and put his massive, callused hand over the camera lens. The transmission ended.

Bianco stopped the playback. "We received a transmission from the *Collins* a while ago. Faden became conscious for a short time. The medical people are still working on him." She removed the first disk and inserted the second. "Let's talk about this," she said, when the playback ended.

Gutierrez nodded.

"Dr. Greer monitored the FS-5 crew and has been treating Faden. After conferring with Dr. Birnbaum, at Bethesda Hospital, we agree that the symptomatology of Faden's condition resembles schizophrenia, though there are a few inconsistencies," Bianco said. "Schizophrenia is a mental illness which affects millions of people. It strikes most often in young adults between the ages of fifteen and thirty, though Faden falls slightly outside that age range. The disease is characterized by severe disturbances in the thinking processes, and behavioral and emotional reactions. Patients in advanced stages are subject to hallucinations, delusions, emotional detachment, and self-neglect. We're now monitoring Faden's response to the classic antipsychotic drug, Thorazine. We have a long way to go before we get to the bottom of what happened at Far Side. But we feel we're on firm medical ground here."

"Did he show any signs of mental illness before he went to the Moon?"

"If he had, we would have pulled him from FS-5."

"You know, it looked to me like one of them threw that thing at Washington," Gutierrez said, shaking his head in sad wonderment. "You knew these people. I mean, they're all astronauts."

"Being an astronaut doesn't mean you're different when it comes to basic human behavior," Bianco said.

"You've all been under the pressure of handling life-threatening situations. It's pretty nearly a requirement for the job, and from what people around here have told me, worst-case scenarios are part of your daily training schedules. The guys who design and run the simulations for you get off on concocting weird combinations of equipment failures, any one of which could kill you if it happened during a spaceflight or at Far Side."

"A simulation is just that," Bianco countered.

☾

"What a waste of my time!" DeSosa blustered. "Toward the end of the interview, I thought I was going to go nuts! We could have been out of here two hours ago . . . we don't have that much daylight left in which to work, and every hour counts."

"I can't fault your logic, but there was no way out of that interview," Tseng said. She and the other crewmen were suiting up in the *Collins'* payload bay in preparation for the second trip to the base. They were wearing only the underwear for their space suits, unitards made of a synthetic thermal knit crisscrossed with flexible urethane tubing that, when connected to a suit's circulation system, would keep water and liquid coolant mixture circulating, and protect the wearer from the lunar daytime heat. Tseng recalled her crime scene investigation under Lol Gutierrez's guidance. Upon close inspection, she'd seen and informed him of the undergarment on Drzymkowski's remains inside the suit. That made it a certainty that he'd gone outside for some reason, and then returned to the base . . . only to be murdered before he could remove his suit.

It was one of the few times when they were not plugged into the ship's COMM link, and, until they activated their suit radios, Mission Control could not hear their conversation—just as well, since they were rehashing the network news program and the TV interview in such unflattering terms.

"While it was not time well-spent, I think it was time that had to be spent," Tseng said. "We're accountable to all the people who sent us up here, not just to NASA and the big corporations who directly service the space program's needs."

"But what purpose did it serve? We did everything but lie outright to them," DeSosa said.

"No, technically, we did everything including lying outright to them," Horo said.

"I take exception to both of those statements," Lebby said. "When I was asked that question about the degree of damage to the base, I could have said, 'Well, Ted, some of the equipment was taken off-line by the FS-5 crew—though, to be honest, there's a question as to why they ripped the wires out and smashed everything to pieces with a ball-peen hammer instead of using the on-off switches. . . .' Would that have sounded better?"

Horo's answer was a good-natured shrug. "The interview would definitely have been more exciting after that."

"They can't know everything we know . . . there would be panic down there," Lebby said. "That's not lying, in my book."

"Is this going to turn into a bitter debate over the public's right to know what's happening, versus our responsibility not to frighten them out of their wits?" Cochagne asked.

"Okay, I retract what I said. Are we going to get on with the serious work?" DeSosa asked.

Tseng unhooked her suit from the special storage bracket on the wall outside the payload bay's air lock and laid out the pieces for inspection. She then removed the suit's drink bag, filled it with a premixed water-electrolyte solution, and replaced it.

As Cochagne passed by her, she felt his hand softly slide across her lower back. An innocent touch to keep from bumping her off-balance when he reached for his helmet? On a mission, there was always a lot of jostling in the close quarters, and there was no privacy. In the course of training together, crews simply got used to a certain level of bodily freedom with one another, but as it had during the interview, the tactile sensation of physical contact with Cochagne made her heart pound, and made her feel lusty and sexually alive. She tried not to look at him, but she sensed he was watching her for a reaction, and it was hard not to blush. She was conscious that the stretch-mesh underwear revealed every contour of her body.

Tseng noticed that Paul Manch had already finished inspecting the pieces of his suit for the telltale signs of wear, damage, and weak spots that would mean death if they caused leaks outside the ship or the Main Dome. The doctor would finish suiting up before her, but she felt no pressure to rush. This was not a task that could be rushed.

Though there was nothing overt about their attitude toward each other, Tseng sensed that there were intense emotions at work between Manch and Greer. They were like two people alone in a crowded room, was the thought that came into her mind. Natural curiosity made her want to know the details from a feminine perspective, but that would mean penetrating the invisible wall of privacy Greer kept between herself and everyone else . . . even Paul Manch, Tseng suspected. The odd part about it was that one did not have to be psychic to know that she was in love with him. Manch's emotions were easier to read, and it was very apparent that he wanted and needed her.

"Is Greer going to be okay by herself with Faden?" Tseng asked Manch. "I know we'll be in constant contact with her on the COMM, but I feel guilty about not being able to spare you from this EVA."

"He's going to be out for hours, but she won't be caught off guard again. I'll go back to the *Collins* as soon as I can." Manch climbed into his suit trousers. "How much immediate financial loss could the Far Side project absorb?"

"That question is out of my domain," Tseng answered, "though I will say that damage assessment is an important priority of the FS-6 mission and, even if the base becomes a temporary liability as a result of this disaster, it's safe to say that it will not be abandoned. In addition to the telescope and the Science Dome lab, the future plans for Far Side include an expansion of the launch and landing facility to accommodate deep space missions, because it's more fuel-efficient, and thus less expensive, to launch payloads into space from the Moon than from Earth."

"What do you think both the short-term and the long-term effects of the FS-5/Far Side disaster will be on the program?"

"Well, obviously we're looking at a number of immediate repercussions," Tseng said. "The number of scientific experiments scheduled for FS-6 were significantly reduced, deployment of the Lunar Telescope has been delayed . . ."

"Today, we're enabling the robot," Horo interjected, "but the test schedule is very, very tight. We have limited 'daylight' in which to work outside, so the number of EVAs has been cut drastically."

"Also, we were planning to follow up on data from FS-5's PERM experiment," Tseng said, "but the instrument package was a casualty of this disaster as well. We may deploy a back-up instrument package at a later date, I don't know.

"As for the long-term effects, there will be a delay in the overall Far Side launch schedule while we investigate what happened. Everything will be pushed back. Eventually, for example, we may lose a number of commercial contracts if we're unable to return to and maintain a practical schedule."

Her own suit inspection complete, Tseng stepped into the trouser section. She checked the degree of adhesion of the biotelemetry sensor leads that were affixed to her skin with spray-on surgical adhesive, then took special care when connecting the tubing from the soft rubber urine collection cup positioned between her legs to the container attached inside the right leg of her trousers. She pulled the upper torso—with the sleeves already attached and sealed—down over herself and connected the water lines from her underwear to the coolant system umbilicals in the suit before locking and sealing the two halves of the suit together at the waist. Next, she put on the communications carrier like a bathing cap, tucking the stray wisps of hair at her ears inside. Last came the thick gloves.

"The PERM experiment has something to do with measuring static electricity?" Manch asked.

"That's putting it in plain English. We're not allowed to do that," Cochagne said.

The statement caused a ripple of laughter among them. "Electrical conductivity is a measure of how easily current flows through a material," Tseng said. "High conductivity means that a material carries electrical current easily and doesn't remain electrically charged. Low conductivity means that the material doesn't easily transport a charge and, instead, remains electrically charged. Moondust contains a high percentage of glass, both impact and volcanic, so the electrical properties of the Moon's surface materials are those of silicates in the total absence of water. There is low electrical conductivity.

"In sunlight, the surface temperature on the Moon rises to one hundred twenty-three degrees Celsius and there is a corresponding increase in the conductivity. In the absence of sunlight, the temperature drops to minus two hundred thirty-three degrees Celsius and the conductivity decreases. We see this temperature-conductivity relationship most dramatically on Earth in winter darkness at low humidity when a static electricity discharge creates a wintertime spark when two charged objects meet."

"Like when two people attempt to shake hands after walking on a wool carpet," DeSosa said.

Manch nodded comprehension.

"The terminator is a moving boundary between sunlight and darkness," Tseng continued. "The charging of lunar soil particles across it could be significant enough to levitate them as much as ten meters above the surface, producing a spectacular moondust storm that would follow the terminator.

"The importance of PERM was that it might have afforded an explanation for a number of phenomena that have not been explained during more than three centuries of ground-based lunar observations. A number of transient lunar events have been recorded—mainly unexplained glows, changes in brightness, and surface obscurations that range in color from reddish to bluish. Previous Moon missions haven't provided us with satisfactory answers to explain the phenomena, but electromagnetic activity on the lunar surface is probably the explanation. Unfortunately, they couldn't put a backup PERM instrument package together soon enough for FS-6, so all we can do is find the 'broken' one and bring it in."

It was time to unpack and enable the robot—though "unleash" was a better description, Tseng thought, glancing involuntarily at the six-foot high machine, which stood immobile, as though "asleep," in its shipping carton and cargo straps. Manch approached the carton. "I can imagine how much money and how many man-hours have been invested in this robot."

"I keep telling Doc that it's all part of a conspiracy, and that she's training her replacement," Lebby said.

Horo ignored the teasing. "Despite advancements in autonomous decision-making abilities, or 'Task Control Architecture' as it's called, artificial intelligence is still incapable of making some types of intuitive leaps, such as making the kinds of decisions that you or I would consider risky. With this unit, we do have flexibility in handling contingencies, plan failures, and unexpected situations, and this robot has a remarkable self-awareness of its own capabilities and limitations. It can learn from its experiences and its mistakes, and it knows when it doesn't have enough knowledge and needs help from a human—it still takes human judgment to oversee the work of this machine."

"Along with the building materials, each mission has transported a major piece of equipment up to Far Side," Tseng said. "The soil mover, the LRV, and a crane are permanently available for use here. The robot is FS-6's contribution to the construction effort, though it's really more of a site exploration and development tool capable of semiautonomous operation."

"And MILTON stands for . . . ?" Manch let the sentence trail off to turn it into a question.

"Mobile Intelligent Lunar Terrain and Outpost site survey, exploration, and sampling Mechanism," Horo said.

Manch opened his mouth to speak. However, Tseng anticipated the question. "How did we get 'MILTON' out of that?"

Manch nodded.

"We needed to convert an unwieldy acronym to a name." Tseng said. "It's both a reference term for us and a group of sounds that the robot's voice recognition system can identify for instruction purposes, and which can't be mistaken for any other group of sounds in its vocabulary."

"How much does it weigh?" Manch asked.

"Up here, a mere three hundred and twenty-eight kilograms," Horo said.

"Arminta has been instrumental in MILTON's development," Cochagne told Manch. "She's spent over a thousand hours of her training time with the robot, three hundred of it in the Mojave, first with the prototypes and then with this unit. The entire FS-6 team has spent time with it in order to help refine the speech recognition system. Now, any of us can control it by voice. It answers by radio with a vocabulary and speech pattern kind of like 'Tarzan the geologist'—not a brilliant conversationalist—but for speed, nothing can compare with voice control communication."

"We've all had training sessions with the robot, and it will respond to anyone, but Arminta's attitude is . . . unique," Tseng said.

" 'Motherly' is the word you're looking for, I believe," Cochagne interjected.

After taking a final visual inventory of her other suit tool pockets, Horo put her geologist's pick inside the special holsterlike pocket attached to her suit. The thirty-five-centimeter-long, all-metal hand tool required special handling because the wedge-shaped pick end was sharp enough to pose a threat for a space-suited astronaut. She made an "okay" sign to Tseng, indicating that she was ready.

Tseng checked her backpack air tanks one more time, then backed up against the PLSS backpack, feeling it snap into place. She lowered the helmet over her head and locked the neck ring. Finally, she switched on the oxygen system. She was in her own environment, unreachable except by radio. She could not smell, touch or hear anything outside her personal "world."

The suit was "broken in" and comfortable . . . and a fitting burial shroud for an astronaut, she reflected sardonically, remembering Drzymkowski.

(

The real-time picture from the robot's solid-state camera was being displayed on an auxiliary monitor, and it revealed that Tseng was shooting the video of the robot that Bianco was seeing on the Mission Control main monitor.

MILTON walked down the loading ramp and onto the lunar surface. To the untrained eye, Bianco reasoned, it was an awkward-looking assembly of machine parts—a mating of a six-legged rover, a portable laboratory in miniature, a machine tool platform with two robot arms utilizing interchangeable grippers, samplers, and tools, and a microprocessor with a sensor array which contained ultrasonic transducers and high-resolution picture, laser, and thermal imaging systems—but it moved with surprising efficiency and an awareness of its surroundings. Indeed, each step was the end result of careful deliberation by the logic circuits which analyzed and made decisions on where to put each footpad based upon a detailed map of the terrain updated every nanosecond by the imaging systems.

To Bianco's technically-trained eye, the robot was poetry in motion and more exhilarating to watch than the best ballet dancer. Its "debut" was an important milestone for the FS-6 mission, and the Far Side program, and coming as it did on the heels of a disaster, it was being celebrated as a joyous event in Mission Control.

Horo was following slowly behind the robot. As if sensing the elation among her colleagues on the ground two hundred thousand-plus miles away, she waved at the camera and said excitedly, "Baby pictures! This is our baby taking his first steps on the Moon!"

Bianco joined in the jubilation and waved to catch the eye of the public affairs officer on duty, a young woman recently promoted to that position, whom she did not know well. She pointed at the TV monitor and made the traditional "okay" sign with her thumb and fore-finger. The woman nodded emphatically "yes" in an-swer. They would be releasing this video to the media within the hour.

Today, James Morris, the NASA administrator, was on hand to beam like a proud grandfather. However, the two anonymous-looking men in conservative suits standing with him, whom Bianco had met only an hour earlier, looked uncomfortable. They were FBI agents and on the outside of an inside joke. For this visit to the Johnson Space Center, which was an official one, Morris wore a well-tailored suit. He and the conservatively dressed agents appeared out of place in the frayed-nerve raw-emotion charged atmosphere of Mission Control, where the long hours with no sleep on a coffee and junk food diet, body odor from layers of perspiration stains, and rolled up shirt and uniform sleeves had become badges of honor for those watching over FS-6.

Bucar's assessment of the quality and deportment of FBI agents was right on the money. The two men looked bewildered, and, as a result of her first meeting with them, Bianco already knew that they had no solid start-ing point for their investigation. So much the better that they didn't, she reasoned in her tactical mind. Agreeing to open the personnel files to them had made her appear affable and cooperative in their eyes; however, in actual-ity, she planned to give them no guidance in wading through the mounds of data in those files. Their fumbling would buy Gutierrez valuable time to investigate the case in his own way.

On-screen, the astronauts were converging on the up-turned LRV. Empty, in lunar gravity, it weighed only ninety-two kilograms, so Cochagne and DeSosa, one on each end, righted it easily.

The picture on the monitor became momentarily unsteady as the portable camera was passed to one of the other astronauts. Tseng appeared in front of the lens and got into the driver's seat of the LRV. "The battery level is down, but I can get it back to the base," she said.

"We'll catch up to you," Manch said. "I want to check on the body bags."

Tseng buckled her seat belt, and DeSosa climbed into the passenger seat of the rover and did likewise. The camera lens followed the vehicle as Tseng maneuvered it through a wide turn and headed it toward the mound where they had placed the bodies.

☾

Tseng climbed out of the LRV and stared at Drzymkowski's body bag, transfixed by a macabre sight to which she could only react with stunned amazement. The dead astronaut's arms were moving into a raised position and his fingers, slightly bent by the construction of the space suit gloves, were pressed against the inside of the body bag. It made the corpse appear as if it were trying to claw its way up from the bag—and the grave—in a desperate attempt to commune with deep space a final time.

"Madre," DeSosa swore, breaking the shocked silence among them.

"I know it's primitive to personalize or 'anthropomorphize' an event or phenomenon which occurs according to the scientific laws of nature and the universe," Lebby said. "Still, the thought of mockery on a cosmic scale enters my mind."

"Proof positive that you didn't trade the right to have 'gut feelings' for a degree in the sciences," Cochagne said.

"Holy sh . . ." Horo began, but caught herself in time.

"What's happening up there?" Christiansen asked in concern.

"We've had a very minor incident of a somewhat bizarre nature here at 'Boot Hill,' " Cochagne said.

"Say again?"

"The heat differential might have resulted in an increase in heat inside Drzymkowski's suit, which caused a pressure spike . . . just enough to dislodge and raise the hands," Manch said.

"It looks like something from the mind of Edgar Allan Poe," Tseng added. She heard the groans in the background at Mission Control.

They watched in silence as Cochagne shot one frame of Drzymkowski with the still camera, and Tseng thought about the astronaut's reference to the site as Boot Hill, a name from the history of the Old West.

The near side maps bore numerous names dating from the earliest observations of Aristotle, Galileo, Langrenus, and Cassini, all the way to the twentieth century, but since the *Apollo* days, local place names near the landing sites had reflected practicality, personal vanity, or a particular sense of humor among the fraternity of astronauts—a desire to laugh in the face of death; a spaceship jockey bravado.

The far side of the Moon was virgin territory, and as such, was a jumble of names. A few major craters along the orbital paths of past missions bore Russian names. When the Far Side Base site was chosen, the Moon base construction crews had all taken the opportunity to put names to things. The South Pole-Aitken Crater, a broad basalt plain, was rimmed three quarters of the way around by craters. On the maps, it resembled a horse's shod hoofprint. Komarov, Grissom, White, and Chaffee were the major craters which rimmed it. Northwest of the Main Dome were two small craters, Peary and Byrd, and they were bordered by Schroeder's Rill, named by Bill

Schroeder, the FS-3 geologist. The Madeline Mountains formed the eastern curvature of the horseshoe, and were named for the wife of FS-4's chief engineer.

. . . And the "flow lobe," fifty meters northeast of the Main Dome, a minute, unimportant feature of the ejecta blanket of South Pole-Aitken would be known as Boot Hill from this time forward.

The nature of opening a new frontier was the same all throughout human history, Tseng reflected. There were always people willing to be the first to go someplace and to face the dangers of the unknown. As a member of FS-1, she had taken those risks without a second thought. Fate and the random "accident" of birth timing had made that mission her "moment" in the history of the space frontier.

FS-6 was also a "moment" in history.

She felt a sense of foreboding. A premonition. Imminent danger was lurking around the next rock and on the other side of a crater ridge. She was split in two by thoughts and emotions. Her intellectual "self" was aware of the ridiculousness and irrationality of the anxiety, but it was helpless to stop the onrush of an adrenergic "chain reaction."

She stood still, unable to move. She was frozen in place. The panic became acute and the realization of ceasing to be crept into her consciousness, followed by a clear and frightening awareness of her flesh decomposing. She was experiencing death without dying.

She could feel the perspiration breaking out on her forehead. Her heart was pounding. She shook herself mentally, fighting harder for control over what she could only think of as a violent "attack" of mental instability; an "episode" that was unmotivated and completely irrational. She had never been plagued by such fears before, even during the few genuine life-threatening experiences she'd had as part of the Air Force Flight Test Group . . .

flying a prototype high over the Edwards Test Range . . .
the computer malfunction that took out her control surfaces . . . there was no panic . . . plenty of time to go
through the emergency diagnostic checklist with Ground
Control . . . plenty of time to look at the results of each
step objectively, without rushing . . . plenty of time to
punch out, and then watch the plane disappear in a mush-
room of red flame on the desert floor.

As rapidly as it had come on, the fear dissolved and
she became aware that the conversation was still going
on around her in normal tones. How long had she been
out of it? In her space suit, she could still appear to be the
woman of stone; the commander; the leader in absolute
control of the situation. No one had to know that, for
a time, the being inside the suit had become a quaver-
ing mass of uncontrolled emotions, numbing fears, and
groundless anxieties.

"I'll take care of Drzymkowski," Manch volunteered. "I want to monitor the pressures and the physical changes."

"I can walk to the PERM site from here," Tseng said.
"Dick, if you'd be so kind as to take the rover back and
plug it into the recharge station."

"Will do. This is the first and last call for luggage going inside," Lebby said. Horo, Manch, and Greer surrendered their Personal Preference Kits, small flight bags
containing personal belongings which the astronauts
wanted with them at the base. Tseng handed Cochagne
the portable camera and her own PPK.

"Dick, Joe, and I will check out the main electrical circuits this morning," Cochagne said. "If the components
are okay, to save time, we'll get the system up and running by jury-rigging with spare parts."

"Lots of luck. The spare parts and supplies are scattered all over the place," Tseng said. "What about the
computer?"

"I'm not going near the mainframe until we're sure of the electrical integrity," Lebby said.

"Think you can build us an auxiliary terminal out of parts?"

Lebby nodded, then emphasized with a verbal, "Yes." Waving a farewell, Lebby climbed into the LRV and drove off toward the air lock with DeSosa and Cochagne following on foot.

Tseng noticed that Manch had turned to face the horizon. He was motionless, as though in a trance, staring at the nearby craters sharply defined by the angle of darkness from the steadily encroaching night terminator line. To Tseng the shadows were a reminder of what little time they had left for outside activity on the mission. She wondered what meaning they held for Manch and what he was thinking.

"EVA-2, Houston. We have a schedule update for you," Christiansen said. "As soon as you have the system up, we're going to schedule a teleconference about Faden with Bethesda Naval Hospital. Also, we would like a few more pictures of the damage in the wardroom. If you could parcel out time in between your equipment diagnosis and repair and reconnaissance of the immediate area, it would be appreciated."

"Roger, Houston," Tseng replied mechanically. She saw Lebby park the LRV. DeSosa and Cochagne opened the air-lock hatch and waited while Lebby connected the rover to its charging station, then they entered. Lebby followed them inside, and slid the hatch closed.

"We're climbing through the air lock . . . and entering the Main Dome now," Lebby told Houston.

"It looks like they had a black mass or something," DeSosa said. "En el nombre del Padre, del Hijo, y de lo Spirito Santo, amen."

Tseng visualized the astronaut making the sign of the cross in his space suit.

"Thanks for the blessing, Father DeSosa," Cochagne quipped.

"I'm telling you guys, I've never seen anything like this. It gives me the creeps. I hope they do send a priest up on the next flight, Jerry," DeSosa fired back.

"They're sending Dave Christiansen. That's good enough," Cochagne said.

"We're beginning pressurization of the Main Dome," Lebby said.

"You would not believe how many dead flies are lying around here," Cochagne said.

"You guys are loading up our schedule pretty good," Tseng told Christiansen. "Is there any spare time left that we can put toward getting the house in order?"

"We need you to hold off on that. No housekeeping until further notice."

"Okay, but we're living at the base as of today," she answered.

"We copy. Just bear with us for a while and stand by on this item."

"MILTON and I will be communicating over suit to suit channel three, for your information," Horo said.

"I'm heading out to find PERM and for a look around the immediate area," Tseng said. "I see the soil mover over there, near the bottom of the construction site. I should check it."

"Sounds like a good plan," Christiansen answered. "One more thing, China. Our biotelemetry showed a sudden increase in your respiration and heartbeat a few minutes ago. Do you happen to remember what caused that? It's happened a couple of times, in fact."

The question was like an electric shock and her involuntary reaction was a childish stab of alarm, as though she'd been caught doing something wrong. "I don't know. I felt hot for a moment or two. A hot flash. That's all. I don't feel like I'm coming down with anything, though."

"Could be a malfunction in your chest pack. Go ahead and replace that CDM unit before you go outside again."

"Right," she said, relieved that Christiansen did not sound suspicious of her vague reply to his question.

Blanket interference over all radio bands for any specific period of time might be an indication that the FS-5 crew had been in the thick of a severe transient lunar event, Tseng theorized, but a communications breakdown owed to a transient lunar event did not adequately explain the missing crewmen, and the deaths and the damage to the base. That was the real mystery to be solved at Far Side—in four days. Any strictly technical problems would be easy to sort out, by comparison.

She stopped walking and turned slowly around in order to shoot footage of Horo and the robot with her PLSS camera. They were moving across her line of vision toward the terraced dunes that formed the rim crest of Chaffee Crater and they were dwarfed dramatically by the Madeline Mountains. MILTON had performed true to its design specs during the training sessions in the California desert, ambulating aggressively through difficult terrain on its two sets of three stacked, telescoping legs with articulating footpads, each leg lifting separately, advancing, then circulating back to its original orientation. Its walking gait resembled that of a cross-country skier, and its linear progress was variable to a top speed of ten kilometers an hour. This compared favorably with some of the caterpillar-tracked and multiple axle, balloon-wheeled vehicles in the program. However, the legged design placed fewer limits on the type of terrain the robot was capable of exploring, sampling, and surviving.

This was of prime importance because, while Arminta Horo would accompany it on its tasks for this mission, it was a permanent resident of the base. It would be working independently, regardless of whether there was a mission in progress or not.

Human supervision, whenever necessary, could be from a remote location—either from Earth, from inside the base, or from an astronaut working elsewhere on the surface. MILTON could decide where to go, how to get there, and which tools it needed when addressing a task—the tools being, in most cases, standard tools integrated into specialized, detachable, and interchangeable appendages called "grippers"—only one of which actually bore any resemblance to a human hand. Each robot arm was multijointed and fully articulating, terminating in a machine tool chuck with a keyway for proper orientation of a tool on the arm. Power and control-contact connection points were distributed around the "wrist-like" periphery of the chuck. Two side-mounted, carousel-type tool holsters rotated the tools into position for pickup by the chuck.

"I'm going to let MILTON drop his pecker . . . er . . . initiate a test sequence here," Horo said. Horo was referring to the eight-foot auger for picking up soil samples which was retracted into a sheath on the underside when not in use.

"I guess we know what's on your mind," Tseng said.

"Did Christiansen hear that?" Cochagne asked gleefully.

"I hope so," Horo said. "Procreation is one thing he has a sense of humor about."

"He has to," Cochagne replied. "The guy's got nine kids."

"That's just the definition of a "good Mormon," Horo said.

"Geez, you play rough," Cochagne chortled.

"I'll have you know that I heard everything . . . and

that I'm going home to see if there are any new arrivals due," Christiansen said.

"Sign off, Dave," Cochagne said above the laughter.

Tseng scanned the horizon trying to find an interesting Moonscape to shoot with her backpack camera. Unlike the pictures from the first Moon missions on the near side, which had featured spectacular angles on the Earth in its phases, the far side exterior shots could only capture and convey the vastness of deep space. But the importance of photography on a mission could not be underestimated. Those shots of the big blue marble, Mother Earth, from the previous century, had proved valuable in stimulating the human imagination. That had translated into continued enthusiasm about space exploration. The era had not yet arrived when everyone could go into space, but because of the pictures, they could still participate in the great adventure.

The best pictures from Far Side Base would be those taken with the Lunar Telescope Array. Everyone at NASA and JPL awaited with eager anticipation the color images of stars and galaxies taken without a thick atmosphere to diffract the light. That was the problem on Earth and in Earth orbit. Chuck MacCallum's forced absence from FS-6 was more of a setback than the general public realized.

As seen from the Moon, the stars were crisp dots in the blackness. No special effects. No "twinkle." Uninteresting? Maybe, but then the night sky on Earth, as seen from Houston, could be considered equally dull at the moment—there was no ghostly, luminous-white orb to be seen in the night sky, merely a waxing gibbous, or three-quarter, Moon.

She triggered the PLSS camera again and pivoted her body slowly in order to pan smoothly across the lunar horizon in the direction of Grissom and White. The horizon always appeared foreshortened in the unfiltered sunlight and from her point of view, there was also the added distortion caused by her space helmet. Improvements in helmet design had widened the astronauts' field of vision, but there was distortion and even local landmarks could appear unrecognizable from certain angles. It was easy to get disoriented—even without the camera.

"China, how long has it been since you took a drink of water?" Christiansen asked.

"Too long," Tseng said, grateful for the reminder. She bent her head slightly and found the straw.

That's when she saw the boot prints which formed a narrow trail toward the northeastern horizon. From the overlapping prints, one individual had traveled it at least twice. Furthermore, the as-yet-unidentified "sojourner" had taken a different return route back to the base. The footprints might be Mobley's. They were going in the right direction for the PERM experiment and the FS-5 commander had been in charge of placing the instrument package. Presumably, he had carried it out far enough from the base to avoid any electromagnetic interference.

"Houston, Tseng. I've found boot tracks and they appear to lead to the PERM site," Tseng said. "Dick, what's the status on the repressurization?"

"We're at one psi. We're going to see if we can shed light on the situation," Lebby answered.

"Okay, I'm going to follow this trail for a while and see if it leads where it's supposed to," Tseng said.

"We copy," Christiansen acknowledged, "but if it begins to look like you're not going where you think you should be going . . . we'd prefer you not to get too far out on foot, by yourself."

"Copy that," Tseng replied.

She made her own parallel path, not wishing to obscure the original trail. To the east, a dull glow caused by the electromagnetic storm of charged dust particles

which heralded the approach of the night terminator, out-
lined the horizon. At Far Side, they would begin to experience the effect thirty hours before the terminator
passed, and for approximately forty hours afterward. The
darkness would be the most dangerous time to be out on
the surface. The Moon's atmosphere was not sufficient
to defuse sunlight. This time of lunar day, the shadows
were jet-black against the glaring whiteness. If the
marker was down, it would be difficult to see the black
box she was looking for until she was right on top of it.
There was even a chance that she might trip over it.

"Interior pressure approaching one point five psi,"
Lebby said. "I'm hitting the light switch . . . and . . .
we've got no light on Level Four."

"Back to square one," DeSosa said.

Tseng studied the terrain in front of her and in the distance. It was with relief that she saw the flag marker. It
was driven deep into the soil so that it would stay erect.
"Houston, I've located PERM," she told Christiansen.
"As I approach, I can see two trails leading from the site.
One turns ninety degrees to the left and runs parallel to
the base before angling back toward it. Here, the boot
prints overlap. We can surmise that someone took
the route repeatedly. A single set of boot prints that
leads northeast and appears to go on forever, disappearing toward the horizon. The optical illusion gives
the impression that the walker continued on, and never
returned."

"A suicide walk," Christiansen said heavily.

"It looks that way." The thought caused Tseng to shudder inwardly.

Taking care to stay in balance, she bent over to examine the instrument package in situ. It was nestled in a
small mound of superfine Moon dust. By Earth standards, the construction of the box appeared flimsy, but
nothing on the Moon had to withstand Earth gravity or

weather. Moisture, a big culprit on Earth, was nonexistent here. Thermal and radiation shielding were the most important considerations, along with contaminants such as dust.

"There's no apparent damage to the case. I'll bring it back with me for analysis. I would like permission to follow those tracks into the 'great beyond,'" Tseng told Christiansen. "I believe we'll find Mike Mobley."

"We copy," Christiansen said. There was a long pause, then the CAPCOM said, "The consensus here is against your going it alone on foot, however. We want to ascertain the working status of the LRV before you plan any long-distance excursions with it today. We're considering scheduling that as a separate EVA, with you and one of the medical team."

"When?"

"You'll have to stand by on that," Christiansen said.

"I know I don't need to remind you that time is against us here."

"We've taken that into consideration, but the immediate safety factor isn't to our liking."

Tseng felt exasperated by the decision. She was poised at the threshold of a discovery, but not being allowed to pursue it. In the end, if she wanted to disregard orders, no one was there to stop her, but that was selfish, unmilitary thinking. There was more at risk than just her life. The lives of those who might be compelled to go after her if something went wrong. She had an obligation to the others. As much as she wanted to go after Mobley, she could not.

She picked up the instrument package and tucked it securely under her arm, then took a last look around the area, her gaze, at last, stopping on the trail of footprints leading away from the base. Every new discovery only added to the mystery behind the accident, the deaths, and the disappearances of Mobley . . . and Takizawa.

Toward the end, why would Mobley have gone EVA except to attempt communication from outside the Main Dome or from the *Aldrin*? From all appearances, he had, indeed, gone on a suicide walk. It was not a pleasant theory to dwell on. "I'm coming in," she said. "The other trail is leading back to the Science Dome. I'm approaching the lunar soil mover, so I'll check out the cab."

"We're at just under three psi in here," Lebby said. "We'll have all the lights back on shortly. Jerry's taking things apart inside the main switch panel."

"Lucky for you I just found a foil gum wrapper in one of my pockets," Cochagne quipped.

". . . and we have main and auxiliary interior lights, Houston," Lebby said excitedly.

"Well done, Jerry," Christiansen said.

Tseng noted the added warmth in the CAPCOM's voice with amusement. Cochagne had the kind of charisma that people responded to—even from hundreds of thousand miles away. Sex education could come early in horse country. As a child she had watched the better colts grow into stallions on her family's Colorado range. Gangling awkward young horses would muscle out into vital male animals, arrogantly aware of their sexuality all of the time, and driven by hot, uncontrollable frenzy when breeding the mares. Cochagne's dark hair and eyes gave his looks a powerful manly intensity that was hard to resist, and physically, he was a well-muscled, powerful male animal with all the bold confidence of a stallion.

She was reminded of how that insight had been put to the test during the FS-1 mission. No weakness could be found in Jack Bucar or in his command decisions. The world political situation that had "spawned" him, and career military men and women like him, was being pacified by the continued growth of multinational corporations whose energies were directed toward profits and new markets, and thus, toward space. The current youthful crop of officers moving up to replace Bucar's generation—herself included—would not have his combat experience. In her belief, his retirement was truly a loss to the nation and to the space program. UBC TV would never know or appreciate the real worth of the man.

The lunar soil mover loomed just ahead of her. It was the primary piece of construction machinery in the Far Side project, and it was parked a short distance down the gaping pit of the Science Dome facing downhill. Both its rear backhoe and its front blade were dug into the surface as anchors. Though it was a big machine, it could accommodate only one astronaut in a space suit at the controls.

Tseng climbed into the cab and toggled the power switch.

The control panel and instruments lit up. "The LSM battery is at thee-quarters charge," she said. "I'm going to drive it up to the charging station."

She rotated the control stick and pulled up the backhoe and the blade, then she pressed the foot pedal. The machine made an initial lurch backward, then climbed powerfully up the side of the man-made crater on its long caterpillar treads. ". . . and it looks like everything is nominal," Tseng said. She backed over the lip of the pit, then, shifted to a forward gear and drove the soil mover to the charging station, a bank of electrical outlets outside the Main Dome, where she parked and shut off the machine.

Looking back in the direction of the Main Dome she could see Manch as a small white shape. He was just leaving Boot Hill.

"I'm finished out here," Manch said. "Are you coming in?"

"Shortly. You go ahead," Tseng answered, waving.

The astronaut waved back at her. "You know, I've

been in this project for a number of years now," Manch
said. "I've seen video of Far Side, and I read all the hype
about the similarities to Byrd's Antarctic base camp . . .
but it really looks like that! I was beginning to think I
would never get to see this place firsthand. It's quite an
impressive layout."

"They made use of a densely pockmarked field of
young, secondary impact craters that are typical of the
topography of the far side. We use this machine I'm sitting in, the Lunar Soil Mover, which came up with FS-2,
to remove the loose top soil and chunks of regolith from a
building site, then, when the habitat structure is in place,
we push the surface material back to provide support, insulation, and radiation shielding for the structure."

"Like planting a seed," Greer said on the COMM.

"You've been eavesdropping," Tseng said.

"I'm bored out of my skull," Greer answered.

"I've been trying to visualize the finished base,"
Manch said.

Tseng pointed toward the construction sight. "FS-7 is
still scheduled to finish the Science Dome, but they'll
have the added job—which was Chris Sweet's job—of
laying the fiber-optic cable for base communications."
Tseng made a big gesture, indicating the *Collins*. "Then,
an upcoming mission is scheduled to make modifica-
tions to the landing pad. They'll be installing a deploy-
able insulated shelter—a 'tent cover'—to protect the
lunar modules against the temperature extremes and
against micrometeoroid bombardment, and, if the program goes forward as scheduled, over the next five years,
new construction will expand the base complex out over
most of the crater field. The new facilities will encircle
the Main Dome, which will then act as the operations
hub. Though the biggest industrial operation planned for
the near future is the facility to manufacture liquid oxygen propellant to provide fuel for deep space missions,

Shimizu, Matsushita, Eastman Kodak, GE, and several other multinational companies are planning manufacturing installations up here."

"Money talks," Manch said. "As with the Space Station, it always comes down to a matter of economics. American taxpayers are not as willing to support the space program with their tax dollars as they are to flock to buy the latest electronic gadget out on the market. So private industry is the only place to go for the kind of money needed for space exploration."

"What about the work schedule restrictions up here?" Greer asked. "As matters stand now, your launch schedules have to be planned so that the best use is made of everyone's time."

"We didn't have those restrictions at the Space Station," Manch added.

"I don't think it's a problem," Tseng said. "Surface activities such as construction, geological core sampling, and mapping and exploration are gradually restricted at the approach of lunar day, because of the extreme heat, and during lunar night, because of the extreme cold, but at the height of those two periods, when crews are confined indoors, the schedule allows us to spend our work time correlating the data gathered outside.

"Even with what you would consider as restrictions, I consider Far Side Base to be a more exciting assignment than the Space Station," Tseng continued. "Look at the long-term effects of a weightless environment on the human body: shrinkage of the heart muscle, reduced blood volume, poor circulation in the lower extremities, bone decalcification . . . those risks are significantly reduced in the Moon's gravity. Besides, the Space Station has a finite life span—though maybe not in our lifetimes—as does any orbiting space station, whereas the Moon will continue to be a permanent outpost and resource."

"Houston, we're at five psi now, so we're going to remove our helmets," Cochagne said on the COMM.

"Go ahead, then," was Christiansen's only comment.

Scant moments later, Tseng heard the sound of gagging in her earphones.

"Oh, God, it stinks like a hundred cats died under the house," Lebby choked.

"After a few seconds, your olfactory nerves will be completely blown and you won't smell it anymore," Manch said. "I'm about done in, just from this short walk," he added. "If ever there was a prime example of the disadvantages of a weightless work environment, it's me. I'm finding even one-sixth gravity hard to take."

"Are you coming in, China?" Cochagne asked.

"Yes, but I'll wait for Arminta." Tseng turned to search the horizon for Horo and the robot and saw them moving steadily toward her in the distance.

"See you at the air lock in five," Horo said.

"Joe and I are going to unsuit in order to inspect the guts of the communications console, so I'm signing off the COMM for awhile," Lebby said.

"Dick, Joe, this is Houston," Christiansen broke in. "How much time are you guys talking about to recover transmission capability?"

"Unless I misdiagnosed this, or we screw up somehow, we'll be on top of it in twenty minutes," DeSosa said. "They're checking the signal through the dish . . . alas, no picture in this switch position. Joe is trying switch position four."

"Nada," DeSosa said, in the background, "Switching to five. Do you think there's a break in the cable?"

"Pray that we don't have to dig it up, Father DeSosa," Cochagne said. "Let's try from the console again."

A burst of static came over the COMM, then Tseng

heard DeSosa say, "Houston, this is Far Side Base. How do you read? Over."

Tseng heard more popping sounds and static on the radio, then Christiansen answered, "Hello, Far Side, this is Houston. We read you. Over."

"Roger," DeSosa said. "We've got a lot of noise somewhere in the system up here. We're working on it . . . I'm switching to the high gain side. Houston, how do you read? Over."

"We're reading you loud and clear."

"Okay, it's clearing up here now. You're coming in loud and clear. We're configured for normal voice."

Tseng turned to see Horo approaching the air lock with the robot. "I really hate the thought of leaving MILTON outside," she said, then she laughed. "You know how mothers are. We hate to let go."

When Tseng climbed through the air lock and into the Main Dome's Fourth Level, she saw that Manch had donned exercise clothing—a soft, fireproofed cotton T-shirt and silky cotton-synthetic blend boxer-style shorts, rather than uniform fatigues. The work lights were on, and one look at his face told her his first breaths of the air inside the dome had made him nauseous. A change of air had only been partially effective, then. Nothing less than a major scrub down of the base would take the lingering odor away. Since FS-6 would not be saddled with any housekeeping, it was another item for the FS-7 "to do" list. The next few days would have to be spent in the midst of chaos, but in the light, the damage looked less horrifying and "spooky," and more random and senseless. Tseng temporarily placed the PERM black box in an empty locker out of harm's way. Horo climbed out of the air lock lugging her rock bag, but made no move to unfasten her helmet. Instead, she remained standing near the air-lock hatch to take in the condition

of the room. "I never thought I'd dread getting out of this
suit," the geologist said.

"Let's get the worst part over with," Tseng said to her.
She twisted her helmet until she heard the click that indicated the release of the locking ring. She saw Horo do
likewise. Tseng heard the faint and muffled voice of
Manch warning them to "take shallow breaths at first."

Tseng shut off her suit oxygen, then lifted the helmet
clear of the ring and removed it, handling it far more
delicately than if it were a crystal fishbowl. She let out
the air she'd been holding in her lungs and slowly in-
haled through her mouth and nose at the same time.

The foul, acrid odor burned the inside of her nose and
traveled up into her sinuses, terminating in a flash of
pain. It was not the sweet formaldehyde-masked death
smell of the morgue or of a biology lab, but the caustic
methane-ammonia-acid smell of the spoilage of lifeless
flesh; of rotting carcasses. The knowledge that it was a
gut-wrenching odor from a moist residue of gaseous decomposition which coated every surface and every object was bad enough. That it would also cling to the skin
and the hair of every person in contact with it was almost
too revolting. Horo gagged and covered her mouth with
her hand.

Tseng fought so hard against the urge to gag and vomit
that the effort made perspiration break out over her
whole body.

The shallow breathing made her dizzy, and there was
no relief from the smell, but the initial shock was past.
She could identify other odors: the Moon's own characteristic gunpowder smell; another heavier odor . . . like
burned bacon fat; the smell of human feces in stagnant
urine that reminded her of an outhouse on a hot day.

The intellectual effort of breaking down the stink into
its component parts, real or imagined, provided enough
distraction for Tseng to overcome the urge to gag. She

dared to breathe deeper and found that she could do it
without a return of the violent nausea, though her throat
felt raw.

"That was tough duty," she croaked. "Shall we get to
that hammer first thing, Paul?"

Manch acknowledged with a nod. "What has Gutierrez decided to do?"

"He's not here yet, but he's on his way, I'm told,"
Christiansen answered.

"Houston, I'm unsuiting, so the next time we talk, I'll
be calling you on the base COMM system," Tseng said.

Horo switched off her suit radio. "It feels good to be
off the hot mode. There's nothing like having every word
overheard in Houston. A little privacy, please!"

Tseng listened to the cross talk between Christiansen, Cochagne, and Lebby for a few seconds, then she
switched off her own radio. The silence felt abnormal.

Manch disappeared down the companionway leading
to the Third Level.

Tseng removed her communications carrier with mixed
emotions. The suit radio had acted as a lifeline with
Earth, but the necessity of having to choose words with
care was fatiguing after so many hours. She could relax
into the mission now, though the transition marked the
end of one ordeal and the beginning of another—the
worst of the discoveries inside the base were behind
them and they could get down to the real business of
making Far Side Base operational again within the formidable time constraints. She and Horo helped each
other disconnect the portable life-support system backpacks. They removed the oxygen bottles and snapped
them into the refill brackets, then they plugged the tubes
from the drain system into the suits' urine collection bottle outlets.

The ambient temperature felt stifling and oppressive.

"It's still hot in here," Tseng said.

"And, on top of that, there are seven of us in here, each metabolizing at a rate of eight hundred BTUs an hour," Horo said. "We're not going to feel any significant cooling until nightfall, a few days from now."

Tseng unlocked, then removed her gloves, and rotated the two halves of her suit apart. She slipped the upper torso section over her head, then climbed out of the trouser section. She found her personal preference kit in an empty suit locker and opened the bag. Following the examples of Greer and Manch, she took out her exercise shorts, T-shirt, and magnetic-soled sneakers.

Horo followed her procedure, then made the same choice of attire from her personal kit. "It's obvious that Jer is putting the moves on you, China girl," Horo said, her voice just above a whisper. "You should go for it."

She had known Horo too long, and they had shared too many intimate details about each other's lives, for her to feel indignation or embarrassment at her friend's outspokenness. Tseng peeled off her cooling undergarment.

Horo pulled off the upper torso of her suit, then stepped out of the trousers.

"I can't make up my mind about him. I feel like my life is a mess and I can't sort out why."

Horo stowed the sections of her suit on a bracket, then stripped off her undergarment. Her voice was still soft, but more emphatic and purposeful, as though they might be interrupted at any moment. "You deserve to be loved—really loved. You deserve every ounce of devotion and attention a man can give you. It sounds corny, but that's how I see you . . . you have so much to offer a man . . . you have an excitement about you, a certain joie de vivre that is magnetic. You are intelligent. You have drive. You have ambition, and you're definitely strong-willed, and that may work against you. You have a certain presence that is electrifying. A quality that is so female . . . so elemental . . . and sexual . . ."

". . . So I should jump into bed with Jerry Cochagne and have a meaningless sexual relationship with a guy who's single but commitment-shy? You have a newly-wed's optimism, but maybe 'true love' isn't possible for everybody."

"Come on! I'm hearing a lot of pain and confusion underneath what you're saying. You project this image of being in control, and of controlling yourself in every situation—whether you need to or not. The trouble is, I see you struggling to keep a tight rein on yourself when Jerry's around. You're working overtime to suppress all of your needs, and, at the same time, you're thinking, 'Thank God the door to my bedroom is guarded by a pair of silver eagles'—and I mean the ones on your collar. Your eagles aren't going to intimidate Jerry Cochagne. He's that kind of man and he wants you."

"What if he just wants the conquest? That's the thing about his playboy personality that really bothers me."

"What bothers you is that he's persistent, and he's systematically chipping away at the protective ice sculpture that you've created around your libido. Cochagne is a threat to your illusion of self-control . . . of being in control. You're afraid. I know, because I was afraid of the same thing once."

Both women slipped into the light exercise clothing, then put on the Velcro-strapped magnetic-soled shoes, which were constructed like heavy athletic shoes. Tseng looked up from adjusting the fit of her shoes to see Horo smiling at her.

"It's been a long time since we've talked like this." Tseng felt a wave of emotion. "Sometimes, I feel you're slipping away. I knew things would change when you got married. I want to hold onto our friendship, and yet I realize that we've reached a turning point in our lives. I'm single and you're not. You have different responsibilities . . . and loyalties. You have less free time."

"Marriage has changed my life and my thinking on a lot of things. I didn't know what real personal freedom was," Horo said. "As a single woman, I didn't have to answer to anybody, I was the master of my own ship, I did what I wanted with my money and my time. I thought my life was fun and exciting, and I didn't want to change it. I even thought that a solitary existence, and the luxury of being able to go to bed alone were the ultimate expressions of independence. I thought I was free, but I was just self-indulgent. It's not the same thing at all. I'm really free now."

"There are those of us who might have trouble with that logic," Tseng ventured wryly, "though having someone with whom to share the responsibilities of life on the planet Earth sounds tremendously liberating."

"It goes way beyond that. For one thing, you don't realize how much you, as a single person, are burdened with the problem of finding quality companionship, and how much time is eaten up and wasted in making yourself available to meet someone."

"I agree with you about that. It's exhausting. Lately, I've lost interest in 'the pursuit.' "

"So you fill up your time with work."

"Do you really think I've done that?"

"I do, and what you've been doing to yourself by taking that road has been emotionally disastrous for you. Single people have to withhold intimacy and affection for self-preservation. They become hardened emotionally. They're not free to open themselves up and completely relax. Part of the burden I mentioned earlier is having to stifle the inner spirit that way in order to keep from getting hurt all the time.

"I'm glad I waited for the right man to come along. It's hard to explain what it's like. He gives himself to me completely, without reservation. Nothing is held back. I've never been closer to anyone. He's a part of me. And

I'm a part of him. We're strong together. Making love is something we do together. There's no thought given to 'technique.' The intimacy has put us on another level. Sex has a dimension it never had before. I hate leaving him for any reason. We're together all the time. He's my most intimate companion. It might not be right for everybody, but it's right for us.

"We've had arguments. It hasn't been all roses. First, he moved in with me; then, he needed a room to set up an office. The only room available was my study. I worked so hard to afford enough room for a study and an office, and now here I was, faced with having to give up the study. I cried. It was so painful to move my stuff out of there and try to make room for it in my office. But I did it because it was necessary to make room for him in my life. I don't know how I lived without him before. We want to be together. We want it to work."

"Why didn't you just live together?"

"That type of relationship was not intimate enough for us. Again, I can speak from experience. I lived with someone for a while. I swore I'd never do it again. People think that, if there's no legal marriage, they have an escape route in case it doesn't work. That means there's suspicion at the very heart of the relationship. It's that false sense of freedom again. They might think they love each other, but they don't love each other enough to have basic trust. How can you ever have love when there's that kind of fear in a relationship? The degree of intimacy just isn't there because the total commitment isn't there."

"And, financially, I imagine it's messier than divorce when you split up," Tseng interjected.

"Yes. I've been there," Horo said. "I'm telling you all this because I want you to know the kind of intimacy I have. I want you to enjoy the happiness I have, too."

"Not everybody can have those things in a marriage," Tseng said.

"But the potential is there. Cochagne might not be the right man for you. You may be right about his playboy attitude. If you don't break this pattern you've developed, you'll never have the chance to know or feel what it's really like to love and be loved completely."

"I don't know how to handle myself with him," Tseng said. She felt a tightness in her chest from the strong emotions and feelings of confusion and anguish.

"Think of this like a new religion, and think of me as a convert who wants to pass on my revelation to you. You're afraid to put yourself out there. You're afraid to let it happen. You're afraid of the change and the uncertainty of an honest relationship. Part of you is about that far from taking a chance on Jerry." Horo held up a thumb and forefinger with a tiny gap between, for emphasis. "The other part of you would like to take him two falls out of three just to show him you're in charge."

The statement made Tseng laugh. "You can tell that?"

"Yep. The harder you fight it, the more it shows because you get more and more uptight when he's around." Horo's expression softened. "The only way you are ever going to turn your life around is to stop settling for 'half a loaf,' and to be strong in the belief that you deserve to be loved; that you are worth any lifestyle concessions Jerry might have to make in order to meet your standards of being loved.

"And be prepared to lose him if he can't see your worth, because if he can't see it, then he's not worth having around. That's how you handle yourself with him."

After a pause, Horo smiled. "It's hard to see how a species with an adversarial attitude toward the opposite sex has survived as long as it has."

"Isn't that the truth," Tseng mused. She felt a relief from tension as she crossed to the hatch, though doubts and fears still assailed her. She needed time to reflect on her discussion with Horo.

She grabbed both companionway safety handrails, but because of the magnets in her shoes, when she tried to skip too fast down the first step, she felt herself on the verge of tumbling. She was prevented from falling by Horo's steadying hand on her shoulder.

On the Level Two main monitor screen, Tseng saw a view of Mission Control through a wide-angle lens. There was no backup for the base's wrecked live footage camera, and one would have to be brought up on a future mission, but Cochagne had temporarily "hard-wired" the portable camera to the operations panel with a power cable for video transmission from this level. He, DeSosa, and Lebby were dressed in the uniform athletic shorts and T-shirts as well. The three men were "mugging" comically for the camera.

"We're getting a nice clear picture. No garbage. Hallelujah," Christiansen said.

"I'll be needing that camera shortly," Tseng told Cochagne.

"Far Side, there will be a delay until Lieutenant Gutierrez arrives," Christiansen said.

Tseng was careful to look for dangling wires when she crossed to the galley, but Cochagne, Lebby, and DeSosa had taped all such hazards up out of harm's way. She plugged the lead of a communications headset into the panel and adjusted the mike. "I would like him to be on hand when we examine his most precious piece of evidence. We'll take a meal break, Houston, and then get on with our schedule, if that meets with your approval."

"Good plan. Listen, the FS-5 personal effects have to be collected and stored for return," Christiansen said.

"I agree, and we'll do that right away. According to tomorrow's schedule, Cochagne and DeSosa will replace the solar panel and check the orientation on the flat-panel radiators. Stored power levels are adequate. We'll have plenty of power into the night phase, and it shouldn't affect equipment. Tomorrow's EVA will also include the LRV checkout. If all goes well, we'll follow those tracks. Unless you have something to add . . ."

"If we do, I'll get back to you," Christiansen said.

Manch took a refuse bag, and brushed dead flies and the half-eaten meal they had found into it. "Is there any disinfectant we can use to wipe off this counter surface?" he asked.

"Should be down in the lower cabinet," Lebby said. "I'd use the hand-vac first, though."

"A brilliant suggestion," Manch replied, with a distasteful look at the dead insects which littered the floor and all the flat surfaces.

DeSosa rummaged through the food packets in the storage lockers located above and over the galley until he found a dried fruit snack. "I've been wanting to try this," he said. He opened the food packet and tossed a morsel of dried fruit into the air. It fell slowly, and as DeSosa leisurely tipped his head back, Cochagne grabbed the still camera, and captured its perfect entry into the other astronaut's mouth.

DeSosa was in front of the video camera, and there was laughter and applause from Mission Control. It was the kind of astronaut antic they loved, Tseng reflected. "Dave, we'd like to set up the tables and chairs on Level Two," she said.

"We have to discuss that," the CAPCOM answered. "Stand by for a bit."

"We're doing that—literally," DeSosa quipped.

Horo unfastened her rock bag and withdrew a plastic pouch, sterilized, then sealed by the robot. It contained a cylindrical core sample of lunar rock. Bubbles of glass reflected the light. "I wanted to show you guys what MILTON and I picked up today. This one is a beauty . . . from a pyroclastic deposit near Grissom. This is a piece of substantial melt sheet." Horo put the sample on the counter, reached into the bag and withdrew another bagged sample, a dullish dark cylinder. "This is a piece of KREEP . . . that's a type of uninteresting basaltic rock," she added dryly, after receiving a blank look from Manch.

"Should you be bringing your rock collection to the dinner table?" DeSosa asked.

"Let's all have 'show and tell,' Father DeSosa," Cochagne said.

DeSosa grimaced. "I knew it was a mistake to open my bag in front of you, but I had to get my clothes out! I'm not that religious. Sure, I was raised as a Catholic, but . . . you know, that stuff doesn't even belong to me. It belongs to my relatives."

"What are you talking about?" Tseng asked.

"That's my grandmother's old Bible," DeSosa said to Cochagne.

"He's also trafficking in St. Christopher medals," Cochagne said.

"They're all for relatives in Mexico who want souvenirs from the Moon."

"You must have at least fifty close relatives." Cochagne said. "Please give me the Salisbury steak and potatoes meal," Cochagne told DeSosa.

DeSosa wrinkled his nose in disgust. "Salisbury steak? Why are you eating that awful stuff? I can't stand that one." DeSosa dug into a storage locker and found the entree. He emptied the contents of all the packets containing the pilot's meal with dessert into a tray with section dividers and placed the tray in the microwave.

"Guaranteed to keep the lead in your pencil, Joe," Cochagne said.

"Speaking of which, I saw a memo recently about a field study that was done on the technical aspects of having sex in microgravity," DeSosa said.

"Sounds like the kind of research the Russians might

have undertaken at the old Mir Station," Horo said. "Make mine the Oriental chicken, Joe."

"China . . . ?"

"Houston, we'll talk to you again after dinner," Tseng said, removing her headset. "I'll have the same," she said to Horo, "and I'll wash it down with cranberry juice."

"I saw some in the cooler," DeSosa said. The astronaut took two containers from the compact galley refrigerator and pitched them overhand to Tseng and Horo.

"Here's to your pH level," Horo replied in a mock toast.

"Yeah, it had to have been the Russians," Lebby continued. "We certainly wouldn't waste time on that type of experiment. Is there another Oriental chicken?"

"We've got enough Oriental chicken up here to last the entire mission. That doesn't include what we brought up with us—they did it in the interest of science. Strictly by the book, naturally," DeSosa said.

"Naturally," Horo echoed.

"And they made detailed notes, no doubt," DeSosa said.

"I'd like to get a look at those notes," Horo replied.

"Maybe Varya Tolstaya can tell you all about it." Cochagne said. "Toss me a cranberry juice cocktail, Joe."

DeSosa launched the juice pouch airborne with an overhand throw. It sailed across the room in a slow arc and Cochagne caught it easily merely by raising his arm in time to intercept the pouch. "I'll make a note to ask Varya when we get back," DeSosa said.

"The information is bound to be out of date, though," Horo said.

"You really think so," DeSosa mimicked interest.

"It might be time for a new experiment," Horo said.

"Don't be disappointed," Manch spoke up, "but Varya will tell you that after less than a month in space her partners couldn't get it up because of reduced blood volume, especially in the lower extremities, and severe electrolyte imbalance; and if any of you guys are thinking about the Mars mission, after two years in space, the circulatory system damage will be irreversible, in all likelihood."

"I believe we've heard enough on the 'sex in space' topic, boys and girls," Tseng said.

"Far Side, I have just been given a note here," Christiansen said. "It's a memo to Dr. Greer from Jonathan Birnbaum at Bethesda, on the 'iconography of the occult.' "

"Houston, *Collins*. Greer here. What's the message?"

"That's it," Christiansen replied. "It just says, 'Terms and symbols consistent with the iconography of the occult.' "

"That's a big help," Greer responded.

"What's the scoop on the teleconference with Bethesda?" Tseng asked.

"We're trying to iron out the time particulars," Christiansen answered.

"Iona, are you having something to eat?" Manch called out from the galley.

"Yes, I just heated up one of those chicken dishes you've all been talking about," Greer replied.

"It's a clean sweep for the chicken—except for Mr. Meat and Potatoes," DeSosa said. "How about a cranberry juice, Pops?"

"Toss it over, amigo," Lebby said. He scooped a forkful of the thick chicken, rice, and sauce mixture and held it up admiringly. "I could get to like it here. Things stay put and don't go floating all over the place like they do at the Space Station!"

"We could use a decorator around here, in my opinion," Tseng said.

"I can't stand any more of this clever humor," Manch said. "I'm going down to Level One to set up my equipment. Jerry, I will need you and your still camera," he added, heading for the companionway.

"It's ready when you are," Cochagne responded.

"What's 'iconography?' " Horo asked.

"A popular social sciences 'buzz' word for the visual symbols we use to describe things," Greer replied.

"Can you elaborate on that?" Horo asked.

"I'll give you an example. How would you describe the American Revolution?"

"A war you guys lost," Cochagne called out.

"At least, after 1812, you Brits had the good sense to quit trying to take the country back by force," Lebby added. "Of course, that's why you've had to buy it up piece by piece ever since."

For the first time that Tseng could recall, Greer laughed with the group. To Tseng it was a positive sign. FS-6 just might mesh after all, even in the short time they had.

"I'll rephrase," Greer said. "What makes the Revolutionary War visibly different from the Second World War, the First World War, the Vietnam War—and the Middle East and Philippine conflicts, for that matter?"

"The uniforms, the weapons, the level of technology," Cochagne said.

"Be more specific," Greer said.

"Okay, I got it," Horo said, "the Revolutionary War is the Boston Tea Party, tricornered hats, Benjamin Franklin, George Washington, the Liberty Bell, flintlock rifles, Valley Forge . . ."

"Those are the things that characterize that period of history in our minds," Lebby said, "but they are also stereotypes."

"That's one way of looking at it," Greer said.

"We're also fairly far removed from that period of history," Tseng said. "Those images represent all the information that remains from that time. The subtler details have been forgotten."

"Iconography evokes an emotional response, certainly a sense of familiarity," Greer said. "These symbols affect us on a subliminal level. Just think how visually upsetting it would be to see a depiction of Benjamin Franklin with an M-16, and wearing a World War Two helmet."

"I like 'Food for the Moon,' " Cochagne said, indicating the phrase scrawled on the wall and other places throughout the base. "There's nothing subliminal about that."

"We'll make that your motto for FS-10," DeSosa said.

"Far Side, Houston," Christiansen's voice came on the COMM. "Lieutenant Gutierrez and Dee Bianco are here."

Tseng washed and stored her meal tray, then picked up her juice container. "I need you," she said to Cochagne.

She regretted her choice of words instantly, when the pilot grinned as though responding to an innuendo, but for once, he did not react with a comeback line. Instead, he met her gaze and held it, keeping her spellbound for a few seconds, before crossing to the communications console to retrieve the video camera.

Tseng's nostrils were assailed with the strong, foul odor of rotten, burned meat. She was in a hurry to reach Level One. Nevertheless, she followed the smell to the recreation area. Dead flies crunched underfoot with each step.

Her first impressions of the room, the site of horrors inconceivable before the events of the previous day, gained while looking through the restrictive faceplate of a space helmet in poor light, were reinforced and augmented by her unencumbered view. Her slow scan took in the piles of paper and debris against the walls. She recognized torn and wadded computer printouts of text and of mapping photographs. She sifted through them and discovered a Nikon F4 camera body, identical to Cochagne's, with a cracked 50mm lens attached. The hard drive unit was missing.

The thrill of finding the FS-5 mission camera sent a shiver of excitement through her, and she picked it up and turned it over in her hands to examine the damage closely. The camera was a loss, but the hard drive might be somewhere inside the base. They had yet to tackle the job of poking through the debris. When the hard drive was located, the images stored on it might fill in the missing details of the disaster.

The sudden realization that she was handling the camera, an object that could be fingerprinted, nearly caused her to drop it. She put it down hastily, angry at herself for the lack of forethought.

The blood on the aluminum strut removed from Ann Bisio's corpse had dried into a hard crust. It stank of decomposed flesh, but it was not the source of the charred grease odor. She looked at the floor, then her glance traveled upward to the dark spot on the ceiling. The soot-blackened, ruined appearance of the prefab acoustical panels gave her an uneasy feeling.

The talk with Horo and the meal break had left her in a positive mood, but as Tseng descended to Level One, a dark depression invaded her psyche threatening to overcome her objective frame of mind. She felt the same icy hand grabbing at her insides as on her first reconnaissance of the area. Negative anticipation filled her with apprehension. Despite the high ambient temperature in the upper levels of the base, upon reaching the bottom of the companionway, she felt chilled.

Manch was appropriating a small area of the ruined lab for his own use, and he had prepared a caddy containing empty containers and vials and bottles of chemicals. Several small machines, which Tseng assumed were

pieces of test equipment, were arrayed atop unopened
supply cases.

She plugged the leads from her portable headset into
the level's wall jacks. "Houston, Far Side. How do you
read?"

"We read you loud and clear," Christiansen responded.
"I have a certain police lieutenant here with me."

"So what has he decided to do?" Tseng asked.

"I want you to go ahead and dust for fingerprints on
the hammer and that aluminum strut," Gutierrez answered directly, over the COMM.

"Lieutenant, I found the mission camera on Level
Two. Unfortunately, I picked it up without thinking. Is it
still worth our time to dust it for fingerprints?"

"What kind of housing does it have?"

"It's textured black plastic," she answered.

"Did you touch any part of the lens or any of the
smooth areas?"

"I don't remember exactly how I picked it up. I wasn't
thinking. I'm sorry."

"Cops do it, too, sometimes, and we're supposed to
know better," Gutierrez said. "We might still get something off of it. Who was using it?"

"Mike Mobley."

"So his prints will be all over it. It's worth looking at,
anyway."

Cochagne descended the companionway. He was carrying the video camera and the FS-6 still camera. Both
pieces of equipment were minus the EVA eyepiece
adapters and the protective shrouds which kept the
lenses free of the ever present abrasive Moon dust. The
pilot squatted down beside her, and Tseng took the video
camera from him. Cochagne put the viewfinder of the
still camera to his eye and focused in on the hammer
experimentally.

"Normally, a very fine powder, usually black, is

brushed lightly over the object," Gutierrez continued. "When the excess powder is brushed off, we get an outline of the fingerprint which can then be photographed."

"We need to find a substitute for the powder," Tseng said. "What about using lunar soil? We could filter it and get a charcoal powder three or four hundred mesh fine."

"What does that mean," Gutierrez asked.

"Approximately twice as fine as baby talc."

"Maybe . . ." the detective replied tentatively. After a thoughtful pause, he said, "Would you happen to have any pencils there? Pencils with soft leads, like drafting pencils?"

"We do, indeed, use drafting pencils. Mike Mobley will have some. I'll check the table."

"If you can locate the sharpener, carbon powder would be the best material for this job."

"I copy you." Tseng moved to the table. She put down her juice container and sorted through the papers. She found Mobley's pencils and an abrasive sharpener tucked between the layers of his papers.

"Houston, this is the Hardy Boys and Nancy Drew calling," Cochagne said. "We've located the pencil sharpener."

Tseng heard laughter in the background at Mission Control over the COMM.

"Good. Do you have anything like a soft brush? A woman's makeup brush for powder or blush will do."

"That's one item we won't have up here, Lieutenant," Tseng said.

"There's no use in getting all dressed up when there's nowhere to go," Manch added.

"I have a lens cleaning brush with a rubber bulb on the end," Cochagne said.

"Beautiful," Gutierrez responded. "Touch the brush to the carbon powder and knock off the excess, then very carefully touch the brush to the handle of the hammer—

don't touch the handle with your fingers—a very light contact is all that's required."

"Paul, you should be the one to do this," Tseng said. "Your hands have the most well-developed motor control."

Manch sighed and flexed his fingers in answer. He took the lens brush from Cochagne.

Tseng opened the pencil sharpener. "It wasn't emptied, so it's full of carbon dust." She placed it within easy reach of Manch, then picked up the portable camera to shoot the physician's efforts.

Manch's hands were steady and precise as he followed Gutierrez's instructions. Overlapping patterns of finger smudges, a few showing whorls and ridges, appeared in powder on the front, back, and sides of the hammer shaft. The heaviest concentrations were on the front and back edges near the base of the tool.

"A lot of people have used this hammer. I'm making a real mess here," Manch said apologetically.

"I'll be the judge of that when I see the photographs," Gutierrez said."

Cochagne changed to a lens for close-up shots and focused down on the shaft. He shot several frames along the length of it.

"I should examine the head for microevidence before we turn the hammer over," Manch said.

"I agree," Gutierrez responded.

They waited in silence while Manch took a magnifying glass, a sheet of paper, a tweezer and a packaged disposable scalpel from his caddy of supplies. The physician spent a few moments bent over the head of the hammer with the magnifying glass, then he placed the sheet of paper against it. He used the tweezers to probe at scars on the head and the peen. Metal flakes and tiny dark particles came off the tool and fell onto the paper. Manch folded the paper and placed it inside a sample container which he sealed and labeled. "I'll examine these scrapings under the microscope," he told Gutierrez and the others. "I'm ready to turn the hammer over."

Manch repeated the process with the carbon powder on the other side of the hammer shaft, and Cochagne shot pictures of that side.

"Is Bob Faden right- or left-handed?" Gutierrez asked. There was a pause, then he said, "Right-handed? Thanks," repeating an off-mike answer.

"We're ready to go upstairs for the strut," Manch said when Cochagne lowered the camera as an indication that he was finished.

"There's a chess set in the CDR quarters," Tseng said. "You might be able to get prints off of the pieces."

"The ones that are light-colored shouldn't be a problem," Gutierrez said.

"We'll add it to the 'to do' list," Manch agreed.

Tseng unplugged the portable video camera and handed it to Cochagne. "I'd prefer to stay down here and sort through Mike Mobley's notes, Lieutenant. Jerry and Paul can handle this job without me."

"That's fine with me, Commander," Gutierrez responded.

"Don't expect any immediate startling revelations from this session, Jerry," Manch said dryly, as the two men disappeared up the companionway. "We won't be 'cracking this case'—as they say in the biz—for a few hours—if at all."

Tseng was startled by the sound of her juice container falling off the table. She remembered putting it there, well away from the edge, yet it was on the floor. The red liquid pumped rhythmically out of the container—it reminded her of a human heart pulsating, bleeding, emptying itself of blood. Drowsily, she watched the liquid spread slowly across the floor . . . she watched until the container was empty, before the idea of disposing of it and wiping up the spill occurred to her. When it did, the sense of profound regret over choosing juice instead of coffee as her dinner beverage was totally out of proportion to the incident.

She could not afford to succumb to fatigue. The realization sparked determination and helped to snap her out of the weird semi-trancelike state. She cleaned up the mess with a compressed fiber cloth and returned to Mobley's worktable. She gathered the top layer of papers into a stack and examined them. The pages were out of order, and they belonged to a computer printout of data recorded by a surface experiment. She tried to correlate the columns of numbers to the known experiments, in particular, the PERM package, but she could find no specific reference to it. She set aside the stack of papers for further analysis and saw a page of handwritten notes tucked into the layer beneath.

Identity: thinking becomes rigid. Shell of flesh. Security blanket. Magnets in the brain. Einstein's theory—energy is neither created nor destroyed.

Metaphysical messages from Mobley?

She was distracted from the papers by the thought that the commander's effects would have to be gathered up and stowed in the *Collins* for return to Earth. She was reluctant to initiate the task, however. An intangible barrier was holding her back, preventing her from moving ahead with her work. Again, she turned her attention to the worktable, but it was difficult to concentrate on anything.

Cochagne descended the companionway. He crossed to the storage boxes and peered at the labels. "I hope they left the photographic equipment alone."

Tseng "ummed" an acknowledgment without looking at him. After a few moments, she heard him tear into a carton. She was used to working with men. She was even used to seeing male crew members in the nude and being nude in their presence. It was routine, and yet, in Jerry's case, the sexual attraction had always been there for her. Now, it was difficult to keep from watching him. She was annoyed with herself for allowing the pilot's presence to create a distraction.

She realized that her jaw was clenched tightly with the effort of trying to forget about him, and that she had read and reread the same line of data on the page she was examining. Annoyed, she bent closer to the paper.

The next thing she knew, Cochagne was moving restlessly through the room. He spotted the photograph of Mobley's family, picked it up, and studied it. "I wonder who they've picked to break the news to them when we find him."

"Someone of comparable rank. My guess is that Dave Christiansen's preparing to do it," Tseng said. She was aware of a strange tension in herself: an apprehension directed at the photograph, and on the fact that Cochagne was holding it.

"I didn't know Mike Mobley before the mission, and I've never met his wife or his kids," Cochagne continued. "My dad was in the military. We lived all over the world when I was a kid. I never really knew my father while I was growing up. If something like this had happened to him back then . . . I don't know that I would have felt anything." Cochagne stopped talking, as if searching his childhood memories for the emotions. "I think I would have felt the same way about his death as I would have felt about the death of a family friend." He set down the picture and approached the worktable.

She was tantalizingly aware of his proximity.

"It may be none of my business, but what made you choose a military career, China?"

"I was hungry for recognition."

"There's more to it than that. You made an innocuous

comment about your family during the interview that leads me to believe relations are strained."

"I've never thought of it as a strained relationship, but I don't get along with my father, and my mother and I were never close—I could never tell her anything I didn't want my father to know, so we just didn't talk.

"They would always make it a point to tell me about other people's children who had done something 'worthy of mention.' It didn't matter what I did, or what I achieved, it was never good enough to please them. I worked so hard as a kid to win their approval, and I felt like such a failure.

"At any rate, I didn't know what I wanted to do with my life. I just wanted to succeed. I knew I was smart. In high school, I happened to meet some cadets from the Air Force Academy. I applied."

"And . . . ?"

"Everyone was in uniform. Everyone looked the same. No one stood out . . . and, for the first time in my life, I was recognized for achievement."

"By kindly Uncle Sam."

Tseng laughed at the reference. "Yes. I worked hard to please 'him.'

"When I got my promotion, a few weeks ago, my dad's only reaction was, 'I guess that's okay, but you'll never become a general.' That comment put my whole life in perspective."

"You're the daughter of a pessimist, and if you look inside of a pessimist, you'll find an unhappy man lurking there," Cochagne chuckled sympathetically.

He was looking at her steadily, and Tseng saw an intensity in his eyes that simultaneously annoyed and inflamed her. "Don't look at me with those bedroom eyes, Jerry. I don't want to be one of your romantic conquests," she said.

Cochagne blinked, startled. "That's a slap in the face."

"Sorry, but you have a well publicized track record."

"Rumors of my reputation have been much exaggerated," he protested. "Unfortunately, I have some failed relationships behind me that, because of my professional notoriety, have gotten more attention than they deserve. That's all."

The strength of the emotion in his voice surprised her. "Why are you making these moves now? Why here?"

"I suppose it's because I consider this the end of our association as coworkers. We're on this mission together, we trained together for it, but in a few more days it will be over. I'd like to pursue other aspects of our friendship."

"I'm not looking for a friendly toss in the hay."

"Neither am I. I've never looked exclusively for that. You have a very bad impression of me," he finished in a wounded tone of voice.

"I can't pursue this now," Tseng said. "The mission is not over for me yet. Do you copy?"

"I copy you, Commander," Cochagne responded with a lazy smile.

Fearing that the pilot might try to prolong the discussion in order to weaken her resolve—which was crumbling with the steadily increasing momentum of an avalanche, she had to admit—she busied herself with the papers on the worktable. A few seconds passed, then she heard him walk away.

Her imagination recreated the looks which passed between them after the discovery of Bisio's corpse. The dark eyes had reached for her, to draw her into him. The incident was ill-timed for a purely sexual ploy. He deserved credit for more depth of character and intelligence than that. She reviewed the thoughts and feelings foremost in her mind during their brief exchange: *should I take him at face value? He makes everything sound too simple. What does he really want from me? What does he see in me?* Though Cochagne was still in the room, Tseng felt suddenly empty and alone . . . and angry that her behavioral yardstick for assessing the feasibility of a permanent relationship was a dysfunctional family that acted glad to be rid of her. For all her efforts at winning their approval, she really couldn't count on them emotionally.

Dick Lebby had his wife and his family . . . there were any number of other men and women around her who had well-rounded lives. That's how it looked to one who was always on the outside. The solitary stranger among them.

Uncle Sam, will you be there for me?

She knew the answer to that question. A few years from now, Uncle Sam would have no use for her. What would she do then? What would she have?

A pension and memories of the great adventure of outer space.

That thought brought back her discussion with Horo.

Her life suddenly looked as barren and devoid of warmth as the Moon's surface.

Who loves me?

She had avoided asking herself that question all her adult professional life. Was it possible to turn her life around at this late date?

The noise of footsteps near the companionway snapped her out of her reverie. She looked up to see Cochagne watching her.

"Dick should be ready to transmit the pictures," he said. "I thought you might want to be around for that."

"You thought right. I'm finished here, for now." She took a last look around the room before crossing to follow Cochagne. This was a dark, cold place conducive to dark, cold, negative thoughts. Why had Mobley chosen it for his quarters?

Lebby was seated at the computer's main workstation.

DeSosa watched the senior astronaut run a diagnostic program.

Tseng's feelings about the machine were mixed: it was one of the base's most vital and sophisticated technical tools, and she was glad to have it back on-line, but seeing it "regain consciousness" made her as nervous as if they had awakened a sleeping giant. Destruction aimed specifically at the computer and its auxiliary workstations by the FS-5 crew was evident throughout the base. Why? Had the giant gone on a rampage?

What could it do? It did not control the base. Unlike MILTON, it was not "aware." It could not arbitrarily decide to shut down critical life-support systems and hold the base personnel hostage. It was a sentry and a regulator for those systems and could alert base personnel to life-threatening faults or malfunctions by means of alarms, but it had no autonomy.

Cochagne inserted and aligned the camera's hard disk in the digital playback/downlink unit. After a short wait, he said, "Houston, we'll transmit those fingerprint photos to you, if you're ready."

"Go ahead," Christiansen responded on the COMM.

Lebby sent the information with a keystroke. The transmission was relayed from the nearest lunar tracking and data relay system satellite and took only moments to reach Earth.

"We got it," Christiansen acknowledged. "We have information for you on the boot prints you found near the rover. One set can be positively identified as Drzymkowski's. He was a big man with a big foot. His boots had to be special-ordered."

"Copy that," Tseng said.

"We'd like to transmit some pictures to you," Christiansen continued. "These are photos you took from orbit. There's one, in particular, that we're interested to hear your opinion on."

"Okay, Houston, shoot," Lebby said.

There was no sound to indicate that the computer was receiving data, but, after a few moments, a prompt on the screen told them that the transmission was complete.

"I wish I could look over your shoulder," Greer said on the COMM.

"I can zap these over to you to view on the *Collins'* computer," Lebby suggested.

"Do you mind?" Greer asked. "I'm fascinated by the process, though all my experience is with medical imaging. I'm interested in the end result, but normally I prefer to leave all the pixels and voxels to the experts."

"A wise decision, and one which provides job security for guys like me," Lebby responded.

"Shall we have a look at our vacation pictures?" Tseng quipped.

"Take a look at frame FS6-dash-zero-seven-three-five six-dash-zero six-niner," Christiansen said. "This is in the area northeast of where you located that set of tracks, China."

At Lebby's instruction, the computer displayed the photo. It showed a flat expanse of lunar terrain broken by clusters of rock formations. The frame's data block displayed the frame number, time, mission data, velocity/height ratio, camera-pointing attitude, fiducial marks, such as the optical axis at mid-exposure, and that it was shot by the *Collins'* panoramic camera, which provided stereoscopic coverage for large-scale topographic mapping and for detailed photogeologic analysis.

"We compared it to the photo mosaic from the FS-2 mapping camera, reference numbers FS2-dash-zero-niner-four-one-five-dash-eight-six-zero through -eight-six-four, but the results were inconclusive. We have no sure way of knowing if we have an object where there was no object before."

"The mapping camera frames have a seventy-eight-percent overlap," Tseng told Greer. "The four-photo mosaic shows the same flat expanse of terrain, but a higher sun angle has obscured the smaller formations.

"Can you go back to our shot . . . or better, let's see a split screen," she said to Lebby.

The computer specialist put the photos side by side on the screen. "We have resolution to less than a meter in a fifty-meter frame with the panoramic camera, but the sun angle has to be just right to identify an object," he said.

"Our pictures were taken at a low sun angle. Those long shadows make everything look different than in the FS-2 mosaic," Cochagne emphasized.

"This could be an astronaut facedown in the dust, or it could be a rock," Tseng said, pointing to the feature pinpointed as the item in question.

"A considerable amount of data can be lost in the process of enhancement," Lebby said. "The JPL techs did a masterful job, but they weren't looking for anything specific. We are. I'd like to take a crack at the original, unenhanced picture."

"In your 'spare time,' " DeSosa said sarcastically.

"Something like that," Lebby answered.

"Rather than having you work on that photo, I need a detailed look at what the terrain is really like in this area," Tseng said. "I'd like to see a topographical contour map."

Lebby responded with his fingers on the computer keyboard. The photo image on the screen was replaced by a representation of the lunar features as defined by contour lines that whorled and snaked around them. It reminded Tseng of the fingerprints on the hammer shaft, but here color shading differentiated the segments for ease of interpretation. "These lines are in increments of ten meters in elevation," he said.

"Increments of half a meter would be better," Tseng

told him. "That will tell me exactly what kind of scenery I might have to maneuver the rover through."

At Lebby's bidding, the features on the map were expanded and the colors adjusted accordingly.

"All this information is acquired from photographs?" Greer asked, astonishment apparent in her voice.

"By knowing the time of lunar day, and then measuring shadows, the computer can give us this elevation and slope information," Lebby told Greer. "Combined with spectrography, and photogeologic interpretation, we can use it to avoid surveying unimportant sites, which certainly maximizes our time here."

"How about letting me see a 3-D rendering with the sun angle as it will be at, say, ten to twelve hours from now," Tseng said.

"Terminator interference is due to affect the area close to that time," Lebby responded.

"I'm aware of that, but I'm still planning an EVA to follow that set of boot tracks until I hear otherwise."

The computer took only moments to compose its artistic interpretation of the lay of the land, complete with the shadows as they would appear.

"Thanks. I'll take printouts of everything to study. How would you rate the computer's performance?" Tseng asked Lebby.

"It's just a bit sluggish, if you can believe that," Lebby said. "My first inclination was to check how much data was stored in memory during the FS-5 mission. It's quite a bit, but the peculiar thing is, there are no picture files in storage. It's as though they've been deliberately wiped. That makes me very curious about the other files they added."

"Far Side, Houston," Christiansen said on the COMM. "We've been determined to get you that teleconference with Bethesda, and persistence has finally paid off. It's scheduled for two hours from now."

"That gives Paul and me time to get back to the *Collins*," Tseng said.

"I can handle this," Manch said.

"Do you know how to operate the camcorder?" Tseng asked.

"I'm sure I can figure it out."

"Right," Tseng said. "I'm coming with you."

"You'll need help moving Faden over here, afterward," Cochagne said. "I'll go along."

"We'll need all the help we can get for that," Manch said.

☾

"This VisionPhone teleconference is a progress report and a round-table discussion of the direction we can help Dr. Greer take with this patient," Birnbaum said. The psychiatrist was seated at a conference table with a group of men and women, whom Bianco assumed were Bethesda Naval Hospital psychiatric staff, but they were anonymous in their white coats.

"It's after eleven PM Eastern Time, and that's an unusual hour for a staff meeting, I realize," Birnbaum continued, "but the purpose is twofold: to let Dr. Greer, our colleague at Far Side, bring us up to date on her progress with the patient, and to actually observe Astronaut Faden during his most active period of the day. Iona, can you hear us clearly?"

"We're receiving your transmission loud and clear, Jonathan," they heard Greer's voice respond, after a small delay.

Bianco leaned back in her desk chair to get a better viewing angle on the TV monitor. On the screen, Jonathan Birnbaum, a short, blocky man in his mid-fifties with kinky steel gray hair, appeared as immobile as a statue and just as unreadable while his assistant made hurried entries on notepad computers. "We've all seen the recent video from Far Side. This teleconference is being held to determine treatment options for Dr. Greer's patient," he said. "Dr. Greer, is the audio still holding up?"

"It's fine," Greer was heard to say.

In a few moments, the setup at Bethesda would allow the doctors to see inside the *Collins,* while the LLM would only have audio over the COMM from the hospital. Bianco's setup gave her video of the *Collins* and video of Bethesda, but she would not be on the COMM.

She'd wanted to view and record the Bethesda teleconference from the privacy of her office, not in front of the techs and personnel in Mission Control. She'd had to bring in extra chairs to accommodate Jack Bucar, Dave Christiansen, and Lol Gutierrez. It was a good thing they were all on friendly terms, she reflected. The four of them were packed together like sardines. "Can you see okay?" she asked them.

"I'm fine, Dee," Bucar replied. "Thanks for going to the inconvenience of letting us watch from your office."

Bianco had not found the time to debrief Jack Bucar since his return to the Johnson Space Center from New York, but she was glad to have the "old man" back. "No bother. I appreciate your time."

In a few hours, Christiansen would be back on duty as CAPCOM. The teleconference was cutting into his rest period, but the astronaut wanted to know—and needed to know—as much as possible. FS-7 was still "go."

She'd included Gutierrez in the group on an impulse. She'd not known what to expect from the detective, beyond his help with the initial discoveries at Far Side. Gutierrez had surprised her by asking to remain at the Space Center to assist the FS-6 crew and to seek out more information. Bianco intended to take advantage of the homicide detective's enthusiasm for the case.

The scene on the monitor changed to a cramped sleep

station inside the *Collins*. Greer stood next to Faden and Manch. The three astronauts faced the camera. Faden wore a hospital gown, opened in the back. Over it, he wore an athletic suit jacket backward. His arms crossed over his chest and the jacket sleeves were pulled to the back. It looked like a good makeshift straitjacket to Bianco. As she watched, Faden squatted and urinated on the floor. He remained crouched and scowled at the puddle he'd just made.

Bianco steeled herself in anticipation of another violent episode. She glanced at the three men with her. Bucar had lowered his head and was massaging his forehead. Christiansen just stared. Gutierrez made eye contact with her, but she couldn't read his expression.

"Faden has not responded favorably to treatment with Thorazine," Greer said. "Unfortunately, Clozapine and the other more effective psychoreactive drugs used in the treatment of schizophrenia are not available to us. Under these conditions, hearing disembodied voices will reinforce his paranoia, so we're going to block the audio from Bethesda for the time being. I've asked Dr. Manch to assist me. Colonel Tseng has the camera, and Cochagne is also here, in case we need help."

Bianco thought Greer's decision a good one, as Faden's eyes darted furtively around the room.

Greer squatted beside Faden. "There's nothing to be afraid of, Bob. I'm here," Greer said. "You are hearing my voice. It's for real."

Faden stared at the floor and said, "Thanks. Lately, I get mixed up about where sounds are coming from . . . and everything is so loud it makes me mad. Like someone turned up the volume all the way. I have to focus all my attention on what people are saying, or I can't understand. Some sounds come from behind my back. If I sit like this, they can't get me."

"I understand, Bob," Greer said. "Where you are is fine."

Faden knitted his brows in concentration. A few moments passed in silence, then he said, "Sometimes, when you're talking, I have to think what each word means. I'm sorry for the delay."

"No problem," Greer said affably.

"If I'm not careful, I'll come apart, and I can't do anything about it, and you can't do anything about it."

"I understand. Can you talk to me about how you feel?"

The astronaut did not answer immediately. He pursed his lips and continued to stare at the floor. His mouth twitched with the strain of working the problem over in his mind.

Bianco watched him with growing apprehension. The question was causing an intense internal struggle for the man. He listened closely as the doctors talked softly among themselves on the COMM.

"Consider that in cases of solipsism, the 'self' cannot be aware of anything except its own experiences and state of being, and nothing is real or exists except the 'self,' " someone from the panel of doctors commented.

"There is clear evidence here in the areas of attention and perception," someone else said in a hushed voice, as though Faden was in a position to overhear. "Normal people reduce, categorize, and organize an otherwise chaotic flow of information from their environment. Here, we've observed the 'flat effect' or emotionlessness of the schizophrenic, in reality, a manifestation of intense anxiety, panic, and internalized hyperactivity. The organism, itself, is in a state of heightened drive."

"In this case, then, you are defining 'sanity' as the degree of capacity to modify incoming data from the sense organs, and attributing the loss of this capacity to . . . what?" someone else said.

"The precise genetic mechanism of schizophrenia causes an imbalance between the sympathetic and parasympathetic nervous system functions, mediated by the neurohumors adrenaline and acetylcholine, respectively," the hushed voice replied. "From the standpoint of medical factors causing the disease, all other aspects of the symptomatology are reactions to this basic disorder."

"But add to that a precipitating event, say, the mission to Far Side, to which Faden had a large anxiety response," Birnbaum said. "Now we have psychological factors causing the disease."

"Jonathan," a new voice said, "I don't think the FS-5 mission itself can be viewed as a precipitating event. These people are monitored for stress every step of the way during training, and Faden showed no unusual reactions in the various simulators. When we talk about psychological factors causing a disease, we usually mean life experiences. An experience stirs us deeply, and our emotional resources are not adequate to cope with it. The severity of the symptomatology can indicate the extent to which we suppress it or reveal it."

Bianco felt frustrated that she couldn't see the speakers' faces, but it was more important to watch Faden.

"In this case," someone else said, "the symptoms resemble those documented in medieval medical journals. At Far Side, I understand there is evidence of satanic practices and rituals . . ."

". . . We're not going to argue the question of whether or not it is possible for disembodied entities to take over the human mind and body, Rick," Birnbaum interjected.

"However," the unknown staff member, identified by Birnbaum as "Rick," persisted, "in some of these cases, where the symptoms are treated in the classical, orthodox, traditional religious manner, a few of these patients do respond. It doesn't prove that possession is real. It's an indication that we're dealing with a particular kind of mental illness: an aberration, an altered state of awareness, and what you or I believe doesn't matter. It's what Faden believes. It's a gray area in terms of therapy, but somewhere, therein, lies the method of treatment that will lead to his recovery."

"I've gone over his records. There's nothing in them that even hints of that kind of impropriety in the past," Bianco said to Bucar, Christiansen, and Gutierrez.

"At first glance, this is coming from nowhere, but as a professional, I know it's just not so," Birnbaum said.

Bianco glanced at Christiansen for a reaction. She could tell that the astronaut wanted them to pursue the topic of possession, but that he was deliberately remaining silent. He watched Faden with something akin to wonderment.

Suddenly, Faden's eyes fluttered. In a trembling voice he sobbed, "They're burning me up!"

"Who is burning you up?" Greer asked soothingly.

Faden squeezed his eyes shut and screamed, "Fire, fire, fire . . ." He followed this by a long, drawn-out moan. The moan died, and he continued with, "He was pouring fire all over me. I ran away when all that hot fire came down on me."

There was a short pause during which Faden hyperventilated, then he rolled his head back and stared at the ceiling blankly, his mouth falling slack. He remained that way for only a moment, then he stood and looked directly at Manch. "Get out of here, you stinking piece of open gut . . . God forgive me! God forgive me . . ." He finished by giggling and twittering idiotically, but in different voices, so that it sounded like a group of people.

A calm, clinical voice from Bethesda said, "In Tourette's syndrome, these types of outbursts of profanities and obscenities, together with grunts, barks, curses, yelps, snorts, sniffs, tics, foot stomping, and facial contortions, begin suddenly and cease just as suddenly."

"Tourette's syndrome is a neurological disease involving a chemical abnormality in the brain, and it responds to drug treatment," Birnbaum said. "I believe we're seeing some side effects of the Thorazine. Tardive dyskinesia can occur with phenothiazines as well as with Clozapine and may not go away after the drugs are stopped. The signs of it are wormlike movements of the tongue or other uncontrolled movements of the mouth, tongue, cheeks, and jaw, such as lip smacking, puffing of the cheeks and uncontrolled chewing movements, uncontrolled movements of arms or legs, loss of bladder control, and seizures.

Further discussion was interrupted as sounds issued from Faden's throat, faintly at first, then louder and louder. Bianco strained to see if the lips were moving, but she couldn't tell. The sounds became a chant with the words run together.

"I'minhellI'minhellI'minhellI'minhellI'min hellI'minhell," the voice out of Faden repeated without even pausing to breathe. Rhythmic at first, the verbal cadence gradually became a monotone chant. It continued for a long time before the voice fell in volume to a barely audible whisper. Suddenly, he shouted, "God of the universe God of Earth God of angels God of devils God of virgins." He doubled over as if in pain and croaked, "God of Satan God of hell kingdom without end . . ." The pain subsided, and Faden continued, "God the father God the son God the holy spirit save this woman your servant because she hopes in you, O Lord . . . Word of God . . . Jesus Christ . . ." Another spasm of pain caused the astronaut to scream, but in a woman's voice. "Leave him alone! Get away from him! Run, Bob! Run! Bob! RunBob! RunBob! RunBob . . ." Faden resumed his chanting.

The discussion among the psychiatric staff resumed then, as though they had paused briefly for a minor interruption.

"A new personality appears to be emerging here," Bianco heard Birnbaum's voice over the view of Faden on the monitor. "We've documented nine of these personae, thus far, and we expect a few of them to be submerged or to disappear, and a few new ones to emerge, before he stabilizes."

Faden's voice had dropped to a whisper again, and he was still mouthing the "runBob" chant. Abruptly, the woman's voice screamed in agony, then Faden fell silent in apparent exhaustion.

Birnbaum and the other psychiatrists were taking Faden's behavior in a matter-of-fact, clinical way, as though it was something they saw every day and talked about casually over lunch, Bianco thought. Were they abnormally blasé, or was she overreacting to the astronaut's bizarre behavior?

She glanced at Gutierrez. The detective appeared totally absorbed and fascinated by what he'd seen and heard. He was taking Faden's behavior at face value and Bianco was struck with how unsophisticated, and therefore, novel, that approach might be in their present company.

Christiansen was another matter. He was energized, or at least impassioned, by his personal interpretation of what he was seeing. Bianco still wondered why the astronaut had kept silent when the discussion turned to the satanic evidence, though she could see the wisdom of it.

"I want to deal with the murders at Far Side for a few moments," Birnbaum said. "Admittedly, one of the weakest points in scientific psychology is the problem of when and how thoughts are translated into action, and why thoughts are translated into open acts in some cases and not in others, and why in this specific case?"

"There's no evidence that Faden committed murder," Gutierrez spoke up. "He's our chief suspect because the evidence looks suspicious, and you have him in the flesh. That makes him a victim, too, in some ways."

Birnbaum continued. "Based on the hypothesis, then, that Faden has committed murder, what made him translate thoughts into action? The psychology of action is an extremely difficult and little understood subject and usually when a murder is committed, the real story is never known. Many individuals have criminal, perverse, sexual, or suicidal ideas in one form or another, but few of them put these ideas into action. Yet there are hardly any clear and well-established scientific data to distinguish the psychological structure of the doers and the thinkers, even when the personalities and situations of the individuals have been fully studied."

Bianco's attention was diverted as, on the monitor, life came back into Faden's slack features. He raised his head, looked directly into the camera lens, and grinned. Did he know what the camera was, and that they were watching him? Bianco felt a chill run up her spine at the implication of being vulnerable to someone as dangerous as Faden might be. Was there such a thing as an "evil" smile, she wondered?

As a Mormon, Christiansen at least, had a secure, well-defined view of the order of the universe—as much could be said of the practitioners of any religion, in Bianco's view. The beliefs of Mormonism were Christiansen's "cosmogony," and in order to be a scientist, the astronaut had found a way to rationalize science and its theories on the structure of the universe with his religion. Perhaps he was, at this moment, struggling with this paradox. Perhaps that was the reason he was choosing to remain silent.

More than likely, he didn't want to jeopardize his position on the FS-7 mission, Bianco reflected. To her, "evil" was strictly a religious term, and its application was to be found in an archaic concept: the war of spiritual opposites in a God-operated universe.

"In the case of an obsessive-compulsive neurosis, a patient is plagued by ideas and obsessions which he feels are entering his mind against his will and are alien to him." Birnbaum continued, "He may commit acts that he feels he must carry out—actually against his will and better judgment. Those are compulsive acts. Obsessive ideas can reach consciousness, but they can't necessarily achieve motor discharge—they cannot make the body obey. So what was the one specific and actual occurrence which, perhaps at the last moment, helped Bob to turn his impulses into actions? In my opinion, we are looking for a precipitating event in which he viewed his actions as the right course . . ."

Birnbaum stopped talking as Faden coughed, softly at first, then harder. Within seconds, he was choking. Blood oozed from his mouth down onto his chin. The picture on the monitor flipped from the *Collins* to Bethesda.

"We just lost our link with Far Side," Birnbaum said.

Bianco's TV monitor went dark.

"I saw cases something like this in the Philippines," Bucar said. "They were diagnosed as suffering from battle fatigue. Ted Guest wants an interview with you, Dee. I'm sure glad I'm not in your shoes on this one."

"What is the 'climate' among the media people?" Bianco asked.

"They're beating the bushes for anything that's newsworthy or spectacular. Let me update you on what's happening with the *Aldrin,* Dee."

"The pictures got to Huntsville, Alabama, with no problems?"

"Yes. Boeing says the structure and the skin appear in good shape. When they get it, they'll go through the cockpit insides. The main engines and the thrusters will go back to Martin Marietta, and IBM will take the computers as soon as they're pulled—and then they'll gut the interior."

"That's a major overhaul," Bianco said.

"I think it's the best thing to do," Bucar said.

"It sounds like you guys are on top of everything." At that moment, Bianco's ear caught the quiet conversation between Christiansen and Gutierrez and she was drawn into it. Bucar, too, stopped talking to listen.

"If I believe in a benevolent father in heaven, a supreme being, who is the force of good in the universe, then can I deny the possibility of an equal and opposite force of evil," Christiansen was saying. "The Bible, the Book of Mormon, and the Doctrine and Covenants, texts which I've relied upon all my life, all deal with this basic idea. The Book of Mormon tells us straight out that, 'Wherefore, all things which are good cometh of God; and that which is evil cometh of the devil.' "

"When all other avenues have been exhausted, we've used psychics and parapsychologists on many impossible cases," Gutierrez said. "They've both verified unpublicized information, and taken the investigation in a direction which we would not have otherwise considered, with some degree of success. But how do you, as a scientist, rationalize your religion with science?"

"No rationalization is necessary. What if this is an opportunity? What if I am to be uniquely privileged with a revelation and a validation of my faith through solid, irrefutable evidence of the existence of God? This is a privilege previously accorded only to the Prophet, Joseph Smith, when the location of the Golden Plates was revealed to him by the angel Moroni." Christiansen shook his head sympathetically. "It's your belief system that might be shattered, not mine. No, the question I'm asking myself is, am I capable of expanding my concept of the identity of the devil to accommodate this new information, or is it beyond my scope of comprehension as a mortal man? Personally, I pray that I have been chosen for a divine reason, just as Joseph Smith was chosen."

Bianco stayed silent. Christiansen was not the first nor the only religious astronaut. During the first lunar landing, more than a half century ago, Buzz Aldrin, too, had tried to comprehend the universe based on his own faith. His feelings about the opportunity of spaceflight had manifested themselves in the act of observing the holy sacrament of communion on the Moon, and he returned to Earth secure in the belief that he had beheld the face of God.

Considering the passion with which Christiansen had spoken, Bianco couldn't help wondering just how eager the astronaut was to behold the face of Satan. He was the commander of FS-7 and the answer to that question might well determine the success of the mission. Was he truly fired with the zeal of a just martyr going into space to confront archetypal evil?

Bianco felt the hairs on her neck stand up at the chilling thought, but she smiled benignly at the two men. On their own, Gutierrez and Christiansen were forming an alliance of sorts. Bianco derived her satisfaction from considering the inherent possibilities in it.

For her private amusement, though, she pondered the irony of the "what if" premise that was at the heart of their discussion. What if Faden was having them all on with a ruse of just such cosmic proportions, and that among all those assembled, only Christiansen was properly oriented and sufficiently "well-versed" to understand it?

PART THREE

Tseng found the odor of urine emanating from Faden's sleep station so overpowering it burned the insides of her nostrils. "This reminds me of an alley I passed by in the heart of New York City, once," she told Cochagne, DeSosa, Manch, and Greer.

"I wonder how Faden will react to his new quarters?" Cochagne mused.

Greer paused in the act of putting Faden's personal belongings into his Personal Preference Kit. "He won't come around for two or three hours yet," she said. "When he does, I want him to see his things. It will lessen the shock, and it may jog his memory."

Cochagne nodded comprehension.

Tseng filed through the five snapshots from Faden's broken instant camera, which they'd sighted during their first look at the astronaut's quarters. The damage to the camera had exposed the remaining unused film inside it.

Two of the snapshots were of Washington and Bisio in happier moments, probably taken early in the mission. Washington wore deep red lipstick in the photo. It was— had been, Tseng corrected herself—like her to bring cosmetics along on a Moon mission. The remaining three pictures were overexposed. The intensity of the light had exceeded the limits of the camera's built-in sensor. She passed the pictures to DeSosa who stood just behind her, trying to look over her shoulder.

Tseng's first look at Faden's sleep station had been through a space helmet. She'd missed the dark gray soot coating the compartment's floor. She watched Manch sweep a sample into a container.

He used a scalpel to scrape at a waxy substance also on the floor. Then he swept the yellowish flakes onto a piece of paper. "This is urine," he said.

"Bodily fluids are an integral part of satanic rituals," Greer said.

Cochagne took detailed pictures of the compartment, and of Manch's work, with the digital still camera.

"That one doctor at Bethesda talked about demonic possession," DeSosa said.

"That would be Rick Masino," Greer said.

"I keep wondering how the situation degenerated into this," DeSosa said. "These were technical people. They were scientists."

"Prior to loss of signal from FS-5, there were symptoms of depression among the crew members," Greer said. "Mike Mobley suffered the most, I think, though he could be rational when he had to be."

DeSosa encompassed the room with a hand gesture saying, "You can't tell me this is the product and the expression of a rational thought process. When I look around here, it gives me the creeps. It's just like what the priests talked about when I was a kid."

"Is Masino a psychiatrist?" Tseng asked.

"He's a PhD psychologist," Greer said. "He did quite a bit of research into the history of mental illness for his doctoral thesis. In the process, he became an expert on paranormal phenomena like spirit possession, telepathy, and psychokinesis. Over the last several years he's published quite a few papers in professional journals citing case studies of schizophrenia among people involved in the occult. You've heard the age-old question, 'Which came first, the chicken or the egg?' That's precisely the

question Masino is asking. Did schizophrenia lead the
patients in the case studies to the occult, or were occult
practices the causal factor for their schizoid behavior?
His search for the answer has aroused suspicion about
his credibility in professional circles."

"He'd have a field day here," Manch said. With prac-
ticed manipulation of the sheet of paper, the physician
shaped a crude funnel and poured the waxy flakes into a
sample container. He sealed it with a rubber stopper and
placed it into a bracket of the caddy that held his instruments, supplies, and empty containers.

"The Catholic Church still practices exorcism," De-
Sosa said.

Lebby and Horo peered in through the doorway.

"We'd like to register a complaint," Horo said.

"We have seven—excuse me, eight—people and one
bathroom and that bathroom is semi-off limits until you
people are through with it," Lebby said.

"I get the message," Manch replied, but his movements were unhurried. He cut a square of bloodied material from a bedsheet, and, using forceps, placed it in
another sample container. He then cut a section of the un-
stained material, placing it into a separate container. "In
this case, where the blood has soaked into fabric, I have
to have an exemplar. A control sample."

"Let me take a look at those computer printouts on the
floor over there," Lebby said, pointing to the wadded papers that had been pushed against the wall.

"Let's not have a lot of foot traffic in here yet,"
Manch said.

Greer gathered the sheets and handed them out to the
astronaut.

Lebby smoothed them and scanned the pages.

Tseng saw handwritten notes and corrections over the
lines of type and symbols.

"This is computer code," Lebby told them. "Bob was

writing a program. Mind if I keep these?" he asked
Manch.

Manch put the sample containers in his caddy and
stood. "Be my guest. I'm finished here," he told Tseng.
"What are you going to do about Takizawa's personal
belongings?"

Tseng looked at the collection of photographs, toiletries, and trinkets spread out on what served as a desk
in the sleep station. Some of the toiletries had Japanese
labels, and there was a picture of Takizawa and his wife.
Among the trinkets, Tseng saw an old round coin with a
hole through the middle. It was a "good luck" piece, she
knew. The coin was worth five yen—"Go-en" in Japanese, a word for good fortune. "Could these things have
been used in the satanic ritual?"

"Things such as hair, or fingernail parings are the preferred items, but I've heard of personal possessions being used." Greer answered.

"This raises yet another knotty dilemma, you realize,"
Manch said. "With or even without Takizawa's knowledge, if Faden performed a satanic ritual with Takizawa's
possessions, then they might be considered evidence in a
murder case. Gutierrez might want these things kept
separate."

"Good point, Paul," Tseng said.

"I'll stay here and finish packing Bob's stuff," De-
Sosa said.

Greer handed him Faden's PPK.

"Have you covered the hygiene station, Jerry?" Tseng
asked.

"Thoroughly," the pilot answered. "I'll see you in
Takizawa's sleep station," he told Manch.

Tseng followed Manch down the corridor and into the
hygiene station. Greer remained in the background with
Horo and Lebby, while Manch entered. He pointed to the
contents of the first aid kit and said, "Anything on the

floor that's not sealed in plastic is not sterile and has to be discarded. I want to take an inventory of what medications are missing."

"I'll separate it, and put what I think should be discarded aside in a trash bag," Horo said. "You can look at it at your leisure."

Manch scraped red-brown stains off of the bathroom mirror with the blade of a fresh scalpel, catching them on a clean piece of white paper. He poured the flakes into a sample container which he then labeled and set aside. "I'm adding normal saline solution to provide a liquid medium for analysis," he explained. He inserted the needle of a hypodermic syringe into the rubber stopper of a bottle and injected air before extracting the clear solution. He then injected the saline into the container and sealed it. "I'll put all the samples in the analyzer tonight, do complete serology panels on the bloods, and then cross-check them with the records of the FS-5 crewmen."

As she watched the physician, Tseng remembered snatches of detail from the FS-5 transmission showing the team dressing Washington's head wound in the cramped compartment.

"If this is menstrual blood, as Paul and I suspect it is, the significance of its use here speaks to what I mentioned earlier about bodily fluids," Greer said. "Women have a special relationship with the Moon. Physiologically, our reproductive cycle imitates the lunar cycle."

"In many cultures, women are considered unclean during menses," Horo said. "They are isolated from the general population for the duration, and must undergo a purification rite afterward."

Greer studied the writing on the mirror. "My questions about this particular act of destruction have to address the perpetrator's state of mind and intent. Unfortunately, it's one of the things we will probably never know. We have this clue staring us in the face, but we don't have any means of interpreting it definitively. For example, was it a woman? In that case, it might be an expression of self-hatred, or deep-seated anger. There were two women on this mission. Which one might have done this? Again, we might have an expression of anger, or a desire for revenge. Another question. Did a male do this? In that case, was it an act directed against the victim, against both women, or against womankind?"

"The bottom line is that Washington and Bisio are both dead," Horo interjected emotionally.

"Yes, of course. I apologize. I didn't mean to get so clinical," Greer said. "However, it would appear that Bisio took part in a ritual, perhaps as the altar?"

"It looks more like she was the ritual sacrifice," Horo said. "What do you mean when you say she was an altar?"

"In satanic rites, the altar can be a woman. There's an element of dark sexuality interwoven with these rituals. The sex is what attracts some people to the occult, in the beginning." Greer paused, then said, "I keep coming back to this phrase, 'Food for the Moon.' It's every-where, and the other obscenities appear to support it. Is this room inconsequential or is it important to the puz-zle? Does the blood have significance as blood? Does it have significance as menstrual blood, or is it an instru-ment of purely incidental, opportunistic destruction? As I look at what's written, I don't get a mental picture of a woman who's angry at herself, but there *is* a violent anger manifested here."

"You're just speculating," Lebby said irritably. "There's no clinical, scientific proof involved in any of this psychi-atric mumbo jumbo about sexuality and perversion. You people can't even straighten Bob Faden out."

Greer's response was a nod of apologetic agreement.

Manch edged himself and Greer out of the small room

and into the corridor. "Three is really a crowd and five is a mob in here," he said. "I want to move on to Takizawa's quarters, so if you'll excuse us . . ." Manch escorted Greer off without waiting for a reply.

As their footsteps retreated along the passageway, Tseng used the washbasin's squirt gun-style water tap to moisten a synthetic wipe impregnated with disinfectant. A few broad wiping strokes cleaned the brown stains from the mirror and imparted a clean, medicinal odor to the room. "Orders be damned, it's not going to be possible to stay in here without concessions to sanitation and comfort," she told Horo and Lebby.

"That has the ring of a command decision," Lebby said. "Mission Control will think we're declaring mutiny."

"You're irritable tonight, Pops," Horo said.

"You're right, and I don't really know why. I've been doing a lot of thinking about where I'm going from here on, however. I love the space program, but my training schedule for these missions has been pretty tough on my wife all these years. I don't know that I want another mission."

"I remember the break up of FS-1," Horo said. "I felt a real sense of loss—like my whole career was floundering. Things were pretty directionless until the FS-6 assignment. I've been trying not to think too far ahead this time."

"Sage advice," Lebby said.

"Well, I intend to use the next eight hours to the best advantage," Horo said to Tseng, as Lebby wandered slowly away. "Where are you sleeping?"

"In the CDR quarters."

Horo made a wry face. "Sweet dreams, then."

"I'm not sleepy yet. I'll follow Manch and Greer around for a while, I guess."

"I've changed my mind. I'll tag along with you," Horo said.

Tseng and Horo met Manch and Greer in the doorway of Takizawa's sleep station.

"I take it you're through in there already," Tseng said. "Did you find anything?"

"Not a thing that can help me," Manch said.

Tseng looked to Greer for confirmation, but the psychiatrist avoided eye contact with her.

"Cochagne's still in there with the camera," Greer said, brushing hastily past.

Tseng wondered if the psychiatrist was chafing over Lebby's comments.

"We're going to see if there's anything in Washington's or Bisio's rooms," Manch said. "Takizawa's things can be removed."

"I'd like to have a quick look around," Tseng said to Horo.

"I'll see you in Washington's room," Horo told her. Tseng's glance inside Takizawa's sleeping quarters took in the characteristics of the room. The Japanese mission specialist's private space emphasized the Asian simplicity designed into the base's personnel quarters by the Shimizu habitat experts. In this case, the feeling was heightened by the framed Ukiyo-e print which Takizawa had chosen to hang above his bed; a scene of a seventeenth century Edo courtesan entertaining a samurai. His cultural past and the future met on a clothing storage shelf: a neatly folded man's gray spun silk kimono in a subdued, monochrome bamboo leaf print, was next to changes of NASA uniform clothing. The only obvious damage to the room was on one wall where graffiti was covered up with lines of black paint. Looking at it, she suddenly felt like an intruder, and her spine tingled with the feeling of being watched, as though any second, Takizawa might return and catch her snooping.

She'd found Shinobu Takizawa bright, capable, and personable on the rare occasions when he'd allowed himself to relax and socialize with his fellow astronauts. There was an invisible barrier that had kept him from becoming completely integrated at NASA, however. In the first place, becoming an astronaut had not been a career choice for Takizawa. It was the job his company had given him.

Tseng was sympathetic to the root of his dilemma. In Japan, loyalty to the company was everything. Loyalty to the group within the company meant survival. That was Takizawa's frame of reference. He had reconciled himself to the way of life of a company employee, but unbeknownst to him, he was a pawn in the grand strategy of the giant entity that was the Shimizu Corporation.

He'd displayed the nervousness of a person under stress, and that was because he'd felt pressured to be a good Shimizu employee and a good astronaut, and these goals were not compatible. He could not reconcile himself to the philosophy that, as far as working in Houston was concerned, doing the best job for the company required forgetting about the company.

Yamato damashii: the Japanese spirit.

Isshokenmei: the concept of committing the whole heart and soul to achieving a goal, as if one's life depended on it. Shinobu Takizawa had done his best to personify both traits. His only shortcoming, in the eyes of his superiors at NASA, was that he'd tried too hard to do the right thing.

The right thing was a subjective judgment call. The right thing in whose eyes? Was he part of the Shimizu team, or part of the FS-5 team? If he identified with the astronauts, it was seen as an act of disloyalty to the company in the eyes of his corporate superiors. The final phase of training for his mission was all-consuming. Contact with the company was virtually cut off. The result for Takizawa was a feeling of complete isolation, outwardly discernible to everyone who came in contact with him.

Tseng's empathy with what she perceived as a sur- mountable cultural barrier had motivated her to intercede and mediate on Takizawa's behalf many times. Mike Mobley had tried to come to an understanding with him in the beginning, but there had been a stubborn inflexi- bility on both sides.

She crossed to the utility shelves, picked up the ki- mono, unfolded it, and shook it out in order to admire the garment. She heard the crackle of static electricity as it fell out. It was not the kimono she'd seen Takizawa wear- ing in the recorded footage of the FS-5 crewmen, but it was the only one on the shelf. She looked for the *obi,* or waistband, and saw it folded neatly behind where the ki- mono had been. The obi was of a stiff, darker gray silk that harmonized with the kimono in a tasteful, under- stated, and definitely conservative way.

Cochagne shot two more frames of the defaced wall, then approached her. "I'll come back later and pack up Takizawa's things," he said. He touched her arm and she saw the bright flash, felt the sting, and heard the crackle of the spark of static electricity that arced between them.

Cochagne pulled his hand back and shook it to relieve the sting.

Tseng laughed and refolded the kimono. She replaced it on the shelf and took a last look around the room. The bed was neatly made, the room uncluttered and fastidi- ous, except for the dead flies that were everywhere. It was a tidiness that was uniquely Japanese, the result of living in a crowded society where privacy was at a pre- mium. From her trips to Japan, and from conversations with Takizawa and Yoshio Adachi, she knew that Far Side Base represented luxury living and a chance for quiet contemplation for the Japanese astronauts.

Tseng and Cochagne found the others still in Washington's room, helping DeSosa put the dead astronaut's toiletries into her kit.

Washington's quarters were the antithesis of Takizawa's, Tseng noted. Outer clothing and lingerie lay strewn carelessly about. Some items were clean and had been pulled from the shelves and dumped on the floor and the bed. Other articles showed evidence of constant wear. A scent of stale perfume, mixed with the odor of perspiration, emanated from the dirty clothes. Washington's book reader, a handheld paperback novel-sized computer screen, was on the table. The reader showed that she'd been engrossed in a trashy romance novel.

Toiletries and cosmetics had been unceremoniously dumped out on top of the table. Horo held up a tube of lipstick in an expensively sculptured gold case. Her eyes looked moist, as though she was trying to keep from crying. She pulled the cap off the tube and twisted the lipstick up. It showed much use. It was the deep shade of red Washington had worn in the snapshot taken with Bisio. "Isn't this just like Louise?" She glanced at the label on the bottom of the tube. "This color is called 'Reentry Red.' "

"Maybe you want to keep it?" DeSosa asked gently.

Horo answered by putting the lipstick in the cosmetic bag. "I can't," she said.

"Think about it," Tseng said.

"Okay," Horo responded.

Cochagne shot the room from different angles. Then, they moved on as a group.

In Bisio's room, Manch was the first to spot a half-empty box of tampons among the personal items strewn about. A stack of colored marking pens and a tablet of drawing paper were on the table. With a sense of dismay, Tseng surveyed and photographed the satanic graffiti written on the walls with the marking pens. The contrast between it and the pictures of Bisio with her husband and her children was bizarre.

"I'm getting tired, and I'm likely to start making mistakes," Manch said. "I'll have another go at this tomorrow."

"I'll take the first watch," Greer said.

Tseng stepped through the privacy curtain and surveyed the CDR sleep station in the soft light from the airline-style light fixtures that were recessed into the wall and ceiling panels. She turned on the reading light that was mounted over the built-in sleeping pallet for added illumination.

She gathered up the clothing scattered around the room, sweeping up and disposing of dead flies as she went along. She spotted the bar from the electromagnetic weight machine sticking out from under a pile of clothing against the back wall and made a mental note to inform Manch of its presence. It had probably been put here for safekeeping after Washington's accident, she concluded.

When she came to the miniature chessboard, she hesitated, then sat down at the table to study the layout. Except for leaving carbon dust on two of the light-colored pawns in their effort to fingerprint and photograph the pieces, Manch and Cochagne had not disturbed the game.

Not a chess player, herself, she could not evaluate the positions of the various pieces, and could not judge the level of play. Was it important? Again, Gutierrez's warning loomed large in her mind. Why had the engineer chosen an antique version of the game, with actual pieces, rather than a modern electronic game? Which pieces had belonged to Drzymkowski, and with whom had he played this game?

The chess game brought Earth to mind for the first time in hours. It was so far away, and Earth priorities, conflicts, emotions, and relationships seemed so unreal and illusory to a lunar inhabitant. This mission was the ultimate "getting away from it all" trip, Tseng reflected.

On a piece of paper, she drew a crude representation of the positions of the chess pieces, then scooped them up and folded the board. She put the game back in its carrying case and placed it, and Drzymkowski's toiletries and clothing, into the astronaut's PPK bag. She left the bag against the wall next to the privacy curtain. Tomorrow, all the personal belongings of the FS-5 crewmen would be stowed in the *Collins*.

Tseng could not allow herself to be intimidated by the compartment. It was just a room where they had found a dead body, and that body was no longer there.

Fewer noises were coming from the passageway. The other crewmen, too, were settling in for the sleep period. Because the air still felt hot, Tseng put only one of the light blankets down on the pallet. She toggled the light switches which automatically activated the room's emergency marker lights. They glowed a dim, unobtrusive reddish orange and provided just enough illumination to prevent disorientation for an astronaut suddenly awakened by the threat of danger.

Tseng stretched out on the bed, her head pillowed on her arms.

She was tired, but her mind was still too active for sleep.

For the last few hours, she had tried to put off a letdown feeling from thoughts similar to the ones Cochagne and Lebby had expressed. She was not naturally given to depression and negative thoughts. Just the opposite. Her optimism and enthusiasm at being a part of the Far Side project had contributed to her present position as commander. To think of Far Side Base as a depressing place was ridiculous, but earlier, prior to the

teleconference, she had ascended from the First Level in
just that frame of mind.

((

It was six forty-five AM Houston time. Bedtime. Bianco
was more than ready for bed. Like everyone else in Mission Control, her body clock was in sync with the FS-6
mission clock. They'd lost touch with outside reality. Far
Side Base was their link to the real world.

The FS-6 astronauts were being allowed an eight-hour
rest period after a nineteen-hour workday. Bianco hoped
that within that time, she would be able to rest, but that
seemed optimistic. This was the only chance she had to
go home for a shower and to pack a suitcase with fresh
clothes, so she had to jump at it.

She slid behind the wheel of her car and inserted the
key into the ignition. Then she heard Gutierrez call her
name. She turned and saw the police detective hurrying
toward her carrying a large brown envelope.

"I have a few questions, Dee," Gutierrez said when he
caught up. "I want to thank you, again. The FS-5 video
was very helpful. I had the rare opportunity of seeing the
victims alive, before the murders. When we investigate a
homicide, unless a celebrity is involved, we don't know
the victim—or victims. I really feel like I know these
people. Maybe that's why I've become so involved with
this case."

Bianco managed a smile in response.

"Am I catching you at a bad time?"

"I was just going home to catch a few hours' sleep and
a shower, but this is important," she said. "I appreciate
the time you're putting in. Please, continue."

"Okay, I'll make this as brief as possible, but why
don't we talk in the car."

Bianco nodded gratefully.

Gutierrez sprinted around the back of the vehicle to get in on the passenger side.

Bianco relaxed into her seat and took a deep breath. She hoped she wouldn't nod off while the detective talked.

"Would you classify Frank Drzymkowski as an aggressive man?"

"Not overly so," Bianco said. "He didn't have to be. He was the boss of a construction crew, so he was a take-charge guy. Stromeyer, Sweet, and Adachi might be more helpful on that score than I can be."

"I'll talk to them, too, but, going on what we have, I want to run a theory by you," Gutierrez said. Drzymkowski's footprints are all around the rover. There was a scuffle between him and at least one other person. At some point, Mobley, the commander, took up residence down on Level One. Drzymkowski's things and his body were in the commander's quarters. In that piece of footage covering Washington's accident, I saw him put his hand over the lens, in effect, overriding Mobley's authority . . . a very aggressive, controlling move."

All Bianco could do was nod.

"Cochagne's pictures show a number of deep foot impressions made by Drzymkowski in the soil next to the overturned rover which suggests he had added weight at that point . . . which leads me to believe that Drzymkowski overturned the rover to prevent it from being taken somewhere. Presumably to the *Aldrin*. The evidence points to a dispute over control of the crew and maybe over command."

"A mutiny by a NASA crew," Bianco said. "It's unbelievable."

"Yes. This is just a hunch, but I think Drzymkowski could have been trying to prevent someone from escaping Far Side.

"I have one more minor question . . . Mobley took the

still photos for FS-5, but Takizawa shot the video. Commander Tseng is in charge of the video camera for FS-6 and Jerry Cochagne has the still camera. How do you determine who does what?"

"It's just a question of who can do the job best. Mobley had more experience as a still photographer. I've seen his personal portfolio. He was very good." Bianco couldn't suppress a yawn.

Gutierrez smiled. "I get the message. I'm outta here."

"You should take the opportunity to get some sleep yourself."

Gutierrez shook his head and held up the envelope in his hand. "I can't do that yet. These are the copies of the pictures that are being sent to the FBI crime lab. I have a good working relationship with the Houston Medical Examiner, and I want her to look at Drzymkowski's head wound and give me an opinion. Also, I have to be at the station before eight in order to get time on the computer that's programmed for fingerprint matching."

Bianco nodded wearily, wishing she had Gutierrez' youthful energy.

And wishing his male pheromones weren't driving her female endorphins so crazy in the confined space. She closed her eyes and rested her forehead on the steering wheel.

"Dee, can you make it home okay?"

Startled by his change in tone, she turned her head to meet his gaze. "I don't have very far to go."

"You could let me drive you home. I could drop you off on my way in."

Bianco answered with a negative shake of her head. She softened the rejection by saying, "If something happens, and they call me, I'll have to get back right away."

"Then you'll call me at the station," Gutierrez said.

She didn't move when he reached to take her car keys

from the ignition. He placed them in the palm of her hand, then gently squeezed her fingers around them.

She couldn't move when his fingertips brushed her cheek as he tucked some stray hair behind her ear.

"Come on. You're in no shape to drive," he said.

☾

It was a bizarre dream, but Tseng had the illusion that she was escaping from it by swimming up through an iridescent blue-green pool of thick, jellied water. She was naked. There was an oppressive sensation of drag and weight on her body, as though she wore several layers of clothing. The effort needed to propel herself through the thick medium drained her. She felt her energy reserves nearly exhausted. She fought suffocation. She longed to breathe deeply, but she dared not draw any of the viscous fluid into her mouth and nose. Only the knowledge of slowly returning consciousness and the anticipation of breaking to the surface of the pool from the deep, deep sleep she was in gave her the will to struggle against the forces threatening to drown her.

In the distance, she saw a figure swimming toward her. She recognized Louise Washington. The dead astronaut was also naked, her face garishly made up with cosmetics, her lips painted a deep red.

Though she could not hear any sound except her own shallow breaths, Tseng saw Washington scream in terror at the swarm of black flies crawling on her face. When the astronaut opened her mouth to scream, the flies darted inside. The bloody "O" of Washington's lips rimmed the cavernous cave of her mouth, and the inside swarmed with flies. The sight was overwhelming. Repulsive . . .

Tseng awoke to a cold, dank darkness. She heard a soft bump against the wall outside the cubicle and she strained her ears to identify the sound. A few moments passed in silence, then she heard the bumping again, but from farther away this time. She could not discern the direction of the sound.

Shadows resolved themselves into objects in the room. She became aware, not of the presence of cold, but of the total absence of heat. She sank downward, through the blue-green gel again. It was hard to breathe. Hard to stay conscious. Was she passing out, or falling asleep . . . or dying? Fear surged through her at the notion of dying.

The dark shadow of a man appeared in the doorway. Tseng sat up.

"Are you okay, China?" Cochagne whispered. "I heard noises outside my room, and when I got up to investigate in the passageway, I heard you talking in your sleep. You weren't saying anything intelligible, but it sounded like you were in trouble."

"I was having a bad dream," Tseng said. She pulled her sleep-tousled hair back from her face. She yawned, arching her body into a stretch that extended her arms upward before she bent them at the elbows and laced her hands behind her head.

Cochagne pulled the privacy curtain closed behind him and approached her. He moved quietly and with a bold self-assurance that startled and amazed her.

She relaxed her body by lying back and supporting her weight on an elbow while she propped her head up with one hand. Her curiosity was piqued as to what Cochagne wanted.

He came close and, for a brief moment, he stood next to her bed pallet looking down at her with a tender, concerned expression, then he leaned over and grasped her free hand in his. The heat of his skin was like a firebrand.

"You're as cold as ice," he said worriedly, and without releasing her hand, he sat down on the edge of her bed.

The musky, male scent of him filled her nostrils. He

rubbed his hands over her arms and her thighs, then moved onto the pallet and lay down next to her. The comforting warmth that flowed into her from his body was an aphrodisiac, and she shivered with pleasure.

She rolled back from him, trying to see his face in the dim light. "What are you doing here?" she whispered, breathless with the heady excitement of awakening sexual desire.

"I can't sleep," he said. "I was so keyed up after we talked down on Level One . . . and, all through that session with Bethesda, I couldn't concentrate. It's important to me that you understand how I feel."

He reached toward her and lightly touched her cheek.

Then he cupped her chin and lifted it toward his face. His touch was firm, but gentle. "This is not a spur of the moment thing with me. Up to now, I've held back because I wasn't sure how to approach you." He fell silent but held her spellbound with his gaze. Suddenly, his desire seemed to overwhelm him like an explosion of fire, and he gathered her tightly to him covering her mouth with his.

She was enveloped in his kiss. She yielded to the pressure of his sensual lips and abandoned herself to his hunger for her.

She did not know how long they remained locked together, but he broke the spell by gently pulling away to look into her eyes. When he leaned toward her, again seeking her lips, she pulled away from him. "Jerry, don't! Not now," she said. Her voice was husky, and the strong tone wavered, betraying the desire, the conflict, the uncertainty, and the turmoil within her. It aroused and frightened her that she'd succumbed to him; that his effect on her was suddenly so . . .

. . . Hypnotic. It had all happened so fast. It left her gasping for breath. Why now? Why like this? She

wanted time to know his body, but he was in the throes of
a sexual desire that he made no effort to control.

She was intoxicated from her own arousal.

"I want you," Cochagne whispered. He pulled her
T-shirt up to bare her breasts, then slid down on her body
and took them in his hands and massaged and sucked
them. His tongue slowly circled her nipples.

Though she knew she should, she did not want to pull
away. *I want to believe in you,* she cried inwardly. He reacted to her unspoken encouragement by pressing himself against her and parted her legs with his thigh. She
could feel his erection against her leg, and it inflamed her
even more. She grasped the folds of his T-shirt and pulled
it off over his head.

He put his broad, bare chest against her, and she felt as
though she would burn up from the sensation of his skin
against hers.

She feared him . . . and wanted him. She reached inside his shorts and grasped him. He groaned with pleasure and thrust his hips harder against her pelvis. His hot
mouth found her neck and he sucked and kissed her skin,
moving downward and across to her shoulder.

He pulled her shorts off and cupped his hand between
her legs, exploring her sex. Despite his sexual heat, his
fingers probed and explored her delicately. Her body responded. The thick and slippery wetness between her
legs seemed to drive him over the edge.

He withdrew his hand and moved up on her until the
tip of his penis pressed against the opening of her vagina.
He remained poised there and raised his head to look into
her eyes.

"Jerry, there's no going back from this," she whispered.

"I know that. It's what I want. You want it, too, I know
you do, but tell me you want it. Tell me you want me."

She closed her eyes. "Oh, God, Jerry . . ." she
breathed. He shook her to make her look at him again.

"Say you want me! Say it," he growled savagely.

She could not speak, as a wave of panic washed over her. It was frightening, delicious. He wanted what she always withheld—her complete surrender. He demanded it.

"Yes, I want you," she said, feeling at once over-whelmed with passion, and released from the tension of trying to resist the desire that raged within her.

He thrust into her, and her intake of breath was made audible by the force of his penetration. She felt herself opened as if for the first time. The sound stirred his desire, and he groaned in ecstasy and plunged himself into her again and again. He grasped the sides of the pallet for support to compensate for the lighter gravity.

"You're mine now," he said.

Cochagne maintained his grip on the edge of the bed to hold them down. Tseng felt his muscles flex with the effort. Feeling his strength increased her pleasure. She wrapped her legs around his buttocks and thighs and held him tightly inside her, while, at the same time, pulling him deeper into her. He was hers, as much as she was his, and she exhilarated and triumphed in taking him. She squeezed her legs forcing his hard shaft deeper within her. It drove him to a heightened frenzy.

To her surprise, he suddenly pulled out of her. He moved down her body and kissed her stomach and her groin. Then, she felt his mouth on the lips of her vagina. He parted them with his tongue and sucked gently on her clitoris.

She felt the tension of her orgasm building and knew that Cochagne sensed her change of rhythm, because he continued his sensual kiss until her climax rushed in upon her like a tidal wave. At the peak of the ecstasy, a sharp electric-erotic current was carried outward through every nerve fiber, and upward in a mind-numbing deluge of pleasure. She felt her entire body release the pent-up

tension and relax, and in the relaxation she was transported to an even higher level of sexual desire. The
anticipation of feeling him penetrate her again caused
her to become the aggressor.

She grasped his shoulders and guided him up until she
felt his hard penis touch her then she raised her pelvis to
take him inside of her again.

He thrust into her again and again until, by the pace
of his thrusts, she knew he'd brought on his own climax.

She heard him gasp and felt him shudder. He buried
his face in her hair. His cries of pleasure were muffled as
his body convulsed in powerful surges and he emptied
the life-creating essence, that he'd built up inside of him,
into her.

The effect of his coming was like the injection of a
powerful liquid pleasure drug in Tseng's veins. Again,
she felt the rush of an orgasm, this one more intense than
the first. The electric pleasure sensation coursed through
her in pulsations of current that exploded in her consciousness rendering her completely exhausted.

She did not know how long they had lain together, still
joined, before she dozed off; but she awoke to find
Cochagne draped across her, his face buried in the crook
of her neck. The sensation of his weight on her added to
her feeling of satisfaction. She listened, but there were
no sounds from outside the sleep cubicle. None of the
other crew members had stirred.

"I'm putting in for a design modification on these
beds," Cochagne said lazily. "We need handholds and
maybe a bar at the bottom that I can hook my feet under."

Tseng was certain she hadn't moved. Cochagne had
sensed that she was awake and had, himself, awakened.

She turned her head and kissed his ear, then she looked
at her watch. Mission Control would be calling to wake

them up in less than an hour. "You'd better go," she whispered.

She felt him stiffen.

"Why?"

"Because, it doesn't look right to have anyone see you leaving here. I'm still in command of this mission, Jerry."

"So? This night didn't change that. Not in my mind, anyway."

"It's bad for morale."

"Whose morale are you concerned with? What about my morale? You want me to sneak out of here like we've done something wrong. That doesn't sit well with me!"

"Don't put it in those terms. I seem to recall that you told me you understood about protocol."

He knitted his brows in anger, then said, "Never mind," and rolled off of her. He snatched his T-shirt and shorts from the bed and slipped them on. "Well, this sure was fun, babe. Maybe we'll do it again sometime, if the schedule permits . . . see you later," he finished, saluting cavalierly. He ducked around the privacy curtain and she listened to his retreating footsteps. She heard him enter his sleep station, then there was silence.

The room felt empty and cold without him. Opening herself to him meant giving him the power to hurt her deeply, and he'd done it. She was angry with herself, because she felt at fault for not knowing how to tread the middle ground between making him feel like a one-night stand and maintaining military discipline.

I want you. You're mine now. The two statements echoed in her mind. There was a danger in taking sentiments expressed in the heat of passion at face value, she reflected.

The old insecurities and habits were resurfacing, but she'd never before felt so burdened by that psychological baggage. Was there a way to apologize? To start over?

If there was one thing that was certain, it was that her relationship with Cochagne would never be the same. There was, truly, no going back from this night.

There was also no hope of getting back to sleep, Tseng admitted to herself. She was awake and she might as well use the time to finish the work on Level One. She slipped out of bed, dressed in her shorts and T-shirt, and strode silently out into the passageway. Just as she reached the companionway, she heard a loud thump against a wall in the direction of Faden's quarters. Curiosity more than alarm motivated her to go back and investigate. It would be to her advantage if Paul Manch, too, was up early to finish his work.

When Tseng drew aside the sleep station's privacy curtain, Greer looked up and paused in the act of loading the hypo-gun. Faden was in a restless, drugged sleep. He still wore his makeshift straitjacket. However Manch and Greer had exchanged his hospital gown for his FS-5 astronaut fatigues.

Greer put a finger to her lips and gave Tseng a negative head shake.

Tseng nodded understanding and remained silent. Greer had evidently not awakened Manch to take his turn at monitoring Faden during the night. This was not the time to ask why, but as Tseng watched, the answer became clear to her.

Faden was having conversations with himself in his sleep in different voices. "Are you a good boy?" he asked himself. "Yes, you're a good boy," he answered.

An argumentative, gravelly Faden voice, which Tseng remembered hearing before, said, "I'm not the only one bothering him! There are six others just as bad as I am!"

"They're dead," Faden shouted at himself angrily in a high-pitched tone that had a feminine quality.

"I'm always dead," a third Faden voice pouted.

"Everybody is coming here . . ." yet another voice interjected, but it was cut off by the gravelly voice, which shouted, "I'm not going to do that! Stop bothering me!"

Tseng heard the simultaneous giggling and twittering of all the voices in response.

Greer put the barrel of the hypo-gun to Faden's arm and pulled the trigger. Faden mumbled something. Then his body relaxed.

"That was the last of the Seconal," Greer whispered.

"What about the Thorazine?"

"All gone. All we have left to give him is diazepam. Fortunately, we have a good supply of it."

"Will it work?"

Greer shrugged. "Diazepam is Valium. All we can do is wait and see if we can control him with it."

Tseng moved silently down the companionway and into the pocket of coldness that was a characteristic of Level One. It was theoretically impossible for the upper three levels of the base to have achieved a thermal equilibrium while the lowest level remained separate and inexplicably cold. Scientific theory could not account for the draft that now chilled her. Gooseflesh rose on her bare legs and arms, but a curious apathy stopped her from returning to her quarters for her fatigue jacket and trousers before proceeding.

There was carbon dust at the spot where the hammer had been. After fingerprinting the aluminum strut, on Gutierrez's instructions, Manch and Cochagne had wrapped it, and the hammer, in paper before removing them. The two items of evidence were stowed on Level Four for transport to the *Collins* along with the FS-5 Personal Preference Kits.

She found Mobley's bag and placed the family picture inside. She checked under the cushions for small items, but there was nothing hidden beneath the makeshift bed.

Where were his toiletries? Toothpaste, toothbrush, soap, maybe a razor—the live footage showed the commander with a beard, but beards on space missions were an afterthought for military personnel—and fingernail clippers. These things were the basics. Tseng eyed the debris scattered around the room. There was so much paper amidst the clutter that a cursory inspection was not sufficient to identify solid items.

Her concentration was broken by the creaking and groaning of the base structure's joints, seams, and flooring above her, as though someone was walking on Level Two. She jogged up the companionway to see who was awake. A look into the wardroom and up the passageway between the sleep stations confirmed that no one was about. She returned to Level One, baffled, until it occurred to her that the sounds were probably being made by the structure contracting because of the steady drop in the outside temperature as they moved into the lunar night phase.

Get organized, she reprimanded herself. The paper debris had to be examined and cleared away.

It was important to gather the printed photographs first, she decided. Most were of the lunar landscape, or of the FS-5 astronauts during EVAs, scanned and printed by the computer. They were proof of Lebby's suspicions that the main computer's memory had been deliberately wiped clean of stored picture files.

Some of the photos were ripped up, and Tseng gathered the pieces and spent a few moments fitting them together like jigsaw puzzle pieces. Problems with the camera had resulted in ghostly background shadows resembling double exposures, and in a light peppering of tiny black-and-white spots in the discarded prints.

She partially completed several black and whites of crew members at work inside the base and posed "glamour shots" of Louise Washington, her hair combed to hang provocatively over one eye, and it struck her that, although all the pictures were printed on the computer's photographic stock, the portraits had a different quality than the mission photos. In the shots of Washington, her lips were pouty and dark—she'd put on her lipstick for the pose—the highlights on her hair and the contrast which emphasized her classic cheekbones were a result of the special lighting effects that were a hallmark of early twentieth century glamour photography. The focus was sharp, but Washington's face had a youthful, sensual softness that indicated the use of a diffusion technique as well. Either a different camera had been used, or, more likely, a lens other than the all-purpose 50mm lens, or the wide-angle 28mm lens the astronauts used to shoot interiors and Moonscapes for documentary purposes.

All of the photos spread out in front of her were more than archival hard copies of digital still camera images. They were art, and classic photography was an especially good pastime for someone expecting to spend two months at a lunar base. It was common knowledge that Mike Mobley had such a hobby, and that the equipment in his home darkroom rivaled that of the best professional film processing labs. There would be a problem with developing and printing standard rolls of film at Far Side, however, and Mobley had taken that into consideration. Photographic chemicals for developing, stopping, fixing, and printing, formulated for use on Earth, in an atmosphere of twenty percent oxygen mixed with eighty percent inert gases at fourteen point seven psi atmospheric pressure, might be unstable or dangerously toxic, even volatile, at Far Side's seven and a half psi oxygen-rich atmosphere. The electronic digital still camera had been developed by NASA to facilitate the interaction and photographic information exchange between astronauts in space and Ground Teams, and to eliminate the hazard and risk of mistakes that could result in injury or ruined pictures due to astronaut error during film processing. Not everyone with the responsibility of mission photography had Mike Mobley's talent, skill, and experience with film.

The pictures of Washington were proof that the person behind that lens was experienced in a style of portraiture that was usually reserved for a fine grain black and white film. Coincidentally, the monochrome image sensor of the digital electronic still camera was capable of very high resolution. That made it ideal for capturing the details of the lunar landscape and, apparently, the human face. Armed with nothing more than a portrait lens, Mobley could easily have used only the mission camera to pursue his hobby, secure and happy in the knowledge that his supply of digital "film" would be unlimited.

The data blocks at the bottom of all the photos proved that they spanned the entire mission up to approximately thirty hours prior to loss of signal with Houston, but, as far as she could see, they shed no light on the disaster at Far Side. The large gaps of time between them led her to theorize that Mobley had taken these prints to his private "lair" in order to analyze his mistakes and to troubleshoot the problem with the digital still camera. As to the reason why some of them were torn up, there were any number of possible scenarios under the circumstances. It was also entirely possible that Mobley had done it in a fit of artistic pique.

Tseng laid the reconstructed photos aside and sorted through all the piles of debris in the room. She found Mobley's toiletries in a shaving kit and more computer printouts. She wanted to find the camera's hard drive, which might still contain the stored digital images for these pictures and for any taken afterward.

Tseng pondered the task of going through the mass of cartons and containers stored on the level in search of the hard drive. She'd come to Level One because she was

agitated and unable to sleep, but that nervous energy was
disappearing, and leaving behind exhaustion and fatigue.
She had a full day's schedule ahead of her, and she was
sleepy. She wandered over to the worktable and sat down
to rest. Unable to keep her eyes open, she folded her arms
on the table and put her head down on top of them.
Blackness closed in on her mind, and with it came a
numbness caused by cold and darkness. This was more
than a drafty room, she mused, it was a pocket of nega-
tivity, where the cold drained her energy as it drained a
battery. Would it be possible to freeze to death here, she
wondered dully?

Though she struggled against the urge to sleep, she
was slipping into a conscious dream state wherein patterns of light exploded in the darkness behind her closed
eyelids and became like the facets of a cut gem. Images
were reflected in the facets which together formed many
composite beings—nightmarish creatures with male and
female sex organs sprawled obscenely and desiccated female breasts covered with coarse hair. Glistening, gelatinous clots of blood oozed from the vaginas and there was
dried feces crusted on their buttocks. The skins were
covered in warts, boils, and infected running sores in
which maggots crawled. Fat, bloated, swollen fingers
and arms and legs transformed themselves into skeletal
members with curved yellow fingernails and toenails.
The beings had faces, but their features were askew.
Some had noses smashed and eyeballs dangling from the
sockets, and cheeks and foreheads gashed open to reveal
parts of the skulls underneath. They were faces that reg-
istered the shock, the terror, and the rage of violent death.
They were faces of a myriad of dead people fighting
to . . . exist? The facets became a kaleidoscope of images seething and boiling up to the surface only to be
overwhelmed and submerged by the sheer masses of
the dead.

Her mind rebelled against the horrors and escaped from the nightmare into the numbness of the darkness and the cold. The effort to awaken made her conscious of an irritating tickle on her forearm. Her skin crawled involuntarily, then the tickling went away. In a moment it returned. Annoyed, she forced open her eyes and saw two flies walking the length of her forearm. She stared in disbelief, and the surprise pumped a small shot of adrenaline into her system. However, the stimulation was only fleeting. An instant later, her metabolism slowed, and her mood plunged as though from the effect of a strong sedative. It felt like something in the room or in the air had instantaneously counteracted the burst of energy.

She brushed at the flies, and they flew off sluggishly. She tried to track them with her eyes, but they disappeared into the shadows where, to her dull surprise, something—a light mist? a vapor plume?—appeared to flutter and undulate in the air current of the ventilation system.

A primal reaction to "the unknown" that had been hovering in the background of her sleepy consciousness burst to the fore, shocking her fully awake. She struggled to her feet and looked hard at the air duct, but there was nothing to be seen now.

Fatigue had affected her vision for a few moments, she concluded. Still, she was bothered by the horrendous nightmare, and by an uneasy feeling about remaining on Level One. The possibility that she might again succumb to the creeping malaise of cold and dampness, and experience more horrors in her dreams, made her yield quickly to the urge to return to Level Two.

☾

In Mission Control, Bianco watched the screen. The techs acquired the live video picture from Far Side Base. On the monitor, Tseng and Horo were at the communications console. Lebby was in the background, at the computer. Bianco noticed that Gutierrez, too, watched the Far Side astronauts and that he also listened with apparent fascination to their casual cross talk, which was coming from the different areas of the base over the COMM.

"Good morning, Far Side," Christiansen said.

Tseng responded with a smile which looked forced, and it disturbed Bianco that her "Good morning, Houston," was perfunctory.

"Are you having any problems you'd like to report?" Christiansen asked.

The concern in the CAPCOM's voice sounded genuine to Bianco. It validated her own reaction.

"Just one," Tseng replied. "Unfortunately, our fly problem has returned."

There were groans from the techs and from the complement of astronauts in the room.

"I saw two down on Level One this morning, and they've proliferated throughout the dome," Tseng continued. "I have no idea how that happened. I thought we had that problem licked, but there it is, so if you have any suggestions, we'd appreciate the input."

"We'll go back to work on it," Christiansen said with a frustrated shake of his head.

"The samples from the writing in the hygiene station are menstrual blood," Manch said. The physician was not on camera, but was speaking on the COMM from the lab he had set up on Level One. "I was able to ID them as Ann Bisio's. The sample from the sheets turned out to be Mobley's blood, however."

The reaction in Mission Control to the news about Mobley was a moody silence.

"We received the latest batch of Jerry's pictures and

we're looking at them," Christiansen said. "Thanks for getting them off to us right away. Compliments of our local expert, we have information about the fingerprints. On the shaft of the hammer there was a good print from Mobley's thumb over Drzymkowski's prints. The implication is that Mike may have been Frank's killer. . . ."

Bianco sneaked a glance at James Morris. The administrator's frown had deepened at the reference to their "local expert," and this revelation deepened it further. For the last hour, Morris had occupied a chair, outside of the group clustered near Christiansen's console, but within earshot. Earlier, on returning to Mission Control, Bianco was informed that the FBI agents, who'd accompanied Morris earlier, had left during the late morning. Just minutes ago, Morris had confessed to her privately that they would shortly be raiding Faden's house for "evidence." Though Morris didn't say so, Bianco concluded that the FBI was in search of something that would support the NASA administrator's theory that Faden was solely responsible for the murders and the disaster at Far Side.

Bianco's instincts told her that the secrecy about the raid was an act of retaliation against her for taking the initiative in bringing Gutierrez in. Morris considered her a threat because of Gutierrez, and a coincidence of bad timing was compounding the problem. Bianco now regretted having spent so much time at home, because the police detective, arriving back in Mission Control ahead of her and carrying the fingerprint results, had unavoidably butted heads with the NASA administrator.

Morris was not keeping his displeasure about the extent of the police detective's input into the investigation at Far Side a secret, but Bianco did not care. Gutierrez was producing results for her.

"What else did he find?" Tseng asked, her voice on the COMM now subdued by emotion.

"On the camera, we have Mike Mobley's fingerprints around the lens hood and on the focusing and aperture rings, but there was a good thumbprint from Drzymkowski on the eyepiece of the viewfinder," Christiansen said. "As for the chess set fingerprints, they are Bisio's. Also, the lieutenant has it on 'good authority' that, as a murder weapon, the hammer is definitely a candidate, in Drzymkowski's case. This same authority is of the opinion that Bisio's abdominal stab wound was very likely not postmortem, and—and this is no real surprise—the aluminum strut has Bisio's and Drzymkowski's prints on it."

"All of this information certainly validates some of our original theories, while blowing others right out of the water," Tseng said.

"Based on the photos, those are the conclusions. Paul, what's the error factor on the blood sample from the bedsheet?" Christiansen asked.

"I'm no slouch when it comes to forensic serology, but I couldn't believe it myself, so I checked those results three times," Manch said. "Judging from the quantity, I would hazard a guess that Mobley received one or more serious puncture or stab wounds."

"He couldn't have walked far in that condition," Tseng said.

Bianco heard exasperation in her voice when she added, "He could have been just beyond my line of sight yesterday."

"We had no way of knowing, and we would have been gambling with your life to send you out there under the circumstances," Christiansen said apologetically.

"I'm aware of that, Dave. What I said was not an accusation."

"The other samples from Faden's sleep station are urine and semen with traces of menstrual blood—again, Ann Bisio's—and ash," Manch said.

Gutierrez's response was instantaneous. "What kind of ash?"

"The lieutenant wants to know more about the ash," Christiansen repeated over the COMM.

"I still have to do a chemical and spectroscopic analysis on it and on the particles I took from the hammer head," Manch responded. "I thought I would get the serology and bodily fluid data in to you first."

"Houston, this is a test of the Jerry Cochagne broadcasting system," the astronaut's voice interrupted over the COMM. "Joe and I are about to go outside. How do you read me?"

"We're reading you loud and clear," Tseng responded.

"This is Houston. We're reading you," Christiansen echoed.

"Testing," DeSosa said.

"We're reading you, loud and clear, Joe," Tseng said.

"We're out of here, then," Cochagne said grumpily.

"We're a bit testy today, aren't we?" Christiansen quipped in a sarcastic voice.

"What gives you that idea?" Cochagne responded flatly.

"Are Jerry and Joe on their way over to the *Collins* with the FS-5 personal effects?" Christiansen asked.

"Affirmative," Cochagne said.

"After the personal effects are stowed, Joe is scheduled to work with Dick to check the edge-on alignment of the flat-panel radiators and to recalibrate the system, if necessary," Tseng said, "and Jerry will commence with the unloading of the supplies and the loading of the trash."

Bianco was amused by Gutierrez's startled reaction to Tseng's comment.

"You have trash?" the detective blurted out excitedly.

"We haven't turned the Moon into a garbage dump

yet," Bianco told him. "They bag it, store it in a shed, and bring it back to Earth for disposal."

"They have to go through it," Gutierrez said, glaring at her with the intensity of a fanatic.

"A month's trash?" Christiansen's tone expressed dismay and skepticism.

"Horo is scheduled for a remote test with MILTON and the data glove," Tseng continued, unaware of the stir in Mission Control caused by her previous statement.

Horo leaned into the camera frame and waved to display the glove, which was hard-wired directly into the computer console for the test.

"Arminta is working with MILTON, the robot, today," Bianco explained. "That glove sends signals to his articulated gripper which duplicates her hand movements. Horo, in turn, is able to feel 'force reflection,' a tactile sensation simulating the forces at work in the remote environment. With the robot's vision system also tied into the Moon base video monitor, Horo can see the lunar terrain through MILTON's eyes, using the total range of his vision capabilities, which includes wavelengths of the light spectrum that are not visible to the human eye."

"We have you scheduled to take the rover out today, China," Christiansen said. "So it looks like Lebby, Horo, and Greer will be the only ones there to hold down the fort for us . . . and have we got a job for you . . . the lieutenant wants you guys to go through the FS-5 trash."

Bianco heard Lebby's voice distinctly when the astronaut said, "What?"

"Have a nice day," Christiansen responded.

"Thanks, Dave," Tseng said, annoyed.

"We're getting interference out here on the high frequency radio bands, Dave," Cochagne said on the COMM. "I thought I heard you say something about the trash."

"You won't be loading it today, Jerry. Gutierrez wants you guys to poke through it," Christiansen said.

Bianco was relieved that Cochagne merely gave a loud exasperated sigh, rather than swearing. "Do we really need to remain on the hot mode? If you need us, you know where to . . ."

"Houston, we've had a glitch here," Horo interrupted.

This time, her voice was bristling with controlled anger and annoyance. "MILTON is not where I left him yesterday. He took a walk all by himself, and he's out about one hundred meters east of here. By any chance, did someone run a program or an unscheduled test sequence during the sleep period?"

There was a moment of stunned silence in Mission Control, then a flurry of activity as bewildered flight controllers scrambled for the hard copy from all the workstation printers, which contained the overnight data on the various systems and experiments that were being monitored from the ground.

"There were no authorized experiments run from here . . . we're checking the logs . . ." Christiansen said. "Shah Zia had the CAPCOM's chair and the green team had the night shift." Someone handed Christiansen a printout. He scanned it, then said, "Nothing here involving the robot at all."

"The possibility is very remote that he's sustained damage from a micrometeoroid strike," Tseng said. "I'm going upstairs to suit up for the EVA. I'll do a visual inspection on him when I go outside."

"So along with our other problems, we have more flies and a renegade robot," Bianco said to Gutierrez. Deep down, she was worried. The FS-6 astronauts sounded tired. The schedule was getting to them. Cramming so much work into just a few days meant pressure with less than enough time for sleep.

Her thoughts were interrupted by the approach of

Yoshio Adachi and Shah Zia. "Dolores, if you have a minute, Yosh and I, we want to show you something on the computer," Zia said.

At first, Bianco had experienced some misgivings about the presence of Yoshio Adachi, a mission specialist from Shimizu Corporation in training for the FS-8 mission. After the FS-6 team's failure to find Takizawa, he'd left, then returned to Mission Control wearing a black armband, a traditional Japanese token of mourning.

Bianco's first reaction was to question the meaning of the gesture. Was the tribute for Takizawa alone, to the exclusion of the other FS-5 team members? That thought had angered her. The anger was dispelled, however, when Adachi proceeded to pass out armbands to the other astronauts as a memorial for FS-5. The gesture had rapidly spread throughout Mission Control as a show of solidarity. One of the flight controllers had located a quantity of black cloth and had cut it into strips for more armbands.

Thus, the twenty-eight-year-old engineer had not made a nuisance of himself on behalf of his company. Though Bianco did not question his loyalty to Shimizu, it was apparent that, unlike Takizawa, "Yosh" Adachi's group identity was solidly with the other astronauts. At the moment, he was content to observe and to comment when the discussion bordered on his area of expertise which was Human Factors and Habitat.

Bianco followed Adachi and Zia back to the computer's main terminal where a photo was displayed on the screen. "This is a shot that Jerry Cochagne took in Shinobu Takizawa's sleep station," Adachi said.

"We were trying to make sense out of it . . . see how this area is painted over? Look what happens if we remove these lines," Zia said.

Bianco watched the computer imaging system remove

the crisscrossing lines, leaving other lines with sections missing.

"If we ask the computer to give us its best guess at filling in the missing spaces in these lines, we get this," Zia continued.

Bianco watched the computer screen as two symbols took shape. "I don't speak Japanese or Chinese—I assume this is Japanese because of Takizawa," he said.

"Yes, this is Japanese writing," Adachi said. "Each of these characters is called a '*kanji.*' Kanji are the Japanese characters that were originally borrowed from the Chinese language. Japanese differs from Chinese because, in addition to Chinese writing, we use two other phonetic alphabets derived from the kanji to express sounds that are unique to the Japanese language, or to write words that are from another language such as English, which have become common usage in Japanese. Here, we see two kanji."

"What does it say?"

"It says 'Shi nobu.' "

"As in Shinobu Takizawa," Bianco said.

"No . . . well . . . yes, but no," Adachi said. "In Japanese, we have words that sound the same, but they are spelled with different kanji, and, because of that, they have a different meaning. Takizawa did not spell his name this way." Adachi reached for a piece of scratch paper and wrote in Japanese. "This is Shinobu," he said, showing Bianco the paper. "This is Shinobu Takizawa's name. The first kanji I wrote is different than the one in the photo, which has a bad meaning. It means 'death.' The two kanji both express the sound, 'shi,' but Takizawa used a kanji which means 'to aim at' or 'to have in view' when he spelled his name. No one would want the death kanji in his name. Takizawa's thinking was not good when he did this."

"What you're saying is that this is graffiti, just like the

other occult words and symbols scrawled all over the walls up there," Bianco said.

"Yes. I think so," Adachi said. "It is an indication that Takizawa was 'sick' like the others."

"Thank you for going to the trouble to do that work," Bianco told Zia and Adachi. "It's still confusing to me how you know which kanji to use," Bianco said to the Japanese mission specialist.

"It's not as hard as it looks," Adachi replied. "The kanji are like the ancient Egyptian hieroglyphs in that they are pictographs. Take the death kanji, for example." Adachi traced his finger across a horizontal line at the top of the character. "This horizontal stroke across the top symbolizes Earth—that is, the ground at our feet. Then, there are two things below that line. On the left side is a symbol of the Moon, or the night." Adachi covered the right side of the kanji with his hand. "The Moon is under the ground here, you see?"

Bianco nodded comprehension.

"By themselves, these two things form a kanji which means 'decompose.' " Adachi lifted his hand to expose the third element of the kanji. "This part, on the right side, represents a man's body sitting upright. In ancient times, a dead body was buried in a sitting position, inside a jar. So we have a dead man under the Earth in the night-time of life, which is Death. That's how we get the meaning of that kanji. Words that have to do with death are spelled with it. For example: 'shitai' is a word for 'corpse'; 'shinu' is the verb 'to die'; 'shigo' means a dead language. Japanese is not confusing. It's very precise."

☾

The condensation inside her helmet visor was a warning sign. Tseng realized she was exerting herself too much in her impatience to rendezvous with the robot. She felt pressured because MILTON's malfunction was causing a delay in her scheduled EVA to find Mobley. She consciously relaxed and slowed her pace. She adjusted the positions of the portable camera and the computer topographical and terrain maps she carried.

The robot turned toward her as though watching her approach.

"What's he doing?" Horo asked.

"He's looking at me."

"That's right, and you look stunning in infrared. He's responded promptly to task instructions, and I've run him through the movement combinations that utilize all his degrees of freedom."

"What would cause him to activate himself?"

"Too bad we can't ask him such a complicated question, isn't it? I'm running his imaging system and atomic absorption spectrometer through the full range. Everything is nominal there, too."

"Let me have him."

"Okay, you have him on channel two."

Tseng switched her radio to the second of the three short-range frequencies.

"MILTON, do you read me," Tseng said.

"Affirmative," Tseng heard the robot's synthesized voice in her earphones.

"Give him an 'identify' task," Horo said.

"Listen," Tseng said. The robot reacted to the command to receive voice instruction by moving itself into the home, or base, configuration which was its neutral, "ready for anything," position.

Tseng pointed out a fist-sized rock to the robot. "What is it?" she said.

A small movement of the robot's "head" indicated that its vision and external laser microprobe were focused on the rock. The microprobe vaporized a micron-sized sample allowing MILTON to employ a direct emission spec-

trometer on the released gas. "Object diameter: six centimeters . . . composition . . . silicon oxide . . . titanium
oxide . . . iron oxide . . ."

"Stop," Tseng interrupted. Reaching down, she picked
up the rock and held it in her hand. "Pick up object."

The robot rotated its tool caddy to replace the core
sampling tool on its right arm. The caddy moved again
and the robot selected a fully articulated five-fingered
gripper with rubber pads on the fingertips. With the tool
in place, the robot moved toward her with spiderlike precision. It stopped one meter away and extended its arm,
smoothly opening the fingers. Tseng felt the pressure of
the contact. The gripper closed around the rock and the
robot lifted it from her hand. The arm retracted a few
centimeters, then, the robot stood silent and immobile,
awaiting the next instruction. Tseng breathed a small
sigh of relief. MILTON could pluck an egg from her fingers, without breaking it, but he could also crush her
hand to a pulp with the tool if there was something drastically wrong with him.

"Release object," she told him.

The gripper opened, and the rock fell to the lunar
surface.

"I can't see any exterior damage to him," Tseng said.

Manch emerged from the air lock and headed toward
the rover.

"Paul and I have to get going," Tseng said. "In terms
of the lunar day, it's getting late. This is the last opportunity we'll have to bring Mike back, and I don't want to
miss it."

"I copy you," Horo replied.

Simultaneously, the robot put the thumb and fore-
finger of its hand into the configuration of an "okay"
sign. The instruction was from Horo via the data glove,
and it gave the robot the illusion of a human response.

Tseng found the gesture amusing, yet disturbing, in

light of their failure to pinpoint the malfunction that had caused it to reactivate itself. Intellectually, the robot was not sufficiently aware to have a personal secret agenda, nor autonomous enough to carry one out. However, the hand sign gave it a sinister countenance in her eyes.

"I'll continue working with MILTON and watch for anything peculiar," Horo said.

"Copy that, Arminta," Tseng said. "I'll drive, Paul," Tseng said to Manch.

Manch put his black bag into the rover's cargo bed and reached out to take the camera from her arms. "I'll help you with this."

Tseng maneuvered herself into the seat. The rover's steering stick was between her thighs. She clipped the real-time computer terrain printouts Lebby had given her into a holder on the vehicle's front safety bar. The physician climbed in on the passenger side.

"You have a lap belt which fastens across your body like this," Tseng told Manch, demonstrating the mechanism. "It's there so you won't get bounced out of your seat."

When Manch was strapped in, Tseng pushed the acceleration pedal, coaxing a smooth forward motion from the rover. Though the LRV was capable of thirteen kilometers per hour, the trafficability factors peculiar to the lunar surface limited their speed to only six. The glass content of the soil made the driving conditions equivalent to maneuvering in icy snow, and hard turns at speeds of over seven kilometers per hour resulted in fishtailing and skidding.

The sun angle changed twelve degrees every twenty-four hours. The shadows made by rocks and outcroppings were longer. It made for poor visibility, and she steered with the attentiveness of a race car driver to avoid the most common hazards, the unobtrusive patches of deep, very soft soil. For the first few meters, she kept a watchful eye on the battery level and the ammeter. Though they were traveling along flat terrain, because of rolling resistance from soil compaction against the balloon tires, the energy expended by the LRV was equivalent to a vehicle on Earth constantly climbing a smooth one and one-half degree slope. She was relieved to see there was no excessive current draw.

"Rover, this is Houston," Christiansen's voice came over the COMM on the high-gain channel. "We'd like you to shoot the satellite and confirm your position."

"I copy you, Dave," Tseng said. She activated the navigation beam built into her chest computer, which sent a signal to the nearest L-TDRS satellite, and received the coordinates of their location on the Satellite-User Geometry Display. "We're point six kilometers northeast of the base."

The lone foot track she and Paul Manch followed angled gradually northeast across the mare basin. At this distance from the base, she and Manch could talk to each other on the narrow band suit-to-suit frequency without being overheard at the base or in Mission Control.

"Something occurred yesterday, during that verbal exchange between Lebby and Greer in the hygiene station," Tseng said.

"Oh, yes."

"Dick's understandably very technical and he called some of her statements into question. There was an awkward moment. Was Greer as offended as it appeared?"

"No, but in those situations, she withdraws into herself. It's a credibility thing. She's remarkably intuitive, but intuition is not provable by scientific methods. Personally, I'm in awe of her empathic ability. I worked closely with her at the Space Station, so I had many opportunities to see her in action."

Tseng had not expected Manch to divulge the nature of his personal relationship with Greer. Though she was admittedly curious, she was relieved that he hadn't. In this professional situation, the physician's discretion was a mark of his character and of his regard for Greer's reputation.

If Manch's assessment could be trusted—and Tseng had no reason to doubt that it could not be—it put Greer's behavior since the start of the mission in perspective. The psychiatrist was understandably concerned about the credibility of her intuitive hunches. It would take an atmosphere of trust to get her to talk freely.

To the east, a dusty haze on the horizon caused by the approach of the night terminator reminded her of the arctic northern lights on Earth.

"What's causing that rippling light effect up ahead of us?" Manch asked.

"It has to do with ionization of the Moon's atmosphere," Tseng answered. "The entire terminator 'effect' will last roughly fifty more hours with peak particle activity around Far Side Base occurring during the next twenty-four hours. At the risk of making a bad joke, what we're experiencing here is, quite literally, the lunar twilight zone, the expanse of pre-darkness preceding lunar night."

"I've never thought about the Moon as having an atmosphere."

"That's a misconception. There are important natural phenomena at work here that indicate the presence of an atmosphere, though it's about fourteen orders of magnitude less dense than the Earth's. Our experiments have detected helium, argon, neon, and hydrogen. The neon and hydrogen are mostly from the solar wind, and some argon is also from the solar wind, but some is also released through radioactive decay of lunar surface elements.

"We already have an atmospheric pollution problem here. For example, a cluster of spacecraft engines releasing exhaust gases will initiate a number of dynamic and chemical processes of direct atmospheric consequence—the exhaust of a vehicle burning liquid hydrogen in an oxygen environment is composed of approximately seventy percent water vapor and thirty percent unused hydrogen, and, when you convert that to particle flow per second for each engine, the flow rates represent extraordinary additions to the ambient lunar atmosphere—and, on top of that, every time we go outside, our suits vent waste gases into that same atmosphere. Some of our most important experiments have been adversely affected by nothing more than 'air pollution.' "

After a pause, Manch said, "In good shape, Mobley could have gone twenty kilometers before running out of air and power. I don't know how he got this far in his condition."

"This is Houston," Christiansen's voice came faintly over the COMM. "Are you reading me?

"I read you, but the static is increasing," Tseng shouted back. "Visually, we're seeing something very interesting out here. Magnetic turbulence is visible as an aurora borealis along the night terminator."

Manch positioned the camera and shot the display of rippling lights, which resembled draperies rustling in a breeze.

"The picture we're getting is full of noise. We can't see anything," Christiansen told her.

"We're continuing on, then," Tseng told the CAPCOM.

"We copy. Can you give me another fix on your position?" Tseng shot the satellite, but this time the readout was unintelligible. "Houston, perturbations in the electron densities in this region are screwing up my Satellite-User Geometry Display," she told Christiansen.

"You're experiencing a degradation of the ranging system signal due to retardation of radio waves passing through the ionized atmosphere," Christiansen replied.

"Free electron density could cause ranging system errors of as much as one kilometer under these conditions."

"We don't have reliable total electron content data to compensate for this condition because of what happened to the PERM experiment," Tseng told Manch.

"So what is Houston saying?"

"That we could get lost if we're not careful."

"How are you feeling?" Manch asked.

"My scalp is tingling, and the old fillings in my teeth feel warm," Tseng responded.

"Same here. Any vision problems such as blinking lights or patterns of light, or even hallucinations?"

"No."

"Me neither, at the moment. We are experiencing low-level electrocutaneous stimulation from the magnetic field, however. In these conditions, the brain cavity behaves like a uniform, spherical-shaped conductor bounded by an insulator—the skull. Hair vibrates at between sixty and one hundred twenty hertz, so that gives us an idea of the strength of the field in this area. It's not yet strong enough to effect the cognitive areas of the brain or to cause stimulation of the visual cortex, which would result in a suppression of visual perception in the form of magnetophosphene light-patterns and hallucinations."

"I'm recognizing landmarks from the computer rendering," Tseng said.

She steered the rover toward the ejecta formation she'd seen in the picture and was soon looking at the object in the orbital photo . . . an astronaut in a space suit lying prone on the lunar surface. The round object a few meters from the body was a space helmet.

"Houston, we've located Mobley. Houston, do you read me?" We've lost Mission Control," she told Manch.

"Why would he come out here like this?" the physician grieved aloud.

"I don't know why he chose this way to . . . he finished it by unlocking his helmet. The pressure inside the suit blew it off."

"He'll be mummified," Manch said.

Tseng took the physician's tone as a caution meant to prepare her for what they would soon see.

Tseng drove the LRV up to the stacked cargo containers sitting outside the payload bay door of the *Collins* just as Cochagne came out with a sealed container. He was unloading the mission's scheduled cargo of electronic components and equipment destined for the Science Dome, and the packaged meals, beverages, and other disposables they had brought with them as part of the routine resupply of Far Side. She had not had the chance to talk to him privately since he'd left her bed, angry and indignant. She dreaded the awkward moment when she would have to speak to him as a crew member, and as if nothing intimate had happened between them. How would he take it? What would his attitude toward her be from now on?

Why did it matter so much?

One disadvantage of being outside the dome for the confrontation was that they would have their gold sun visors down. Each helmet would reflect the mirror image of the other and hide the face within. He would not be able to see her true emotions, and it would be impossible for her to gauge his reaction. She hoped she could put the right amount of sincerity in her voice.

"China, what do you think about, 'Food for the Moon: we deliver,' as a motto for FS-10?" Cochagne asked in an amused tone.

She was completely disarmed by the warmth in his voice.

She'd prepared arguments to combat stinging anger,

and even indifference—whether feigned or real—but she had no strategy for this show of affection. Though a tense knot inside her stomach unraveled, she was annoyed at herself for being sucked in by the astronaut's lethal charm.

"If everyone at NASA had your sense of humor, it would go over big," she answered lamely.

"It's too bad about Mike," he said. "I heard your cross talk with Houston. There was a lot of static on the COMM." He was facing her, and it appeared to her that he was watching her climb out of the rover.

She pretended not to notice by picking up a container, which was very light in lunar gravity, and placing it in the vehicle's cargo bed. "The signal degradation was quite a problem, and we're going to be unable to adjust the ranging system, until we get some data on total electron content through each stage of the terminator pass," she said. "That's why the PERM experiment was so important. Unfortunately, the schedule doesn't allow me any time to take it apart to see why it failed, let alone to fix it in time for it to do us any good. FS-7 will have to redeploy the experiment."

She worked with him, loading the supplies into the LRV, and enduring an awkward silence. Finally, she said, "Did you hear how we found him?"

"His helmet was off. I couldn't hear what happened after that very well."

"He looked like an Egyptian mummy . . . completely desiccated. When we picked him up, we were just handling the weight of the suit. He weighed nothing."

"Did you leave him on Boot Hill with the others?"

"No. We took the body inside. Paul wants to examine it. He took the video camera for his report to Houston. I didn't realize until now just how much I wanted to find him, to bring him back, and to take him home."

"I read you," Cochagne said. Instead of continuing his work, he stood still, facing her.

"Come inside with me for a minute, Jerry. I have something I want to say to you." Tseng crossed to the payload bay hatch, but turned to look back before entering the LLM.

She saw Cochagne put the last container in the LRV, then he turned and followed her inside.

Tseng lifted her gold sun shield in order to see inside the darkened ship. Only the emergency markers glowed, as the major systems inside the *Collins* were powered down when they moved to the base.

Cochagne, too, had raised his sun visor upon entering the payload bay, and she turned and met the astronaut's steady gaze.

They spoke at the same time. "I want to apologize . . ."

"I owe you an apology . . ."

"You first," Cochagne said.

"I'm sorry about this morning," Tseng said, taking care to keep the sudden, strong emotion she felt out of her voice. "I said some things which sounded insensitive, and, in retrospect, they were insensitive. I insulted you by making it sound like you were just a one-night stand. That was the farthest thing from my mind. I don't want there to be any awkwardness between us. Can we still be friends?"

"No," Cochagne said, shaking his head for emphasis.

Tseng felt her stomach twist with a pang of disappointment, but before she could turn away, Cochagne put his hands on her shoulders and pulled her as close as the chest computers on the front of their suits would allow. It was impossible to feel anything so subtle as a loving touch through the space suit, but she could feel his warmth and desire in the solidness of his embrace. "I want more than that," he said, "and when I want something, I'm not that easily discouraged. The only thing standing between us is . . ."

He hesitated, and she could see that he wanted to kiss her and she wanted him to. Her knees felt weak. Her heartbeat quickened.

". . . this God damned space suit," he cursed, then burst into laughter.

She had to laugh with him, at the absurdity of the moment.

"My turn," he continued. "It was very self-centered and narrow of me to get angry the way I did. I don't know where that mood came from, really. The truth is, I do have a reputation—though undeserved—that can't do you any good at this time. I'm comfortable with the idea that what we feel should be between us, especially now. And we can hope that no one on the ground was paying too much attention to our vital signs in the middle of the night."

Cochagne climbed into the passenger seat of the LRV for the ride back to the base.

"We'll pick up the FS-5 trash on our way in," Tseng said.

"I'm really looking forward to that job," Cochagne responded with good-natured sarcasm.

"Think of it as an exercise in contemporary archaeology." As Tseng drove away from the *Collins,* an unexpected pressure on her arm threw her slightly off-balance and caused her to turn toward Cochagne. Despite the difficulty presented by the bulky pressurized suits, he had hooked his arm through hers. Their proximity to the dome meant that the only way to keep the moment private was to say nothing on the radio, so they rode the rest of the way back in silence.

She wondered why she was finding the prospect of

falling in love with Cochagne more unnerving than anything she had yet experienced at Far Side.

((

"Thanks for taking time out for my call," Jonathan Birnbaum told Bianco. The Bethesda psychiatrist smiled back at her affably from the office monitor. She'd taken his call in the privacy of her office for reasons of security, but she welcomed the chance to get away from the tension-charged atmosphere of Mission Control even for a short time.

"What's the latest on Far Side?" Birnbaum asked.

"They've run out of Seconal and Thorazine. They're giving Faden diazepam. Fortunately, they have a large supply of that."

Birnbaum responded with a worried shake of his head.

Bianco felt a frisson of anxiety race up her spine at the prospect of a new problem to deal with at Far Side.

"During the teleconference, Faden talked about 'burning up' and 'coming apart,' " Birnbaum said. "Has he said any more about that?"

"From what I understand, that personality did manifest itself," Bianco said. "The dialogue was consistent with what we've been hearing from him. However, several of his personalities have been in conflict over the last few hours."

"Would you mind if I looked in on him?" Birnbaum asked.

Bianco weighed the question for a moment. "We can arrange another teleconference with Bethesda, if you'd like."

"I was thinking about flying into Houston."

"That would make it much easier."

"It's less . . . complicated . . . for me, too. I'll clear my schedule immediately."

"Thank you, Dr. Birnbaum." Bianco said. She paused to gather her thoughts. She'd picked up on the subtext of Birnbaum's comments. He didn't want his staff involved this time. "We know, in broad strokes, some of the things that happened to FS-5," Bianco said. "However, I can't stress enough how badly we need the details that Faden has locked up inside his head, in order to complete the picture."

"And I'm confident that we'll get them," Birnbaum responded. "It's just a matter of time."

"Time is the one thing that may be in short supply," Bianco said. "I'll get back to you with the schedule." She disconnected the call and leaned back in her chair. Alone with her thoughts, the social restraints gone, strong emotions boiled over inside her. Birnbaum was optimistic about Faden, but she couldn't see the basis for that optimism, and she'd worked hard to control and suppress the anger and frustration building up over the lack of concrete results in solving the mysteries at Far Side. It was hard for her to remain positive. Faden's case appeared hopeless. She had to find a way to turn the situation around. Negative thinking would not produce the answer. Bianco switched off the monitor and left her office, determined to walk off the unproductive emotions before they took hold of her.

☽

Tseng's first impression, upon descending to the Third Level, was that something about the room had changed. It looked homier. The foul stench of death was diminishing because of frequent filter changes in the air purification system. However, for a crewman coming in from outside, the first breaths of the air inside the Main Dome were still difficult to endure.

She'd just about decided that the room was gaining its

homey warmth purely from human occupancy, when she realized that the difference was actually due to the addition of a few basic pieces of furniture, such as the chairs for the computer and communications consoles, which Lebby, Greer, and Horo had retrieved from Level Two during her absence. That the astronauts, tired of waiting for the go ahead from Mission Control, had taken the initiative, Tseng had no doubt. What did the Ground really know of their discomfort? They were occupied with more important problems.

Under Lebby's watchful eyes, Horo used the Far Side computer's vast imaging capabilities to view and interpret the recorded data from the robot's cameras.

"Dick and I have been talking about MILTON's little problem," Horo said. "He thinks it's in the software."

"A program can look perfect and check out exactly right, but a series of keystrokes in a certain order will trigger a glitch that's embedded so deeply that it could be completely overlooked. It can turn out to be something as minuscule as having two lines of program code transposed."

"What can we do about it?"

Horo shrugged. "Yesterday, I shut him down using voice command. Today, we shut him down manually. We're now waiting to see if he turns himself on."

"What's this about an autoerotic robot?" Cochagne called out, as he descended the companionway stairs from Level Four.

The quip drew a belly laugh from Horo.

"The garbage awaits our inspection upstairs," Cochagne said.

"Greer already took the bagged trash that was inside the dome when we got here down to the wardroom," Horo said. "She and Joe are sorting through it. Dee Bianco wants another teleconference with Faden," Horo added. "Dick and I figured you'd want to get it out of the way as soon as possible."

Tseng shrugged. "Has Houston put it into our schedule yet?"

"Tentatively," Horo said. "They're just waiting on Birnbaum, the psychiatrist. Greer asked me to ask you if we could make the teleconference two-way."

"The disembodied voices problem?" Tseng asked.

"Uh-huh."

"I'll pass that along," Tseng said. "How's Bob Faden?"

"In and out," Lebby said. "They've run out of everything except diazepam, you know."

"I know," Tseng said.

Tseng surveyed the accumulation of trash. "Let's get this place in order, then, and let's confine this job to one area."

"I copy you," Cochagne responded.

"What's the status on the computer?" Tseng asked Lebby.

"I've been checking the files. Nothing's been lost, but some things have been added—both program and document files. That program that Bob wrote—you remember the pages of code in his sleep station—it's a game. The document files with it are just garbage . . . pages of nothing but lines of random letters and numbers. I'm going through them anyway." Lebby brushed impatiently at a fly which had alighted on the keyboard. It flew up, circled the keyboard with apparent aggravation, then, as Lebby sat back in his chair, it realighted. "Hearty little buggers, aren't they," he said.

"Have you eaten?" Tseng asked Horo and Lebby.

"A little while ago," Horo answered. "You guys must be starved."

"I know I am, but before I do anything about it, I'm going down to Level One and check on Paul's progress. Can you show me the game later?" Tseng asked Lebby.

"We can all figure it out together," Lebby said.

Tseng fastened the Velcro closures on her jacket in anticipation of the damp, chilling cold of Level One, glad that she had stopped by her quarters to change into the regular NASA uniform with long pants, before making the descent. She was still at the top of the companionway when she heard Manch's voice.

"There's an inexplicable temperature differential and a dampness here," Manch said. "Although Cochagne's systems checks have indicated that the environmental sensors are functioning within acceptable parameters on all levels, there's something wrong."

"I'm told that any moisture is going to cause that body to deteriorate rapidly," Christiansen's voice came over the COMM.

"The lower body, which was not subjected to direct bombardment by gamma rays, is already under attack by mold, fungi, and microorganisms," Manch told him. "I wouldn't be surprised if the flies are the carriers," he added.

When she reached the bottom of the stairway, she saw that Manch was wearing a radio headset and surgical gloves, and that he was leaning over Mobley's brittle, desiccated body which was on the worktable.

Manch had the body on its back, just opposite of the way they'd found it. In death, Mobley had flung his arms out and had fallen facedown, but the hard torso of the suit had caused the neck to hang forward, and the head to drop with the face turned slightly to the left. The corpse had dried and hardened in that position, making insertion into a surgical bag impossible. Tseng surmised that Manch had spent nearly all his time, up to this point, at the task of removing the PLSS backpack and then unlocking and pulling off the sleeves and the gloves, and pulling down the trouser section of the suit in an effort to avoid breaking any part of the fragile body. Tseng saw a heavy coating of dried blood on the inside front of the trousers.

"Houston, Po has just joined me," Manch told Christiansen.

Tseng plugged her own radio headset into a jack and said, "Hello, Dave. Is Lieutenant Gutierrez with you?"

"We couldn't get rid of him if we wanted to," Christiansen said, his tone pleasantly gruff.

Manch's reaction to the comment was a sly wink at her. Tseng gave the physician a nod of acknowledgment. The CAPCOM's implied acceptance of Gutierrez meant that the young police lieutenant was rapidly integrating himself into the Mission Control team. He was becoming an insider. One of them.

"Do you have a time for us on that teleconference?" Tseng asked.

"Sorry, no. We're still trying to put it together," Christiansen said.

"Keep me informed . . . and one more thing," Tseng said. "Under the circumstances, we think you should plan on making this a two-way teleconference."

"Greer thinks there could be a problem with Faden and disembodied voices, like the last time," Manch said. "It's a concern."

"Copy that," Christiansen said.

A swarm of flies circled lazily over the corpse just out of Manch's reach. Whenever they landed, he stopped working to brush them away, and he vented his annoyance by periodically reaching up to bat at them futilely.

The sight of the bearded, long-haired, mummified corpse, as well as the sight of the dead commander's papers piled on top of a nearby carton to raise the video camera to the proper level for a hands-off recording of the examination produced a sharp pang of anxiety for Tseng, because of the work yet to be done in sorting through them.

Tseng peered inside the hard shell torso through the lower connecting ring at the waist. The torso looked cavernous. The dried, stiff body appeared ancient. The head and neck were blackened by direct exposure to the sun. The skin had shrunk, making the facial features look distorted. However the corpse was still recognizable as Mobley.

The lips were pulled back from the teeth. The eyeless face was hardened into a grin. Mobley's hair and beard were bleached and brittle. The exposed skin below the neck and on the hands was dried to a nutshell brown color. Spots of encroaching blue mold were visible on it. The skin had shrunk away from the nail beds, giving the fingernails a clawlike appearance.

There was a large container on the floor to catch the liquid dripping out of the umbilical from Mobley's cooling undergarment. The knit fabric wrinkled and bagged around the shrunken human husk, except in the chest and lower torso area where there was a hardened black stain. The point of origin appeared to be the upper left side of the solar plexus, the direction of the heart.

"I will have to cut away the undergarment fabric to get a look at the wound," Manch said.

"I'll get a close angle on this for you, Houston," Tseng said. She picked up the camera and focused the lens on the blackened area. Manch bent down close to the body. He reached inside the suit from the bottom of the torso section to cut through the undergarment material with a pair of surgical scissors.

Though the instrument was sharp, it was tedious work for the physician to cut and peel away the knit fabric without accidentally puncturing the body or cutting the coolant tubing.

Manch peeled away the section of undergarment to reveal that, in the wound area, it was stuck to a thick gauze pad. The gauze was also hard with dried blood, and it was stuck to the corpse's skin.

"The wound is dressed," Manch told the listeners in Mission Control. He traded the scissors for a scalpel to cut away the bandage and Tseng saw a deep, wedge-shaped gaping wound beneath.

"Houston, I'm looking at a wound channel which has shrunk to one and a half centimeters in length," Manch said into the mike. "It's difficult to determine the exact depth, though the angle of penetration is in an upward direction toward the rib cage and chest cavity. This is an antemortem wound, and quite serious. It could have been sustained several days prior to his going outside the last time, and it was apparently reopened by strenuous physical activity while he was in his suit."

"If he lost a lot of blood when he was wounded, wouldn't he have been very anemic from then on?" Tseng asked.

"Yes," Manch answered. "The wound, itself, was made with a curved, wedge-shaped, single-edged instrument. This is definitely not a knife wound, as skin shrinkage has caused the edges of the wound to pull apart, and I'm seeing radial cracks and fissures around the perimeter. Though this certainly has the characteristics of a life-threatening wound, I think the actual cause of death has to be attributed to asphyxiation and decompression from exposure to the lunar atmosphere," Manch finished.

"The lieutenant says to be sure and check his pockets," Christiansen said.

"I copy," Tseng said. She put the camera down and checked the suit utility pockets. "There's nothing unusual. He's got his surface tools, and that's all," she reported.

"Wait a minute," Manch said. "That holsterlike pocket

on Mobley's suit—I saw a pocket like that on Horo's suit. She carries a hand pick in it."

"A geologist's pick," Tseng said. "Mobley was the FS-5 geologist. She opened the flap of the holster, and grasping the head, removed the pick from inside. She grasped the shaft and offered it to Manch for closer inspection, but when the physician picked up a utility towel and placed it in the palm of his hand before grasping the shaft, she knew immediately the implication of his action, and knew she'd made a mistake.

The resulting pang of anxiety prompted her to say, "I'm sorry. I keep forgetting that this is a murder investigation."

"What's happening?" Christiansen asked on the COMM.

Manch turned the tool in his hand thoughtfully, examining it from all angles, then he pointed to, but did not touch, the pick end. "I'm reasonably sure that a tool such as this one could have made Mobley's wound," he said. "The head of this pick was probably wiped clean or washed, so I may not be able to make a definite determination on that." Manch put the pick aside and approached the body. He studied the wound, then his gaze traveled upward to linger a few seconds on Mobley's mummified face. "As for the circumstances under which Mobley received the wound, I can only guess," he said slowly, "but my gut feeling is that it was an accident, pure and simple. "I can't really put my finger on why I think that. I suppose it's because, judging by what I see, it just adds up that way."

Tseng mused about the coincidence of Manch having voiced her own thoughts about Mobley, but she elected not to discuss it on the COMM.

She had witnessed stranger things on Level One.

"Thanks for all your hard work, Paul, and you, too, China," Christiansen said.

"Houston, I want Jerry to get some stills of Mobley,

and then, I think, we're open to suggestion as to how you want us to proceed," Tseng said.

"What's your feeling on it?" Christiansen asked.

"We should put him back inside his suit and get him outside," Tseng responded. "The process of deterioration is advancing rapidly in our oxygen-rich environment."

"You'd better get on with it, then," Christiansen said.

"We'll be in touch later," Tseng said. She removed her radio headset. "I'll get Jerry."

On Level Two, she found Greer, Horo, DeSosa, and Cochagne surrounded by loose refuse and sealed bags of trash. Flies swarmed above and around them. "What have you found so far," she asked them.

"Banana peels and apple cores, some food packages that look Japanese, computer printouts, and two empty bottles of sake . . . as you can see, we still have quite a bit to go through," DeSosa answered, gesturing at the pile of still unopened garbage bags.

"The flies could have come up on the fresh fruit— someone's private stash. That's going to be a big 'no no' from here on. Let me see the Japanese food packages." Tseng said.

Horo handed her a stack of colorful plastic refuse and she recognized envelopes for instant miso soup, and packages for dehydrated noodle soup, tofu, flavored rice, and curry.

"Do you know what they are?" Cochagne asked.

"I can read the labels fairly well because of my background in Chinese and what little Japanese I know . . . see this word . . . *oishii*. That means delicious. All packaged foods produced in Japan have that on the label. It must be mandatory."

Greer picked up the sake bottle and turned it over in her hand. "Did Takizawa bring this food and the sake up in his personal preference kit?" she asked, as she unscrewed the cap.

"Leave the cap on," Tseng cautioned her. "We have so much patchwork circuitry in operation that a spark could ignite the alcohol fumes in your face."

Horo showed her a package that pictured a bowl full of what looked like black beads. "What's this stuff?"

"It's called *hijiki* and it's a type of seaweed. The dish is preprepared and packaged like this so that all Takizawa had to do was rehydrate it in water, then microwave it."

"Did you study Japanese?" Cochagne asked.

"No, I picked it up in the course of my martial arts studies and on trips to Japan. I love it there, and I love the Japanese people."

"You grew up speaking Chinese at home," Greer said.

"No, I studied it in school. I studied everything I could about the Chinese culture hoping to please my father. The result was that I have more classical knowledge than he does. Because he only knows his own dialect, he has trouble understanding me if I speak to him in scholar's Chinese, so he gets annoyed when I do."

"I thought you were half Vietnamese," DeSosa said.

"Before the war, the Vietnamese merchant class was mostly Chinese. My father was a child at the time of the Vietnam War. His family owned a nightclub, which they lost after the fall of Saigon, but they got out with a great deal of their wealth in precious stones sewn into their clothes. They saw the way things were going early on and bought a big boat. That's how they made their escape."

"In style," Horo said.

"It was still a dangerous journey, from what I understand," Tseng said. "Where's Dick?"

"He got a brainstorm a few minutes ago, and went back up to Level Three to do some work on the computer," Horo said.

"I hate to stick you guys with this job," Tseng said.

"Sure you do," DeSosa replied sarcastically. "I can see that you're just dying to dive into this stuff."

Tseng stifled a laugh at the astronaut's tone. "We need some stills taken of Mobley," she told Cochagne.

As she descended the companionway to Level One, a hopeless, depressed feeling of having failed weighed heavily on her mind. There was no logical reason for it. Negative emotions were triggering a physical response. It occurred to her that the symptoms resembled premenstrual syndrome, an annoying malady with which, at times, she was all too familiar; a condition where emotions were often triggered by changes in body chemistry, rather than by actual situations and outside stimuli.

She was gratefully distracted from her thoughts by the sound of footsteps on the stairs. Cochagne was descending, carrying the mission camera. He was followed by Horo and Greer. She saw Manch's mood brighten at the sight of Greer.

"What brings you down into the catacombs?" Tseng asked.

"We're taking a break from garbage duty," Greer said.

"This is not much of an improvement," Manch replied. Cochagne crossed to the worktable. Manch handed him a surgical mask. "If you're going to get in close, wear this," the physician said.

"How's our boy, MILTON?" Tseng asked Horo.

"So far, he hasn't moved a servo," Horo replied. She looked at the corpse with a sad expression. "It's a shame. Why did he commit suicide like that?"

"At the end, he was severely anemic from loss of blood. His thought processes would be very much affected by that condition," Manch said. He held up Mobley's geologist's pick for Horo to see before placing it inside a plastic bag. "As for the injury he received prior to his suicide, this tool may have been involved somehow."

Horo frowned and raised her eyebrows in response.

"Arminta, what was your personal assessment of Mike Mobley?" Tseng asked.

"Dedicated, intense, energetic, no nonsense, inflexible at times . . . you and the red team got to know him better than anyone."

"What's your analysis, Po?" Manch asked.

"Prior to FS-5, he was a professional colleague," Tseng answered. "We had a good, but distant, working relationship, but he was not the kind of man you could really get close to. He was not able to express himself too well, verbally, on any subjects except lunar science and photography. It was only because I was the principal CAPCOM that I really got to know him. Even toward the end, I thought we had a good rapport, and yet, I now know that there were things he was not telling me." She crossed to the stack of papers removed from the table and searched through them. She withdrew the notes she'd found among Mobley's papers and showed them to Horo, Manch, and Greer. "As it turns out, he was more of a deep-thinker than I gave him credit for."

" 'Magnets in the brain,' " Horo read aloud.

"I'm reminded that, when I was at Caltech, there was some research going on based on a theory that there are magnetic sensors in the brain itself," Tseng said. " 'Magnetites' was the word coined for them."

"In mineralogy, magnetite is ferrosoferric oxide, an oxide of iron," Horo said. "It has the power of being attracted by a magnet, though it has no power to attract particles of iron to itself unless it becomes magnetized, in which case it's called lodestone."

"Oxides of iron have been identified as part of the brain's makeup," Greer said. "Supposedly, the number of these brain 'magnetites' varies per person—that is, not

all brains are endowed with the same quantity of iron oxides. The Russians have been exploring the connection
between the ability to turn psychic energy into physical
energy—to move objects, as in psychokinesis—and
brain chemistry characteristics for decades."

"There was a guy—I forget his name—who could
melt spoons and deflect compass needles," Horo said.

"I believe he was exposed as a charlatan," Greer said,
"but, at any rate, the ability to do that is supposed to be
the result of 'thought pressure.' "

"If one subscribes to the magnetite theory, that would
be a form of magnetomotive force," Tseng said.

"There have been studies linking brain cancer and
leukemia with exposure to high tension power lines,"
Horo said. "Certain individuals were found to be more
prone to it than others, and children were the group most
seriously affected because their magnetic susceptibility
was much higher than that of the adults tested.

"An outside electric field produces a surface charge on
the human body," Manch said. "Earlier today, Po and I
experienced an outside environment in which the static
charge was probably a million times greater in magnitude than what we might normally be exposed to on a
routine basis. The corresponding physical effects were
greater by the same order of magnitude. There is actually
a perturbation of the environmental electric field by the
body which looks like this." Manch drew the outline of a
human body on a piece of paper, then he drew a series of
vertical lines. The nearer the lines were to the body, the
more they bent toward it, and, above the shoulders, they
were no longer vertical, but angled sharply toward the
top of the head.

"Magnetites in the brain, in the presence of an electric
field should behave like electromagnets according to
Maxwell's equations," Tseng said.

"I thought that was Lenz's Law," Horo said.

"No, Lenz's Law has to do with the direction of induced electromotive force, which is described by Faraday's Law," Tseng replied. "It's Maxwell's equations that actually describe the magnetic induction of current."

"MRI, Magnetic Resonance Imaging, uses the hydrogen atom to make images, but I don't think it's by induction," Manch said. "The body is mostly water, so, during the test, the machine surrounds the body with a powerful electromagnetic field. This aligns the protons of the hydrogen atoms in the direction of the field's poles. A radio signal is beamed into the magnetic field, which knocks the protons out of alignment. When the beam stops, within milliseconds they go back into place releasing energy and thereby emitting faint radio signals of their own. A computer translates the signals into an image of the area scanned, which reflects the hydrogen or water content of the tissues. Water density is greater in the gray matter of the brain, in particular, and electrical currents have been detected there and in the spinal cord, though we're talking about field strengths of less than a thousandth of a microvolt." The physician mopped his forehead.

Tseng noticed that he looked flushed, and that he was perspiring freely. "Are you feeling okay, Paul?" she asked.

"I suppose not, since I'm in a cold sweat."

"You wore gloves to work on Mobley, but you didn't put a mask on," Greer said. "You've been disturbing the skin surface and breathing in the airborne spores from the mold growing on the body, and that's dangerous."

"I tried wearing a mask, but they couldn't understand me on the COMM," Manch said.

Tseng had seen the physician's eyes watering as he studied the notes. Now, he rubbed them with a vigor that revealed his annoyed agitation.

"I'm definitely having an allergic reaction to something," he said. "I'm not going to be able to work down here anymore today."

"You need to give it a rest, Paul," Horo said.

"I have so much to do . . . I still have to analyze that ash I found in Faden's room. I took a sample of the burned spot in the recreation area to run a comparison on them."

Tseng's attention was suddenly drawn to Greer. The psychiatrist looked pale, and she hugged herself as though from a chill.

"Is something wrong, Iona? You look very uncomfortable," Tseng said.

"You'll have to excuse us, but I think I should get Paul out of here," Greer responded.

"I'm not through yet," Manch protested.

"Jerry and I can take care of the body," Tseng said. Manch nodded. He and Greer ascended the companionway together.

(

They were nearing Boot Hill when Tseng said to Cochagne, "Let's put him next to Washington, rather than Drzymkowski." Tseng winced at the burst of static in her earphones when the astronaut responded with, "Do you think he has a preference?"

"I have one. I guess that's what counts."

"There's a lot of noise on the RF channels," Cochagne said.

"Let's get this over with," Tseng said. She squatted in unison with Cochagne and they set Mobley's spacesuited body down gently beside Washington's. Tseng took out her utility knife, and Cochagne helped her to roll the body over on its side. She used the blade to force open the suit's oxygen inlet valve so that air trapped inside at the dome's seven psi atmosphere was evacuated, creating a vacuum inside the suit.

It didn't hurt this time, did it, Mike? was the bizarre thought that came into her mind as she saw the suit's flexible material collapse, but, instead of the sense of completion and finality that she'd expected, she had the distinct, unsettled feeling of having left unfinished business behind her.

With hunger gnawing at her insides, Tseng picked impatiently through entrees in the galley storage cabinet and settled on the spaghetti and meatballs.

Horo approached and looked over her shoulder, then reached around her to take out a package of apple cobbler.

Tseng gave her friend a remonstrative frown. "Didn't you tell me you had dinner already?"

Horo grinned impishly. "I'm hungry again. I don't know why . . . well, yes, I do. When I was running, in college, and in the Olympics, I would get hungry like this, but I was burning up a lot of energy then. Unfortunately, my brain doesn't seem to know my body's not in training for athletic competition anymore. When my energy level is like it is right now, I'm conditioned to eat. I shouldn't eat. You're welcome to the cobbler."

"It's just nerves," Tseng said.

"It's a high metabolic rate," Horo insisted. "I feel . . . you know . . . 'wired.' "

Tseng smiled sympathetically at her friend. "I don't know what to tell you—I feel just the opposite of wired," she said, reaching back into the cabinet for a bag of coffee. She opened the vent hole and put it in the microwave. While the coffee was heating, she emptied her entree and the apple cobbler desert into a tray. The coffee was hot in seconds, and she removed the bag and inserted the meal tray into the microwave oven. She heard footsteps on the companionway and saw Cochagne emerge from below carrying the camera's hard drive.

"I want to transmit these pictures of Mobley now, before the interference gets too bad," he said.

Carrying her coffee, Tseng, along with Horo, followed Cochagne to Level Three. The astronaut gave the camera's hard drive to Lebby, who inserted it into the computer's playback/downlink unit.

At the communications console, DeSosa reacted by initiating the COMM link on the high gain channel. "Houston, this is Far Side Base, do you read?" he asked.

A loud burst of static in response caused DeSosa to grab for his controls, then they heard Christiansen answer, "Far Side, Houston."

"Did the info on what we've found in the trash so far get through to you?"

"Say again, Far Side."

"The trash list."

"Affirmative. We have it," Christiansen responded.

"Houston, we're about to transmit some pictures to you . . ." DeSosa said.

"Say again, Far Side, your transmission is breaking up," Christiansen interrupted.

Tseng crossed to the communications console and stood sipping her coffee and listening worriedly to the exchanges between DeSosa and Christiansen.

"Repeat. Stand by for Jerry's photo transmission."

"We read you," Christiansen confirmed. "We're standing by to receive and we have something to send as well. Dee Bianco says you can put it in your graffiti file."

Cochagne's photo transmission took only moments, and then they received Christiansen's acknowledgement.

"We're getting something," Lebby informed DeSosa. ". . . problems . . . your transmission . . ." Christiansen said.

"Say again, Houston," DeSosa interrupted, annoyed.

". . . breaking up . . ." There was a change in pitch in the static, then they heard Christiansen's voice over it. "Far Side, Houston. Do you read?"

"We read you, Houston, but there is a lot of interference."

"Say again, Far Side."

Tseng crossed to the communications console and donned a headset. "Houston, Far Side. Po, here. We're battling electromagnetic interference up here. Listen, is there a decision on the teleconference?"

After a short pause, Christiansen questioned, "How soon can you be ready?"

"We're ready any time. Let's get on with it," Tseng replied.

"We'll see you in fifteen."

"Copy that," Tseng said. "What about our mission status?"

"Negative. . . . status is under discussion at . . . is time. You . . . to stand by."

"We're anticipating loss of signal prior to peak passage of the terminator. Over," Tseng said.

"Affirmative on LOS, Far Side. Can you boost your signal?" Christiansen asked.

"Affirmative, Houston," DeSosa said, deftly resetting the console switches. "How do you read?"

"Far Side, we read you, but there's still interference."

"We're maxed-out on the high gain side," DeSosa said.

"Is Paul Manch close by?" Christiansen asked.

"Negative," Tseng said. "We put Paul to bed a while ago. He wasn't feeling well."

"This wasn't communicated to us," Christiansen said.

Tseng bristled at the implied criticism. "We didn't think it was anything to get excited about. We feel it's a temporary condition and something the medical team can handle."

There was a noticeable pause before Christiansen

continued in a calm, matter-of-fact tone, "We copy, Far Side. Something we'd like to draw your attention to . . . it isn't meant to criticize, it's just an observation. We're a little concerned. Earlier today, we noticed a tendency toward irritability in certain crew members that got our curiosity aroused. Since then, we've been kicking around some theories as to why that might be happening at this stage of the mission, since there's an obvious parallel with the FS-5 psychological profiles. Is Iona Greer available?"

Greer ascended from Level Two, but remained standing at the top of the companionway.

"She's here now," Tseng said. Intuition and experience told her that the perceived problem was bothering the ground team perhaps a bit more than they were willing to let on. A glance at DeSosa's reaction to the comments reinforced her suspicions. Lebby, Horo, and Cochagne had stopped what they were doing to listen to the exchange on the COMM.

"How's Paul doing?" Christiansen asked. The question was followed by a loud burst of radio static.

Greer crossed to the communications console. DeSosa gave her a headset. "He's got some symptoms of bacterial infection and a low-grade fever," Greer said into the mike. "I pumped him full of antibiotics. He's resting."

"The ground support medical team has confirmed your decision," Christiansen said.

"Houston, we'll be back to you in ten with Faden," Tseng said.

"Copy that," Christiansen said.

☾

The picture from Far Side that appeared on the main monitor shocked Bianco. They'd strapped Faden to a chair on Level Three. He wore the makeshift straitjacket over his FS-5 fatigues. Bianco noticed that, under his fatigue shorts, he wore one of the diapers designed to be used with a space suit.

"Don't bother me. I need rest!" Faden growled at the camera.

Greer responded with her most benign, professional smile. She stood next to Faden while the other FS-6 astronauts found their own positions in the communications center from which to observe. Tseng had the camera, Paul Manch was conspicuous by his absence.

Gutierrez remained standing near Birnbaum, while Christiansen sat at his CAPCOM station. Bianco had sought the chair farthest away from the camera trained on them and sending their video to Far Side. Off to the side, a second monitor showed the picture Far Side was receiving. At the moment, the tech behind the lens transmitted a long shot of the assembled group in Mission Control.

Faden looked into the camera, then he turned his head to stare at the monitor. They watched him. He watched *them*. Bianco felt uneasy at the man's scrutiny.

Christiansen waved to the camera and said, "Hello, Bob. It's Dave Christiansen. I'm CAPCOM on this shift, and I thought we'd pay you a visit." He gestured at Gutierrez and Birnbaum saying, "We brought along a couple of friends of ours. This is . . ."

"I know who they are," Faden frowned at the camera menacingly, then he turned his attention back to the monitor.

Bianco checked Gutierrez's and Birnbaum's reactions.

The detective's expression reflected only curiosity.

Birnbaum crossed to Christiansen and whispered something in his ear.

Christiansen nodded assent. "Bob, I want you to know how sorry we are about what happened to your friends at Far Side," he said.

"Food for the Moon," Faden responded, but in an aggravated voice that was not his own.

Bianco marveled at how the enigmatic phrase took on a chilling connotation when spoken by the astronaut. However, it was as though he was merely the mouthpiece, but not the speaker. An angry male personality had surfaced, and had dominated him in order to be heard.

"So, Bob, you say you need rest. Haven't you been getting any sleep?" Christiansen asked.

"Hell, no! Can't you hear them singing?" Faden responded in his own voice with a look of incredulity.

"I . . . I'm afraid your hearing is better than mine," Christiansen said uncertainly, turning to look at Birnbaum for guidance.

Birnbaum's expression was unreadable to Bianco.

"I listen to the sounds all the time," Faden continued in a chatty tone. "We can be having a conversation, like we are now, but I can hear all the noises going on from every room on every floor."

"Since you're so talkative, do you feel like talking about Far Side, Bob?" Birnbaum said aloud.

"It's hard for me to think," Faden said, and he grimaced.

It occurred to Bianco that Faden's twisted facial expression was for show, so that they could see and appreciate what a great effort thinking was for him, and not push him. He really wanted them to back off.

"My brain is going so fast. So fast. So fast. So fast . . ." Faden continued to repeat the phrase, and the words tumbled out of his mouth in such a rapid patter that his grimace gave way to a smile of enjoyment at his own cleverness. ". . . So fast. So fast. So fast. So fast. Like an engine. Like a rocket engine. Like a nuclear rocket engine . . . Whooooshshsh!"

Without warning, a sly look replaced the merriment on Faden's face. With a hard look at them, a different voice said, "People are afraid of the dead. Do you know that, Dave?"

The change of personality in Faden was sudden. In Bianco's opinion, the personality of this speaker was aggressive and overbearing, and obsessed with Christiansen, because the statement and the question were a direct challenge to him.

A quick glance at Birnbaum told her the psychiatrist had interpreted the situation similarly, and that he was carefully considering what strategy to use in dealing with it.

Gutierrez shifted his body position, so that he was facing the monitor, as if sensing a physical threat.

Christiansen seemed reluctant to pick up the spiritual gauntlet Faden had so arrogantly flung at him.

Bianco was keenly aware of the nuances of the interplay. For Christiansen, she reasoned, it was not so much a personal reluctance to believe in the veracity of the behavior he was witnessing from Faden as it was a reluctance to accept the challenge of a confrontation with the personification, if not the embodiment, of evil without a sign from "above" that he was, truly, the chosen champion of "the good," and that Faden was truly what he appeared to be. The history of the astronaut's religion would have taught him to expect a "revelation," and he seemed sincerely reluctant to go forward into battle without one. The irony was, that if Christiansen's preconceived notion of what form the revelation would assume was too rigid, he would fail to recognize it and to take appropriate action. Bianco wondered if Christiansen was cognizant of that irony, and if the fear of missing his opportunity was part of his inner struggle.

Her thoughts were interrupted by the unnatural sound of Faden's voice.

"Are you afraid of the dead, Dave?" the astronaut taunted Christiansen.

In the instant of time that Christiansen took to respond, Bianco knew, instinctively, that a decision had finally been made and that Christiansen was gathering himself and calling on his inner strength and faith before speaking.

"No. I'm not afraid," Christiansen said with sincerity. "Those of us who have faith in our Lord, Jesus Christ, know that the Heavenly Father has a plan for us."

A wildly exaggerated look of enlightened astonishment came onto Faden's face. He spoke in a hushed tone, as though the statement had been a profound personal revelation for him. "I have too many thoughts, Dave," he said in his own voice. "I have to think about what those words mean. What they really, really mean. What . . . do . . . they . . . mean? The meaning. I have to think about the meaning. I've got to be better prepared when people talk to me. I've got to be ready for these things."

It was too forced and melodramatic to be sincere, Bianco thought. The two sides, which, much to her own surprise, Bianco could only think of as "good" and "evil," had clashed, and a battle was now under way.

"Dave . . ." Birnbaum began warningly.

Faden cut him off in a loud, harsh voice. "Dave, Dave, Dave, David, King of Israel! I've got a surprise for you! Hey, Joe Smith, you dirty animal, you leaky bag of shit and piss. You're the stinkingest bag of rotten flesh that ever came out from between the fat, smelly legs of a woman, but you're here with us now, so say something to one of your flock, Jooooooseph!"

A guttural Faden voice said, "We put one over on them, Dave. All those Latter Day Whores . . . they're juicy cunts, aren't they, Dave? They came to worship my cock and balls! All day and all night . . . poom poom poom poom," Faden made obscene thrusting movements with his hips and groin to the rhythm of the words.

"Poom poom poom for Jesus . . . oh, Jesus, let me give it to them!"

Christiansen's eyes sparked with surprise and anger at the blatant attack.

"That's enough on this subject," Birnbaum said sternly.

On camera, Faden continued moving his pelvis in the obscene rhythm. "Poom poom poom poom poom . . . ah-hhhhh!" he groaned in ecstasy.

There was every indication that Faden had had a sexual climax.

Christiansen could not hide his disgust, and his face was bright red with embarrassment, shock, and righteous indignation.

Greer said, "Dave, if you could refrain from any religious references, I would appreciate it. In these instances, Faden reacts to religious symbolism in a predictable way, given the symptoms he's manifested all along. On a certain level, he's cognizant both of the symbol, and of the relationship between himself and the symbol."

Christiansen acknowledged Greer's comment with a shrug of his shoulders like a fighter told to go back into his corner until the next round. Bianco saw beads of sweat on the astronaut's forehead.

Faden's legs sprawled open. Several voices giggled and twittered in amusement. Faden puffed out his belly and then expelled gas in a long fart. "You believe in your precious God and in Jesus . . . that Jesus, you know, he has this thing against flesh."

Birnbaum shook his head in annoyance.

"Can we open the window?" Cochagne mumbled, voicing the nausea everyone at Far Side but Faden was obviously suffering.

"They don't open, for reasons that I'm sure are understandable to you," Lebby answered sarcastically.

"Cut the chatter," Tseng said.

Meanwhile, Faden was totally self-absorbed, giggling and muttering to himself.

Bianco blinked, startled as Gutierrez strode toward the camera and looked into the lens to catch Faden's attention.

He said, "So, Bob, who else have you got in there with you besides Joseph Smith?"

"All his precious saints are here," a Faden voice said, indicating Christiansen by a jerk of his head. "You're just like me, Dave!" the 'Smith' voice hissed.

"Who are they?" Gutierrez persisted.

"Don't tell him a fucking thing," a different Faden voice answered.

Gutierrez took out his pen and notebook, and wrote hurriedly for a moment, then he said mockingly, "You're a fake and a liar, Bob! Why don't you stop this act?"

"I believe he's had enough of this," Greer warned.

Birnbaum opened his mouth to speak.

Gutierrez held up a hand to interrupt him.

Christiansen took them off the COMM.

"In my line of work, when you bring certain people together and create a situation, and things start to happen, you let them happen," Gutierrez said. "As long as you can maintain control, you let the thing run its course and you see what develops out of it. Whether accidentally, or on purpose, by bringing Christiansen and Faden in contact, you've created a situation where Faden is motivated to talk. If we could just have a few more minutes with him . . ."

Gutierrez turned to her. Bianco's intuition told her to trust his instincts. She nodded assent.

Gutierrez said, "Please keep talking to him about the Lord, Dave."

Christiansen opened the COMM. He started to speak, then changed his mind. He seemed unsure of what to say under pressure from Gutierrez.

It was the first time Bianco had seen the astronaut nonplussed.

"Your Lord likes it in the ass, Dave!" a rough Faden voice mocked.

Christiansen turned his head away, as though to physically ward off the hate and the filth that Faden was directing at him.

Gutierrez motioned to the tech behind the camera to move in on Christiansen.

He moved forward obediently.

Christiansen looked into the lens, but he was now clearly annoyed that what he considered an act of faith was receiving a base secular endorsement.

Faden screamed in terror. He twisted his head around, away from the camera, and cowered. "Make him go away. He's torturing me," he sobbed.

"How is he torturing you?" Gutierrez asked.

"By watching me," the voice answered. Several of the other voices whined and twittered nervously in sympathetic response.

"What are you doing?" Greer hissed. "I want all of you to stop this right now!"

Bianco got up from her chair. "I'll take full responsibility, Iona," she said.

"I don't care," Greer responded. "He's my patient!"

"Everything's under control," Birnbaum said to Greer. "I just don't think this will accomplish the objective," he told Gutierrez.

"Just go with it for a little while longer," Gutierrez requested.

Christiansen began, "Bob, if you believe in the Lord . . ."

Bianco could see that Faden eyed Christiansen suspiciously. Suddenly, a stream of vomit exploded from Faden's mouth, soiling him and the floor under him.

Horo gagged in revulsion.

"Too bad, but I haven't found Jesus because I'm not dead," a Faden voice said.

The voice was defiant, yet Bianco was sure she saw fear in Faden's eyes . . . fear of the struggle that was taking place within him. She noticed that two flies were buzzing and circling excitedly in the air over the yellowish vomit that ran down Faden's chin and soaked into his clothes.

Gutierrez moved closer to Christiansen in order to draw Faden's attention. "Who else is in there with you, Bob? Is Ann Bisio there?" he asked.

"No," a Faden voice responded.

"Is Frank Drzymkowski with you?"

"No."

"Is Mike Mobley with you?"

"Is Shinobu Takizawa with you?"

This time, there was no answer from Faden.

"Who's in there with you?" Gutierrez persisted.

Again, there was no response, but a violent tremor ran through Faden's body. He twisted his head and turned his face away from the camera. "My beautiful bones . . . my bones are burning," a plaintive voice whined. "Look at that fire! The whole place is on fire! I'm burning up! My eyes are on fire! I can see myself coming apart! I'm coming apart and my bones are burning!" Faden screamed in terror and agony.

"So you were in a fire. Do you know what happened after that?" Gutierrez asked.

"I went to sleep, but I woke up again because I wanted to live. They thought I was dead, but I wasn't!" the Faden voice sobbed, "I lost my body! I lost my body!"

"If you lost your body, where are you now?" Christiansen asked.

"I don't know."

"Look around you. Who else is with you?" Gutierrez coaxed.

"I don't know them."

"If you're Takizawa, speak to us in Japanese," Gutierrez demanded.

In an instant, Faden's personality changed. He turned his face back to them, smiling slyly. Then he glared at the camera. "Give me something to drink. I want some wine!" a familiar voice said.

"It's the personality that is calling himself Joseph Smith," Christiansen said. "You know you can't have any wine," he told Faden sternly.

"I want it! Give it to me now, and I want cigarettes and a whore, too, or I'll kill you!"

"You're not Joseph Smith! I don't believe he's there with you!" Christiansen challenged.

"Get Takizawa back," Bianco whispered furtively.

"You think he thinks he's possessed by Takizawa?" Birnbaum asked.

"The name triggered that persona last time," Bianco said.

"Let me speak to Shinobu Takizawa," Christiansen told Faden.

Faden's body went limp. The whining voice said, "I'm very weak. I'm afraid of the others."

"Who are the others?" Gutierrez asked.

"Food for the Moon," a different voice answered.

"I'm always dead," another voice pouted.

"I've lost my body!" the Takizawa personality complained, then burst into sobs.

"In that state of mind, he's focused only on the fire," Bianco whispered. "It's as if that personality is in shock."

"Shut up and behave yourself!" a gravelly Faden voice commanded the sobbing Takizawa persona.

"This is quite a seance you're conducting," Birnbaum grumbled. "I hope you're satisfied!"

Faden was turning his head restlessly from side to

side. Greer approached him and placed her fingers on the
astronaut's throat to check his pulse. Seemingly satisfied, she frowned and brushed at the flies circling
above him.

In his own voice, Faden moaned, "Dave, will you take
me with you?"

"Answer him. Tell him you'll take him with you,"
Gutierrez urged Christiansen.

Christiansen ignored Gutierrez's coaching. Instead, he
put his hands together and concentrated with an attitude
of fervent prayer. His brows knitted in deep concentration, and his lips moved, but the words were inaudible.
Bianco could only feel an intensity that was hypnotic to
her, and, likewise, no one else dared to break the "spell."
There was a hushed silence in Mission Control.

Faden's smile was cherubic, but Bianco noticed a
black speck between his lips which drew her curiosity.
She felt revulsion as the speck emerged from his mouth
and flew upward to join the flies over his head.

In an instant, his cherubic smile disappeared, and
Faden raised his head and fixed the camera with a harsh
unblinking stare. "Are you trying to exorcise me, Dave?"
a deep-throated Faden voice growled at the astronaut.

Faden's eyes were hard and lacked any emotion
Bianco could recognize as being compassionate or even
human.

"Man is inherently evil, Dave. If he were not, then he
would not have to be taught 'good,' " a Faden voice said.

For the first time, fear showed in Christiansen's face.

Faden flexed his body and lunged forward against the
straps that pinned him to the chair with such force, that
the chair bucked. He lunged forward and fell back, then
forward, then back again, and, each time the legs of the
chair left the floor. Abruptly, he stopped.

Bianco saw Faden's eyes grow wide with terror, as if
from something only he could see. He screamed, and, to

Bianco's ears, it was the simultaneous scream of all the voices inside of him.

It was a scream which lasted longer than Bianco thought humanly possible.

☾

"Houston, your transmission is breaking up again," Tseng said.

"We copy. We'll make this as br . . . possible," Christiansen said. "We'd like an update on Bob Faden's condition."

"He's resting quietly, for the time being," Tseng said.

"No more teleconferences," Greer said.

"None scheduled," Christiansen said.

"Stand by, Houston, while we make another storm-time correction," DeSosa interrupted, adjusting a bank of dials on his console.

"Far Side, do you read?" Christiansen's voice came through a diminished, but steady, hiss of radio static.

"We're reading you," DeSosa said.

"By our present calculations, we will have loss of signal at one hundred forty hours: thirty-five minutes Mission Elapsed Time. You are also coming up on termination of solar power array input at one hundred forty-six hours: fifty-seven minutes MET, at which time you will go to stored power for the Lunar Night Phase, Far Side. We would like you to take some time, now, to review your LNP power usage requirements. Your house-keeping loads, including life support, water processing and O_2 recovery, your main interior lights, your auxiliary interior lights, your cooking and refrigeration and your data system and instrumentation controls and displays will have priority, but you should scale those to a minimum. All user loads, such as EVA support activities, science activities and FS-6 mission servicing activities should be carefully prioritized and kept at a bare minimum."

"We copy that," Tseng responded.

"Also, concerning your situation, we feel that, under current conditions, an enclosed metal structure such as the Main Dome might act like a 'Faraday cage,' where a tremendous field of positive ions would be generated within the dome by the movement of the solar wind and energized dust particles across the outside surface. Even under normal conditions, your air would get saturated with positive ions, depending upon the level of activity going on and the number of people in residence, so the ionizers—the negative ion generators which are part of your life-support system—maintain a healthy balance by charging your atmosphere with negative ions."

"Yes. The Far Side system is modeled after the one at Space Station," Tseng said, not bothering to disguise her impatience.

However, Christiansen continued doggedly, "Yes. In their case, again, they're breathing temperature-controlled, recirculated air, which, if not for the ionizers, would contain a high concentration of positive ions because of the effect of the solar wind passing over the structure.

"Your current situation is worse by an order of magnitude, and if this type of positive ion field is building up inside the base, it can have a number of adverse effects. It can lower the oxygen level in the blood and increase the accumulation of serotonin and other neurotransmitters in the brain. Too much serotonin can result in chronic fatigue, loss of concentration, slowed reactions, depression and, in particular, irritability. An increased concentration of other neurotransmitters such as epinephrine and norepinephrine would have an adrenergic effect—

that is, they could cause a type of 'fear-anxiety' adrenal reaction."

"That's the 'fight or flight' reaction," Greer interjected. "When we perceive a threat such as from a situation or a natural enemy, it's the adrenal cortex that primes us for action. It's called an adrenocorticotrophic reaction, and it's an automatic response."

"We think that if the output of negative ions can . . . increased, it might lessen the physical side effects . . . you," Christiansen said.

"Each ionizer has a fixed output of only two meters in any given direction." Cochagne grumbled with uncharacteristic petulance.

"We think the increase . . . accomplished by doubling the number of units in the system. You . . . ould have everything you need to do that stored . . . Level One . . . cause the last three missions, counting yours, have . . . ansported primary life-su . . . ort system electronic components for the Science Dome up . . ."

"The containers are down there," Cochagne said. "Do they realize that it will take quite a while for this to have any real effect?"

"We have them," Tseng told Christiansen.

"We'd like you . . . do that."

"We copy." Tseng recognized that this was an order that was being diplomatically worded as a request. The ground team was coaxing them into cooperation.

"That's the best . . . come up with at this time, Far Side. When do you think you . . . get to . . . t?" Christiansen persisted.

"I'll get on it ASAP," Cochagne said grudgingly.

"We . . . cop . . . F . . . Side. Over," came the response from Houston.

"They think that cleansing the air is really going to solve our problems?" Greer asked.

"An ionizer doesn't 'cleanse' the air," Lebby said. "It

neutralizes the positive ions by generating negative ions."

"I hate make-work projects," Cochagne grumbled.

"They must be favoring a 'GO' through loss of signal, or they wouldn't have asked us to make the modification," Horo said.

"I agree," Tseng seconded. "It's in our best interest to get it done."

"What did they send us?" Horo asked.

With a few keystrokes, Lebby brought a photo onto the computer screen.

"I took that shot in Takizawa's sleep station," Cochagne said.

"There's so much distortion in the image," Lebby said disparagingly.

"They did a piece of work on this," Cochagne said. "Look how they brought out what was underneath the crossed-out area."

"What does it say?" Horo asked.

"Takizawa was screwing around with the spelling of his name," Tseng said. "Print it out for me, will you, Pops? I'll look it over later."

"Right away," Lebby answered, keying the computer.

Tseng remembered the snack that she'd fixed for herself and retrieved it from the galley microwave. It was cool, but she was too hungry to reheat it.

"Can I show you that program now?" Lebby asked her, when she returned to Level Three carrying her tray.

"Yes, let's see it."

Lebby keyed the computer and a colorful game board appeared on the screen with the letters of the alphabet, the numbers from zero to nine, and the words "yes" and "no." An area at the bottom of the screen was designated as "Message line."

"That's a Ouija board," Tseng said.

"I'll be damned, but that's what it is," Horo affirmed.

"I haven't seen one of those in years, and I've never seen one on a computer."

"Does Greer know about this?" Tseng asked.

"No."

"I'll get her," DeSosa said.

Tseng studied the screen and ate her food in a thoughtful silence until DeSosa returned followed by the psychiatrist.

"Dick found this on the computer," Tseng told her.

"A Ouija board."

"What does it do?" Lebby questioned.

"It's what's known as an automatism," Greer said. "It's a form of automatic writing."

"My friends and I used one in an attempt to contact the spirits of dead relatives and rock music stars," Horo said. "That's what it's for . . . to communicate with the dead."

"Did you get any response?" Cochagne asked.

"Our board must have been a dud."

"The problem with automatisms is that certain personality types can become addicted to them," Greer said. "In my opinion, the allure and the danger of this game, especially to young people who are strongly suggestive and highly imitative, is a subject that has never been adequately addressed. Parapsychologists have supposedly documented contemporary incidents of poltergeist activity, where young teenagers, thought to be the cause and the focus of the activity, have been linked to use of a Ouija board. Bodily injury, destruction of furniture and property, 'apports'—feces, urine, pools of water which appear out of nowhere, and small objects which disappear and then reappear somewhere else, sometimes having moved through solid walls or containers—are all reported to be part of this phenomenon.

"All the hocus-pocus stuff aside, what nearly all of these kids have in common is very low self-esteem. They may perceive—rightly or wrongly—that they are not accepted by adults and by their mainstream peers, and they are attracted to the board as a way of conjuring up 'friends' from the spirit world as confidants. Any response they get is really their subconscious crying out for acceptance and ego reinforcement, but, in some cases, repeated use of the Ouija board has had the rather serious consequence of fostering the development of multiple and split personalities. From time to time, we also see cases of something we call a mediumistic or possession psychosis, where the subject believes that he or she is possessed by a spirit contact, or even by a demon."

"Is that what Rick Masino was alluding to during the teleconference with Bethesda?" Tseng asked the psychiatrist.

"Yes."

"I can't make this work from the main computer keyboard," Lebby said.

"The board game we had came with a pointer," Horo said. "All the players put their fingers on it, and then, everybody concentrated on the question they want to ask a particular spirit."

"In this application, we'd need a user interface such as a light pen or a mouse," Tseng told Lebby.

"Automatic writing with a computer," Horo said. "It looks like a complicated program."

"I think I understand how this works, and it's not complicated," Lebby said. "Anyone at Faden's and Bisio's level could write this kind of thing in about two hours."

"Nice graphics," Cochagne said.

"You're too easily impressed," Lebby said dryly.

"I believe the document files that Dick found which look like series of random letters and numbers are transcripts of the 'game sessions,' " Greer said. "I want to see them, and I would like to know how they were made, which means seeing this game in operation."

"I don't want to tie up the main computer with it, but

I could put together an auxiliary terminal with a mouse as a user interface for you to play around with," Lebby told her.

"I don't think we should mess with it," DeSosa said.

"Faden never said anything about a Ouija board program to me, neither did Mobley, and yet, he must have known about it," Tseng said.

Cochagne yawned and stretched. "Well, folks, this has been loads of fun, but I have work to do."

"You don't sound very optimistic, Jerry," Lebby said.

"I'm not. I think the level of saturation we'll get from the ionizers will have a negligible effect."

"I'll give you a hand," DeSosa said.

"If you don't, he won't get his beauty sleep tonight," Horo teased.

Far Side's "basement" seemed even more damp, cold, and tomblike than usual to Tseng as she descended the companionway with Cochagne and DeSosa.

When they reached Level One, they were surprised to see that the stacks of loose papers, which Manch had moved in order to use the table for the postmortem on Mobley's body, were scattered throughout the room, as though by a strong wind.

The makeshift worktable was lying on the floor. The boxes of lab supplies, that had been its corner supports, were stacked vertically and precariously on top of the bed cushions, and, as they watched, the tower of boxes swayed, wobbled unsteadily, and collapsed. When the topmost box struck the floor, they heard glass breaking inside.

"This is the kind of thing that happens when you play with a Ouija board," DeSosa said.

"I prefer to think it was the result of human carelessness," Cochagne said.

Their inspection of the contents of the box confirmed the destruction of a large quantity of laboratory glassware.

Cochagne crossed to a stack of payload containers. He scanned the inventory lists posted on the lids, then pulled out one of the containers and opened it. "This is it: the Air Revitalization System Assembly. There are four units here. One for each level of the Science Dome." He reached into the container and lifted out a flat base with square modules and electronic black boxes, attached to it.

The job of mission commander required a detailed knowledge of every individual crew member's job and a familiarity with all the vital base systems. Tseng refreshed her knowledge of the assembly by quickly tracing the connections and circuits for the odor control canister, the dehumidifier, the fan, fan filter, and fan silencer, the catalytic containment burner, the depolarized CO_2 concentrator and the ionizer. Some of the units were linked by wires and lengths of pipe or tubing, while others, including the ionizer, were "stand alones."

"You're the base systems engineer, so what's the best way to do this?" Tseng asked Cochagne.

Cochagne took a screwdriver from his tool kit and removed the ionizer unit from its base. "We're going to wire these units onto the ARSA boards on every level. It's a simple connection, 'quick and dirty,' as we say in the trade."

☾

Christiansen, Stromeyer, Sweet, MacCallum, Weinstock, Gutierrez, Bucar, Fay, Zia, Ramirez, Adachi, every flight controller, every scientist, and every person in Mission Control—Bianco felt the heavy pressure of their expectations of her as a crushing weight. They awaited her decision to continue the mission, but she was not through considering the alternatives.

"In the *Apollo* days, before the L-TDRS system was put into orbit to maintain constant communications, a forty-five minute Loss Of Signal was routine when spacecraft went around the Far Side," Bucar said. "They just sweated it out.

"Certainly no one came back from those early Moon missions crazy. What happened to FS-5 was not a result of LOS. LOS is the result of certain conditions that exist during periods of high electromagnetic activity associated with the lunar day-night cycle. In the case of Mike Mobley and his crew, we also had a random set of circumstances dictated by the human element. The question that we don't have the answer to is: why did we have murder and mayhem up there with FS-5?"

"We'd hoped to have more insight into the human factor in the problem before now, but the way the schedule has worked out—" Bianco left the sentence unfinished in order to get her thoughts on a more practical track. "At this point, the schedule is irrelevant. My feeling is that this is a different crew. They're fresher, more alert. They haven't been up there a month. They haven't been worn down by problems. There's also a different combination of technical specialties and a different personality mix on the team."

"There's no sense in polling them," Bucar said. "The level of professionalism that kicks in in these situations will result in their presenting a united front and in their voting to see this through. The decision has to be ours," Bucar added.

Gutierrez nodded comprehension. "Police officers react in much the same way when confronted with a dangerous situation on the job," he said. "Let me bring you up to date as far as what I've been doing," he continued, addressing the group. "I've seen the videos and the stills of the FS-5 mission, and I've studied the evidence gathered thus far by the FS-6 crew . . . I've come up with some possibilities based on that, but they move the main focus of the investigation away from Bob Faden.

"In the matter of Frank Drzymkowski's murder, fingerprint evidence strongly suggests Mike Mobley as the
perpetrator. I think Mobley may have had several very
strong motives for killing Drzymkowski, not the least of
which was an ongoing struggle for power and authority
between the two men.

"There's evidence which connects both Drzymkowski
and Faden with Bisio's murder, but fingerprint evidence
targets Drzymkowski in the stabbing. At this stage, we
can't be absolutely certain that Bisio's wound was received antemortem, but that is a bet, based on an expert
opinion. Drzymkowski's motive for this is as yet unknown, and there are other gaps in this scenario because
of the unexplained disappearance of Shinobu Takizawa.
The circumstances of Louise Washington's death also
disturb me greatly, and then, there's the fire.

"Let's talk about the rover first. The original theory
was that there were at least two persons involved in an
altercation which resulted in the lunar rover being overturned. My conclusion is that there were three individuals involved. Faden had to be one of them. I believe Mike
Mobley was the third party, and that Mobley's actions resulted in Bob Faden's being shut up inside the *Aldrin.*

"I've been wanting to work backward to the event that
set things in motion, but, until now, I just didn't have
enough information. My gut feeling is that the deaths
were the accidental result of an initial problem or mistake which was concealed from Mission Control, and of
a series of subsequent desperate attempts to cover up for
later problems and complications, some of which might
even have happened because of that first event.

"None of the deaths appear premeditated. Rather, the
evidence suggests that they were spur-of-the-moment
acts of violence between people who knew one another
very well. That's the most common type of murder. In
these cases, the crime scene is littered with evidence and

clues to the identity of the murderer, because there is no plan made, ahead of time, for covering up the act. Attempts to cover up, after the fact, are hastily conceived and usually ineffective because they're so obvious.

"When the psychiatrists at Bethesda talked about Faden, they used the term, 'precipitating event.' I am trying to look at this whole situation from that point of view: what was the original event or act that set things in motion, and which provided the motives for the other acts committed? It looks to be Mike Mobley's injury. Paul Manch is of the opinion that it was an accidental injury. Of course, we don't know that for sure at the moment, and we may never know for sure. From his subsequent actions, I don't think we'd be far off target exploring that scenario, however. As for casting Frank Drzymkowski as a key factor from then on, I would have to say that I'm definitely leaning in that direction.

"What part all the occult practices play in this, we don't yet know, though the focus of that part of the investigation falls on Bob Faden for reasons that are obvious to anyone who's seen him in his present condition. The motivation for his activities is again unknown; however, we do know that he had an obsession with Shinobu Takizawa. Was there a close friendship between them? The individuals I've questioned about that say 'no.' There was a working relationship, but Faden and Takizawa had very little or nothing in common. In fact, Takizawa was not very communicative, in general, which proved to be a problem during the training phase of the FS-5 mission, from what I've been told. God, I wish I knew how his disappearance fit into this," Gutierrez said, with a sigh of exasperation. "Bob Faden is the key to that." He looked at them apologetically. "I was hoping to make this as brief as possible."

"It sounds like you're on a roll, Lieutenant," Bucar said.

Gutierrez responded with a shrug, then he continued. "Though the exact chronology of events is unknown, there are several things we do know: at some point, Mike Mobley became seriously injured, and Shinobu Takizawa disappeared, or was murdered, and the body hidden; Ann Bisio was stabbed by Drzymkowski; there was a confrontation outside the dome, between Mike Mobley and Frank Drzymkowski, which resulted in further injury to Mobley. There was a final confrontation between them inside the base, which resulted in Drzymkowski's death. It was probably a continuation of the altercation which began at the rover.

"Having looked at the photos of Mobley's body, it's obvious to me that, had he not committed suicide, he would have bled to death from reopening his wound. He would not have had the strength to fight off a man of Drzymkowski's physical stature for very long. Thus, he resorted to the use of a formidable weapon—say, the hammer—on Drzymkowski.

"That's why I can be reasonably certain that Mike Mobley's death was the last link in a chain of events that took place within a very brief time period. Why did Mobley go on his suicide walk and leave Washington behind? Perhaps, he did not know that she was still alive. The circumstances of her discovery by the FS-6 crew lead me to think that this was the case, and that Washington sustained certain of her injuries in defense against an unknown assailant. Shutting Faden up in the *Aldrin* was a death sentence. What led him to make that decision? I've said about all I can say at this point. I have some new evidence—the results of an examination of the FS-5 trash, but I don't yet know how it fits in."

"Forgive me if I find some of that hard to accept," Bucar said. "Clearly, something horrendous happened up there, but this was a NASA crew. A crew of professionals. The vast majority of these people are either in the military, or have had experience in the military, and they are, or were, officers. You're talking about people who believe in, and operate by, a very rigid code of conduct and strict rules of discipline.

"Just taking the flight crews, for example: many of us have backgrounds that include combat and/or hundreds of hours in the air on flight test duty, which requires test pilot school. Now, the survival rate in test pilot school has been as low as about one in three. That means one out of three candidates in that class lived through the course to graduate, and yet, the competition to get into flight test is incredibly fierce. And I'll tell you another thing, you come out of the experience either knowing people and/or knowing stories about people who, when they knew they were going down in flames, continued to monitor their instruments and relay the information back to the tower until they hit the ground."

"Then let's ask ourselves this: what would it take to overwhelm that kind of discipline?" Gutierrez asked.

"Nothing short of major brain damage," Bucar responded sarcastically, then, turning to Bianco, he shook his head worriedly. "A decision to bring FS-6 back now will result in a setback for the program, but, by the same token, our people are not expendable in the interests of science."

"If we're going to give them the order to pull out, we have to do it soon," Christiansen said.

The CAPCOM had surrendered his chair to Bahija Fayyad hours ago, but had remained in Mission Control to offer technical assistance, and also, Bianco was sure, to add a "spiritual" power to their efforts in his way of thinking. Several times, Bianco had seen him in an attitude of fervent prayer.

She recognized the irony in the situation, for, while the assembled scientists, astronauts, and technicians might soon be standing helplessly by, and anxiously sweating

out the period of radio silence, Dave Christiansen would
be engaged in "purposeful" activity—never mind that it
was purposeful only in a very narrow, subjective way, it
was purposeful to him. In his mind, did Christiansen
think of prayer as an active solution to the problem? If
so, rightly or wrongly, he had the only positive attitude
in the room.

She was not really concerned with Christiansen, however. She was thinking of the FS-6 crew and feeling frustrated that the only action for her, at the moment, had the
earmarks of inaction.

The International Space Station had been considered
the technological wonder of the turn of the century. Far
Side Moon Base was another technological step outward, and it also represented another foray away from
the nest of Earth for mankind—Mike Mobley and his
crew, and Tseng and her crew were all fledglings of a
space traveling species. . . .

Technology had let the FS-5 astronauts down, and it
was letting FS-6 down, too. Survival would not depend
on it, but on human powers of perception and interpretation, and on logical reasoning and personal courage; it
would depend on people.

"I am in favor of extending the mission for an additional forty-eight hours despite the pending LOS period," Bianco said. "My only concern is Bob Faden. If
they think they can handle him, then I say it's a go."

Christiansen and Bucar nodded acceptance of the decision. Gutierrez nodded agreement with it.

☾

Tseng luxuriated in the comfort of warm water cascading
down her body from the handheld, controlled-spray
showerhead. The head was attached to a flexible water
hose, so that the water could be directed precisely where

it was needed for greater efficiency. The water itself was not a problem at Far Side, because it was a natural by-product of the fuel cells. Recycling waste water, however, was another matter, and the length of a shower was limited by the capacity of the waste water system.

She leaned against the shower stall and closed her eyes. Cochagne's estimate about the time needed for the additional ionizers to reach an adequate saturation level had been too conservative, she reflected.

Cochagne. Whenever she thought about him, she couldn't help remembering the feel of being in his arms; of the way he'd touched her.

With a start, she realized that she'd dozed off with the water running. She turned the water off and hung up the showerhead, then dried herself under the blower.

With the mission extended for two more days, frequent changes of clothing would create additional laundry that would only add to the disorganized clutter inside the base, she reasoned. Intending to put her shorts and T-shirt back on, she reached out of the shower stall to where she'd left them. Her hand groped in vain. Puzzled, she leaned out of the shower stall and saw them on the floor, out of reach.

A glance up at the mirror made her freeze, and raised the hairs on the back of her neck. The word DOG was scrawled across it in deep red crayon or wax. When she approached closer, she knew by the smell, even before wiping at the writing with her finger, that it was lipstick. Reflected on the opposite wall was the phrase, Food for the Moon. The cover of the first aid kit was off and the remaining contents were, once again, scattered on the floor on top of her shorts and T-shirt, along with the contents of the trash bag which Horo had filled with the first aid items to be discarded.

Tseng could hear movement and voices from the level above. Lebby and Cochagne were still awake. For a moment, her own anger and sense of outrage flared at the possibility of being the target of a prank and the graffiti as a joke. Indignation tempted her to wipe the mirror clean, but she resisted the impulse. The paranoia was unwarranted and served no purpose other than to obstruct logical thinking.

Annoyance with the unknown prankster was tinged with disbelief at finding evidence that Washington's tube of lipstick was still here, and not with her things on board the *Collins*.

This was out of character even for Cochagne's or Horo's senses of humor. On the surface, the incident seemed trivial, but was it? All one needed to do was to look around the walls of the Main Dome for an answer to that question, she concluded.

Tseng put on her clothes, then moved silently down the corridor to Greer's sleep station. She knocked softly on the wall next to the privacy curtain.

"Who's there," Greer called out sleepily.

"It's Po. I want you to see something."

"Just a minute," Greer whispered back, more awake this time.

When Greer pulled back the privacy curtain, Tseng motioned silently for the woman to follow her.

In the hygiene station, Greer stared unblinkingly at the mess from the first aid kit, and the mirror, for a few moments. "My opinion is that this writing is meant to be "God," spelled backward," she told Tseng. "It's fairly clichéd evidence for occult activity—I use the word 'evidence' with great reluctance. It's so childish. I can't imagine who among this crew would do this. If we didn't know better, the implication would be that one of us is a Dr. Jekyll and Mr. Hyde type."

"How long since you checked on Bob Faden?"

"I don't know. Paul insisted he could look in on him, so I could rest . . ."

"How long were you asleep?"

"I . . . I don't know."

Before Tseng could respond, the noise of Horo and DeSosa emerging from their sleep stations destroyed the link between herself and Greer. What's more, she had the distinct impression that the woman was retreating even farther back into her protective mental shell because of the intrusion.

"What happened in here?" Horo exclaimed. "Joe, look at the mirror and the wall!"

DeSosa turned pale and crossed himself.

"I don't understand . . ." Horo said.

"Did you put that lipstick in the bag with Washington's things?" Tseng asked her.

"I thought about it, like you suggested. I decided I wanted it as a keepsake," Horo said.

"Do I smell something—like plastic or wire insulation—burning?" DeSosa asked, looking around the room, then out into the corridor.

Tseng saw thin billowing puffs of white smoke wafting toward them from the recreation area.

"Jer! Smoke from below," they heard Lebby exclaim from Level Three.

"Get the extinguisher," Cochagne called back.

Tseng ran toward the hatch. "Bring the camera," she yelled upward, before turning to follow Horo, who was already in flight toward the recreation area.

A stark naked Bob Faden watched the smoke curling up around the pile of furniture and refuse that had remained untouched on the orders of Mission Control.

Tseng had expected to find something smoldering, rather than actually on fire, as only fireproof materials were used in the interior, but hot blue flames shot up from the vicinity of the burned spot on the floor. The smoke was noxious, and, though it did smell like burned plastic, there was an underlying odor of charred bacon fat as well. Faden turned and smiled at her.

How had he removed his clothing and restraints?

Lebby ran in carrying the CO_2 fire extinguisher.

Looking pale, Paul Manch staggered in. "Faden is . . ." His sentence choked off when he saw the naked astronaut and the fire.

Cochagne came down the stairs cradling the camera under his arm. Tseng took it from him and shot Faden, then Lebby spraying out the fire.

"Have you ever smelled anything so foul?" Horo asked.

"Yes. I've worked in burn wards," Greer said.

Lebby continued to shoot the flames with the fire extinguisher until they were completely smothered.

Tseng circled to get a better angle on the fire. She caught the movement of a large solid object out of the corner of her eye. The next instant, she was knocked off her feet as DeSosa crashed into her. The blow sent her to the floor, the camera flew out of her hands.

She lay stunned, her mind blank from the shock, then she heard a babble of voices, with everyone talking at once. "She's coming around!"

"It just stunned her," Horo said.

"China!" Cochagne groaned worriedly.

"Thank God," Lebby said. "How's DeSosa?"

Tseng felt strong arms helping her sit up. Her vision cleared and she saw Cochagne's worried face close to hers. "What happened?" she asked.

"Faden ran into me," Lebby said. "This flew out of my hands and hit DeSosa." Lebby picked up the extinguisher, which was lying on its side against a wall. "The impact knocked him into you."

Greer ran into the room carrying her black bag. Tseng waved her away, toward DeSosa. "Where's Faden?"

"Paul's got him back in his quarters," Greer said. "We gave him another dose of medication."

"It happened so fast," Horo said. "There was no warning."

"How do you feel, Joe?" Greer asked.

"My right side is sore," the astronaut answered with difficulty.

"It's a miracle you weren't killed by that blow," Lebby said to DeSosa. "The extinguisher was literally torn from my grasp . . . the rate of linear acceleration must have been . . ." Lebby couldn't finish the sentence.

DeSosa put his hand on his forehead and felt for a bump. "God, my head is throbbing . . . and my shoulder aches."

Greer removed his hand and replaced it with her own. "You have a bump all right. I can feel it."

Tseng watched a fly land on the injured astronaut's face.

DeSosa brushed at it; however, the gesture was uncoordinated. The astronaut looked around the room with an unfocused expression. Suddenly, his expression changed to distress. "Tell me again, what happened?"

"He has a mild concussion," Greer said. "We'll have to keep a close watch on him for the next few hours."

"God! It's starting, just like with FS-5!" DeSosa said. "There was something I wanted to tell you . . . before the fire. About the lipstick. I put it in Washington's PPK. I found it in her sleep station. I thought it was a mistake."

"When was this?" Horo asked.

"I don't know. My head hurts."

"I need help to get Joe to his room," Greer said.

Lebby and Horo moved in to help Greer steady DeSosa on his feet.

"How's Paul doing?" Tseng asked Greer.

"He says he's feeling okay. I'd better go help him with Bob."

"Where's the video camera?" Tseng exclaimed, searching the room with her eyes.

"It survived," Cochagne said.

"That's a relief." Tseng gestured at the loose refuse and the bags of trash around the room. "This mess is adding to the chaos. After we finish going through it, I want it out of here. Right now, let's see if we can still raise Mission Control."

☾

The video replaying on the monitor in Mission Control documented a fire inside the Level Two recreation area. The transmission was bad, and the footage was askew with lines of static. Bianco heard Lebby, Horo, and Cochagne yelling at Faden in the background. Then there was a dizzying, spinning blur, and the transmission ended.

"That's all we got before LOS," the tech told Bianco apologetically.

PART FOUR

There was a flurry of nervous activity in Mission Control though Far Side Base was LOS, and would remain so for many more hours. To Dee Bianco's experienced eyes, "the jitters" were evident in the flight controllers and the astronauts who were part of the ground team. Some, like Yoshio Adachi, Shah Zia, Al Weinstock, Ignacio Ramirez, and Chuck MacCallum lingered past their shifts though the situation was not expected to change for many hours.

MacCallum, the astronomer, sat at a flight control station, working on a personal computer he'd set up on top of the console. Weinstock, a physicist, looked over his shoulder, interested in what was on the computer screen. From a distance, the physical contrast between the short, balding physicist and the red-bearded, Viking-like astronomer reminded Bianco of a fairy tale she'd read as a child, called "Jack and the Beanstalk." Everyone was making the best of the situation, but no one liked the waiting.

Bianco wandered toward the CAPCOM console where Dave Christiansen sat and pulled up a chair in preparation for the vigil ahead. Christiansen's reaction to her presence told her there was something on the astronaut's mind. "How's it going, Dave?" she asked casually.

"Just waiting for them to come back on the COMM," Christiansen answered. With a nod of his head, he indicated a tightly clustered group of flight controllers and computer techs. "It's mostly busy work that's going on here. They're having minor problems at one of the telemetry stations, but they think they've got a handle on it."

Bianco did not reply to the comment. Instead, under the pretext of watching the activity in the room, she waited for the astronaut to choose his own moment.

Christiansen seized his opportunity as soon as the normal movement of personnel near the CAPCOM console took them away and out of earshot. "Dee, when FS-6 comes back, I'd like to go and see Bob in the hospital, and maybe talk to him," he said. "I believe that he can be reached through the power of Jesus Christ."

"Are you asking for my permission to pray for him?"

"I suppose I am. Yes."

Bianco had anticipated this question. "As an official gesture, I think it wouldn't be appropriate," she told the astronaut, "but I do feel it's important for you, as the commander of FS-7, to follow Bob Faden's progress rather closely from here on in, and I'm going to help you establish some lines of communication where you can work with the people at Bethesda and work with Bob on a one-to-one basis. While you're doing that, at some point, you can decide, on your own, privately, to do something or not to do it."

Christiansen acknowledged her decision with a nod.

Bianco checked her watch. "The red team is taking over in forty minutes. Where do we stand in the countdown for AOS?"

"Acquisition Of Signal will be somewhere around one hundred sixty-seven hours Mission Elapsed Time."

"Roughly, another twenty hours. It's going to be a long day."

Across the room, MacCallum and Weinstock were attracting other astronauts to their discussion and computer display. Bianco got up from her chair and joined them. She noticed Gutierrez enter, take a purposeful look around Mission Control, spot her, and wave. Bianco waved him toward the MacCallum-Weinstock group.

"We're looking at a computer model of the Earth and its magnetic field." Bianco responded to the unspoken question in Gutierrez's eyes. The detective looked at the computer screen with a puzzled but interested expression. "This graphic representation has to do with the problems at Far Side . . . but I know you didn't come here to look at computer models."

"An FBI raid on Faden's house this morning is being featured on the news," Gutierrez said. "I thought you would be watching it. So far, the UBC coverage has been pretty decent."

"Ordinarily, it wouldn't occur to us at all," Bianco said. Inwardly, she was taken aback by the detective's announcement that there had been major media coverage of the FBI move.

"Let's see what's going on in the outside world," a flight controller said sarcastically, crossing to switch one of the TV monitors at the perimeter of the room to receive an outside signal.

"This is a UBC news special broadcast: Crisis at Far Side," an off-camera network announcer said over the shot of the Moon that came up on the screen. "Here's Ted Guest."

There was a noticeable drop in the noise level in the room as conversations stopped and the attention of people in the vicinity who were idle at the moment focused on the monitor.

On the screen, the network cut from the Moon shot to a studio interior. Guest sat at a news desk looking worried and somber. "As I sit here, Far Side Base is experiencing LOS. That acronym stands for Loss of Signal, a relic, certainly, of the *Apollo* program days.

"The vigil has begun in Mission Control. They are waiting to reacquire communications with the Moon base. On everyone's mind, I'm sure, is the knowledge that FS-5 never reestablished communications with Earth following LOS. Indeed, all but one member of that crew died under mysterious and still-unknown circumstances.

"There has been an attempt to follow up on Commander Mike Mobley's whereabouts, and from what we understand, his body has now been recovered. We're hoping to get the details shortly. That leaves only Shinobu Takizawa unaccounted for, and there's speculation tonight as to whether FS-6 will be brought home short of achieving the goal of finding that missing crew member. On Capitol Hill, there's already talk of delaying the FS-7 mission indefinitely."

Christiansen pursed his lips.

"We've been trying to keep you posted as to all the latest developments in this story. According to a tip from a government official, who wishes to remain anonymous, the FBI suspects Bob Faden in the deaths at Far Side Base. Today, the big news is that an FBI search of Bob Faden's home has uncovered a possible link to the occult in this bizarre case. We switch you now to a special report from Houston with our correspondent, Beverly Ochoa."

The scene changed to film shot from a vehicle moving through a suburban neighborhood. Bianco recognized it as one of the "astronaut villages" near the Johnson Space Center. Such affordable tract housing made it possible for the newer NASA employees to be near their homes and families. Bianco recalled the years she had lived in a similar neighborhood. Her neighbors had all been involved in the space program. It made for a tight-knit community.

"The Faden family has been living in this quiet neighborhood in a quiet Houston suburb for the past three years," Ochoa's voice-over continued. "Thanks to an anonymous tip, our camera crew was on the spot, and this was the scene here, earlier this morning."

On the screen, the news vehicle pulled up in front of Faden's house at the same time as two unmarked sedans. All the car doors opened at once, disgorging a squad of clean-cut men in dark suits who converged on the front door.

"An hour and forty-five minutes later, this is what we saw," Ochoa said. The picture cut to the front of the house from another angle, indicating a passage of time between the shots. The FBI agents emerged from the front door carrying bundles of papers and a wide, thin, rectangular box. The camera got a clear shot of the word "Ouija" in huge ornate lettering which decorated the lid, before the agent carrying it turned the box around to hide it from view.

The camera cut to Ochoa. The reporter looked into the camera and said, "The question is, why are NASA and the FBI interested in these particular items, which they will undoubtedly tag as pieces of evidence in the Far Side investigation? When we interviewed the wife of Astronaut Faden, this was her only comment."

A shot of the front porch showed Maggie Faden standing tearful and trembling, supported by the arm of an elderly woman—perhaps her mother, Bianco thought. A crowd of reporters pressed in.

"It's just a stupid game," Maggie Faden sobbed.

Bianco sighed, impatient with the melodrama.

"Do you think it was a mistake for Morris to go public with this?" Gutierrez whispered to her.

"I think both James Morris and I want to do what's expedient to get the Far Side program back on track. I have my priorities as an engineer and James Morris has his as a politician."

"And his priorities call for the blame to rest on Faden's shoulders."

"Something like that. In light of the work you've done,

his conclusions are not well-founded, but they reinforce his priority: to keep things moving forward."

"When this is all over, for my own peace of mind, if nothing else, I'd like to verify my conclusions and to be able, then, to 'close the book' on this case," Gutierrez said.

"I'll do what I can to see that the political climate around here doesn't interfere with that," Bianco said.

On the TV screen, the scene changed to an exterior of an old Victorian-style mansion. "The Ouija board is supposed to be a communications device for talking to the spirits of the dead," Ochoa continued with her off-camera voice-over. "It's used in seances . . . and it's an age-old favorite at Halloween parties. For the details, we contacted Madame Irena, considered a world-famous spiritualist, medium, and expert on the occult."

Bianco heard a buzz of surprised conversation from the people behind her as the scene changed again, and the camera pushed in on an ancient, white-haired woman wrapped in a fringed shawl and seated in a heavily carved high-backed chair.

When she spoke, it was with a thick, Crimean accent. "The Ouija board is a device—or instrument—used by an individual who is seeking to free his subconscious mind by releasing it from the control of the conscious mind. It is necessary to do this in order to enter a psychic state where actions are not controlled by one's own will but by the will of a spirit."

The camera angle widened to include Ochoa, who was seated in front of a table upon which a large antique game board lay open. "Okay, we have this board and this piece is the planchette," she said, holding up an opaque triangular plastic piece with rounded corners and a large see-through plastic circle in the center. Bianco judged the equilateral sides to be seven centimeters. Ochoa looked into the camera and said, "Could we get an overhead shot of this?"

The view changed as the camera tilted to show the features on the board. The letters of the English alphabet and the numbers were large and rendered in an elaborate antique script.

"How old is this Ouija board?" Ochoa asked the woman.

"Very old. More than a hundred years, but the device, itself, is much, much older—more than two thousand years old."

"What do I do with it?"

"You would put the planchette on the board and rest your hands on it. It absorbs your psychic vibrations. Your mind must be relaxed and your thoughts blank in order for you to become an empty vessel for a spirit, who will guide your hand along the letters of the alphabet and the numbers to communicate with you, and to answer the questions you put to it. You would see the message letter by letter in the middle of the planchette."

"There would be someone taking notes for me each time the planchette stopped on a letter or a number?"

"Yes. I am not advocating the use of this device by the average person, you understand. It is very dangerous to consider it a toy."

Bianco studied the reporter's rapt expression, but she could detect no patronizing smile or other sign of disbelief. She appeared genuinely captivated and enthralled by the woman's arcane knowledge. "Either the intelligence behind TV news is on the decline, or, we have to give Ms. Ochoa credit for her acting ability," she told Gutierrez.

"Don't laugh, but there have been cases where police departments have used mediums and psychics to find murder and kidnap victims and missing people," Gutierrez said. "When all else fails, we are ready to make 'the leap.' How open would NASA be to that kind of experimentation?"

"Totally unopen. Completely closed," Bianco said.

"There are cases where truth really is stranger than fiction, however," Gutierrez persisted. "Our statistics show that a lot of weird things seem to happen during the full Moon, for example. Violent crimes, in particular, go way up. Do we have an explanation for why that occurs? No. Do you?"

"I don't believe in Satan. I do believe in sociopaths," Bianco said.

On the TV screen, the old woman leaned forward in her chair, as though intent on mesmerizing the young female news reporter with her eyes. "Between the world of the living and the 'realm' of the dead, there is a kind of outlaw territory or 'no-man's-land' that is populated with 'lost souls,' " she said. "Some of these died suddenly and violently. They are accident victims and murder victims, suicides and vicious, psychopathic criminals executed in this life for their crimes, and still others," the woman paused for emphasis and frowned, ". . . they have never been human."

"Are you referring to what we call 'demons'?" Ochoa asked.

"Yes. When these lost souls are able to find and attach themselves to a sympathetic living person—and I mean a person who is attuned to the negative flow of psychic energy in the universe—via the Ouija board, they are then able to give vent to their violent and destructive natures without any restraint. You see, positive and negative psychic energy is all around us. We make jokes about how differently optimists and pessimists see the world, but psychically speaking it has a basis in fact. A person who is depressed and contemplating suicide is going to radiate negative emotions. That person is going to tap into the negative energy flow and give off negative soul vibrations. Those negative vibrations can then attract the soul of a dead person who actually did commit suicide. They are attracted like magnets. This shell of flesh we call our body is our identity, our security blanket, but it means nothing to the disembodied entities. The physical body is not very important. We place too much importance on it. It is excess baggage. This is ancient knowledge lost before recorded history. Western religion reflects a distorted version of it," the elderly woman finished.

Bianco heard the noise of the people around her drifting away from the monitor. They were literally and symbolically turning their backs on the media's presentation.

Bianco shook her head in disbelief at the theatrics of the old woman on the screen. "The only significance of the Ouija board, to me, is that Bob Faden was so inclined as to have such a thing in his possession," she said to Gutierrez.

"It's not a crime."

"It's certainly an aberration, to my way of thinking."

"Do you think Faden's having a Ouija board is, in itself, an indication of something like a latent mental instability?"

"All I know is that we screen for character abnormalities that could lead to a mental or emotional breakdown in a life-threatening crisis and that, somehow, Faden just got by us."

"Does that mean you'll be adding the question, 'Do you now own, or have you ever owned, a Ouija board?' to the astronaut application?" Gutierrez asked.

Bianco saw the glint of humor in the detective's eyes. "At the moment, I'm sorely tempted," she answered on the same level. "This hoopla about the supernatural is embarrassing to me and to the program." With a sweeping gesture at the TV monitor, he added, "These people are making a big deal out of this because they don't have anything else to report on."

Bianco guided Gutierrez back in the direction of Mac-Callum and Weinstock, who were again discussing the model on the computer screen. Behind her, Guest's voice was cut off in mid sentence as someone turned off the monitor.

"So, now that we've heard from the lunatic fringe, have you got anything new to tell me?" Bianco asked.

"Just an observation," Gutierrez said. "In light of Paul Manch's postmortem on Mobley, I watched the last FS-5 transmission again. If you'll remember, when we saw Mobley, he'd wrapped himself in a blanket. In some of the other footage, he looked like he was suffering from being cold. When they were treating Washington, the sink in the hygiene station had blood in it. My guess is that Mobley had already received his injury prior to that incident, and that he was having a problem controlling the bleeding. Loss of blood, and the subsequent anemic condition, would cause a decrease in mental capacity and a drop in body temperature. That would definitely account for his feeling cold. Why wouldn't he report something like that to Mission Control?"

"That's easy. It would cause the mission to be aborted. Obviously, he was confident that he would recover."

"I don't know if we'll ever know how he got hurt," Gutierrez said. "There was an attempt to cover up the fact that he was hurt—and seriously—and it had to have been a conspiracy by the whole crew. I'm sticking with my theory about the mutiny, but my feelings about Drzymkowski's original motive have changed somewhat. Being the kind of man he was, if he saw a decreased mental capacity in Mobley that he felt was life-threatening to himself and the other crewmen, he would deem it necessary to forcibly take command of the mission. I can't say that I would blame him."

Gutierrez took out his notebook and flipped to a page three quarters of the way through. "I made a list of the things they found in the trash," he said. "I'd like you to look at it and tell me anything about these things that strikes you."

Bianco took the book and glanced at the items noted. "The consensus is that unwashed fresh fruit is the cause of the fly infestation up there," she told Gutierrez. "The only thing that's really disturbing to me is the sake."

"Because of the possibility of drunkenness among the crew?"

"No, because of the alcohol. Substances that we take for granted, and which are stable in the Earth environment, can behave very differently in the space environment. The classic example is a solution that was developed for defogging the visor of a space helmet. This happened early on in the space program, but it's something that we constantly have to remind ourselves about. The defogger was invented so the visor would stay clear when an astronaut was engaged in heavy exertion during an EVA. The stuff passed every test they gave it, so they tried it out on a mission.

"The astronauts suited up and went outside the spacecraft, and their eyes stung and watered uncontrollably. No one had thought about the possibility of the stuff outgassing in the pure oxygen atmosphere inside the suits. It was a life-threatening situation, because here they were floating around in space hooked to a tether, and they couldn't see the spacecraft. Finally, they were able to get back inside. There was talk of aborting the mission, but the decision was made to just cancel the rest of the space walks, which crippled it anyway. It was a real setback.

"With the potential of an electrical arc from the equipment at Far Side, and the danger of static discharge, there's always the chance of a spark that could ignite alcohol fumes," Bianco finished.

"Alcohol fumes are a danger here on Earth," Gutierrez said. "There are strict laws about ventilation and occupancy in bars and nightclubs that are the result of legendary—and very lethal—alcohol fires that have claimed hundreds of lives. The alcohol fumes rise to the

ceiling and stay there, if the place isn't properly venti-
lated. Someone lights a match and . . . suddenly, the
place is an inferno. Sake is normally drunk hot, too."

". . . increasing the amount of alcohol vapor," Bianco
said. "Takizawa is undoubtedly responsible for taking it
up there."

"Okay, so it's a possible cause of the first fire at the
base," Gutierrez said. "It's fortunate that it didn't spread.
I understand that there is some concern right now about
another fire that broke out just before you lost contact
with the base?"

"Yes."

"Any idea as to how it might have started?"

"No, unfortunately. Though they have the means to
extinguish any fire that might occur, we're still very concerned," Bianco said.

"I know that's an understatement," Gutierrez said
sympathetically.

Instead of a verbal response, Bianco solemnly nodded
her appreciation of the sentiment.

Gutierrez allowed the next few seconds to pass in silence, then he said, "I may have given you the wrong impression a few minutes ago. I don't believe in the
supernatural. About using psychics . . . it's . . . well, like
I said. Occasionally, we get lucky."

His lips curved into a smile that Bianco found unsettling. His eyes said it was meant exclusively for her.

"I wanted you to know, because what you think matters to me," Gutierrez said in a lowered voice.

She sensed a disturbing warmth from him, disturbing
because it was so satisfying. So calming. She'd had a
similar feeling when he'd driven her home. It was the
feeling of being special and of being under his protection. Unsure of what to say, because she was afraid of
reading too much into the compliment, Bianco responded with a polite nod. "I said I don't believe in Sa-

tan. The truth is, I don't have any strong religious beliefs one way or the other." Bianco glanced at the computer screen. "What I believe in is the fundamental science illustrated in this computer model."

Weinstock and MacCallum exchanged amused looks.

"She believes in a universe composed of good old maxwellian plasma," MacCallum said.

Weinstock laughed out loud. Adachi, Zia, and Ramirez chortled.

"Science humor," Bianco said.

Gutierrez's face reddened. The reaction prompted Weinstock to quickly add, "This is the gospel according to James Clerk Maxwell, a nineteenth century physicist who derived some mathematical equations that describe the relationship between electricity and magnetism . . . you know, an electric current moving through a conductor, like a wire, for example, produces magnetism—a magnetic field—around the wire. If we move a wire across a magnet, current flows in the wire. It's the theory that moving magnetism produces electricity, and moving electricity produces magnetism. This relationship has far-reaching consequences—and it has reached out and bitten us pretty hard at Far Side, I believe."

"You'll have to explain what that means," Gutierrez said apologetically.

"I'm not sure you need to get into it any further than that for the purposes of your investigation," Weinstock said.

"Let me be the one to decide that," Gutierrez said.

Weinstock shrugged good-naturedly. "Maxwell's equations also describe how, when the current in a wire changes direction, the magnetic field around the wire collapses and builds up again with the opposite polarity," he said. "This changing magnetic field, in turn, sets up an electric field which collapses and reforms every time the magnetic field does. So, a whole chain of alternating electric and magnetic fields is built and decays, and the resulting energy of those fields propagates through space as electromagnetic waves." He stopped to note the detective's reaction. As Gutierrez appeared to be following his explanation, he added, "Radio and TV signals are an example of waves propagating through space."

It amused Bianco that the astronauts listening to them were moving in closer, eager to be involved in the indoctrination of a neophyte into solid scientific principles. She suspected they were especially eager to put Gutierrez in touch with the real world after having seen the media reports that sustained the public interest by emphasizing old superstitions. "The equipment breakdown at Far Side represents another failed attempt to cope with a persistent technical problem which has plagued engineers since mankind harnessed electricity: the malfunction of electrical equipment due to electrostatic discharge," she said. "The earliest examples of attempts to deal with the problem come from the records that were kept of the ways people tried to shield buildings from lightning strikes. Remember Benjamin Franklin's lightning rod?"

Gutierrez nodded.

"On a more sophisticated plane, with the advent of integrated circuits and computers, and the miniaturization of electronic components, the sensitivity of electronic equipment to electromagnetic interference has increased.

"Far Side Base is jam-packed with complex, sensitive and fragile electronic equipment that allows the astronauts to live and work in a very harsh environment in which they would, otherwise, perish immediately upon exposure. We have to tightly control this situation by shielding certain electronic components to keep the equipment operating as it should."

"As for the lunar environment, what's on this computer

screen represents the near-Earth region of space," Mac-Callum said, directing Gutierrez's attention back to the computer screen. "This blue-and-white marble is the Earth, and you can see the Moon out here in its orbit. As for these other lines and crosshatched regions—for the purpose of this explanation, let's say that this is a model of the aerodynamic shock wave formed by a blunt object in a wind tunnel. The wind source is the Sun, and the wind is the solar wind, a high-temperature, electrically charged—or 'ionized'—gas that is constantly being ejected from the Sun. That's what I meant by 'maxwellian plasma': a plasma is a gas with electrical properties and, as such, it can change the state of electrical charge of any atoms with which it comes in contact. My maxwellian plasma is more commonly called ionizing radiation."

"So, the solar wind, your 'maxwellian plasma,' is constantly blowing past the planets and other objects in our solar system," Gutierrez said to the astronomer.

"Yes." With his finger, MacCallum traced the heavy black line in the computer model that was bent into a parabolic curve around the Earth. "This curved line represents the shock wave that occurs when the solar wind encounters the Earth's magnetic field. It occurs on the side of the planet that faces the Sun. We refer to it as the 'bow shock.' It's like the bow wave created by a boat going through the water."

"With no magnetic field of its own, the Moon, of course, gets the full force of the solar wind during most of its orbit," Weinstock interjected. "Its atmosphere is completely ionized—that is, it's highly charged, electrically."

"To give you an example of the impact these conditions can have on a planetary environment, the reason there is life on our planet is because the Earth's magnetic field acts as a solar windbreak," MacCallum said. "It prevents the solar wind from interacting with our lower atmosphere—the part that's breathable to us—and from gradually stripping it away. That process is called isotopic fractionation. I see your eyes are glazing over . . ."

"Do you have to know all of this to be an astronaut?" Gutierrez asked, awe in his voice.

"No," Bianco responded. "This kind of knowledge is job-specific."

"A mission specialist would not necessarily have to be strong in this area unless it was important to his or her work," Yoshio Adachi volunteered. "However, if you hang around with these people often enough, you pick up a lot of good information."

"In the early days, they tried to cram this stuff into the heads of Air Force test pilots, but not anymore," Weinstock said. "The basic training course for mission specialists is about a hundred and twenty hours total, and it focuses mainly on what you have to do to maintain your survival."

"Things like how to put on a space suit . . ." Ramirez interjected.

". . . How not to have an embarrassing accident with the plumbing," MacCallum quipped, winking at the group of astronauts.

"How to clean up if you forget that part of your training," Weinstock countered, with a chuckle.

". . . and tips on how to eat, how to get around, how to walk, when that's possible . . . that sort of thing . . . just about anyone from any walk of life can work in space," Bianco said.

"Age is becoming less of a factor," MacCallum said. "They've taken up people with medical conditions because their expertise was needed. That's what qualifies someone to work in space: their area of expertise."

The other astronauts made signs of agreement.

Weinstock turned his attention back to the computer model. "I'll just finish this by saying that, without a strong magnetic field to shield our atmosphere, conditions on the Earth would closely resemble those on Mars. Mars has a magnetic field, but it's minuscule compared to the Earth's, so Mars has been losing its atmosphere to the solar wind for the last several million years."

Gutierrez frowned in concentration. "The solar wind can't do that to the Earth because the Earth's magnetic field . . ."

". . . the magnetosphere . . ." Weinstock coached.

"The magnetosphere acts like a blunt object inserted into the flow of the solar wind. So the solar wind is forced around the Earth."

"Watch what happens when I put it all in motion," MacCallum said, his fingers ranging like spider legs over the computer keyboard.

Gutierrez studied the moving model. "The Moon passes right through the Earth's magnetic field here— opposite the daylight side."

"That region is referred to as the geomagnetic tail—or magnetotail," Weinstock said. "There's actually an exchange of plasma between the Earth and the Moon that occurs at that time. It's a unique situation in the solar system, as far as we can tell."

"So, what is the effect of this on Far Side?" Gutierrez asked.

"Obviously, there was a need to shield the equipment from the known electromagnetic interference from the lunar environment, as well as from internal electrostatic discharge," Bianco said. "We went to a great deal of work to do that both on the ground and in our orbital data relay system. The lunar communications satellites had to be designed to be able to relay base communications under these conditions, so we'd always be in touch with Far Side."

"Theoretically, we figured that about the only time the system might go down is when a dynamic change occurred in the environment such as a solar flare," Mac-Callum said. "Then, communications might go to hell."

"We thought solar flares were the only serious dynamic change that might impact the lunar environment and our communications, but we were wrong," Zia said.

"A dynamic change in the environment also occurs during the passage of the day-night terminator," Weinstock said. "In this case, it's the effect of the temperature differential between lunar day and night that changes the conductivity of the lunar soil. Heat improves the conductivity, the cold causes it to retain a powerful static charge during the lunar night phase. Right at the line between day and night there is so much electromagnetic activity that it actually causes a magnetic storm. What we're calling 'the terminator effect' actually begins forty hours before the passage of the terminator and lasts approximately thirty hours after it."

"It has turned out to be the unpredictable ingredient in our maxwellian kettle of soup," Bianco told Gutierrez. "With FS-5, we were hoping to get a handle on it by means of the Particle Event Rate Monitor Experiment— the PERM instrument package, but it stopped transmitting data at the critical time. We're reasonably certain that the effect of the passage of the terminator, and the resulting magnetic storm, was what initially affected the Far Side equipment. The physical damage to that equipment, and the deaths, occurred during loss of signal, and that aspect of the problem is totally perplexing to us. We don't have a clue about why that happened, or why Faden is acting the way he is."

☾

Tseng stepped out of the air lock and onto the lunar surface. Obsession had kept her awake through her badly needed sleep period. Had they overlooked any clues to the strange behavior of the FS-5 crew and their deaths that might have been left in the *Aldrin?* There was still time for one last EVA.

She'd tried not to awaken the other sleeping crewmen when she had made her way to the Fourth Level. There was no way to slip quietly out of the base. The hydraulics, pneumatics, and the opening and closing of the air-lock hatch all made noise. She'd felt driven to get out before anyone could stop her. She'd accomplished that.

She decided against taking the rover and started for the LLM on foot. She tried to stay clear of the wall of roiling dust shot through with a bluish aurora that undulated like a drapery in a wind. Still, she could hear minute dust particles impacting against her visor.

Beyond the zone of twilight, she saw the dark line of demarcation that was the night terminator creeping toward the base. It was about an hour away, she guessed. Ahead of her, the *Collins* and the *Aldrin,* awash in the magnetic dust storm, appeared indistinct and far away.

There was a burst of hissing static in her earphones which stabilized to a dull, ever present roaring sound. The sound was at just the right level to set her nerves on edge. She checked her suit computer. The information was unreadable. However, the suit's life-support systems functioned, so she pressed on despite the odd physical sensations she was beginning to experience. It felt as though hands were stroking her skin in an upward direction, toward her head. She felt a tingling sensation in her groin, the back of her neck, and across her scalp.

At first, the realization that, no matter how fast she walked, the ship was moving away from her, caused her to chuckle in amusement. However, as minutes passed, the thought that she would never reach it would not leave her mind. Amusement dissolved into concern. She began to question the wisdom of her journey. Was she becoming disoriented?

The hissing in her headset now became a rhythmic

sound, like someone inhaling and exhaling in long, labored breaths through an oxygen mask. There was no escaping this assault on her ears. She broke into a fast, limping trot, then into a run.

With great relief she saw the *Aldrin*'s payload bay hatch looming ahead of her. She triggered the manual-open sequence and climbed gratefully inside the cavernous space. The heavy breathing sound in her ears subsided. She closed her eyes for a few moments and took deep breaths to regain control of herself. When she opened them, she saw burning wax candles arranged around an altar draped in heavy black cloth in the middle of the payload bay. A nude woman was lying on the altar. Her eyes were open and staring, as if in a trance, at a shadowy figure in priestly attire standing over her. The figure held a jeweled dagger poised above her abdomen.

Bisio lay on the altar. Bisio *was* the altar.

The scene was an impossibility, yet the payload bay was now the inside of a high-ceilinged cathedral. At first, Tseng could not recognize the shadowy "priest being," as his facial features were constantly shifting. Then the features rearranged themselves into familiar configurations— Mobley, Drzymkowski, Washington, and Takizawa.

In slow motion, she saw the dagger descend toward Bisio. The sight made her feel suddenly faint with fright. Her vision swam, momentarily. When it cleared, it was she who was lying nude on the altar, watching the swiftly descending dagger. In the last instant, as it plunged into her, the dagger was transformed into an aluminum strut.

She awoke to reality as if from a deep sleep. She was still in her space suit, and sitting in the *Aldrin* payload bay. Instinctively, she looked down to check the elapsed time on her suit chronometer and was glad to see it functioned again, along with the rest of her suit displays. The hallucination had lasted only seconds, but she had experienced the full horror of it, as though it had happened in real time. Her heart pounded with such force she feared it might burst. The sudden thought that Washington had gone into cardiac arrest from fear was accompanied by a sharp pain in her chest.

Willing herself to get up, she unclipped her flashlight and switched on her backpack lights.

The interior of the ship had been ransacked, the payload bay walls defaced with graffiti written in black marking pen. Had Faden done all this during his imprisonment? *Food for the Moon* was written repeatedly, along with the same occult phrases, symbols, and obscenities found inside the Main Dome.

Near the end of the mission, the FS-5 astronauts might have transported and stored personal possessions inside the LLM that they intended for use during the trip home. Tseng hoped to spot these things. There would also be records and data. Most of all, she hoped to find that information.

The heavy breathing in her earphones started again, growing in volume until it became earsplitting. She had the urge to take off her helmet. She wanted to rid herself of the Snoopy hat and headset, now pressing too tightly against her ears. Her skin tingled maddeningly.

She fought to hold onto reason. Perspiration broke out on her forehead from the effort. The noise in her ears would not subside.

Her heart still pounding, she made her way forward.

Without the lights and the life-support systems in operation, the *Aldrin*'s mid-deck was inhospitable. It was so dark and cold. . . .

It was strange to be so aware of the cold through a space suit . . . her reason told her that the cold was inside her enclosed environment, not inside the ship. She adjusted the temperature control knob on her chest computer to maximum heat, and felt the chill subside.

Maneuvering through the ship's mid-deck habitat section in a space suit was difficult. She felt tired by the time she ascended onto the flight deck, and settled awkwardly into the command seat. For a few seconds, she peered out through the flight deck windows that had been defaced with obscenities, trying to see the base. Then she concentrated on her purpose. She took her time and studied her surroundings, looking for anything unusual. The clipboards holding the flight crew checklists had been removed from their brackets and tossed on the deck. She retrieved them and flipped through the information. Nothing out of the ordinary had been added to them. She replaced them in the brackets.

She couldn't shake the conviction that something about the *Aldrin* was the key to the Far Side disaster.

Even she'd begun to think in those terms.

The damage to the command console appeared superficial, but there was no way to tell visually. What if the ship's main controls were damaged, leaving FS-5 with no means of escape? What would Mobley have done in his diminished physical and mental state? Would he have had the presence of mind to leave a message for the rescue mission that would surely follow? Putting herself in his place, she would have done that. What form would that message take? The most logical place to look for it was in the *Aldrin*'s computer.

However, logic had deserted FS-5 at the end.

She had her hand on the "power on" switch for the flight control console, but a forced inclination to be cautious stopped her from activating it.

She considered the electromagnetic storm outside. If she gave in to obsession and powered up the *Aldrin* now, the high electrostatic charges might induce voltages in the ship's control circuitry that could short-circuit the smaller and more fragile electronic components. If she closed the switch, the power surge might cause them to fail. The data she searched for would be lost. That would be disastrous.

She withdrew her hand from the switch, shaking with fright at having so narrowly avoided an error in judgment. She struggled to her feet. Had Mobley had the presence of mind to make the same assessment? If so, what would his thinking have been?

Tseng left the flight deck with a feeling of relief, but with her curiosity unsatisfied.

She lumbered onto the mid-deck to continue her search—for what she didn't know. Only vague intuition motivated her to wander into the galley. Discarded food wrappers, remains of partially-eaten meals littered the area. The wardroom table was cluttered with wasted food and its packaging. It didn't make sense.

She peered into the hygiene station, but turned quickly away in disgust. How long had Bob Faden been imprisoned inside the ship? Long enough to have done all this damage himself?

She became aware of a mild ache in her joints, and of feeling hot. The ache she recognized as the onset of "the bends"—nitrogen boil-off inside her tissues and blood—because she hadn't taken enough time to pre-breathe pure oxygen before going outside.

She felt desperate with the need to find the answers in a hurry. She moved to the sleep stations. They'd been ransacked. Someone had been searching for something. For what? And who had searched. Faden? Mobley? Another FS-5 astronaut? Drzymkowski? It could have been any one of the crew members. What would be so damaging that it had to be destroyed? Photographs, perhaps? Were there more pictures?

She had yet to find the hard drive from Mobley's camera.

She was cognizant of suffering from body aches. Her physical condition worsened by the second. To avoid serious, debilitating complications, she would have to return to the base sooner than she wanted to. She fumbled with her controls to reduce the temperature inside her suit. She was too hot. The suit was restrictive. Oppressive. Smothering. Fury rose up in her at being imprisoned inside such a tight shell. It felt like the bulkheads were closing in around her.

The need to get out of the *Aldrin* suddenly became overwhelming.

Outside the ship, Tseng was again enveloped in the leading edge of the magnetic storm. It seemed more intense now. Despite that, being on the lunar surface was a relief after her vivid hallucination and her claustrophobic attacks.

Flashes of bluish light that originated from deep inside the storm drew her attention. They fascinated her. While she watched, the lights appeared to coalesce. A hulking human form materialized as though approaching from out of a thick fog. An astronaut in a space suit walked slowly toward her. At first, she thought it was someone from the base searching for her, but as the figure drew nearer, she saw something was wrong, or rather, unnatural about it.

The image was not solid. It resembled a hologram.

She saw writhing blue tendrils of the magnetic aurora through it. A bluish aura surrounded the figure and it appeared not only to move through the dust storm, but also to draw an existence from it. Tseng stood still and waited, her fascination riveting her to the spot. The heavy breathing in her ears was a roar.

The figure stopped a few feet away. She could clearly see a familiar face through the helmet visor. It was Drzymkowski. He smiled at her. Tseng switched her RF selector, trying all three suit-to-suit channels in an attempt to communicate with the apparition, but there was only static and the breathing sound on all channels.

This is a ghost, her imagination insisted, even as her sense of logic tried to comprehend its existence by comparing it to other acceptable phenomena in the known universe.

This had to be another hallucination. She felt a nervous excitement tinged with a fear of the unknown.

A spreading discoloration on Drzymkowski's skin drew her attention. The flesh on the astronaut's face was decomposing. Tseng's wonderment metamorphosed into horror, yet she did not run from the sight of the flesh sagging into gelatinous, rotten, pulpy globs and falling off until all that remained was the grinning skull. The figure inside the suit became unsteady as the skeleton lost its supporting flesh. The monstrosity that, only moments before, had been Drzymkowski, turned away from her and walked jerkily toward the base.

Tseng ran in long, lumbering strides to catch up with it; to try to get a closer look. However, the figure remained just ahead of her like a mirage. Then it changed direction and walked into the thick of the electromagnetic storm . . . and disappeared.

Tseng sweated from exertion. Moisture condensed on the inside of her helmet faceplate. The urge to pursue Drzymkowski and to seek out the explanation was strong.

Somehow, she knew further exposure to the magnetic field might result in a complete loss of reason. Her mind pictured Mike Mobley unlocking his helmet to let the lunar atmosphere in. The thought that she might do something equally fatal, if she were to become completely disoriented, sent a wave of fear through her.

Two more figures materialized inside the storm. They, too, were in space suits, and streamers and pinwheels of light undulated and spun off from them like Saint Elmo's fire. One raised a hand and pointed at her. Streamers of fire shot from the gloved fingers like jagged lightning bolts.

She moved toward the phantoms, determined to catch

and to touch them. As she drew near, they did not turn
and disappear into the storm. Instead, they continued to
approach. She squinted to read the names stenciled on
the helmets.

Cochagne. Horo.

She approached them and reached out. Her gloved
hand shot jagged streamers of fire at them. Then she felt
the solid contact of live bodies. They were not phantoms
out of the magnetic dust cloud.

Tseng tried the suit-to-suit channels, but her earphones
were filled with the hiss of radio static. The two astronauts pointed at their helmets and shook their heads—
too much interference for communications.

Cochagne and Horo gestured toward the base. Tseng
nodded comprehension and fell into step beside them.
How could she tell them what she'd seen? She analyzed
the possible scenarios. Would they think something was
wrong with her? They might believe she was losing her
mind, as Mobley had.

They were all scientists.

There had to be a scientific explanation for what she'd
experienced. There had to be a plausible explanation for
the space-suited phantom.

Manch and Greer were waiting on Level Four when
Tseng emerged from the air lock with Cochagne and Horo.

Manch was unsteady on his feet. His skin was a pasty
white, and there were dark circles under his eyes. His
sandy hair was dark and greasy from perspiration.

Tseng unlocked and removed her helmet, and said,
"What are you doing out of bed, Paul?"

"I don't know. I feel like shit," Manch said.

"Those are the exact words I would have used to describe how you look," Cochagne countered.

"There was a big commotion in here after you all left,"
Manch said. "I couldn't sleep through it; besides, I had

work to do. The results of my analysis on the scrapings from the hammer head and from Mobley's pick revealed organic materials present."

"Isn't that what we were hoping to find?" Tseng asked.

Manch gave a grim nod of agreement. "That was the easy work. The hard work was the analysis of the ash samples taken from Faden's sleep station. The presence of animal fat and carbonized proteins in both that sample and the sample from the burned spot in the recreation area is disturbing to me, in that the middle of the recreation area is a peculiar place to hold a barbecue."

Cochagne and Horo had removed their helmets, and they were unlocking their gloves.

"You shouldn't have followed me," Tseng said to them.

"We heard the air lock cycling," Horo said. "First, we tried getting you on the radio, then we suited up."

"Why did you go out?" Cochagne asked.

Tseng saw worry in his eyes. "I went back to the *Aldrin* to check on something," she said. The excuse sounded lame and evasive as she voiced it.

"And what was that?" Cochagne persisted.

The emotional atmosphere felt heavy with suspicion and apprehension, and the steady, expectant gazes of the other crewmen seemed accusative to Tseng, perhaps, she reasoned, because of her own guilt feelings. Cochagne and Horo were justified in being angry with her. She'd pursued a course of action, which, in their eyes, had necessitated a risk to their lives. She understood that they felt they were owed an explanation . . . and they were.

She remembered her earlier apprehension about giving an account of what she'd seen to the other astronauts. That anxiety was gone. The desire to share the experience with colleagues who would apply their scientific reasoning to her "encounter" had replaced the paranoia. "I'm just going to lay this out for you . . . my objective for going to the *Aldrin* was to look for anything that might shed light on what happened here. I didn't find anything, but I'm convinced that we have to find the hard drive to Mobley's camera."

Over the sounds of annoyance, reprimand, and astonishment from the other crewmen, Tseng said, "In retrospect, it was a dumb thing to do. However, that's not the strangest thing I have to tell you about. I had problems while I was in the ship. I hallucinated. When I went outside, I saw what, for want of a better word, I will call Drzymkowski's ghost."

"You *were* hallucinating," Manch said.

"Maybe."

Greer took her wrist and felt for a pulse. "Your heartbeat is very rapid."

"Yesterday, you said something about an adrenal response to electromagnetic stimulation," Tseng said to Greer.

"Adrenocorticotrophic," Greer corrected her.

"I mentioned to you that electromagnetically induced currents in the brain and visual cortex can also cause magnetophosphene hallucinations," Manch said. "Currents which are strong enough to cause hallucinations and prolonged adrenal stimulation can also induce cardiac arrhythmia. At least the three of you didn't die of heart failure or the bends out there. The bad news is . . ."

The interior lights dimmed and flickered. Tseng checked her chronometer. "This is termination of the solar power array input, a scheduled switchover of our power supply to stored power," she said to reassure Manch and Greer, who had paled visibly. In her rough estimation, the flickering lasted for another five seconds before the lights stabilized and remained on. Another check of her chronometer confirmed the time. The transfer had lasted longer than she'd been told to expect by Mission Control, but it was not unusual for equipment in service to develop its own minor idiosyncrasies.

A fly landed on Manch's forehead. He shook it off and ran a trembling hand along his brow. "Okay, get those suits off, so we can administer steroids and check you over . . . and I want the three of you back on oxygen right now, and for at least an hour!" he added.

The ambient temperature in the dome had remained high, despite the repositioning of the black body radiators outside and Cochagne's system adjustments inside. Tseng quickly dressed in shorts and a T-shirt and descended the companionway to Level Three ahead of Cochagne and Horo.

She found Lebby at work with a small screwdriver on the open housing of an auxiliary computer terminal. The electronic circuit boards were in place, and Lebby had connected a trackball mouse to the machine.

Bob Faden sat in a chair opposite the computer screen. He glowered at the machine, unaware of anything or anyone else, it seemed to Tseng. His straitjacket was askew, and he was naked from the waist down. Tseng looked from Lebby to Faden and back again with raised eyebrows.

"He hasn't been a problem, so far, except that he refuses to keep his shorts on," Lebby said.

"He's quite an escape artist."

"Indeed," Lebby said. "Manch and Greer are exhausted. We can't keep him tied down. He has to eat and . . . this way, all of us can keep an eye on him."

"As long as he doesn't set any more fires, or become violent . . ." Tseng warned.

"We have him on a combination of things—liquid cold medications and odds and ends Paul and I had in our medical bag," Greer said, ascending from Level Two. "We put together a kind of 'serenity cocktail.' "

"What about the vomiting and the incontinence?"

"Side effects of the initial doses of diazepam we gave him," Greer said. "I believe his body has adjusted to it now. He hasn't had an accident in several hours."

Tseng eyed Faden suspiciously.

The astronaut appeared content just to stare at the screen. The only remnant of his past hyperactivity was a constant rhythmic, nervous jiggling of his legs.

Tseng indicated her tacit okay with a shrug. Then she turned her attention back to Lebby. "According to the computer, termination of the solar power array input was nominal," she said, studying the mainframe's display panel. "Between you and me, the switchover took a long time."

Lebby shrugged. "We've patched together enough of the wiring that it doesn't surprise me. The changeover was still within acceptable parameters. Otherwise, we would have had an audible alarm." After a pause, he said, "While it's true that you don't need anyone's permission to go EVA to the LLM, in the future, you might let us know that you're planning to take an evening stroll."

"Your chastisement is acknowledged and accepted," Tseng said.

With a few keystrokes, Lebby brought a game board up on the auxiliary terminal's screen. "I've got the Ouija program working," he said. The senior computer specialist rolled the trackball mouse around with a rapid hand motion. An arrow zigzagged across the screen. He slowed the movement and stopped the arrow on the letter "M." He clicked the mouse button and the letter appeared in the message block at the bottom of the screen. "That's it," he said.

Horo and Cochagne descended the companionway from Level Four.

"Is anyone going to try the game?" Cochagne asked.

"I have no real desire to," Greer responded. "The importance of this discovery is that Bob Faden chose an unscientific and unorthodox method to deal with an unexplainable situation in which he found himself. While this Ouija program is not the cause of his mental illness, his psyche has taken refuge in it and in the iconography of the occult to such an extent that he exhibits all the classic symptoms of demonic and spirit possession."

Tseng glanced at Faden. "It's got his attention," she said to Greer.

The astronaut's nervous leg jiggling had stopped. He stared at the Ouija board without blinking.

Greer moved a chair in front of the terminal and sat next to him. "Perhaps this is the breakthrough I've needed," she said.

"Or it could be the disaster we don't need," Lebby interjected.

"This is the first time he's been quiet, Dick," Horo said.

Greer ignored Lebby's gibe. "Let me know if he shows signs of becoming agitated," she said. She put her right hand on the mouse and closed her eyes. When she moved her hand, the pointer fanned over the alphabet. When she stopped, the pointer was on the letter "Z." Greer clicked the mouse button and the letter appeared in the message block. She repeated her actions, periodically stopping to click the mouse button, but the letters appearing in the message block did not spell any words.

After a few minutes, Greer opened her eyes and looked at what she'd written. Then, she looked at Faden. The astronaut sat like a statue and scowled at the computer.

"No change," Horo said.

"Perhaps your technique lacked a certain sincerity," Lebby said to Greer.

"It's too soon to tell," Greer said.

Tseng turned to see Paul Manch watching them from the companionway to Level Two.

"Now that you've seen the computer program work, you can take a look at these," Lebby said. He handed

Greer a stack of computer printouts. "They're Ouija messages I found stored in a subdirectory of this program."

When Manch joined them, Tseng asked, "How's Joe?"

"I just checked on him. His eyes are clear, not blood-shot, which indicates that he has only a mild concussion," Manch said. "He'll have to suffer with a headache for a day or so." After a pause, he said, "I want to know more about your 'ghost.' "

"It seemed very real to me," Tseng said, continuing her earlier discussion of what she thought she'd seen outside. "I was afraid, at first. Maybe I'm rationalizing, but it looked real. It was like watching a three-dimensional recorded message with the magnetic storm as the imaging system."

"What is the 'soul'?" Manch asked. "Is it a form of electrochemical energy, such as what we detect in the spinal cord and in the brain? Is there a life-force residue?"

"We are composed of atoms," Horo said. "In the structure of an atom, we have charged electrons orbiting a nucleus which contains protons in equal proportion to electrons. Atoms tend to combine into molecules. Within a molecule, the nucleus of one atom feels itself attracted by the electrons of the adjacent atoms, and for a solid to be bound as a unit, the atoms must fit together in such a way that the forces between the positive and negative charges of neighboring particles can bind it cohesively. That's what holds rocks together, and it's the force that holds us intact. It's the fundamental glue of our universe."

"The concept of this life energy being imprinted with a memory of physical existence is intriguing," Manch said.

"Any reference to the supernatural leaves a bad taste in my mouth," Lebby said. "All things are bound by the laws of the physical universe."

"There may be laws we don't understand yet," Manch said. "Theoretically, these undiscovered laws may form the basis of certain myths which have been perpetuated because of documented phenomena and sightings."

"Has there ever been a sighting that wasn't open to dispute by the nonbelievers?" Lebby asked.

"How is it possible to believe in God and, at the same time, deny the existence of the supernatural?" Manch asked.

"I'm not disturbed by the notion that I may have hallucinated out there. I felt the kind of fear . . ." Tseng searched for the words, ". . . it went beyond the knowledge that here was something potentially harmful and beyond my ability to control . . . it was like a fear of monsters hiding under the bed, and 'things that go bump in the night.' That I could fall prey to it is disturbing."

"The fear of the unknown is an ancient fear," Lebby said. "Animals automatically fear the unknown, and it is a mechanism of their survival. However, over time, they learn to function with more confidence because they accumulate knowledge in the form of experiences in the process of living. That's adult maturity.

"We're supposed to be the intelligent species, but our solution to the problem of the terrors of the unknown has been to consistently institutionalize that fear in the form of religion. We've been doing it for six or seven thousand years or longer, and," he encompassed Faden, the computer terminal, and the graffiti on the walls with an expansive gesture, "I think this occultism thing can be lumped into the same category. This particular mythology pervades our thinking in all kinds of insidious ways. The deaths and the physical damage to the inside of the base are unexplained, but well within the realm of human actions."

"You sound like a Confucianist," Tseng told Lebby. "They felt that popular Chinese folk religious beliefs in the gods and in the existence and immortality of the soul led to superstition, and undermined the basic ethical principles of human behavior by shifting the moral responsibility for all actions from man to spiritual beings."

"Perhaps we can look at this age of religion as a growth phase of a species that is thousands of years old, yet still in its developmental childhood, because its nature is to know 'why,' " Greer said.

"I think that the belief we can talk to disembodied spirits is a symptom of the fear of the end of consciousness, and an inability to accept mortality," Horo said. "The fear of death is the fear of ceasing to be. We see the visual horrors of the grave, but we know our awareness is what makes us unique. We want that awareness to continue after death. As a species, we can't face the possibility that it won't."

"How do we know that it doesn't?" Manch asked.

"There's no one *alive* who can resolve this, is there?" Cochagne chortled.

"You've just hit upon the reason both the priesthood and talking to the dead have been lucrative businesses for several thousand years," Lebby said.

"Where's Dave Christiansen when we need him?" Horo asked.

"We don't need him. We've got Joe DeSosa," Cochagne responded.

"I'm not about to tear down Joe's beliefs," Lebby said, "especially when he's not here to defend them."

"But you have your opinion. We all understand that," Horo said.

"Look at all the different life-forms we have on Earth," Lebby continued, "Insectile, reptilian, mammalian, avian, aquatic, bacterial, viral, plant life—we're land mammals, but, in the majority of cases, the others represent life with a different metabolic process than ours. That's only a sample of what we may come in contact with when we head for the distant stars.

"This age of religion we're in will end. I believe that

the universe is going to prove a strange and exciting place, but, I also think that, at the moment, our technology is dangerously far ahead of the collective level of human intellectual sophistication. We're certainly not going to make any rapid progress when we're so quick to attribute everything new we experience to supernatural causes. This is a psychological barrier that mankind as a whole must transcend."

"Theologians are fond of using the findings of archaeologists to validate the Bible," Horo said. "Archaeologists, on the other hand, start with the Bible, and the works of other ancient historians like Josephus and Herodotus, and use them as guidebooks for identifying the lay of the land in the hopes of finding the lost cities of the ancient Middle East. If we employ a similar logic to this situation, we might identify the mythology common to ghost sightings, and then construct a theory based on the scientific principles that might make it possible in this universe and on our Moon. I'm saying let's remove the superstition and get down to the physics and chemistry."

"Spirits are sighted on dark and stormy nights," Lebby volunteered.

"And in fog," Greer said. "Certain parts of England are quite famous for them, particularly the lowland areas where the air is quite dense with water vapor."

"Under certain conditions, water conducts electricity," Cochagne said.

"We have the exact opposite condition here," Tseng said. "However, the Earth's atmosphere is ionized during an electrical storm, and the lunar atmosphere is also subject to ionization. The atmospheric conditions under which I saw my apparition are characterized by a specific electron density and a high rate of particle activity. We have a correlation there."

"I've heard of a valid scientific theory which states that we are still living with the noise of the big bang, but that the waveforms are now so small that the sound is inaudible to us," Tseng said. "We're living amidst the sound waves of every sound ever made or uttered . . . the sound of every tree that has ever fallen in the forest, the sound of every cannon ever fired, every bomb that has exploded, every word ever spoken, etc. Why couldn't the same conditions apply to the release of energy at the moment of death?"

"What you're saying is that we should be living with the dead all around us, too, and not just in the ground," Lebby said. "You're postulating that everyone who has ever died is still part of the 'ethereal' environment."

"Why not, if we live in a universe where energy can't be created or destroyed and all molecules are recyclable?" Horo asked. "If the essence of a person is this electromagnetic energy plasma, like what we saw, it could linger on a long time after death."

"A mass of plasma would gradually lose cohesion and shape, and would eventually disperse, but it might take centuries or millennia for the dispersion process to be complete," Cochagne said.

"On Earth, there could be discarnate souls all around us, all the time, which lack the ability to manifest visually except under certain conditions," Horo said. When Lebby groaned in response, she added, "I'm trying to come up with a theory that's peculiar to death on the Moon, where a set of conditions exist that affects energy waves and records patterns in a magnetic medium."

"This discussion is starting to give me a headache," Lebby grumbled.

"I keep coming back to 'Food for the Moon,' " Tseng said. She glanced at Faden. "I can't shake the notion that it's fundamental to all of this."

"If what you're all postulating is true, you're talking about a fate that I consider to be worse than death,"

Lebby blustered. "I can't think of a worse state to be in than that of having to endure a lingering, deteriorating intellectual awareness while my electro-spiritual essence disperses on the solar wind."

"Only if there is a comparable state of awareness to that of life, in death," Cochagne said.

"Jerry, that implies that, rather than being circumstantial, there might have been an intent behind this hallucination China saw," Lebby argued. "Intent implies that there's an intelligence at work. Forgive me if I find that a little hard to deal with."

"A member of FS-5 was the first human to die on the Moon," Manch said. "There's a question on which death occurred next, but the order isn't important to this discussion. The statement in Mobley's notes about Einstein's theory might be relevant to this. There's been a great deal of life energy released here in a relatively short period of time, and if energy is neither created nor destroyed . . ."

"It turns to heat and raises the entropy of the universe," Lebby said flatly.

"It's clear that we're not going to discover the secrets of the universe in the brief time we have up here. Sorry, folks, but it's not going to happen on this trip," Tseng said. "Personally, I'm willing to leave that job to better minds. What we can do, and what our job is, at this stage of the mission, is to document anything that takes place."

"I disagree," Greer spoke up. "It's clear, from the things that have happened, that we're in real physical danger here. I think we should discuss whether or not it might be best to leave Far Side with the information we have. We can make sure that the next crew that comes up here is better prepared than we are."

"Are you afraid that we're all going to murder each other at the stroke of midnight?" Cochagne asked.

The color drained from Greer's face. "The physiological and psychological effects on us that might cause us all to hallucinate make it imperative that we give careful consideration to our ability to survive the next twenty-four hours. We owe it to our colleagues to come back with the data we have."

"I have to be realistic. What Greer is saying has merit," Horo said.

"Based on what we already know, I think you're exaggerating the risks," Lebby said to Greer.

"Tell that to Mobley, Bisio, Washington, Drzymkowski, and Takizawa . . . and to Bob Faden, too," she fired back at him.

"We can all see the wisdom of the case you're trying to make," Manch said.

"The conditions outside being what they are, we don't have a choice right now," Tseng said. "I think trying to leave will be riskier than sticking it out. A few hours from now, those risks will diminish."

"It's pretty bad out there," Cochagne finally said, nodding in agreement.

Horo's shrug indicated her acceptance of the situation. "I just hope we're not going to spend the entire sleep period staying awake to wait for something bizarre to happen," she grumbled.

Upon entering the recreation area, Tseng walked into a wall of fetid hot air. Cochagne, Horo, and Manch followed her down to Level Two, and their reaction showed equal concern.

"The heat in here is from the decomposing organic materials," Horo said, indicating the sealed garbage sacks. They were puffed out from the buildup of gases inside.

Tseng saw the video camera lying on the floor and picked it up. She shot a few seconds of footage of the garbage sacks, then played it back in the camera as a test. The picture was grainy, but the camera was undamaged.

"Oxidation is so rapid in this atmosphere that we could get spontaneous combustion at any time, especially in any exposed oils and fats," Cochagne said.

"Let's take the sacks that look inflated, go through them in a hurry, and get them out of here," Horo said.

"At present, we can't risk another trip outside," Cochagne said.

Manch's reaction was a worried frown of agreement.

"As a safety measure, we can put the garbage inside the air lock and then depressurize the chamber. No combustion will occur in a vacuum," Tseng said.

"Good plan," Horo said. "However, Lieutenant Gutierrez never told us exactly what we are looking for."

"So we'll take note of everything," Tseng said.

Tseng was alone in the recreation area. She'd divided up the chore of searching through the remaining garbage sacks with Cochagne and Horo. They'd finished before her and were hauling the first load of garbage back up to the Fourth Level for temporary storage in the air lock.

So the garbage, itself, would be under vacuum when the air was evacuated inside the air lock, she loosely tied the necks of the garbage bags. She batted at a swarm of flies, then she stood up straight to stretch and to massage her back, which was stiff from working hunched over while examining the refuse and repacking it.

She'd just picked up as many sacks as she could carry and was heading for the companionway, when she heard DeSosa bellow in pain. She dropped the sacks and ran toward the sound. As an afterthought, she returned for the video camera.

At the entrance to the communications specialist's sleep station, she met up with Lebby, Horo, Cochagne, and Manch, who'd also come in response to DeSosa's yells. Greer joined them with Faden in tow. She'd made extensive notes on the computer printouts Lebby had given her, Tseng noticed.

DeSosa stood in the center of the room clutching his shoulder. "I was just lying here, asleep, and that fell off the wall and hit me," he said in a whining tone, gesturing over his shoulder to indicate the large, solid wooden crucifix and its shiny brass figure of Christ that lay on the bed. The fastener DeSosa had used to hang it on the wall lay next to it.

Tseng stepped aside for Manch, then entered DeSosa's room behind him. Greer followed her. The other astronauts remained outside. They guided Faden to the front, and crowded into the doorway to view the scene inside. However, Faden wasn't content to stand with them. Instead, he wandered into the room, a vacant expression on his face.

Manch peeled DeSosa's hand away from his shoulder to reveal a large red welt.

"You're lucky it didn't hit you in the head or put out your eye, Joe," Cochagne said.

"One concussion is enough, thanks," DeSosa quipped.

The astronaut's quarters reminded Tseng of a monk's cell. On the wall opposite where the crucifix had hung was a framed picture of Christ, and there was a well-used King James Bible on the tabletop. A small swarm of flies buzzed excitedly over it. Individual insects alighted on the cover, scurried across the title with a deliberateness that Tseng found annoying, then flew up to rejoin the main swarm.

"Have you found anything useful in the computer files?" Tseng asked Greer.

"Only the later entries are intelligible," Greer said. "Unfortunately, we have answers here, but no questions. However, judging by the dates and times and the sheer volume of material, just prior to leaving the base, Faden was spending all of his time on the computer."

"Why was the computer a deliberate target of the destruction?" Horo asked.

"I can see how Faden's obsession with the game might have gotten on someone's already frayed nerves," Lebby said. "In the end, the motive for the destruction could have been simply to prevent him from using it anymore."

"That's pretty drastic," DeSosa said.

"If the situation was perceived by someone as drastic . . . drastic situations call for drastic solutions," Cochagne said.

"The Ouija messages are the basis for the things that Faden has been saying," Greer said. "There are more than a few references to Takizawa's death by fire, specifically by spontaneous combustion, and to 'burning up' and 'coming apart.' "

"There are other nonsensical messages interspersed throughout," Manch said.

"For a brief time, Ann Bisio was a 'player' on the Ouija board," Greer said.

"I find the concept of spontaneous combustion of a human being impossible to believe," Tseng said.

"Though there are recorded cases of spontaneous human combustion, mostly from the late nineteenth and early twentieth centuries, they're not eyewitness accounts, so it's hard to give credence to that information," Greer said. "There was a spiritualist renaissance of sorts about that time and a great interest in the orthodox scientific community in psychical research. Spiritual mediums and seances were quite the vogue. It's hard to give credence to much of the information and documentation, and I'm afraid that's all I know about the subject. Faden's messages establish clearly that Takizawa died during the time that the base was out of communication, however. That's when the references to fire and to burning up begin. Faden started to get clear answers to his inquiries after Takizawa died, and he believed he was communicating with Takizawa's spirit."

"Reading these messages is like experiencing consciousness on another level," Manch said.

"How valid can his information be?" Tseng asked.

"If we believe that this is a sort of diary, that this is Faden in touch with his subconscious rather than with a spirit, we can believe certain things provided we interpret his meaning correctly. That doesn't necessarily mean interpreting his messages literally."

"The trick is knowing when to take him literally," Tseng said.

"But we do know that Takizawa's death coincided with the active phase of the electromagnetic activity and the kinetic energy phenomenon, and that he died in a fire," Manch said.

"Yes," Greer confirmed. "Strange things happened afterward, too. In one message, Bob referred to a visible sign which he believed was from Takizawa. It's apparent that Bisio and Faden didn't always 'connect' with the spirit of Takizawa during these sessions. There were, evidently, 'others'—meaning, I suppose, other sentient incorporeal entities—who interfered with, and disrupted their seances."

"Takizawa's was the only crew death alluded to in the Ouija messages," Manch said. "That leads me to believe that he was the first to die."

" 'First man to die on the Moon' is a dubious distinction for him," Tseng said.

"You know, a flash fire could look like spontaneous human combustion," Manch reflected. "When a person is on fire, the body fat burns. Any clothing present acts as a wick. The ash samples from the burned spot in the recreation area and the odor of burned fat in there suggest that, in all probability, that's where his death occurred."

Tseng's mind recoiled at the unusually vivid image of Takizawa on fire created in her imagination by Manch's statements. More disconcerting, the mental visualization of it left the impression of a real memory of the incident.

Movement caught Tseng's eye. She looked past De-Sosa to see Faden wander to the bed and stare down at the crucifix. Before she could call Greer's attention to him, Faden calmly began urinating on the religious object, saturating DeSosa's bedding.

DeSosa, wild-eyed with rage, lunged at Faden. "You crazy son of a bitch!" he screamed.

Manch blocked him and held him.

Greer pulled Faden away from the bed. However, he continued to empty his bladder on the floor, unaware of Greer or anyone else.

The other astronauts made sounds of disgust.

DeSosa became more infuriated. "Get him out of here before I kill him!"

"Calm down, Joe," Manch said.

"Look what he did! Look what he did!" DeSosa ranted. "It's sacrilege!"

"Joe, he can't help himself," Greer said in a placating tone.

"Get him out of my sight," DeSosa threatened, red-faced with anger.

"You need to calm down, Joe," Manch insisted. "We have diazepam in pill form. Ten milligrams. Why don't I give you one?"

"I'm all right! I don't want anything," DeSosa yelled. "I have to be awake in case something happens."

"Nothing's going to happen," Greer said.

"You're not going to turn me into a vegetable . . . like him!" DeSosa shouted. The astronaut opened and closed his fists spasmodically and looked at Manch and Greer as though he expected them to attack.

"No one's going to force you into anything, Joe," Tseng said, taking a step toward him.

It was an aggressive move, she realized too late. De-Sosa sprang at her, enraged, his fists doubled to strike at her face.

Though caught by surprise by the sudden, violent attack, Tseng expertly sidestepped the astronaut's lunge. She was clutching the video camera in her right hand, but she easily turned DeSosa's fists aside with her left by an openhanded slap block.

In the Moon's gravity, the move caused DeSosa's forward momentum to send him past her. Lebby had to jump aside as DeSosa stumbled into the passageway and crashed into the wall opposite his sleep station. The move caused Tseng to fall backward, opposite to the direction of the force she'd just exerted. The resulting headlong backward dive sent her flying toward the bed. She had to let go of the video camera to tuck and roll with the impact, but she recovered herself quickly. Manch and Greer crowded past her and out into the passageway. Manch had the hypo-gun in his hand.

From the sound of his impact against the wall, Tseng expected DeSosa to stay down, but he struggled to his feet. He cradled his head in his hands and grimaced in pain.

"The activity is making your headache worse, Joe," Manch said.

Like a maddened bull, DeSosa struggled upright to charge again.

"I'm sorry," Manch said to DeSosa, when he put the hypo-gun against the astronaut's arm and pulled the trigger. The effect was instantaneous. The astronaut's tension and anger appeared to drain out of him.

"This is adrenal overstimulation," Manch told them.

"Physical tolerances of electromagnetically induced currents in the brain can vary from person to person. We'll have to watch out for each other over the next few hours."

DeSosa groaned and said, "Am I going to fall asleep?"

"No. You'll just feel relaxed, like we told you," Manch said.

DeSosa nodded comprehension. "That's good. I don't want to sleep anymore until we get home. I've been having these dreams, you know. All kinds of violent things happened to me in them."

Manch lifted DeSosa to his feet. The astronaut swayed uncertainly, and Lebby moved to help support him.

"Let's get him back to bed," Manch said.

DeSosa shook them off. "No. I don't want to sleep!"

Cochagne sniffed the air. "Do I smell smoke again?"

Tseng and Horo followed him out into the passageway. Thick noxious clouds curled and billowed toward them from the recreation area.

Long before they reached the fire, they were choking from the smoke. Despite the discomfort, they pressed forward. Horo grabbed the CO_2 fire extinguisher and sprayed the area around the trash sacks. The floor around her blazed with burning refuse. Lebby arrived with a second extinguisher. Tseng shot video footage of the combined efforts of the two astronauts while they put the flames out.

DeSosa stumbled into the room followed by Manch, Greer, and Faden.

"The trash caught fire," Lebby said excitedly.

Faden looked at his surroundings with dulled awareness. Tseng wondered if the astronaut knew where he was, or that anyone was in the room with him. He worked his jaw in a chewing motion punctuated by repeated lip-smacking. What had Birnbaum called it? Tardive dyskinesia?

She saw fear in DeSosa's eyes as he surveyed the damage.

"I can't stay in my quarters . . . by myself," he said. "There's something about this place . . ." He let the sentence trail off. He chose his next words with difficulty. "One moment everything is normal. The next moment, flames just shoot up from something, or things hit you when you're asleep, or you think you see someone and they're not there . . ."

"Who did you see?" Tseng asked.

"Louise. I thought I woke up. Washington was there. She looked at me. That's all. She just stared at me. It must have been a bad dream."

"It was no dream," Tseng said. "You're not the only member of this crew who's seeing things."

In response to DeSosa's puzzled frown, Greer said, "Something happened to Po. I'll explain it to you."

"Let's get these sacks out of here before we burn ourselves up," Cochagne said.

"I don't want to take any chances," Tseng said. "All the trash goes into the air lock, including ours."

"I don't much like the idea of blocking our only exit from here with sacks," Lebby said.

"We could have MILTON take it out from his side," Horo said.

"He could do that?" Manch asked.

" 'Garbage man' is currently not one of his subroutines, but I can teach him in a matter of a few minutes using the data glove."

"You know, I could get used to having a robot around the house," Cochagne said.

"I'll help," DeSosa said.

"No, you won't," Manch said.

"We need to feed Bob now," Greer said. "We could use your help, Joe."

DeSosa nodded.

* * *

Cochagne, Lebby, and Horo helped Tseng move the trash up to Level Four. A short time later, the air-lock chamber was full. A thick swarm of flies had followed after them. Tseng silently vowed to trap as many of the insects as possible in the air lock. She waited patiently until they followed the garbage into the chamber before she shut and secured the inside air-lock hatch and initiated the cycle to purge the air. She turned to Horo. "Time to wake up your pal outside."

"Okay, let's do it," Horo said, and headed for the companionway with the others following.

When they reached Level Three, Horo, Lebby, and Cochagne went directly to the computer. They busied themselves with the data glove, and hardly took notice as, from Level Two, heavy footsteps were heard in the galley. The crash of furniture against a wall followed, a moment later.

Tseng descended to Level Two to check for damage, but could detect nothing amiss. Greer, Manch, and De-Sosa watched Bob Faden feed himself. They'd removed his jacket so he could eat. The astronaut appeared to be doing so calmly. He wore his T-shirt and they'd induced him to wear his fatigue shorts. *How long will he keep them on?* Tseng wondered. The other three astronauts looked ready to pounce if he showed signs of becoming agitated.

"We're ready to go," Horo called out from above.

"You'll want to watch this," Tseng told the astronauts in the galley. She snatched up the video camera, then ascended the companionway to Level Three.

For the record, Tseng shot a few seconds of footage of Horo and Lebby looking scientific and serious. The computer screen displayed an indistinct, grainy picture of the outside in a slow panning shot that stopped on the entrance to the Main Dome. It was the view through MILTON's eyes. As Tseng and the others watched, the robot slowly closed in on the precipitator and the air-lock hatch.

"At least he's on the move," Lebby said tensely. "We weren't sure we could get a signal through to him."

"It's a good thing he stayed close to the dome," Tseng said.

"We're reaching him via that antenna outside the air lock," DeSosa said.

Several moments passed in silence while they waited for the robot to reach and pass through the precipitator, and stop in front of the air lock.

"This is where it gets tricky," Horo said. She wiggled her fingers in the data glove experimentally. The robot mimicked the gesture with its fingered gripper. Horo extended her arm and hand slowly and carefully until the robot's gripper touched the hatch. "I've made solid contact," she said. "I can just barely see the latch," she added.

Horo moved her arm and hand, leading the robot's gripper to the mechanism. At least a minute passed, in Tseng's estimation, during which Horo—and MILTON—fumbled at the latch mechanism in an effort to properly align the fingers of the gripper. The geologist's patience was finally rewarded when the robot unsealed the hatch and slid it open. Horo sagged in her chair, perspiration running down her face and body, and Tseng could see how drained she was from the effort of concentration.

The robot moved slowly forward and stopped.

"The proximity sensors have stopped him here . . ." Horo began, but ceased further comment as the machine moved jerkily forward. With the data glove, Horo mimicked reaching for a trash sack. When the robot's gripper made contact, she said, "MILTON. Pick up object," and closed her gloved fist around the neck of an imaginary trash sack.

The robot grasped the neck of the trash sack in the air lock and lifted it.

For the next few minutes, Horo and Lebby concentrated on instructing the robot how to deposit the sack on the surface to one side of the air-lock hatch.

"Let's see if he's got it now," Horo said when they'd finished. She gave MILTON the command to repeat the routine.

Tseng cheered with the others when the robot walked obediently to the air lock and picked up another sack. Horo sat back in her chair and relaxed. "I've been doing some thinking about what we talked about after Po's trip to the *Aldrin*—that the existence of ghosts could be explained by quantum mechanics."

Lebby frowned and grumbled, "I'll grant you that. Einstein took some heat from the scientific community when he set out to describe the quantum nature of light. He was building on the work of another physicist, Max Planck, and he was proposing that light is a particle phenomenon and that it is made up of particles that Planck called 'quanta.' In saying that, he was agreeing with Newton's theory about the nature of light, but Thomas Young had already proved that light is a wave phenomenon.

"To make a long dissertation short, Einstein was able to prove that light is both a wave and a particle phenomenon. It was the quantum theory which won him the Nobel Prize, and it's now accepted, among physicists, that light behaves like both a wave and a particle phenomenon.

"So, with particle-wave duality, the precedent has already been established in physics for a theory that can acknowledge, accept, and actually address the duality of a phenomenon like what we're experiencing up here."

"He's saying that he can accept what some might choose to call paranormal phenomena as falling into the realm of quantum physics, but not as Halloween hocus-pocus or religion, both of which are based on unscientific leaps of faith," Tseng said.

"And, in this case, where does this duality come in?" Greer asked.

"What we have seen can be an energy phenomenon and it can also be . . . a human characteristic which further defines the complex nature of our biological existence," Lebby said. "After all, we are truly the children of the 'big bang.' The elements in our bodies were formed in the vacuum of space. We're made of the stuff of the cosmos."

"In fact, this experience might vastly expand the definition of 'life' in the universe to such a degree that it could make God scientifically palatable as a life-form even to Dee Bianco," Cochagne said jokingly. "Dick, when we get back, I'm going to put a new sign on your office door that reads: 'Lebby's Theory of the Universe Repair Shop: Quantum Mechanic on duty.'"

"In a quantum universe, it may be possible for someone to be insane and spirit-possessed at the same time," Horo said. "The human eye is sensitive to only a narrow band of wavelengths along the electromagnetic spectrum. That's what we call visible light. Remember 'Raging Martians Invade ROY G BIV Using X-rays and Gamma Rays'?"

"The order of the electromagnetic spectrum," Tseng said. "Radio, Microwave, Infrared, Red, Orange, Yellow Green, Blue, Indigo, Violet, Ultraviolet, X-rays, and Gamma Rays."

"Things are happening and the cause is 'invisible' to some of us," Horo said. "Po saw Drzymkowski outside, but Joe said he saw Washington inside the base. They could have been hallucinating, or it might just mean that something's taking place in an area of the spectrum that we can't see all the time. Some initial activity may be taking place in the infrared part of the spectrum, that is, in the long wavelengths."

"A plausible theory," Cochagne said.

"I would like to pursue it," Horo said.

"How?" Lebby asked.

"It means bringing MILTON inside and using his vision system in combination with the computer to view the phenomenon in the infrared part of the spectrum," Horo said. "We can hard-wire him to the computer. We can go directly through the central processor. All we really want to do is see with his eyes."

"Because of the safety risk, I have to think hard about bringing him in here," Tseng said.

"He's the only piece of test equipment we've got for this," Horo persisted.

"I'm not dismissing that possibility, I just have to weigh all the factors," Tseng said.

"What's this about? Are you talking about bringing the robot in here?" Manch asked, ascending from Level Two with Greer, Faden, and DeSosa.

Tseng wondered why they'd left Faden in his T-shirt and shorts without his makeshift jacket restraint. The astronaut smacked and popped his lips continuously and appeared not to recognize anyone nor did he exhibit any awareness of his surroundings.

As if reading her mind, Greer said, "He tore the jacket a while ago. It's useless now. We'll have to come up with another way to restrain him, if need be."

"I want to employ MILTON's vision system to look around at what's happening, using the part of the electromagnetic spectrum that the human eye can't detect," Horo told Manch.

"How can you get him inside?" Greer asked. "How will you get him down the companionway?"

"Getting him in here isn't the problem," Tseng said.

"We've had him climbing and descending stairs since he learned to walk," Horo said.

"I can see the merits of doing this," Tseng said. "There's a question in my mind of how risky it might be, though, since he's malfunctioned once already."

Horo turned to Lebby for support. "I don't think there's any risk, if we hard-wire him to the computer, Dick."

"That's doable," Lebby said, his eyes alight with what Tseng interpreted as the excitement of the scientific challenge.

Cochagne wrote hastily on a piece of scratch paper. "I'm calculating the floor loading." After a pause he said, "There's no risk of structural damage to the base."

"Are there any objections?" Tseng asked.

"He's not going to bust the place up, is he?" DeSosa asked.

"His proximity sensors prevent him from crashing into things," Horo said. "Once we have him connected to the computer, we'll have direct access to his microprocessor. Come on, guys . . . we've got the equipment to take a look at this from the scientific side," Horo coaxed.

Tseng glanced at Cochagne. He nodded approval.

Horo flexed the data glove.

From the robot's movement, Tseng knew that MILTON was stepping over the lip of the air-lock threshold.

"I'll be damned! He figured out what to do," Cochagne said.

"That's it . . . one leg at a time . . . good boy," Horo coaxed. More tense moments passed while the robot moved inside the air lock.

They got a panoramic view of the inside of the chamber as it rotated its torso one hundred eighty degrees and slid the hatch shut at Horo's direction. The video picture cleared.

Another rotation of the torso brought the camera around to face the inside hatch.

Horo collapsed back in her chair from fatigue.

"One thing bothers me," DeSosa said. "MILTON has the capacity and the capability to memorize routines and to learn from his experiences."

"His input data scanner will monitor an operator control sequence, read in the required data for learning and decision making, and organize the data as input to future decisions," Horo said.

"We just showed him how to get inside the dome," DeSosa said. "He can now come in or go out whenever he wants to."

"The idea of MILTON's using the air lock like a 'doggy door' is amusing, but the key word in your sentence is 'want,' " Horo said. "He's not that autonomous. Any self-motivation he has is limited to carrying out the operational goals in his task programming as a geology teleoperator."

"Can autonomy be learned?" DeSosa asked.

Horo remained silent for several seconds, deep in thought, then she said, "Yes and no: No, in that he can't get a notion in his head to do something for the sake of his own curiosity or edification, and he can't choose to arbitrarily expand his repertoire of operational goals. Yes, in the sense that he knows the relationships between his sensors and his effectors—his manipulators and tools—and he can use his sensors to assess a task and select the proper tools for it, but, again, his decisions are related to a very narrow range of operational goals such as learning to search for a particular type of object with regard to size and weight, and learning a sequence of pickup and handling motions involved in collecting the object. He does have the autonomy to refine a series of instructions I give him in order to generate the smoothest and most efficient trajectory of motion for his manipulators and tools, and in the process of carrying out a task, he can recognize when he is about to exceed the boundary of his reach or step into a crater, or fall on his face, and modify his movements accordingly, without my help."

"I was under the impression that he has a glitch in his programming," Greer said.

"The problem may not be with his programming," Lebby said. "In light of the electromagnetic activity we're experiencing in here, I've been thinking that he may have just suffered what's called a 'bit-flip' or a 'single-event upset.' A single charged particle like a heavy ion or proton can invade a microelectronic circuit and deposit a transient charge to momentarily change the binary logic state of the circuit, creating a temporary false datum."

"If that's the case, then it's not a big deal," Horo said. "On a future mission, they'll retrofit his processor with heavier shielding and that will be the end of his problem."

"They'll do the same thing with the domes and that will be the end of our problems," Lebby said.

"We hope," DeSosa interjected.

Tseng ascended to Level Four and slid the air-lock hatch open. For a few seconds, she met the robot's mechanical stare through the lens of the video camera. MILTON broke "eye contact" with her, however, and small movements of the head and camera lens eyes indicated that the microprocessor mind was active and that it was mapping, recording, and analyzing the new surroundings. She backed up, widening the shot.

The only means of voice communication with the robot was via the COMM, and, as there could be only one controller for the robot at a time, Horo was the only one now wearing a portable radio headset. "MILTON, forward," Tseng heard her tell the machine.

Tseng kept the camera on the robot while it picked its way gingerly out of the air lock and moved into the room. Then she stopped shooting. She slid the hatch shut and purged the chamber of its atmosphere.

When she turned to watch the robot's progress, the brilliant flash of Cochagne's camera strobe in her face blinded her for a few seconds, but she was glad the astronaut was also capturing the moment for "history" by taking pictures of Horo and the robot with the still camera.

At Horo's direction, MILTON proceeded to the companionway. As she'd predicted, the robot did not hesitate at the stairs. Its spiderlike descent to Level Three was slow, but sure, every movement calculated with machine precision.

MILTON's "studied" panoramic glance around Level Three looked sinister through the camera lens. While it didn't exactly put Tseng's nerves on edge, it was with difficulty that she shrugged off an imagination-inspired paranoid suspicion about the motivation behind the machine's behavior. She'd half-expected Faden to react to the robot as a demonic presence, but he appeared unaware of it and fully self-involved. He lived only in the twisted reality in his own mind.

"So far, the focus of the activity we're interested in has been down on Level Two," Horo said. "That's where I think I should take him first."

"I would like to know why that is," Cochagne said, "And why I feel ... peculiar ... when I'm down on Level One."

"The bodies were found on Level Two, and the fire that killed Takizawa occurred there," Greer said. "We've already had two fires, and DeSosa has had his share of . . . accidents. Those sites are certainly associated with a great deal of negative psychic activity."

"Bah and humbug," Lebby grumbled.

"As for Level One, we don't know what happened down there," Horo said.

"Maybe Drzymkowski died on Level One," Manch said.

"I don't think so," Tseng responded. "I think he was killed on Level Two, very near my quarters, if not actually in the room. Mobley came down to Level One a final time. He dropped the hammer there. Then, he felt he had to put his things in order before he went outside."

"It's cold down there," Manch said. "Mobley was anemic from loss of blood. He would have had a hard time maintaining his body temperature. He would feel the cold."

"According to the mythology of the supernatural, we've got it backward," Horo said. "Consider that, when Mobley lived down there, Level One was not cold. He was cold because he'd lost blood. The coldness that is there now . . . well, I've heard stories about places that retained those kinds of characteristics after a person's death."

"What has gotten into you, Arminta? Lebby snapped. "Why are you coming up with all these way-out theories all of a sudden?"

"It's just a carryover from what we were all talking about earlier," Horo said. "My thought processes are still working along those lines. If we're quantum beings and we were created in God's image, then God must be a quantum being, too. If God exists . . . If we hadn't talked about it, and if I hadn't seen certain things with my own eyes, I wouldn't be giving any thought to what we call the supernatural! I'm actually surprised at how much I remember about the old superstitions because I haven't pursued this since I was a kid."

Cochagne cocked an eyebrow questioningly. "Exactly what have you seen?"

"I've seen what's gone on around here," Horo said defensively. "I've had my share of nightmares about dead people, too . . . and I believe Po. I believe she saw Drzymkowski."

"Then why haven't I seen any of these hallucinations and ghosts?" Lebby challenged. "I'll tell you why. It's because I don't believe in them!"

"It may just be your age," Greer said. "Serotonin levels in the brain diminish as we get older."

"So, when all you youngsters go berserk, it will be up to the old fart to save the day?" Lebby said sarcastically.

"I wouldn't have put it quite that way, but yes," Greer said.

"The strictly scientific theories don't seem to cover the situation adequately, or, as you've said, Dick, modern science could be inadequate to this task," Manch said.

"Enough of this," Tseng said. "Before we take MILTON downstairs, I would like a thorough diagnostic run on him up here."

"I copy," Horo said. She and Lebby immediately occupied themselves with the details of the robot's construction that would effect the task of hard-wiring it to the Far Side main computer.

DeSosa sank gratefully down in the chair at the communications console and felt at the bump on his forehead. It had darkened into a large bruise.

"How's your head, Joe?" Tseng asked him.

"I still have a headache, but that shot Paul gave me has made it bearable," DeSosa said.

"You remember what happened?" Cochagne asked.

"Oh, I remember! I have a bad temper, but I've never been that angry before in my life. I couldn't control it," the astronaut said, enunciating with care. "I was mad enough to kill."

"I noticed that you put up all that stuff in your room that you said belongs to your relatives," Cochagne said, in a gently chiding tone.

"For all the good that did," DeSosa said.

"You told me you weren't very religious."

"I'm not, Jerry," DeSosa said. "This is going to sound stupid, but old habits die hard, I guess. With all this stuff happening, I figured it wouldn't hurt to be safe . . . just in case . . . you know. Man, was that a stupid idea."

"Do you remember actually getting hit?" Cochagne asked.

"I was sound asleep, I swear, though I remember I was having a bad dream and seeing Washington. I keep having the same dream over and over: someone is chasing me . . . to torture and kill me. We're in space suits, outside. The dust is so deep . . . like quicksand in places. I keep getting bogged down. I'm running so hard through this deep dust, but the other guy is gaining on me. It's so cold . . . I'm really struggling . . . I think my heart is going to explode . . . then I wake up—only this time the pain and the cold were real. When I saw that it was the crucifix that hit me . . . what a bummer."

"Joe, did your ghost appear to ripple like a curtain in a breeze, or was it static, like a 'traditional' ghost?" Tseng asked.

"Funny you should mention that. It undulated like your curtain," DeSosa said.

"The aurora borealis you see is in the visible part of the spectrum," Cochagne said. "The parts of it that you don't see are in the ultraviolet and infrared ends. Beyond infrared radiation you have microwaves and then radio waves. An aurora borealis appears to undulate because of the different superimposed frequencies."

"Radio waves are on that same cycle," DeSosa said.

"Which could create a radio noise that sounds like breathing," Tseng said.

"The activity we're hoping to see through MILTON's eyes is taking place somewhere along the spectrum between the red end of the visible spectrum and these radio waves," Horo said.

At that moment, a fly landed on the robot's camera lens and walked across it. It was joined by a second fly which then proceeded to mate with the first.

"Has there ever been a study linking electromagnetic activity with the rate at which flies reproduce?" Tseng asked.

"Yes. I think they studied that years ago on a *Skylab* mission," Greer said. "I can't recall the results."

"Flies don't seem to need much outside stimulation to do their thing," Manch said.

"What's the status on MILTON?" Tseng asked.

"We're ready to go when Jerry's finished," Horo said.

Cochagne took the strap of the still camera from around his neck and held it out to Tseng. "If you need something to do, you can take a look at what's on the hard drive while you're waiting."

Tseng inserted the digital still camera's hard drive into the playback/downlink unit for viewing. Lebby, Manch, Greer, Horo, and DeSosa clustered around the viewer in excited anticipation. The images were disappointing, however. In some of the frames of DeSosa's sleep station, there were phantom outlines which made the images look like pictures of ghosts, "time sequence" shots, or double exposures. All the shots were grainy, but the quantity of grain increased progressively from the sleep station images. It was especially pronounced in the shots of MILTON. Those were peppered with tiny black-and-white spots.

Tseng made hard copies of the images for Lebby's perusal and analysis.

"These areas that are full of pinholes are the result of excessive noise during the time the image was being digitized," Lebby said, indicating the peppered areas. "We call this 'shot noise.' "

"You must be defining 'noise' in a way I'm not familiar with," Greer said.

"Noise refers to extreme random-intensity variations in brightness of adjacent pixels in the uniform regions of an image," Lebby said. "It indicates an instability in the camera that is due to the intrusion of incident charged particles."

"For my money, we have too many free-ranging photons and electrons around here," DeSosa interjected.

The comment drew a chuckle from Lebby. "This degree of damage is easy to clean up with the computer. All it takes is time."

"A few of these look like double exposures," Manch said.

"Except with the digital camera, there's no film to get hung up and double-exposed," Lebby said. "We're probably looking at motion blur, and that can easily happen in a situation where the light levels are low and the exposure time is long enough for camera motion to have occurred with respect to the scene."

"But Mike Mobley had the same problems, and he was a pro," Tseng said. "You're certain the noise problem is in the camera, or could it be in the playback/downlink unit?"

"In the camera," Lebby said confidently. "It's extremely vulnerable to ambient conditions."

"If that's true, the electronics in the video camera are just as vulnerable as those in the still camera," Tseng said. She removed the video camera's hard drive and inserted it into the playback/downlink unit. She played back pieces of the stored footage from DeSosa's sleep station and the robot's entry on an auxiliary computer screen. The results were similar to the still photos and showed a steady increase in noise from the pictures of DeSosa's sleep station to the shots of the robot, which were all but obscured by electronic "snow."

"This would seem to support your opinion," Tseng told Lebby. She replaced the hard drive in the camera, then thumbed the power switch to the off position before putting the lens cap on.

"Won't the robot's cameras be affected?" Manch asked.

"MILTON's vision system is more heavily shielded because he's an outdoor kind of guy," Horo said, "but we may see noise."

"I'm going to suggest that FS-7 bring up a film camera," Tseng said.

"Dave Christiansen will be the new 'landlord of flies,' " DeSosa said, watching the swarm of insects circling over them.

Horo chortled.

"Sorry, but I don't get that joke," Lebby responded.

"It's biblical humor," Horo said.

"The Old Testament tells of a Philistine god called Baalzebub. In Christian mythology, he's associated with the demonic. The name means 'lord of flies,' " DeSosa told him.

"Oh," Lebby grunted.

"The results of the diagnostic show the circuits are intact," Cochagne said. "According to the computer, we have nominal redundancy in the backup systems."

"Bit-flips are not going to show up during the course of a normal diagnostic routine," DeSosa said.

"If that is, in fact, happening, then the shielding is woefully inadequate and this equipment is too sensitive for a reason, or reasons, we'd better figure out," Lebby said worriedly.

Horo sat down at the computer and, with a few keystrokes, brought the view through the robot's cameras onto the computer's main screen. She waited until the other astronauts had gathered around her before speaking. "I've instructed MILTON to do a continuous scan of the room in the infrared band and to gradually and systematically try longer and longer wavelengths."

In MILTON'S view, red objects appeared orange; greens and blues as black; yellows as white; other colors in shades of muddy gray against a reddish background.

To make a comparison, Tseng looked away from the computer screen. There was nothing abnormal about the room in visible light, but on the screen, lines, which had the appearance of layers of stratified air, began to appear in the picture. By the time DeSosa came into MILTON's line of sight, she could see lines of energy converging around his body, as though he were a magnet in a bed of iron filings.

"Certain special pigment molecules in MILTON's vision system contain magnetic information. They're sensitive to this area of the spectrum," Horo said. "Migratory birds and animals also have these pigment molecules, which is what allows them to navigate using the Earth's magnetic field like we might use a compass."

"We're actually seeing the perturbation of electromagnetic energy around the human body!" Manch exclaimed.

Tseng stepped in front of the robot's cameras and looked at herself on the screen. While she was in the robot's line of sight, she moved her arms and her body and studied the effect of her movements on the lines, which formed an energy corona around her body, until the sweep of the robot's cameras moved her out of its visual frame and passed on to Faden.

There was a collective gasp of wonder from the astronauts at the strength of the pattern around him that undulated and curled into a torus shape.

"The visual window we're looking for will probably

not extend into the wavelengths beyond one centimeter," DeSosa said. "After that, you'll be picking up more and more electromagnetic distortion."

"I think you're right, Joe," Horo said, "and, geologically speaking, Far Side Base is sitting on top of a mascon—a solid foundation of ferrous material capable of being affected by an electromagnetic field. That can only be compounding the effects of these conditions."

"Okay, I'm satisfied that this is going to work," Tseng said.

Tseng waited at the bottom of the companionway on Level Two, alert for any sign of threatening behavior in the robot, but MILTON descended the stairs methodically, then, under direction from Horo via a radio headset, it ambled toward the wardroom.

Cochagne, Lebby, and DeSosa had preceded MILTON down the companionway to Level Two, carrying the auxiliary computer terminal components Lebby had pieced together from spare parts and the connecting cables. Now, DeSosa and Cochagne helped Lebby bring the terminal on-line.

DeSosa reached down to pick up a shiny metallic object from the galley floor. He held it up for them to see. "It's Washington's tube of lipstick," he said triumphantly. He took off the top and twisted the base of the tube. The lipstick rotated up into view. It was worn to within a centimeter of the base.

"Haven't we been within sight of one another, more or less, since the fire in the recreation area?" Horo asked.

The question hung in the air, and remained unanswered, as Greer and Manch descended the companionway with Faden.

"He's been out of our sight several times," DeSosa said, nodding at Faden. He placed the lipstick tube down on the galley countertop.

"Look, let's table the issue of affixing blame for something trivial and get on with what we're trying to do," Lebby said impatiently.

At that moment, the main and auxiliary interior lights went out, and the computer terminal flickered off. A sudden ambient quiet told Tseng that the level's fan had stopped. Almost at the same instant, the main computer's emergency klaxon sounded to warn them of the electrical system failure, and the resulting loss of current to the environmental control and life-support systems.

Tseng rushed up the companionway to Level Three with Lebby and Cochagne. They covered their ears with their hands against the earsplitting alarm which continued for five painful seconds before the current was rerouted to the emergency circuits and the vital systems and the auxiliary lights came on. The main computer's caution and warning indicators pinpointed the location of the electrical system failure, while reminding them that only stored power was available.

Tseng took a deep breath, relieved that they again had fresh air circulation.

"The fault is in circuit T-311," Lebby said.

Cochagne looked up and indicated a block of four ceiling panels above them. "I have to remove these to get to it," he said. He frowned and added, "It's not one of the circuits we had to patch."

"Shall we get to work on it, Jerry?" Lebby said to Cochagne.

Tseng heard the fatigue and exasperation in the computer engineer's voice and saw them reflected in the tired, haggard expressions of both men.

Tseng returned to Level Two. The area's video monitor was connected to MILTON's vision system, and, since the limited illumination provided by the auxiliary interior lights did not affect the infrared picture, every detail of the darkened room could be seen through the robot's electronic eyes. However, a small amount of noise could be seen in the picture.

Horo was tapping frustratedly at the keyboard of the computer and frowning at the screen. The Ouija board graphics displayed on it were bright and glaring in the semi-darkness. It made Tseng's eyes ache to look at the screen.

"When the terminal rebooted itself, this is what came up on the screen," Horo told her. "I can't get rid of it."

"Why did that happen?" Tseng asked.

"How in the hell do I know?" Horo growled moodily.

"Calm down," Tseng said. She approached and studied the screen.

"It's behaving like a software virus," DeSosa said.

"The Far Side computer system has the capability to run some programs simultaneously, so I'm going to try to push the game aside," Tseng said.

Horo moved to give her access to the keyboard. She had spent many hours with Lebby learning the intricacies of the base computer, but now, as she tried all the combinations of commands that the computer engineer had taught her for similar emergencies, the Ouija board remained stubbornly fixed on the auxiliary terminal's screen. It was as if the program had been designed to nullify all her efforts to end it. "All we have right now is a straight video hookup between the monitor and MILTON's vision system," she said to Horo. "If we can't tie him into this computer, how certain are you that we can safely control him?"

"To be honest, I can't be at all certain of anything under these conditions," Horo said in an exasperated tone. "Does that mean we have to shut him down?"

"No, it doesn't mean that," Tseng answered. "I'm as anxious to get the data on what's happening as you are." A glance at the monitor showed her the magnetic lines of force that surrounded everyone in the room as they came within range of the sweep of the robot's stereoscopic cameras.

"We don't really need the computer in order to record the data," Horo said. "We're covered as far as that's concerned. What MILTON sees gets stored in his memory, and he's operating on his own power supply."

"The safety considerations are staring me in the face," Tseng said. The air had turned cold, and Tseng felt her energy and body heat draining away. It appeared to her that the others, too, were feeling the sudden cold. The fog of their breaths hung in the frozen air and diffused the light in the room.

Suddenly, they heard a startling series of rapid, loud pounding noises from the level above.

"That's Jerry," Tseng hastily reassured the others.

"Is there a problem with the power?" Manch asked uneasily.

"No," Tseng said. She deliberately kept her eyes averted to avoid betraying her own concern. However, Horo's expression told her that she was not fooled.

Tseng felt relief when the main interior lights flickered, then came on, adding credence to her claim that nothing was wrong.

"We've got something happening here," Horo said, with both anticipation and trepidation in her voice. She pointed to the video monitor, where, in MILTON's infrared view, the air around the galley storage lockers rippled as though it were a detail in a desert mirage. In visible light, a small spark of static electricity snapped near a metal hinge of one locker and, for a brief instant, in the robot's view, a gas plume appeared around it. Then, with a loud "crack," the locker erupted like a volcano spewing meal packets upward and outward into the room. A foul odor of vaporized polystyrene plastic packaging assailed Tseng's nostrils.

DeSosa, Greer, and Manch were all speaking at once, expressing their amazement.

"Energy is being harnessed in a complex process that is resulting in the movement of objects and the release of heat and light," Tseng said. "Did anyone notice how cold it got just before this happened?"

"I was wondering about that, but I thought it was just another malfunction," Manch said.

Horo carried on a staccato dialogue with the robot. Only she could hear its side of the conversation, but Tseng caught the words, "replay, heat scale, surface rendering, and color palette," and knew the geologist was calling for a display of the data from the machine's thermal infrared multispectral mapper for scientific analysis.

The real-time picture on the monitor was replaced by the robot's recorded footage of the explosion running in slow motion. Around the edge of the monitor screen, multiple graphs plotting the time sequence, thermal and spectral distribution curves, and brightness values were displayed.

"The spectral analysis of the gas: carbon dioxide and trace amounts of neon, argon, and helium," Horo said.

"The latter three are the principal gases found in the lunar atmosphere," Tseng said.

"What's happening?" Cochagne called down from Level Three.

"We can't be sure yet," Tseng called back.

"That was incredible!" Greer exclaimed.

Tseng glanced at Faden. An eerie awareness of what was happening had replaced his vacant expression.

Cochagne and Lebby descended the companionway to Level Two. Lebby was carrying the small camera he kept in the pocket of his space suit, the one Tseng had seen him use during the memorial service for the FS-5 astronauts.

"I remembered that we do have a film camera available, after all," he told her.

"Good thinking, Pops," she responded. "How much film do you have for it?"

"I brought two extra thirty-six exposure film cassettes, and there are twenty-nine exposures left on the cassette in the camera."

"Okay, you're now in charge of the FS-6 mission photos," she told the senior astronaut. "I'm glad you were able to repair the damaged circuit so quickly," she said to Cochagne.

Cochagne shrugged and scratched his head, perplexed. "No repair was necessary. We opened up the ceiling, and I was about to check that section of wiring when the lights came on again. I checked the connections anyway. Nothing was loose. I don't quite understand it, and I don't like it."

"Bit-flips," Lebby said.

"Shhhhh!" Horo hissed at him, and pointed to the center of the room where something Tseng could only define as an energy mass was forming.

The robot's cameras zoomed in for a closer shot, then the real-time picture was replaced with a detailed surface rendering of the phenomenon showing it to be composed of a dense gaseous mass of energized particles. In addition to graphs plotting the thermal and spectral distribution curves, the robot displayed a pseudo-color map showing the continuously changing temperature relationships within the energy mass.

Lebby moved stealthily forward with his camera. Tseng hoped that his presence would not affect the phenomenon. The knowledge that the robot and the other astronauts were also observing the phenomenon made it easy for Tseng to react to it with excitement and curiosity. She was not completely without fear, but it seemed like a natural reaction attributable to the need for caution. They were face-to-face with "the unknown."

DeSosa crossed himself, then approached the apparition and put his hand and arm into it. He made several passes through it in every direction. Lebby captured his actions with the pocket camera.

Tseng looked for any reaction to the human contact, but it appeared that the mass was merely rendered momentarily unstable by the disturbance. DeSosa flexed his hand and arm experimentally, then shrugged at them to indicate that he was feeling no ill effects.

Faden approached the mass like a man walking in his sleep. He touched it, and he did not retreat when it disintegrated around him, but Tseng was alarmed to see an expression of horror come onto his face. As evidenced by the real-time scene through the robot's infrared-filters, Faden was suddenly the sole object of attraction for a host of indistinct, gaseous masses. Faden beat and swatted at the air around him, but the more he fought to drive off the phantoms, the faster they closed in on him. They threatened to overwhelm him like a pack of hungry wolves.

"My God! What's happening?" Manch cried, rushing toward Faden, but the astronaut was blind to his surroundings. He looked at Manch in fear, without recognition. Then he lashed out with his fists, catching Manch in his rib cage.

Manch stumbled backward, groaning in pain.

With a terrified yell, Faden retreated, covering his head and face with his arms. As the astronaut's struggles brought him closer to her, Tseng felt powerful tingling sensations. Static electric discharges stung her skin with tiny pinpricks of pain and every hair on her body stood on end. Dizziness overcame her, and her senses numbed.

The next thing she knew, there was a heavy, suffocating spray of water in her face. She saw that she was on the floor outside the hygiene station, and Cochagne was directing the spray from the showerhead at her. Thoroughly soaked, she sputtered and sat up, yelling, "Jerry, what the hell . . . ?" Then she saw that Manch, Greer, Lebby, and Horo had thrown Faden into the water spray and Cochagne was also aiming the nozzle on him.

Faden put up his arms to protect his face against the suffocating impact of the water. He tried to retreat from it, but backed into DeSosa's waiting grasp and was shoved back into the water.

Cochagne kept the showerhead aimed unrelentingly at them. Within seconds, everyone was completely soaked.

"That's enough!" Lebby shouted.

Cochagne went into the hygiene station and turned off the water.

Faden lay on the floor, exhausted.

"Why did you do that?" Tseng sputtered.

"A good soaking was the only thing we could think of to neutralize the energized field enveloping you and Faden," Lebby answered.

Though she felt waterlogged, Tseng managed a smile of relief. She looked out into the passageway between the sleep stations and saw that it was flooded with water.

Manch crouched down and winced with pain. With his left hand, he probed gently at the right side of his rib cage.

"Are you all right, Paul?" Greer asked, immediately alarmed.

There was an exchange of furtive glances between the physician and Horo, Cochagne, and Lebby.

"Faden packs quite a punch," Manch said to her. "I think I have a cracked rib, that's all."

Emotion brought tears to Greer's eyes. "I was so frightened . . ." She threw her arms around the physician's neck and sobbed into his shoulder.

"I know," Manch said gently. "It's okay."

It was several seconds before Greer could recover her composure.

To Tseng's amazement, Faden shook himself and stood. When he spoke, there was a tremor in his voice, but he sounded completely rational. "It was so weird . . . I saw Louise Washington," he said. "I saw the FS-5 crew. They were dead . . . and there were others with them— other . . . ghosts . . . I mean. I don't know . . . was it all in my mind?"

"I think we all saw something on the monitor," Cochagne said. There were affirmative nods from everyone in response.

Faden walked toward the sleep stations. "I want to be alone for a while," he said over his shoulder.

"Is *this* the breakthrough you've been hoping for?" Lebby asked Greer in a bitter tone.

"I'm not sure," Greer answered.

Lebby removed the camera from the pocket of his wet uniform shorts and looked at the film count indicator. "I covered it all pretty well, I think. There are only six exposures left in the camera. It'll be interesting to see what shows up on the film."

"You mean we won't know if we're all crazy until we get back to Earth," DeSosa said.

"What's in MILTON's memory will be the test of whether or not we're crazy," Horo said.

"I'm starting to chill," Greer said, shuddering involuntarily. She rubbed her arms for warmth and mumbled, "I'm going to get rid of these wet clothes," as she walked away from them.

"I was thinking," Manch said slowly, "Washington must have regained consciousness after Mobley left. She was injured, weak, and alone here for God knows how long. During that time, she must have witnessed scenes and images of her dead crewmates that looked like the 'ghosts' Po and Faden saw, and all the while, she was s from hunger and dehydration." Unexpectedly, the physician's voice broke with emotion. "She didn't know we were there to save her. She thought we were ghosts. That's why she screamed . . . and why she died screaming." His sad expression deepened. "I think I had better examine Bob Faden."

"I'll go with you," Tseng said.

"Are we going to set the equipment up on Level One?" Horo asked.

"I can't do any more science right now," Tseng answered reluctantly. "I'm really exhausted."

"We've got to work out a schedule, so we can rest in shifts," Cochagne said.

Greer was still in her wet clothing and standing, as if mesmerized, outside the sleep station that had belonged to Washington. The privacy curtain was open. From inside the room, Tseng and Manch heard feet scuffing the floor. When they joined Greer, they saw that she was attentive rather than "entranced." Greer turned to them and gestured for silence, then she returned her steady gaze to the inside of the sleep station.

Bob Faden sat on the bed scrutinizing his face in the mirror of a makeup compact he was holding in his hand. Flies were swarming around him, but he seemed not to notice or even to feel them when they alighted and crawled on his bare skin. The astronaut had taken off all of his clothing. Takizawa's silk kimono was draped loosely over his shoulders. He glanced up as though annoyed at the intrusion from outside and Tseng was shocked that, while the face was Faden's, the expression on it was strangely not his. He'd put mascara on his eyelashes, and black eyeliner, and he was dabbing powder blush on his cheeks from a compact. Washington's cosmetic bag lay open on the tabletop. The tube of lipstick, now completely used up, was lying discarded on the

floor. A partially opened food package lay with it. Tseng
cocked her head to read the contents. Apple cobbler. The
discarded dessert seemed out of place in the dead astronaut's quarters. Tseng picked it up and knew that the
wrapper did not contain apple cobbler. She'd found the
hard drive of Mobley's still camera.

Faden had applied the remaining "Reentry Red" lipstick with feminine precision. As if to check the effect of
this handiwork in the mirror, he formed his lips and
mouth into a round "O" shape, and Tseng recognized the
face of Washington she'd seen in her nightmare. Faden
smelled of sweat and perfume, and the odor was familiar
to her, she realized, because she had smelled it during
their examination of Washington's sleep station.

Faden looked away from them and became engrossed
in his reflection in the mirror once again.

"How did he get these things?" Manch whispered.

"He could have gotten to the FS-5 personal preference
kits before they were stowed in the *Collins,*" Tseng
replied. "Who would think to check them?"

"Look! What do you want?" Faden asked them in an
annoyed tone.

"Bob, after what you experienced, I think you need to
rest," Manch said.

"Why do you think I'm a man?" Faden asked, genuinely shocked.

"Where did you get that?" Manch said, pointing to his
groin.

Faden looked down at himself and was immediately
horrified at the sight of his male organ. "I don't want a
man's penis!" he cried and tears came to his eyes and
streamed down his face. His eyeliner ran, creating sooty
rivulets on his cheeks.

Greer and Manch moved toward Faden, but the astronaut stood up and pushed past them. He walked swiftly
out into the corridor.

Tseng could not help but notice that his movements were uncoordinated. *A woman trying to control a man's body,* she thought. She bounded after Faden and caught up to him before he reached the galley. Greer and Manch joined her, but to Tseng's surprise, they did not try to detain Faden.

Horo had disconnected the robot from the video monitor, and he was responding to voice command instructions from her. DeSosa, Lebby, and Cochagne were hunched over the auxiliary computer terminal which continued to display the Ouija board graphics.

"I can't find Mike," Faden sobbed to the astronauts. They could only stare back at him in shock. Faden seemed not to notice. He stopped crying and, after dabbing at his cheeks with the edge of the kimono, said with an air of grim resignation, "They're ghosts, aren't they! I forgot that they're dead!"

Faden had a clear view of the computer screen and Tseng saw his demeanor suddenly change as he became aware of what the screen displayed. He pointed at it and raged, "That's an evil thing!" at Lebby.

Faden rushed at the computer and, though Lebby tried to stop him, he tore the power cords and cables from the computer, picked it up, and dashed it to the floor. It bounced in the light gravity and he fumbled and caught it. He slammed it down and stomped it with his feet, and then beat at it with his fists.

Cochagne grabbed Faden, but the astronaut seemed to have acquired superhuman strength. He wrested himself from Cochagne's grip and dashed purposefully toward the companionway to Level Three.

"Stop him! He's heading for the mainframe," Horo yelled, charging forward.

Tseng placed the camera hard drive on the galley countertop and bounded toward Faden. She managed to grab his legs as he was ascending the stairs. She dragged him back down, but he caught at the safety railing and held on. Manch reached her and grasped the astronaut by his kimono.

Faden kicked furiously at them. DeSosa joined the fray and pulled at the astronaut's legs.

Faden lost his grip and they dragged him down, tumbling with him onto the wet floor of the passageway between the sleep stations, but the astronaut wrestled free and scrambled to his feet. He took an unbalanced step, slipped, and fell under the legs of the oncoming robot.

There was no time to ponder why the robot was still on the move. Tseng could see it was as much of a surprise to Horo as to everyone else.

Faden lay stunned in a prone position on the floor as one of the machine's footpads descended onto his head. In less time than it took Horo to recover and shout a voice command at the robot, the footpad came down squarely on the side of Faden's head.

MILTON was not programmed to know or to take into account the frailties of human flesh, and, in that infinitely small, decimal fraction of a second, Tseng anticipated the horror of seeing the astronaut's head crushed like an eggshell by seventy-three kilograms of the machine's weight pressing straight down on it.

As if in slow motion, Tseng saw the robot shift its weight into the step . . .

. . . and stop. It looked down at the object under its foot, then, it took two steps backward, crab-stepped sideways, and continued past the prone astronaut.

"How come MILTON was moving toward the companionway?" Tseng asked Horo.

"I don't know," Horo responded worriedly. "It could have been something I said—a word combination—we were all screaming and yelling . . . or, with all the static, his radio receiver could be picking up parasitic wave oscillations, I suppose."

Tseng could see that her friend was still shaking from the close call with Faden.

"You realize, his proximity sensors wouldn't have stopped him," Horo said nervously. "He made a decision based on what he'd learned about his surroundings. In analyzing the new terrain in which he found himself—that is, the terrain inside the base—he must have concluded that, except for the stairs, it was consistently flat. He's programmed to always choose the easiest route, so, when it came to a decision between going over the obstacle under his foot—Faden—or going around it, he decided to back up and go around it. The important thing, to me, and the fortunate thing for Faden, is that MILTON chose a course of action based on something he'd learned! I wouldn't wish it on Bob, but it was sure a better test situation than anyone could have devised." Turning to the robot, she said, "MILTON, listen." When the machine had moved smoothly into the home configuration, she said, "Shutdown."

To Tseng's relief, the robot obeyed the command dutifully and became immobile.

"That's a good little soldier," Horo told it.

Weak with relief, Tseng trembled as she assisted Cochagne, Lebby, and DeSosa to pick Faden up from the floor. The astronaut was semiconscious and moaning softly.

"What's happened to him?" Lebby asked Greer. "Why is he dressed like this and all painted up?"

"If I tell you that he's had a psychotic episode, will that satisfy you? Will it make you feel better?"

"That's psychobabble," Lebby responded angrily.

"Yes, it is," Greer retorted.

Cochagne slung Faden's right arm across his shoulder. Tseng helped to support his weight on the other side and, together, they walked him slowly down the passageway toward his sleep station.

A blast of cold air against her face and exposed skin sent a shiver of alarm through Tseng. A blinding flash of electricity arced through the air. She heard a whooshing sound and felt the pain of a hard, glancing blow across her left shoulder. She reeled backward with the impact and fell to the floor, simultaneously hearing a bellow of pain and a loud thump behind her. This was followed by yells of surprise and alarm from DeSosa, Greer, Manch, Lebby, and Horo. The main and the auxiliary interior lights went out, plunging them into darkness and setting off the main computer's emergency klaxon.

Tseng struggled to her knees and saw Cochagne writhing on the floor with his hands over his face. Blood streamed from between his fingers and onto the floor.

Manch rushed to Cochagne's side and elevated his head, then he pried the astronaut's hands from his face. Greer, DeSosa, Lebby, and Horo moved to attend Faden.

The speed of the accident left Tseng stunned and dizzy. Her shoulder throbbed, her ears rang and there was a tingling sensation inside her head as well, but she was more concerned about Cochagne. His face and eyes were already puffed and swelling, and he would soon have two black eyes. She had never seen the handsome, jovial astronaut incapacitated in any way, and the feeling it created within her was one of intense anguish. She felt strong instincts of protectiveness for him as well. Her throat tightened convulsively as she struggled with the unaccustomed emotions.

"I've got one hell of a headache," Cochagne said in a nasal tone of voice. "I bet I look like I've just gone fifteen rounds with the world's heavyweight champ, too."

The comment made Tseng grimace.

Seeing her reaction, he chuckled self-consciously and said, "You can't think of me as just another pretty face from now on. See? Everything happens for the best."

Cochagne gritted his teeth and made a wry face as

Manch probed the area around his nose gently. "Your nose is broken, but I'll pack it and plaster it and give you a shot for the pain, and you'll be as good as new," he told Cochagne.

"Faden is dead," Greer said. The pronouncement was a jolt to Tseng. Because of her concern for Cochagne, she had not noticed, until now, that, while Faden, too, was lying on the floor, his head was resting on his shoulder in an unnatural position. His eyes were open and glassy-looking. Horo and Lebby were crouched down over him. Their faces told of their shock.

"What happened?" Tseng asked.

"I saw the whole thing," Horo said. "There was an electrical arc."

"I felt something," Tseng said, massaging her shoulder.

"When the current struck Bob, his head came back and slammed into Jerry's face. That's how his nose was broken."

"It happened so fast I can hardly believe it," Lebby murmured.

In spite of Greer's pronouncement, Faden's death did not seem real to her either, Tseng realized. She watched several flies scurry across the floor and wade into Cochagne's blood. Like happy bathers at the beach, they washed their feet and rubbed their heads and reveled in the sticky, gory pool. It was an invitation to more flies. These flew down, landed in the pool, performed their sanguinary ablutions, then flew over to alight and crawl on Faden's face.

Manch brushed away the flies and gently closed the dead astronaut's eyes.

Her emotions were in rebellion at the suddenness of his transformation from a human being to a broken, kimono-clad mannequin in garish makeup that was now sprawled grotesquely on the floor in front of her. This was a different state of matter . . . this state known as "death." The finality of it made her feel weak, and powerless, and cold. She only wanted to think of Faden as alive, and, with every passing second, the body on the floor was becoming more of an inanimate object to her because there was nothing to animate the features and the limbs in all the ways that were familiar to her from the years of living, training, and working in close quarters with . . . him? Where was he? She felt disconnected from the thing lying on the floor.

"The current must have stopped his heart," Manch said.

Tseng felt Cochagne's eyes on her. She turned her head to meet his gaze and tried to give him a reassuring smile.

"I want to do a postmortem on him right away," Manch said. "I'll need help to move the body down to Level One."

"Should we use a stretcher?" Lebby asked.

"It's on Level Four," Horo said.

"We can roll him onto a blanket and carry him in that," Manch said.

"I'll get something," DeSosa said. He crossed to his own sleep station and returned with the sheet from his bed. He spread it out on the floor next to the body.

"We'll move it onto the sheet, but I want it moved carefully," Manch said.

The physician's choice of words did not escape Tseng. Manch, too, was relating to Faden's body as a lifeless object.

"Someone will have to support the head," Manch continued. "Okay . . . three people, one on each end and one to support the middle."

Lebby reluctantly grasped Faden's shoulders and waited for Manch and Cochagne to grip the ankles. Tseng moved to support the lower torso, while DeSosa held the head steady. They lifted the body together on a count of three. It was more difficult than Tseng had imagined it would be. The body was completely flaccid.

Faden was literally dead weight. Horo grasped the wrists to fold the arms over the chest but, abruptly, she and Lebby both let go of the body, and the shoulders and upper torso fell to the floor.

"He moved!" Lebby said.

"I felt his arms move," Horo echoed.

"Are you sure he's dead?" Lebby asked in a frightened voice. His face was ashen.

"Yes, I'm sure," Manch said patiently.

Greer confirmed the statement with a nervous nod.

"There are two kinds of death," Manch said. "One is somatic death, where the person irreversibly loses the sentient personality. That is an event characterized by loss of consciousness, the inability to be aware of or to communicate with the environment, and an inability to respond to sensory stimuli or to initiate any voluntary movement.

"The other kind, cellular death, is a process not an event. Certain tissues, like muscle tissue for example, live on for hours, even days, after cardiovascular activity ceases. Muscles are capable of contraction for many hours, especially if the deceased exerted himself prior to death. These postmortem muscular contractions are called Sommer's movements."

Lebby and Horo approached the body cautiously and resumed their positions. Working together, they lifted the body onto the sheet. Then they put the two halves of the sheet together to make a sling.

☾

Upon walking into Mission Control with Gutierrez and Christiansen, Bianco was immediately aware that their arrival breathed life back into an atmosphere of worry, inactivity, and exhaustion. Christiansen went directly to the CAPCOM console to resume his duties, releasing

Shah Zia. With hours to go until the window opened for the reacquisition of a signal from Far Side, no one wanted to leave the control center unless ordered to do so. Christiansen put on his communications headset so as to be ready for the first break in the silence.

Bianco had been aware of a marked difference in Christiansen since his encounter with Faden. Though the astronaut had applied his knowledge and professional experience to the discussion and detailed analysis of Faden's bizarre responses to his presence and to Gutierrez's questions, he'd been more subdued in his manner and opinions than Bianco had ever known him to be. Now, as Bianco prepared to resume the vigil for FS-6 in her accustomed place, near the CAPCOM console, she thought she recognized the need to bolster Christiansen's spirits. "You have to think of tonight as a breakthrough, Dave," she said. She accepted Christiansen's nod as an acknowledgment of the compassion motivating the statement, rather than as agreement with it.

"You've lived by a set of beliefs and teachings, and I know you have a perception of 'good' and 'evil.'" Bianco hesitated, wanting to chose the right words and feeling suddenly awkward because she was out of Christiansen's league when it came to the subject of a God-operated universe. "Maybe you had a perception of how it was going to be to actually confront evil in its personification, and the way things happened with Gutierrez and Faden . . ." A bemused smile came onto Christiansen's face, and she hesitated, worried now that she was in danger of offending the astronaut.

Instead, Christiansen leaned back in his chair and regarded her with an attitude of straightforward earnestness. "When that teleconference ended, I felt like a failure," he said easily. "I felt that I had been put to the test, and that I had failed. But I'm coming to terms with it, because I realize that, to arrive at such a conclusion, is to be guilty of an offense against God. That offense is vanity. '. . . and they that are rich, who are puffed up because of their learning, and their wisdom, and their riches—yea, they are they whom he despiseth; and save they shall cast these things away, and consider themselves fools before God, and come down in the depths of humility, he will not open unto them.'

"If I take pride in my piety and in the degree to which I am able to live my faith, then, despite my good intentions, I lack humility, a quality that is essential to a true understanding of the teachings of the prophet."

"By 'the prophet,' you mean the teachings of Joseph Smith," Bianco said.

"Yes, but I should really have said 'the prophets,' because God's message has reached mankind only through prophets." A wry expression came onto Christiansen's face, and he added, "I believe that this is at the root of a lot of intellectual skepticism about the existence of God. If there was an answer to the question of why divine communications are always filtered through the minds of a few such individuals, could you believe in God?"

Bianco decided not to rise to the challenge and said, "I'm afraid I have many more serious doubts that would have to be satisfied."

Christiansen bobbed his head as though having predicted her response. "What you haven't asked, is: am I convinced Faden is demonically possessed, because I have a religious point of view? I've been asking myself that and other questions since the teleconference, when I first saw the condition Bob is in. I've done a considerable amount of studying in an effort to find answers.

"Most of the time, the New Testament makes a clear distinction between insanity and demonic possession, as in Matthew, chapter four, verse twenty-four: 'And his fame went throughout all Syria and they brought unto him all sick people that were taken with diverse diseases

and torments, and those which were possessed with devils, and those which were lunatic, and those that had the
palsy; and he healed them.' Jesus was, himself accused
of being either insane, as in Mark, chapter three, verse
twenty-one: 'And when his friends heard of it, they went
out to lay hold on him: for they said, He is beside himself,' or possessed, as in the verse following that one,
'And the scribes which came down from Jerusalem said,
He hath Baalzebub, and by the prince of the devils
casteth he out devils.' The line between insanity and possession is blurred in John, chapter ten, verse twenty,
however: 'And many of them said, He hath a devil, and is
mad; why hear ye him?'

"Did spirits communicate to us through Faden? Did
Takizawa send us a message through Faden? Intellectually speaking, we can't know for sure, because these are
symptoms of schizophrenia, and it is a very real condition. Can we believe what we heard? Religiously speaking, Satan is the father of lies, so, again, can we believe
what we heard?

"Did insanity cause Faden to seek out and experience
the powers of darkness through a Ouija board, or did
seeking out and experiencing the powers of darkness result in insanity? The result is the same in both cases;
however, the first scenario does not depend on faith in
the existence of beings whose plane of existence is the
spiritual realm, and the other does.

"Chapter nine of the Book of Mark contains a lengthy
version of an incident also mentioned by Matthew and
Luke, about Jesus' encounter with a child that was possessed by a 'dumb spirit.' The passages tell of how the father brought the child to Jesus, and of how the child
experienced a fit of possession right there in front of him.
The child threw himself on the ground and gnashed his
teeth and foamed at the mouth. The child had been possessed as an infant, and the spirit had a history of causing

the child to do suicidal things in an effort to make him destroy himself. The apostles had already tried to drive out this particular spirit and they had failed, so the father brought the child to Jesus. Jesus drove out the spirit, and there were lessons in the act for the father of the child and for the apostles, but what makes the incident stand out in my mind, is Jesus' reply when the apostles asked him 'Why could not we cast him out?' Jesus said, 'This kind can come forth by nothing but by prayer and fasting,' the implication being that this spirit was different than others the apostles had successfully cast out in Jesus' name. I have to admit that I keep coming back to the meaning of that.

"One thing about the experience with Faden . . . I was struck with the realization that I, and those I know and associate with in the Church, have an understanding of spiritual concepts derived from reading the scriptures. We also have an understanding that is the result of studying the Book of Mormon, the Doctrine and Covenants, and the Pearl of Great Price, the other three great books of our religion. This is intellectual understanding, though it can bring about an intense emotional experience. Take a simple concept like 'the power of God,' for example. We read about how it is exemplified in the creation, in the miracles of Christ and in the resurrection of Christ, and we are filled with reverence and euphoria at what we perceive the power of God to be. Each one of us tries to imagine the power of God, but, eventually, we run up against our own individual limits because we have no real, practical, firsthand understanding of the terrifying magnitude of the power of God. I've thought about this many times when I've been up in space or in an airplane where I can look out over distances that are vast, but there, too, I run up against the limits of my physical senses to perceive the size and magnitude of God's creation."

"It's the difference between putting your finger into the flame of a match and knowing the pain of fire, and reading about how, if you put your finger in the fire, it will burn you," Bianco interjected. "One results in first-hand knowledge, the other intellectualizes an experience for the reader."

"Precisely. So I will try to intellectualize an experience I had tonight in those terms. If I've been burned by the match and you haven't, my experience automatically isolates me from you emotionally and intellectually. You might listen to my explanation of the experience in the hope of overcoming the barrier between us caused by your lack of firsthand knowledge. You might also envy me for that knowledge. What you may not fully compre-hend is that the firsthand knowledge I have might very well be a burden for me because of the isolation and be-cause of the effort I must make in trying to relate the ex-perience in a way that you can understand.

"As revelations go, it was rather a simple illustration of something at my level of ability to comprehend which is at a very, very elementary level in the total scheme of these things. The combined power of the dumb spirits in-habiting Faden is so infinitesimally small as to be almost nonexistent as compared with the power of God. Yet tonight I beheld the total destruction of an intelligent man, and in doing so, I beheld that infinitesimal measure of the power of God as surely as if I had placed my finger in a match flame and felt pain.

"This experience, multiplied infinite times is the bur-den of knowledge of the full power of God placed upon the prophets of the Bible. That it was a terrible thing to bear is clear from the tragic details of their lives re-counted in the Scriptures. It brought them isolation from the rest of mankind, and at the same time came with the commandment to communicate important knowledge, so that others might gain a small measure of enlightenment. Who would be so vain as to seek out and to glory in such a life? Only a false prophet, I believe.

"Isolation, ridicule, being the object of fear and hatred . . . Joseph Smith was assassinated while in jail by a mob who hated and feared him. I had no basis for understanding his burden and his struggle in the depths of my soul until now. When I reread his words, it will be as though for the first time."

The thing that disturbed Bianco was that the astronaut's eyes did not burn with their usual self-righteous zeal. Instead, they reflected a great weariness, much emotional turmoil, and a sadness that was heavy and even poignant. She was prevented from delving further into Christiansen's impressions on the Faden incident by the approach of Gutierrez.

"Jack Bucar is calling from the UBC studio," the detective told her. "They said you can take it over at the flight director's console."

Bianco nodded her thanks.

"You look like you could use a break," he said in a tone she'd come to recognize as a polite don't-argue-with-me. "Have you had dinner yet?"

Bianco realized she hadn't thought about rest or food in hours. "No."

He moved closer and leaned down to whisper in her ear. "Can you 'order in' at a place like this?"

His warm breath in her ear sent shivers up the nape of her neck. He straightened, and his lips curved into a mischievous smile. The personal attention was unexpected. Bianco found it invigorating, and she rose to his challenge. "Just what did you have in mind?"

"Dinner for two, your office?" he murmured.

"I'll see what I can do," she said, feeling suddenly more alive than she'd felt in hours . . . and in years, it seemed.

(

Tseng was ahead of Cochagne, DeSosa, and Lebby as the four astronauts ascended the companionway to Level Three, and she was the first to discern the sound of radio static that mimicked heavy, raspy breathing. "Listen," she hissed, drawing their attention to it.

"There's an open COMM channel," DeSosa said incredulously.

They peered cautiously up through the Level Three hatchway, and Lebby swore under his breath. The computer's main screen displayed the Ouija board game. "What that machine needs is a diversion," he said.

"A task that will occupy time and memory," Tseng said. "How about photographic analysis?"

"That would do it," Lebby said.

"I'll be right back," Tseng said.

She navigated her way to Level Two by flashlight and retrieved the apple cobbler package she'd found in Washington's room from the galley.

"This is the hard drive from Mobley's camera," she told Lebby, handing him the package.

"Bob Faden had this," Lebby said. "Let's see what's on it."

In the light from the screen and the orange glow of the emergency markers, Tseng thought she saw a swarm of flies. She played the beam of her flashlight through the darkened room to confirm the sighting. That the flies were airborne was a good sign. The sudden drops in temperature that preceded what she was now calling static events made them fall from the air like tiny black hailstones.

"It looks all clear to me," Cochagne said. Nevertheless, they crawled on their hands and knees across the floor to minimize the chances of getting struck down and killed as Faden had been. No place was "safe" for them inside the base.

DeSosa crawled directly to the communications console and switched off the radio.

Lebby crossed to the computer. "This time, the problem is in circuit T-357," he said, taking the information from the caution and warning panel. He busied himself with connecting the camera hard drive, and began typing furiously on the keyboard. Moments later, the first image replaced the Ouija board on the computer screen.

"The images are in the order they were taken, and they range over a twenty-eight-hour period," Lebby said, a few minutes later. "We've got the first one coming on-screen now."

It was a glamour shot of Louise Washington, her pouty lips defined by lipstick. The data block recorded the frame number, the date, and the time.

"In Mission Elapsed Time, this is about nineteen days into the mission," Lebby said.

"That was just like Louise," DeSosa said.

The next picture was of the brooding face of Drzymkowski, annoyed at having his picture taken. The one following it showed the engineer making a threatening gesture at the camera. He was dressed for a workout, and, indeed, the following shot showed him "pumping iron" on the electromagnetic weight machine, using the long lat bar. He was sweating profusely and his teeth were tightly clenched. His fanatical effort could be seen in his eyes, which looked as though they might pop out of their sockets, and in his facial muscles which were locked in a maniacal grimace. The huge muscles in his arms were "pumped up" and well defined. The veins were prominent. To Tseng, the image appeared to characterize the obsessive side of the man and to foreshadow his subsequent violent actions.

Next was a picture of Bisio and Faden. It elicited gasps of surprise and shock from the other astronauts, as it showed the two in an affectionate embrace that hinted of shared intimacy. They were unaware of the camera. Faden's hair was dirty and stringy and he had two-days' growth of beard. Bisio was equally unkempt.

"There is a small amount of noise in the picture," Lebby said, pointing out areas of the image which were peppered where pixels were missing.

The following pictures were of the same quality. One showed Takizawa, dressed in a bamboo leaf-print kimono, in his sleep station eating rice and dried fish from a ceramic bowl with wooden chopsticks. An elegant ceramic decanter and small matching cup were next to the bowl. The expression on his face showed annoyance at the invasion of privacy.

"This is a sake warmer and a sake cup," Tseng told them, pointing to the decanter and then to the cup. A "pinup" style picture of Washington was followed by a picture of the astronaut, grim-faced and working with her tools on the communications console. Both pictures were remarkable only for their grainy quality, the consistent amount of electronic noise, and the double-exposure effects in them.

There was a shot of Faden and Bisio working on the computer, then a picture of Mobley taken on Level One. He was sitting on his bed, cross-legged. His beard and the pale, drawn look of his face gave him the appearance of an Eastern mystic. Manch pointed out the small, dark stain on the astronaut's shirt in the area where he had found the serious wound during his examination of Mobley's body.

"The MET is nineteen days, twenty-two hours," Lebby said.

"This could have been taken shortly after he received

his wound, or else he'd reopened it and was bleeding through his dressing," Cochagne said.

"This looks like a self-portrait," DeSosa said. "He set the timer and then got in front of the lens."

There were nods and grunts of agreement from the other onlookers.

A shot at an angle past Bisio seated at the computer showed the screen with a game board displayed.

The next picture showed Washington and Bisio in the recreation room. Bisio was pulling Washington's hands away from her forehead. Washington was in obvious pain.

"This was taken right after her accident," Lebby said.

The following picture bore out his statement because it showed the red-stained hygiene station washbasin and mirror with the words, "Food for the Moon" in identical condition to the view in the last live footage they'd received from Far Side.

"This is the closest we've come to being able to establish a time frame. These two shots are our benchmark," Tseng said.

"They were taken nine and five minutes prior to LOS, respectively. LOS occurred at twenty days, two hours, eighteen minutes, MET," Lebby said.

The next shot was another Mobley self-portrait taken on Level One. The astronaut had a blanket wrapped around himself and he looked cold, exhausted, and depressed.

A shot of some occult graffiti on the wardroom wall came up next in which "Food for the Moon" figured prominently.

"This is two hours after LOS," Lebby said.

The next shot showed an angry Drzymkowski examining the wall moments after the previous shot, according to the data block. There was a time gap of three hours, then a grainy shot of Bisio and Drzymkowski playing chess in the CDR quarters. Bisio was obviously furious with her hulking opponent.

There was a time gap of an hour between the chess picture and one of the hygiene station featuring more writing on the mirror and walls. A shot of Washington and Bisio breaking up an argument between Drzymkowski and Faden, taken ten minutes later, followed it.

A shot of Drzymkowski pulling down a block of ceiling panels in the recreation room came up on the screen.

"The MET, here, would be twenty days, seven hours, forty-seven minutes," Tseng said.

After a gap of five hours, a series of three shots, spaced within five minutes of each other, showed the big engineer doing electrical work inside the opened space. The series ended with a shot that showed electrical wires left hanging down from it.

"It wasn't like Frank to be sloppy in his work," Cochagne said, shaking his head in bafflement. DeSosa nodded in agreement.

Next came an image of the FS-5 crew members looking on. It showed Takizawa in a dark-colored kimono in the background, holding his sake cup. These images were shot through with noise.

There's almost a day between these shots of Takizawa," Tseng said.

The shot that followed showed Drzymkowski pouring sake on Takizawa's head from the bottle. Takizawa's expression showed rage.

Another frame from a different angle showed Faden, Bisio, and Washington, with a bandage on her forehead. The data block showed that it was a reaction shot of the astronauts, upset by the sight of Takizawa and Drzymkowski.

The next picture made them gasp in horror. It showed Takizawa's kimono on fire with the other astronauts scrambling to smother the flames.

"This is twenty days, twelve hours, fifty-five minutes MET," Lebby said.

"Go to the next one," Tseng said, her voice trembling. But the next image showed a break in time of fifteen minutes. Takizawa, burned almost beyond recognition, was still on fire, despite continuing efforts of the other astronauts to extinguish it. It appeared that he was either falling or trying to rise from the floor. The shot that followed it confirmed that Takizawa was trying to stand. In the next shot, taken fifteen minutes later, they viewed the smoldering, charred, and blackened remains of the astronaut.

DeSosa turned away from the computer screen.

"See if you can print all these out," Tseng told Lebby.

"There are more pictures," the computer specialist said. After queueing up the previous images for the printer, he brought the next image onto the screen. It was of Drzymkowski in his space suit carrying a bulky trash bag into the air lock on Level Four. "We're at twenty days, thirteen hours, ten minutes MET," he said.

The picture that followed was of the death kanji painted on Takizawa's wall. It was peppered with noise.

"This is two hours later," Tseng said.

"These pictures show a pattern of steadily increasing noise," DeSosa said. "I'm glad we saw them before someone cleaned them up, because I think that this is important."

Lebby nodded. "It's an indication of charged particle interference while the image was being digitized."

A shot of Bisio at the computer with Faden looking on, came up on the screen next, followed by one of Faden at the computer with Bisio looking on taken half an hour later. Both astronauts were scantily clothed, and they looked haggard. The next shot was of the computer screen with the Ouija board displayed. The letters and numbers were still discernible despite much noise, but the message block was not readable.

There was a break of two hours in the time sequence of the images, then a shot of Bisio in her room, dull-eyed and trancelike, came on the screen. She was writing on the wall with a marking pen. This image was followed by a shot of Faden's room showing the pentagram on the floor.

"This is twenty days, eighteen hours, twenty minutes MET," Lebby said.

Another Mobley self-portrait came up. The time interval was two hours. The level of noise nearly obscured the details, but Tseng could see that, despite being wrapped in his blanket, Mobley looked chilled, weak, and feverish.

The final image was a grainy, noisy shot of Faden's room that showed Bisio and Faden looking wild-eyed and frightened at being caught by the camera in the midst of an arcane ritual. Bisio was holding the aluminum strut over the pentagram like a wand.

"We're at twenty days, twenty-one hours, ten minutes Mission Elapsed Time," Lebby said.

"Had Drzymkowski gotten his hands on these pictures, I believe he would have destroyed them," Tseng said. "He might well have torn the base apart looking for the hard drive."

"By this time, Mobley couldn't be sure that any of them would survive to tell what happened," Cochagne said, indicating the picture. "Sometime between twenty days, twenty-one hours, and approximately twenty-one days, two hours, Mission Elapsed Time, Mobley removed the hard drive from his camera and hid it."

"Faden's imprisonment was a spur of the moment thing caused by some event," Cochagne told Tseng.

Tseng nodded with dawning comprehension. "If we

can believe some of what he said, then he thought someone was going to kill him—possibly because he'd witnessed something or, based on these pictures, because he
was involved in something which infuriated someone.
Mike Mobley tried to save his life and save the pictures
that would tell what happened."

They were silent for a few moments.

"I have to open up that wall to get to that circuit,"
Cochagne said at last, pointing to an area that had been
painted over with the number, six-six-six, the occult
graffiti that Greer had called "the devil's number." He
paid no heed to the writing and, after rummaging through
his toolbox, he attacked the nuts holding the panel in
place with a ratchet and a socket.

His eyes were slits in his swollen face, and Tseng noticed that he fumbled several times when trying to place
the socket over the nuts. Such clumsiness was not normal
for him. "Can you see?" she asked.

"I can see well enough to do this," he growled back
at her.

Despite the fumbling, within moments, he had the
panel off. Tseng aimed her flashlight beam into the space
behind the wall panel, but then had to help him locate the
bulk connector for the bad section of wiring by its number. He tackled the job of checking the wires and connections with a test light. He'd no sooner started when
the auxiliary interior lights flickered and came on.

"I'll be a son of a bitch," Lebby said.

"There's a serious problem here, and I'll find it if I
have to rip this whole place apart," Cochagne said, pain,
as well as anger and defiance, in his voice.

Tseng felt an icy wind on her face. "Get down!" she
shouted at the men while, at the same time, dropping
back into a prone position on the floor and covering her
head with her arms.

DeSosa, Cochagne, and Lebby did likewise just as a spark snapped from underneath the computer chair.

"Thank God that one was a fizzle," Cochagne said.

"Don't kid yourself," Lebby retorted. It took a hell of a lot of energy to do that!"

"The terminator may have passed over us, but that won't be the end of our woes. I think we're going to be dealing with the aftereffects, in the form of electrostatic charging and discharging, for at least another twenty hours," Tseng said.

They stayed down, alert for any sign of another phenomenon, but Cochagne soon became impatient to resume his task. In dropping to the floor, he'd scattered the nuts from the access panel. He fumbled badly while trying to gather them up and, when he dropped the ratchet, he felt around for it like a blind man.

Tseng crawled on her hands and knees to the companionway. "Where are you going?" Cochagne called after her.

"I'm going to look in on the autopsy," she lied.

Faden's naked body was stretched out on the reassembled worktable inside a surgical bag. Horo, Manch, and Greer had not removed the garish makeup from his face, and, as the dead astronaut's skin had already taken on a lifeless, waxy quality, he looked like a wax museum dummy.

The last member of the FS-5 crew . . . dead. Even as she stared at the body, Tseng could not shake the feeling of disbelief. She'd heard about amputees who continued to feel the presence of a lost limb. She still felt Faden's living presence among them.

"We've just finished here," Greer said.

"The shot you gave Jerry for the pain is wearing off," Tseng said. "Can you give him another one?"

"Will do," Manch said.

"We found some pictures that pretty much tell the story of what happened. Dick will print them out as soon as he can," Tseng said. "You two are getting a lot of experience at doing autopsies by flashlight," she quipped, indicating the one Horo was holding. "Under normal circumstances, we would take him out to Boot Hill, but we can't risk the trip right now. How long before it starts to get unpleasant with him in here?"

"If we leave him down here on Level One, the cold temperature should slow down the deterioration," Manch said. "The normal onset of rigor mortis begins anywhere from three to six hours after death, for example, but, in this case, I think it will be closer to the six hour mark before we see the first signs of it. On the other hand, if it were hot down here, we would be seeing those changes already."

At that moment, Faden's body rolled off the table with a sickening plopping sound, and landed on the floor faceup. The sudden shock and revulsion caused them to spring back and away from the corpse almost as one. Manch stared at the body and then started to laugh. Tseng's own laughter died in her throat as the corpse sat up jerkily and the head rolled down to rest on the chest. The movement was accompanied by the sound of bones grinding together in the neck. The body pitched forward, then rolled into a limp sideways somersault. The sequence was repeated. Stunned, they watched the corpse move along the floor a short distance, toward the companionway to Level Two, like a rag doll buffeted by gusts of wind. At length, it lay still again.

A look of horror came onto Greer's face. Her knees buckled, and she collapsed loosely to the floor.

Manch was the first to reach her side. She was conscious, but dazed, and the physician had to help her to sit up.

"It's not Sommer's movements, Paul!" Greer said to

Manch. "We're . . . under supernatural assault! I feel like I actually made contact with some . . . thing, just now. There was an intelligence present in my mind . . . it was of a very low order . . . ." Greer hesitated, and Tseng saw fear in the woman's eyes when she added, "I've never encountered such feelings of contempt for 'life.' "

"You've spent too much time with that Ouija board," Manch said worriedly.

"Yes, but you know I wasn't trying to communicate with any 'spirits,' " Greer responded. "This presence . . . it was just there for a few seconds, and then it left my consciousness."

"We're all feeling some effect from the electromagnetic activity," Tseng said. The words were meant to be placating, but she was still trembling from the effects of seeing Faden's corpse move, and they sounded strangely hollow to her ears.

"Oh, my God," Horo gasped, backing even farther away from the corpse in horror. Through the clear surgical bag, Tseng saw Faden's left foot making slow circles as a result of a spasmodically rotating ankle joint.

Horo was mesmerized by the sight of Faden's moving foot. "Isn't there some way we can get this body out of here?" she asked. "I . . . I don't think I can live with this!"

"Please, we have to get away from here!" Greer pleaded. "The body . . . it's . . . it's possessed! If we don't get out of here . . . ." She stopped in mid sentence, staring transfixed at the body as it suddenly sat up, then flopped over in her direction. She backed away from it, but it rolled jerkily, as if in pursuit. Greer screamed in terror.

"Can't you sedate her?" Tseng yelled at Manch, who was frozen to the spot and staring at Greer, dumbfounded. The shock of her raised voice galvanized the physician into action. However, when he loaded an amp of liquid diazepam into the hypo-gun, it was with violently trembling fingers.

Horo covered her ears with her hands. "I can't stand this," she said through gritted teeth.

Manch strode toward Greer. She backed away from him screaming, "No! Don't put me to sleep! "I'll die! We'll all die if you don't listen to me! You've got to listen to me!"

A container slid across the floor to impact against the wall with the sound of breaking glass, but Manch was not deterred. He reached Greer, grasped her arm firmly and pressed the hypo-gun against her shoulder. Tseng heard the hiss of the pneumatic charge, and Greer's muscles relaxed. Manch caught her and clutched her tightly to his breast. He kissed her forehead, and tears cascaded down his face.

The sound of footsteps on the Level Two companionway broke the silence. A second later, Lebby, DeSosa, and Cochagne appeared at the top of the stairs. Lebby, acting as a guide, had a firm hold on Cochagne's arm.

"We heard a lot of shouting down here," DeSosa said.

"We've got everything under control," Tseng said. She was aware of a sudden quiet that now seemed to pervade the room. Faden's corpse had ceased to move. Perhaps they had, indeed, already survived the worst of the terminator effect.

Horo, too, was aware of the change in their environment.

"Is it over?" she asked.

"Not quite," Tseng responded. "I estimate that we've got between ten and fifteen hours to go before we'll even start to get communications back."

"I'll put Iona to bed," Manch said.

"Maybe we can all get some sleep now," Tseng said. "God knows I need it!"

* * *

Tseng heard the slow, measured rhythm of her breathing. Then, out of the blackness of a deathlike sleep of exhaustion, there came a dull awareness that she was in bed, and in her quarters. She looked around the darkened room and wondered why the details of it looked so distorted, as though she were inside an amusement park fun house, or behind the lens of a camera. For no apparent reason, there were strange and monstrous shadows in the room. Tseng looked for the light source and saw a plasma field building up in the middle of the room.

Mike Mobley appeared. He was wearing his space suit, and he was walking purposefully, though the image stayed in the same place in the room. Another space-suited figure materialized in front of Mobley. It was Drzymkowski, and he was striding toward Mobley, his face twisted in anger. The figures had the same holographic translucence as all of the ghostly images she'd seen, but here, they were also surrounded by a ribbonlike energy corona which flickered and undulated like the aurora borealis. Mobley reached out to stop Drzymkowski, as if trying to block his way, then the two men faded out of existence, but the amorphous plasma field remained. Fascinated, she watched it and saw the energy being released by the billions of atomic particles moving in a frenzy of excitement and colliding with each other over and over. She watched it with no awareness of passing time until Mobley's head appeared in it and floated in the air in front of her for a few seconds before the eyes and other soft tissues exploded, leaving behind the mummy's grisly death mask. Even as this image dissipated within the plasma, another formed. The half-rotted corpse of Ann Bisio was sitting cross-legged in the center of a pentagram and examining the aluminum strut protruding from the gaping wound in its abdomen. The sound of deep-toned male laughter echoed around the specter.

Another image of Mike Mobley took form. Tseng felt

the fear-shock release of adrenaline. He was coming
toward her with a hammer held tightly in a raised hand.
She tried to retreat from it. Then she saw that the intended victim was an image of Drzymkowski. The construction engineer's ghost was in his space suit, but he
was carrying his helmet under his arm. He was laughing
at the approaching Mobley.

She became aware of herself, suddenly, and felt a stab
of panic because her heartbeat was not inside of her. Instead, it felt like someone was pounding on her chest
with a clenched fist. She saw Faden standing over her.
The astronaut was in the bizarre makeup and clothing in
which he'd died, and he looked frightened and confused.
Mobley, Drzymkowski, Bisio, and Washington were advancing toward him from all directions at once, and
Tseng caught glimpses of a myriad of horribly disfigured
corpses hiding behind them. She was the observer. The
camera. Yet, though she could not see her body, she had
an awareness of it, and she felt it respond. She reached
out for Faden, but was physically pulled away from
him. Fear and instinct made her resist and fight back with
all the power and speed of which she was capable.
She wrenched herself free and drove fast combination
punches into her nearest assailant. Her fists made contact
and she heard dull thuds of impact. She shifted her
weight and delivered a straight kick to the midsection of
the specter. She saw Bisio fly backward and disappear
even as she was propelled in the opposite direction from
the force she had exerted. She landed hard on her side
and rolled up into a crouching position to spring, but her
assailants had closed the gap created by Bisio's absence
and they were nearly on top of her. She scrambled backward and then, when they were upon her . . .

From far away, she heard Cochagne's voice. She woke
up and found herself on the floor of the darkened CDR
quarters. The temperature in the room was icy, but she

was sweating and feverish. She existed in real time, yet, she could neither explain nor deny the pain in her knuckles and toes that testified to having lashed out with physical force. That such intensity was possible in a hallucination was terrifying. Did it signal the beginning of a descent into madness? No. The pain was real. She heard a frantic buzzing noise above her head. A swarm of flies were slow-moving black dots on the ceiling. She heard movement on Level Three.

Moving as silently as possible, Tseng stepped through the privacy curtain and out into the passageway. She was not yet out of control, she reassured herself. Muffled voices were coming from above. Pain caused her to examine her knuckles closely. They were skinned, bruised, and swollen, evidence of the likelihood that, in the throes of her nightmare, she had attacked the wall.

At the top of the companionway, she saw Cochagne and Lebby in silent contemplation of DeSosa, Horo, Manch, and Greer who were all seated at the main computer. The Ouija board game was on the screen. Greer looked exhausted and feverish, but she was awake and coherent. Her fingertips were on the trackball mouse, Horo's, DeSosa's and Manch's hands were placed lightly on top of hers. Greer's and DeSosa's eyes were closed, but Horo and Manch watched the screen.

"Is anyone there?" Greer asked. Greer's fingertips moved on the trackball. On the screen, the mouse pointer ranged over the alphabet, the numbers, the words "yes" and "no," and the question mark and exclamation point at random.

"We want to contact Bob. Everyone should concentrate on Bob," Horo said.

"I feel a contact," Greer said. She looked weak and feverish, as though in a trance state. Greer's hand moved on the trackball. The pointer moved randomly for a few seconds, then slid down to the word "no." Feeling the trackball stop, Greer clicked the mouse. She opened her eyes to look at the message block. " 'No,' " she read aloud.

Greer closed her eyes again. "Who's there?" Presently, her fingers moved the trackball and the pointer ranged back and forth across the alphabet twice before she clicked on A and then, B. The letters appeared in the message block.

"A. B. Are you Ann Bisio?" Greer asked.

The pointer sped toward the "yes," overshot it, then came back to stop on the word. Greer clicked the mouse and "yes" appeared in the message block. Suddenly, without prompting, Greer's hand moved over the trackball again. The pointer moved around the board more deliberately this time, stopping on the letters W, H, T, P, L, C, T, H, and S, and the question mark.

" 'Whtplcths?' " Horo read aloud.

"It's a question," Manch said. "I can't figure it out."

"It's a kind of shorthand . . ." Greer began, then she stopped speaking because her hand rolled the trackball again. The letters W, R, M, I, and the question mark were clicked on, and appeared in the board's message block.

" 'Wrmi?' " Horo said.

"You're getting nowhere with this," Lebby said.

The comment broke the "spell" among the players. Greer awakened from her dreamlike state and looked in their direction. "That's not so," she replied, her temper suddenly flaring at the interruption. "The Ouija messages I read from the Faden-Bisio sessions were in this form. 'Wht' could be 'what,' 'plc' is probably place, so the message is, 'What place is this?' "

" 'Wrm i? Wr . . . m . . . i?' " Horo tried the combinations, then she said, "Wr . . . where m i . . . where am I?"

Greer's hand moved. The letter I was clicked on, and appeared in the message block. There was a pause, then D, E, D were clicked on in quick succession.

" 'I ded,' " Horo read aloud. "I dead! I'm dead!" Greer's hand moved, and the letter U followed by the number, 2, were clicked on.

"U two," Manch said aloud, then, "You, too! No. We're alive. We came to rescue you, but we were too late. I'm sorry."

"Isn't it just like the dead to forget how to spell," Cochagne mumbled.

They waited, but there was no movement for a full minute.

"No more sarcastic remarks," Horo said. "It creates bad vibes."

"Sorry," Cochagne whispered.

"I'm getting interference from 'others,' Greer said. "I don't understand it. How could other spirits of the dead be here?"

"Think of how many people die every day on Earth," Horo said. "That energy is released into the atmosphere, and it becomes part of the plasma. It could possibly have structure, for a while, as a magnetic record. A 'ghost.' "

"There is interaction between the Earth and the Moon on the atomic level," DeSosa said. "There are periods where the Moon passes right through the Earth's magnetic field."

"All kinds of energy, including this kind, could conceivably become trapped in the magnetic field," Manch said.

"When conditions are right, it's seen on the Earth," Manch said. "This phenomenon then becomes the basis of the mythology about death and the supernatural."

"That would mean that the energy of the people who have died up here is trapped along with energy picked up from the Earth's magnetic field," Greer said.

"Let's not get carried away with this," Lebby said agitatedly. "I remember that you told us that Faden was probably in touch with his own subconscious through the Ouija board."

"I believed it at the time, but now . . . I have these feelings. I don't know what to think," Greer responded. "I was driven to come up here and try to work the board. I feel a kind of heightened psychic power."

Greer once again collapsed back into the computer chair with a blank expression on her face. The psychiatrist's hand moved on the track ball and she clicked the mouse. A sequence of letters appeared in the message block. UWHORU?

" 'You. Who are you?' " Horo translated.

The trackball mouse appeared to roll under Greer's fingers to the letters P and L, and ION A.

"Can you tell us what happened to you?" Manch asked.

The trackball moved, but the pointer simply ranged back and forth over the alphabet without stopping on any letters. "What is the last thing you remember?" Manch persisted. Again, the pointer wandered across the game board randomly.

"Your questions are too complicated," Horo said.

Did Frank Drzymkowski kill you?" Manch asked. The pointer sped to the word "Yes" and stopped.

"So far, it hasn't told us anything we didn't already know or suspect," Tseng said.

Greer stood up abruptly, then sank limply back into the chair and moaned, "There is rage here . . . and hate!"

"Oh, God! It's starting again," Horo whispered.

"Is someone angry?" DeSosa prompted.

"Yes, he's very angry at me. Things are happening. He says I'm the cause." A note of fear crept into Greer's voice as she added, "He wants to kill me."

"Who is it that's angry?" Manch asked.

Greer gripped the sides of the chair with such force

that her knuckles turned white. She wanted to speak, but it was as if her jaws were locked shut.

Greer's hand rolled over the trackball mouse and clicked on the letter D. The lights flickered and went out, and the computer screen went dark. "He's here," Greer sobbed into the sudden, deadly silence.

"Did life support go out again?" Tseng asked Cochagne.

"It's the fan circuit," the astronaut swore.

"Something's going to happen," Greer yelled. "We're all going to die! I know it!"

Tseng felt the hair on her skin and scalp tingle.

Invisible fingers pressed at her temples.

"What's happening?" Horo said in a distressed tone. "My God! I can't think!"

"We might have another static field building up in here," Cochagne said.

The lights flickered and came on and the computer screen came to sinister life displaying the Ouija board.

"We've got several problems working against us," Cochagne said. "This is a long shot, but I want all the ionizers from every level brought up here. It's the only way we can get enough negative ion concentration to regulate our brain chemistry, so that we can keep from going nuts. I can't see very well, so I'm going to need help."

"I'll start down on Level One," Tseng said.

"The second thing is that we need to pull the plugs on all our electronic equipment until this is over," Cochagne continued. "That means the computer, the communications equipment, and everything that has current going through it."

"That's a good idea," Lebby said. "We can keep life support going without the computer."

"We'll just stay here, on Level Three, until this is over."

At that moment, the lights flickered and went out, plunging them once again into darkness.

Tseng shuddered at the cold she felt from the darkness all around her on Level One and tried to ignore the feeling that she was being stalked. Her scientific mind resisted using the word, "absolute" to describe the cold, but this was surely the cold of the grave, a voice—in reality, her thoughts—told her, as she marveled at the way her flash-light beam was being absorbed by the "abyss." Why was there such utter blackness; such a total absence of heat and light? Not even the glow from the emergency lamps appeared to penetrate it. The flashlight beam fell on the still corpse of Faden. There was an unnatural rigidity about the body now.

From every direction, Tseng heard the sound of labored breathing, punctuated by screams of agony. The smell of burned human flesh made her want to gag. Sometimes the screams died out to be replaced by soft whimpering and sobbing. A familiar voice—a woman's voice—pleaded for her life, then, she heard multiple thumps followed by the impact of a large object on the wall on Level Two above. There was an audible reaction near her which sounded like twittering laughter.

She understood that these things were from the iconography of her own imagination. She was creating these terrors in the darkness, she repeated to herself while her bruised and swollen shoulder throbbed to the beat of her heart.

Her heart was pounding because the basic knowledge of her mortality made the fear of death an inescapable burden, a burden impossible to share with anyone, the idea coalesced in her mind. It was emphasized by her persistent inner voice playing the devil's advocate.

A feeling of aloneness, and the notion that it was forced upon her by the shell of flesh that was her body, caused anxiety to well up in her. Her mind perceived that the faces of Cochagne and Horo were pale with the strain of their aloneness.

With the thought came the sensation of weight. The weight of her thoughts was draining energy from her. Heaviness . . . oppressive weight on her mind . . . Mobley's walk to oblivion . . . the only way out. . . .

Each of them was trapped inside his own mortal husk. Together but alone . . . "Oh to be free of such an onerous burden . . ." the voice inside her whispered with forceful insistence.

Tseng forced herself to concentrate on the task of removing the Level One ionizers. She had only just removed the black boxes from their assembly when she sensed a presence in the room and turned to see ghostly images of Louise Washington and Bob Faden, visible in every detail, against the backdrop provided by the far wall. The phantoms' bodies were opaque and their clothing appeared as though made of a diaphanous silk chiffonlike material. It was like seeing holographic images captured as they died, for the manifestation of Washington was screaming in soundless terror just as she had done until heart failure, and then death had silenced her, and Faden, his head hanging to one side, was in the bizarre makeup and clothing in which he had died.

She waved at the ghosts and called them by name repeatedly, but they seemed obsessed with their own misery.

Faden gave no indication of an awareness of her; instead, he was preoccupied with touching and probing at his corpse. There was a panicked desperation about the phantom's actions that she could feel as well as sense. It was more than just an empathic reaction on her part. It was a perceptible mood that pervaded the atmosphere of Level One.

At length, the distraught wraith lay down on top of the

corpse; then it sat up. When this failed to raise the body, the persistent apparition lay down, then sat up again. The stiffened, dead flesh did not respond.

Tseng was distracted from watching Faden by the movement of Washington's ghost toward her. Again, she heard the pleading, cajoling voice in her mind that sought to convince her to seek peace in death.

She heard the clatter of feet on the stairs, then there was a bright flash of light which nearly blinded her. Warm flesh took hold of her hand.

"It's okay, China," Lebby said.

Tseng clasped the astronaut's hand tightly. "What did you see? If you saw something, anything, tell me!" she pleaded.

"It . . . it was like a cloud . . . I can't describe it any better than that," Lebby stammered, regarding her worriedly. "Whatever that was, I got a picture of it!"

"Okay, that's it," Cochagne said, looking around Level Three at the ionizers, visible in the subdued light of the emergency markers. The units were strung together like Christmas tree lights. "Still, to get the full benefit of this beefed-up, retrofit super-ionization system we've created, we have to remain within the two-meter boundary of the units, because we still don't have the kind of capacity that will give us a sufficient level of negative ions out in the middle of the room."

"Nevertheless, I feel a whole lot better already," Horo said.

"So do I," DeSosa said.

Tseng nodded in agreement and saw Cochagne grimace in what, for his swollen eyes, passed as a wink at her.

Manch sat back against the wall and pulled Greer closer to him.

There was a heavy, thumping noise from a level below,

then silence. A moment later, they were again distracted
by the sound of heavy footsteps and, again, they were
coming from Level Two. For the first time in hours,
Tseng felt clearheaded enough to know that there was
something different about the sound. In the next instant,
the smell of burning plastic prompted her to descend the
companionway stairs at a run. Reaching the bottom, she
saw MILTON with Horo's radio headset dangling on one
manipulator, and saw the robot's cameras and sensor array turn in her direction. Intuition told her to dive to the
floor just as the beam of the laser microprobe sliced
through the air, passing just a few centimeters above her.
The beam struck the base of the wall beyond her, burning a hole in the material. Tseng remained still as the robot scanned in both directions, as if looking for her, then
turned and walked toward a wall partition. A half meter
short of colliding with the wall, the robot stopped. The
cameras looked in all directions again, as if confused,
then the laser beam burned a hole in the partition. The robot pondered the information for a fraction of a second,
then brought a manipulator to its tool caddy. It quickly
exchanged the gripper that was on it for a drill motor
with a five-centimeter drill bit designed for cutting into
lunar rock, and drilled a series of holes into the partition.
The other manipulator chose a parallel jaw gripper from
the caddy, and taking a firm hold on the partition by
means of the drilled holes, MILTON applied brute force
to tear the drilled section out.

   She heard the clatter of footsteps on the companionway. "Stay back!" Tseng shouted at the other astronauts.
"MILTON has gone a little crazy!" She was relieved
when, after ripping and tearing large jagged pieces out of
the partition, the robot gave up the strategy and backed
away from the obstruction, moving off in the direction of
the wardroom and galley.

   Horo came down through the hatchway, reached the

bottom of the stairs and crawled across the floor a short distance in pursuit of the robot to observe its behavior. After it had nearly collided with the wardroom table, and had then burned a hole in it, she said, "His vision system is malfunctioning. It's the same thing that happened to the digital cameras. He's blind, so he's relying on his radar and his laser probe to fill in the gaps in his information in order to find his way around. What got him moving again?"

"He might have picked up a false signal on his radio. There was a COMM channel open upstairs a while ago," Tseng said. "I don't know how that happened."

"Either we've got to get him on the radio, or I have to get close enough to him to shut him off," Horo said. Without waiting for a reply, she sprang nimbly to her feet and sprinted toward the robot. Its reaction time was faster than that of the ex-Olympic athlete, however. With methodical precision, MILTON quickly turned and shot his laser at the oncoming astronaut, hitting her in the thigh. Horo stumbled, yelping in pain. MILTON tracked her movements and fired a second time, striking her in the heel. She managed to duck behind the wall partition separating the wardroom from the recreation area just as the robot burned a hole in the floor where she'd stood a moment before.

"Joe! Get MILTON on the radio!" Tseng called up to Level Three.

"I'm trying to do that! I can't find the channel he's on," DeSosa called back.

"MILTON would be scanning all the frequencies, trying to establish radio contact," Horo called out. "There must be too much static interference. He's blind and deaf."

"How are you, Arminta?" Tseng shouted.

"Okay. Just some burns," Horo replied.

"Don't try that again!" Tseng reprimanded.

They studied the robot as it walked toward a wall, stopped, and drilled a hole in the wall. There was an eruption of sparks, and Tseng was aware of a deadly quiet that could only mean a life-support system failure. "He's hit a vital circuit," she called up to the astronauts on Level Three. "I want everyone to suit up in case the skin of the dome is breached! She heard Cochagne swear, then she heard the sound of his footsteps across the floor.

"I've got to try again," Horo called to her.

"Wait," Tseng called back. "If I distract him, are you close enough to get to him?"

"I think so," Horo answered.

"Okay, just hold on. Don't do anything until I'm ready," Tseng cautioned. She fought off a wave of dizziness by panting for breath. Had the robot's drill already pierced the skin of the dome? If so, how long would it be before she and Horo felt the onset of the bends from the drop in pressure, or blacked out from oxygen starvation?

"I can't breathe," Horo panted.

"It could be from lack of air circulation," Tseng said. She tried to think, but her mind was muddled. If she could throw something at the robot to get its attention . . . she looked around for a heavy object, but it was hard to see in the darkness, and lights popped, flashed, and sparkled in front of her eyes. A plasma cloud drifted across the floor, carried on an icy breeze. She followed the movement and saw a large black cylindrical object almost within reach among some debris in a corner of the room. Her vision clouded, and, for a moment, she thought she saw the face of Mike Mobley in the energy mass. She felt a stab of panic. She was hallucinating again, this time from oxygen starvation. The robot had punched a hole in the skin of the dome.

She moved sideways on her belly, then had to curl up and roll toward the wall as the robot turned toward her and fired its laser. She felt a searing pain across her ankle.

"Were you hit?" Horo panted.

Fighting for breath, Tseng reached out to grab the black cylinder. As her hand closed around it, and she felt the weight, she knew it was Mobley's camera lens. Why hadn't she found it before, she wondered dully. "Get ready," she shouted at Horo. She lobbed the lens, grenade-throwing fashion, on a trajectory across the machine's sensorframe and shouted, "Go!" as the robot turned, tracking the flying object. Behind it, Horo's lithe shadow bounded out of hiding and momentarily merged with the back of the machine. MILTON became immobile.

"I pulled his power supply lead," Horo said.

Tseng felt on the verge of passing out. From far away, she heard lumbering movement and saw a space-suited figure clumsily descend the companionway holding two of the portable oxygen tanks with masks used for EVA pre-breathing. From the awkwardness of the descent, she knew it was Cochagne before she read the name on the helmet.

☾

". . . ston . . . ar Side Ba . . . . read?"

Bianco was dozing when Tseng's voice broke radio silence in Mission Control, but the shouts of wild jubilation, and the sobbing and other expressions of unbridled joy from the flight technicians and astronauts keeping vigil, which erupted and threatened to turn the room upside down brought her instantly awake. A feeling of relief washed over her.

"Far Side, Houston. We have reacquisition of your audio signal at one hundred sixty-six hours: thirteen minutes Mission Elapsed Time," Christiansen said into the

CAPCOM mike. "God bless you and thank you for a job well done."

"We're . . . little worse . . . wear," they heard Tseng answer.

"Faden . . . dead."

The words rang loudly through Mission Control, but they were all too high on adrenaline for the shock of even the loss of a friend and colleague to bring them all the way down. That would come later, Bianco knew. Right now, they were celebrating the living.

"We . . . nformation . . . or you on . . . happened to . . . S-5 . . . LOS. . . . schedule?"

"We've decided to let you pack up and come home on the first flight you can catch."

"Say again, Houston."

"Come home!" Christiansen shouted.

". . . unable to . . . kizawa's body."

Bianco approached the mike.

"Dee Bianco wants to talk to you," Christiansen said.

"I know you must feel badly about Faden, and about not finding Takizawa," Bianco said. "We took it into consideration, but we feel you've done enough—more than we could have hoped for. We're deeply grateful."

". . . ay again . . . ton."

"We're glad you're okay!" Bianco shouted.

"We . . . ave a . . . bet . . . communica . . . window in a couple of . . . transmit . . . pict . . . video . . . then. As for . . . ow, it's just good . . . be back . . . n touch. We . . . aven't . . . any rest . . . ast couple . . . days . . . here. . . . busy, so, before we close . . . shop . . . do that."

"We copy you, China," Christiansen answered. "Lieutenant Gutierrez is here, and he's looking very relieved and happy to hear from you, too."

". . . copy, Houston. Over."

Bianco had noticed Gutierrez standing in the background during the initial moments of jubilation in

Mission Control. He hung back from joining in the cele-
bration. She motioned to the detective to join her and the
group of astronauts at Christiansen's console. "With the
media focused on rumors of cults and devil worshiping
in the highest circles, and every crazy psychic and as-
trologer haranguing us on the news, saying it's technology's fault that this whole thing happened because
we're upsetting the psychic forces of nature, I don't envy
Po and her crew," she told the assembled group. "I've
heard more theories about demons and the realm of the
dead than I care to repeat. They've just been through an
electromagnetic storm—I'm not going to tell them about
the media storm that's waiting for them yet. They'll find
out soon enough when they get back here." The comments drew laughs from her listeners, except for Gutierrez. "You look a bit lost, Lieutenant," Bianco said.

"I guess that, right now, I'm feeling like routine police
work will never be the same," Gutierrez said quietly.

"Uh-oh, it's a case of that old post-mission depression
syndrome," Christiansen said.

"You might want to be on hand after the rest period,"
Bianco said. "A considerable amount of information will
be transmitted to us that may help you wrap this up. As
for this new 'psychological problem' you seem to have
developed . . . get back to me next week. We're going
to need a mission specialist with your qualifications on
FS-7," Bianco said. She was rewarded by seeing Gutierrez's eyes spark with renewed excitement and curiosity . . . and something else, something personal.

EPILOGUE

Tseng took a last look around Level Four. She was about to climb into the air lock when a fly landed on her helmet faceplate. She was momentarily distracted from her thoughts by the vain hope of carrying the insect with her into the air lock and, thus, to its death in the vacuum of space.

"Far Side, this is Houston," she heard Christiansen's voice in her earphones. "At one hundred eighty hours: twenty-two minutes, MET, you are GO for egress and GO for launch."

"I copy, Houston," Tseng answered. "The rest of the crew has already departed for Boot Hill. Of course, you realize that if we have a cold start failure, this will be an exercise in futility, because we won't be going anywhere for about eight more days."

"We'll be standing by, down here," Christiansen said.

"Roger, Houston," Tseng said. She took another look around, unable to shake the uncomfortable feeling of having left something behind . . . something unfinished. It was more than just the effect of Faden's death.

MILTON's drill had not penetrated the skin of the Main Dome. After shutting down the robot, she and Horo had suited up, and, together with Cochagne and Lebby, they'd made the necessary repairs to the severed wiring to restore the base's life-support system and the lights.

The activity had helped to pass the time until AOS, Acquisition Of Signal, with Mission Control.

There was something unfinished, she reminded herself.

They were going home without Shinobu Takizawa. One of Faden's Ouija board messages had hinted that there was a message from Takizawa . . . a message from beyond the grave. Greer had interpreted the clue to mean that they would literally find a message about Takizawa left by Faden at the urging of his subconscious. If there was one, they'd missed it.

She climbed into the air lock and slid the inside hatch shut behind her. She activated the controls to purge the chamber, and sat back to wait.

"China, I have an idea," she heard Cochagne's voice.

"Go ahead, Jerry," she answered.

"We can transport the bodies to the *Collins* in one trip if we use both the soil mover and the rover to carry them."

Tseng quickly fathomed the idea Cochagne had in mind. "You'll use the blade as a stretcher?"

"Yes. Where are you now?"

"I'm in the air lock," Tseng said. She adjusted her body position and a small object slid out from under her boot. She bent over and, after some difficulty, picked up a small metal piece. She recognized it as one of the St. Christopher medals DeSosa had brought to the Moon with him. The small, nickel-sized medallion had obviously fallen out of the astronaut's PPK. She had not noticed it upon getting into the air lock. Knowing that St. Christopher was the patron saint of travelers, and, smiling at the irony, she opened the sleeve pocket of her suit and dropped the medal into it.

There were many ironies about the mission, she reflected. They were going home with the remains of the FS-5 crew, except for Takizawa. Perhaps FS-7 would find clues they had overlooked. Certainly, Greer's mediumistic ravings could not be taken seriously, and neither could her own dreams and hallucinations, although— and this was another irony—Greer had, indeed, displayed a kind of misguided clairvoyance in predicting that something was going to happen that would endanger all their lives. That it was the malfunction of the robot, and not the supernatural assault the psychiatrist had envisioned, convinced her that, in the light of restored reason, the disaster prediction had been pure coincidence. The robot's memory record of the phenomena seen during the passage of the terminator was of scientific interest, but it was inconclusive, and, thus, hardly illuminating. It fueled her doubts that the pictures from Lebby's pocket camera would reveal anything substantive. It seemed that all their speculation about ghosts and the supernatural, while intellectually challenging, could be chalked up to the mass hysteria of temporarily unbalanced minds. . . .

That point of view represented the opposite extreme, she reflected. They had explored myths in search of the underlying science. True, some things remained unexplained, but, based on her own experiences, she could honestly believe that the answers lay somewhere in their collective theories.

At any rate, they had survived the robot catastrophe, and AOS had restored communications with MILTON as well as with Mission Control. Its sight restored with the decrease in electrostatic interference, it had obeyed Horo's precise instructions in helping them to repair some of the damage it had done. Afterward, it had left the dome under its own power and was now a stoic, silent witness to their departure preparations.

Her thoughts returned to the mystery of Takizawa's disappearance. Faden had fooled himself into thinking that he was communicating with Takizawa's incorporeal essence—his soul. How had he been able to fool himself

about a message from the dead Japanese astronaut? The
notion that death could automatically bestow a stronger
desire to communicate, as well as a greater fluency in
English on the deceased, so that he could express himself
more readily and more eloquently in the afterlife than he
ever had while he was alive, was preposterous.

She reviewed her conversation with Greer in which
the physician-psychiatrist had revealed the existence of
the message—was that the word she had used?

No. Greer had said that one of Faden's messages had
referred to a sign from Takizawa.

Her imagination immediately pictured the death kanji.

Faden could neither speak nor write Japanese, but
Takizawa's was a mind that could express a complex
thought in a single kanji.

Her logical, scientific mind balked at the implication
that the death kanji was, in fact, the sign from Takizawa.
She knew the meanings of the symbols—called "radi-
cals"—that were its component parts . . . the Moon under the Earth . . . to decompose; the nighttime of life . . .
a buried man . . .

It was evidence that, like Faden, Takizawa had been
preoccupied with the notion of impending death.

A buried man . . . She remembered the lunar soil
mover as she had first seen it at the construction site.
Now that was a tangible clue to dwell on.

Tseng climbed out of the air lock and switched on her
PLSS lights to illuminate the darkness for a few meters
in front of her. In the distance, she saw the other sets of
lights. Cochagne was driving the lunar soil mover
toward Boot Hill. She waved at him, and motioned
toward the pit that was the foundation for the Science
Dome. "Jerry, I have a hunch that I want to follow
through on," she said.

Cochagne met her at the lip of the pit, but she did not
pause there to explain. Instead she motioned him to fol-

low her down into the man-made valley. "When I found the soil mover, it was down here, at the bottom," she told him, gesturing at the floor of the pit. "It was facing downhill, as though it had been used and then abandoned by someone in a hurry. I didn't think anything about it at the time, but those circumstances are bothering me now, and I want to check out even the remotest possibility. I won't get a second chance at the problem."

"Far Side, Houston. We're standing by. What are you up to?" Christiansen asked.

"We're checking something at the construction site," Tseng answered tersely.

At the bottom of the pit, she followed the pattern of the tread marks with her flashlight and saw a piece of a plastic trash sack protruding from the ground, exposed, perhaps, by the movement of surface dust particles during the magnetic storm.

"China, what's going on down there?" Lebby asked.

Tseng glanced up to see the senior astronaut, against a backdrop of bright stars, descending the slope of the pit followed by the others. "There's something buried down here," she told them.

"Cochagne squatted down and brushed around the plastic with his glove. The gesture exposed more of the bag and the edge of a buried hand spade.

"I want to remove the loose material around this bag carefully, so that we don't break it accidentally," Tseng told Cochagne as she squatted next to him. Before unearthing the bag, she used her own gloved hands to scoop away the soil from around the buried hand spade. She freed the tool and picked it up, turning it over in her hands to examine it from all angles. "If we dig around this area, odds are we'll find more hand tools," she said.

"The hand tools were missing from Drzymkowski's space suit when we found him," Cochagne said.

"I had the same thought," Tseng said. "He started out

to bury something in a garbage bag with his tools, but he must've been feeling impatient, or very frightened, so he finished the job with the lunar soil mover."

"Did he think he could hide something by burying it like this?" Horo asked.

"This was not the act of a rational person," Tseng said. "None of these people were rational at the end." She set the spade aside and carefully brushed away the soil around the bag. Cochagne followed her example.

When DeSosa and Lebby reached them, they, too, knelt down to carefully dig around the bag, which was loosely sealed, probably calculated to maintain a vacuum inside. The feel, and then the sight, of a hard, rotund object concealed inside near the top caused Tseng to shudder. It took fifteen minutes of careful digging to free the bag, but, by that time, she already knew that the hard, rounded object was a human skull.

Tseng fumbled nervously with the bag seal, then opened the bag and looked inside. The badly burned skeleton had been interred with the ashes from the body, and with the fire-blackened shards of an empty sake bottle wrapped in the tatters of charred Japanese silk. "Houston, we have just found the remains of Shinobu Takizawa," she told Christiansen. Cochagne fingered the burned silk.

With communications restored, they had given Mission Control the opportunity to see Mike Mobley's last pictures. That Takizawa, in his madness, had so accurately described his own fate was another of the ironies of the FS-5 disaster, Tseng reflected.

Tseng adjusted the position of her body in the command pilot's couch. She and the other astronauts were strapped in and waiting for the launch countdown to resume from a hold ordered by Mission Control. It had already lasted five minutes. The tasks of picking up the mess in the payload bay, and then loading and securing the remains of their colleagues inside, had consumed her attention for the last two hours. There had been no time for nostalgic rumination about leaving the Moon, perhaps never to see it again from this vantage point. However, the waiting was trying her patience and causing her to reflect on such things, now, and on the events of the mission.

She smiled to herself, remembering the comic scene that had accompanied Horo's farewell to MILTON. She'd captured her friend's tearful handshake and speech of motherly advice to the machine with the portable video camera.

And what of Horo's advice to her? The mission had pulled her away from the earthbound personal problems she'd felt mired in.

A strong urge caused her to turn and look at Cochagne, sitting in the pilot's couch next to her. She was pleased and comforted to find him looking at her.

What were the chances that their relationship would work, once they returned to Earth? It was impossible to predict, but she had never before felt both the inner peace and the exhilaration she did when she was near him, and surely, that was a good sign.

"*Collins,* Houston," she heard Christiansen's voice on the COMM. "Sorry for the hold. We're looking forward to a perfect launch . . . Stand by to resume launch countdown. Five . . . four . . . three . . . two . . . one . . ."

"We have ignition," Tseng said, feeling the familiar and reassuring vibration. ". . . and we have liftoff!" she added as the *Collins* rose toward the stars leaving the *Aldrin* behind as a lonely sentinel.

OTHERLAND

TAD WILLIAMS

In many ways it is humankind's most stunning achievement. This most exclusive of places is also one of the world's best kept secrets, created and controlled by The Grail Brotherhood, a private cartel made up of the world's most powerful and ruthless individuals. Surrounded by secrecy, it is home to the wildest of dreams and darkest of nightmares. Incredible amounts of money have been lavished on it. The best minds of two generations have labored to build it. And somehow, bit by bit, it is claming the Earth's most valuable resource—its children.

☐ **VOLUME ONE: CITY OF GOLDEN SHADOW**   UE2763—$7.99
☐ **VOLUME TWO: RIVER OF BLUE FIRE**   UE2777—$7.50
☐ **VOLUME THREE: MOUNTAIN OF BLACK GLASS**

UE2849—$24.95